BRITANNIA:
THE WARLORDS

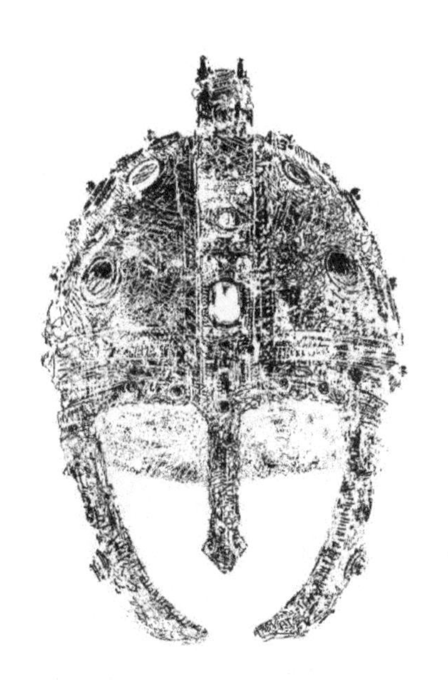

BRITANNIA: THE WARLORDS

RICHARD DENHAM

&

M J TROW

ISBN 978-1-913762-54-4

First published in 2016.

This edition published in 2020 by BLKDOG Publishing.

A catalogue record for this book is available from the British Library.

Cover art by Andy Johnson.

www.blkdogpublishing.com

THIS SERIES IS DEDICATED TO TRISTAN

CURA DAT VICTORIAM

OTHER TITLES IN THIS SERIES

BRITANNIA: THE WALL

BRITANNIA: THE WATCHMEN

BRITANNIA: THE WARLORDS

WORLD OF BRITANNIA

LIBER I
CHAPTER I

Aquileia, at the mouth of the Natiso

The torches of the Emperor's camp guttered in the warm wind from the south, the light like a thousand eyes watching from the far lagoons. Theodosius had forbidden festivities. The wine and the women and the song would come later. For now, there were to be solemnities, Christian services for the dead. In the dim light of his tent, the candles glowed tall and straight and he looked at the face on the painted glass he carried, smiling at the baby who smiled back at him. Little Honorius, his youngest, his favourite, his best. Difficult to believe the little one with his dimples and his curls would be an emperor one day.

But all that lay in the future, if God willed it. For tonight, Theodosius had more pressing business. He heard the barked command of the guard outside and the tent-flap flew back. Quintus Phillipus stood there, fist thumping on his mail shirt and the arm extended.

'Salve, Imperator.' The man was formal, as always and his dark eyes burned brighter than usual. Theodosius nodded in salutation and waited. 'You have something for me?' he asked.

Phillipus clapped his hands once and stood aside. A soldier marched in, his boots still stained with the blood of the men he had killed that day. In his hands he held a platter, draped with a cloth. Theodosius recognized the scarlet at once. It was a vexillum of the old II Augusta, the banner of a legion that guarded Britannia, that outpost of empire Theodosius had all but forgotten about.

The emperor nodded and Phillipus whisked the flag away. There, sitting on the platter like the centre-piece of some mad cannibal's feast, was the head of Magnus Maximus, the usurper; the man who had dared declare himself first Caesar and then Augustus. His dark hair lay matted with blood and his teeth glinted through the parted lips. Theodosius crossed the tent and stooped a little to look into the eyes. Even now, now that the heart had stopped and the brain was still, even now with the dust of death brushed across the eyeball, even now the arrogant bastard stared back at him.

'Do you think this is over, Theodosius?' the Emperor heard the dead man say, his voice burning into his soul so that his heart jumped and his pulse raced. 'Do you think this will ever be over?'

Theodosius snapped upright, hoping that no one else in the tent could hear the scream inside him.

'Doesn't look so big now, does he?' Phillipus sniggered.

His emperor spun to face him. 'He looks bigger hacked to pieces than you and me with our bodies intact,' he murmured. Phillipus stood to attention. It had been a long day, a long campaign. Everyone was a little on edge. Theodosius suddenly needed air and he swept out into the night.

Ahead the lagoons shimmered under a fitful moon, the clouds lurid silver as they passed, saluting the victorious emperor, Theodosius, whom men would now call the great. Around him, the camp was settling to sleep, medici still patching and stitching, slaves still digging the pits for the dead. Theodosius saw the standards of his legions clustered on a hill, the eagles silhouettes against the imperial purple of the sky. The whinnying of horses took his gaze across to the cavalry lines where those strange, fierce little men called the Huns were lying between their horses' legs. The ponies were still saddled and bridled, as was the Hunnish custom, those peculiar iron hooks they called stirrups dangling from them. Theodosius found himself smiling. What a ridiculous idea; it would never catch on.

Then another horse caught his eye; Magnus Maximus' grey and across its bloodied shoulders, the headless corpse of its master, ripped and riddled with arrows, the arms dangling to one side, the feet to the other.

'Phillipus,' the emperor raised his voice a little, as the grey snorted and shifted the load across its back.

'Sire.' The man was at his emperor's side in an instant.

'At first light,' Theodosius said, 'We will bury Magnus Maximus according to his custom. They say he became a Christian towards the end, but we all know that's nonsense. He was a soldier. We'll use the rights of Mithras, one last time.' He closed to the grey, stroking the animal's warm muzzle and patting its cheek under the bridle's gilt fittings. 'Sic semper tyrannis,' he murmured. Then he straightened and shouted so that all men could hear.

'The head of the usurper, Magnus Maximus, will be taken to Britannia, where he began this doomed mission to unseat Gratian and to unseat me. It will be carried throughout that God-forsaken province as a reminder to all that there is but one Emperor of Rome.'

Then he lowered his voice and murmured to Phillipus, 'You will take it, Quintus. You will speak for me. Do you want the Huns as an escort?'

Phillipus was horrified, especially by the smirk on his emperor's face.

'A joke, Quintus,' Theodosius chuckled. 'I would wish all kinds of hell on the people of Britannia, but I draw the line at the Huns. And when you come back, let it be with news of how loyal Britannia is to me.' He felt the little boy's portrait still in his hand. 'And to mine.'

Londinium

Chrysanthos the vicarius had spies everywhere. That was why he was vicarius and how he kept watch on the provinces at the arse-end of Theodosius' empire called Britannia. News had reached him in mid-Septembris that a ship had left Belgica flying the emperor's colours and butting into the German Sea. It had landed at Regulbium where the Baetasian cavalry watched it drop anchor and the oars slide to the upright.

The tribune of the Baetesians had sent a galloper north-west to the marshes south of the Thamesis and the word was brought to the vicarius.

'Quintus Phillipus,' Chrysanthos nodded to the man, still swathed in his travelling cloak and already finding the climate of Britannia far too cold for him.

'You are well informed, sir,' Phillipus stood to attention. 'I assume you are the vicarius Britanniarum?'

'Chrysanthos,' the man smiled and held out his hand, 'and feel free to assume what you like.'

Phillipus shook it.

'How was your crossing?'

'Appalling.' Phillipus wasn't smiling. He barely knew how. Nothing about this place appealed to him. The German Sea had been a bitch, the ship's fare revolting. He had brought a hundred men of the Heruli with him, crammed on those slippery decks, hard riders who had campaigned with Theodosius and would now have to buy new horses in Britannia. But Quintus Phillipus was not a military man, for all he wore the uniform of the Schola Palatinae, the emperor's bodyguard. That was for the look of the thing; a man with a sword at his hip tended to command more respect. He wasn't even sure about the quality of the wine Chrysanthos offered him now, but he took it anyway.

'Have you eaten?' the vicarius asked. 'I have a table prepared next door.' He glanced at the guards at Phillipus' back. 'I expect we can find some scraps for your people. The kitchens are that way.'

Phillipus didn't move. Neither did his people. 'I'll come to the point, vicarius,' he said. 'This is not exactly a social call.'

Chrysanthos sipped his wine, if only to prove to Phillipus that it was safe. 'Don't tell me I have displeased the emperor in some way.'

Phillipus did not care for the smirk of unconcern on the man's face. The trouble with Britannia was that it was too far from Rome – and further still from Constantinople, where Theodosius increasingly made his home these days. 'I have brought you a present,' the emperor's man said.

'How touching.' Chrysanthos lounged on his couch and gestured to Phillipus to do the same. Instead, the man clicked his fingers and one of the guards held up the bag.

'Hold out your hands,' Phillipus said.

Intrigued, Chrysanthos put down his cup and sat upright, hands extended, palms up in front of him. The guard reached into the leather and hauled something out. It was a human head and the guard held it up by the hair. He dropped it unceremoniously into Chrysanthos' hands.

'Behold,' Phillipus said softly, 'the head of a traitor.'

Chrysanthos felt his pulse jump and he caught his breath.

'Magnus Maximus,' he said, his voice barely a whisper. The hair had dried to black straw and the skin was brown leather. The eyes were sunk deep in their sockets and the dead man seemed scarcely to recognize his old vicarius at all.

'The same.' Phillipus took Chrysanthos' offer and sat, languidly sipping his wine. 'You aided and abetted him.'

'Did I?' the vicarius was a man used to recovering quickly from shocks; he had done it all his life. He nodded to a slave, half-hidden in the shadows and the man relieved him of his grisly burden.

'That,' Phillipus stopped him with a snapped word, 'stays with me.'

Both his guards moved forward and took the head from the slave. For a moment, the man stood his ground, jaw flexing, waiting for the word of command from the vicarius. 'Now, Clitus,' Chrysanthos smiled, 'these gentlemen are our guests. It's only right they keep their toys.' The head disappeared again into the leather bag.

'Oh, this isn't a toy,' Phillipus corrected him. 'It's a symbol of the futility of going up against the emperor. My instructions are to display it in each of your provinces. Here in Maxima Caesariensis, then Flavia Caesariensis, then …'

'Yes, thank you,' Chrysanthos stopped him. 'I *do* know what they're called. Good luck with that, by the way.'

'What?' Phillipus paused in mid-sip.

The vicarius helped himself to grapes on the low table in front of him. 'Well, you see, the late Magnus Maximus was pretty popular in all my provinces. Oh, he had some local difficulty in Britannia Prima, but that all ended rather well. No, more than a few of my subjects …'

'*Your* subjects?' Phillipus interrupted.

'Sorry,' Chrysanthos smiled. 'Slip of the tongue. The *emperor's* subjects. More than a few of them elected Maximus Caesar and joined him on his little adventure. Even the Hiberni.'

'Yes,' Phillipus said, straight-faced. 'We buried them.'

'Well,' the vicarius spread his arms, 'fortunes of war, eh?'

'And you, vicarius?' Phillipus sat upright now, looking hard at his host. 'Where did you stand in all this? Did you elect this rebel Caesar?'

Chrysanthos frowned. '*Please*,' he said. 'I am the vicarius, the emperor's deputy.'

'Ah,' Phillipus was a politician. He could fence all day with this man. 'But *which* emperor?'

Chrysanthos was serious. 'There is only one; surely you know that, Quintus Phillipus?'

'*I* do,' the man answered. 'The question is, do the peasants around here know it? I'm here to remind them.'

'Are you?' Chrysanthos poured more wine for himself but none for his guest. 'You and your hundred men?'

It was then that the vicarius heard a strange sound, one few men ever heard. It was the sound of Quintus Phillipus laughing. 'I am merely the advance guard,' he said. 'There'll be thousands following.'

'Really?' Chrysanthos said, knowing full well that his spies had only reported a single ship. 'Well …' he smiled and reached across, topping up Phillipus' cup, 'perhaps I was a little hasty. And to answer your question more fully … no, I did not elect Maximus Caesar. He was a law unto himself; as you say, a rebel. A man, even a vicarius, can do only so much. We heard he defeated Gratian's army.'

'He did,' Phillipus acknowledged, 'before we cut him down.'

'Of course. Listen, my man here will see you to your quarters. I think you'll find the basilica comfortable, but if not, my house is your house – the governor's palace. Your men will be quartered in my own stables.'

'I'm touched,' Phillipus nodded, though clearly he wasn't.

'Tomorrow,' the vicarius said, 'we'll talk more. I think the Forum here in Londinium is the best place for the head, don't you? Every day is market day. If it's speeches you want, I'll have my praecone do the honours. Oh, you'll write it, of course.'

'Of course,' Phillipus scowled. What was going on? The vicarius had turned on a solidus and something didn't sit right with that.

'Clitus, see our guest to his quarters.' Chrysanthos stood up and extended his hand again. 'My man is at your command, Quintus Phillipus, and, in the name of the emperor, allow me to welcome you to Londinium.'

They shook hands and saluted each other and the emperor's messenger followed the slave into the shadows.

From other shadows a figure emerged, soft, sensuous, her hair a golden mane over her shoulders.

'Well?' Chrysanthos poured another cup of win and passed

it to her.

'Well, he wasn't very nice, was he?'

There was the briefest of silences and then they both burst out laughing. 'That's what I love about you, Honoria,' he said, stooping to kiss her bare shoulder, 'your innate grasp of political reality.'

'Ooh,' she tapped him playfully. 'I love it when you use big words.'

They laughed again.

'Seriously, though, Chrysanthos,' she said. 'Is he trouble? For us, I mean?'

'For us? No.' The vicarius looked into the middle distance where Phillipus and his men were walking their horses across the courtyard. 'Trouble? Well, that depends.'

'On what?' Honoria asked.

Chrysanthos turned back to her, sighing like a man with a plan forming in his mind. 'On that wayward son of yours. Have you seen Scipio recently?'

CHAPTER II

The lights burned bright in the Hen's Tooth that night and the laughter carried to the cobbled street outside. Drunks caroused along the gutters, pawing their women under dark arches, vomiting into the rivulets that ran to the banks of the Thamesis. A raw wind had risen along the river, gusting sharply as it whistled around the great wall towers that Theodosius' father had built twenty years ago. The rain was falling in torrents over the city, bouncing off the roof tiles and thudding on the leather awnings of the street market stalls. Far out to the east, it drifted lazily on the wind, driving into the blackness of the forests there and pattering onto the endless mud of the marshes. Curlews hid in the reeds with the corn-throated bitterns and the ghostly owls stayed in the warmth of their barns.

Another bird out of the weather sat on the strapped wrist of a young man in the Hen's Tooth. The hawk sat upright, its talons hooked into the leather, its head hooded with a plumed cap that covered its eyes. The young man yawned and stretched, watching the bird flap and squawk, jingling the bells on the hood.

'He's not coming, Scip.'

The young man turned at the mention of his name. 'He'll be here, Caius,' Scipio nodded, watching the door. 'He won't be able to stay away.'

'On a night like this,' the other man said, swigging his wine, 'He'd be mad to try.'

'Half Londinium's riding on this,' Scipio said, passing the hawk to a minion. 'Metellus won't get another chance.'

The older man looked at him. 'He has a chance, does he?'

he asked, smiling.

'No,' Scipio said. He half turned as a half-naked girl brushed past him, trailing her fingers across his shoulders and into the dark ringlets of his hair. She was a little unsteady on her feet, what with the giddiness of the wine and the exercise they had both had earlier in the evening.

Scipio smiled up at her and slapped her buttocks. 'Not just now, lover,' he purred. 'Business.'

He heard his friend's chair scrape back. 'Well, well,' he said, 'look who just walked in.'

Scipio did. The door was still open and the wind was unsettling the candle flames of the taverna. A giant of a man stood there, with others just as big behind him.

'Salve, Metellus Scaevola,' Scipio said. He hadn't moved but the girl sidled away. She had seen this man before and many like him. They stank of sweat and ale and their hands were coarse and everywhere. She glanced furtively at Scipio. He looked so small by comparison, so … beautiful. She didn't want to stay and see what was going to happen in the next few minutes. She didn't want to … but she did.

'Bitch of a night,' Scipio smiled as Metellus hauled off his dripping cloak and threw it at an attendant.

'You said it,' Metellus nodded. He wasn't looking at Scipio. He was counting heads. He'd been here before, to the Hen's Tooth in the Black Knives' patch. Time was, he'd have cracked a few heads, slit the odd throat and claimed it as his own. The girls would be his and the wine. Robbery with violence. Nothing easier. But it was all about politics these days. When Scipio's papa had been the Consul of Londinium, it was easy. Leocadius Honorius had been with the Black Knives himself and as long as he got his concession, of the grain imports and the woollens and the timber taxes, he had more blind eyes than an earthworm. But now that bastard Chrysanthos ran the place, there was no Consul, just a by-the-book vicarius with that thing Metellus hated most, an honest streak.

So now it was all about territory and the lawless days of the free-for-all had gone forever. So now it was about not losing face. Now it was about teaching this whelp who was the dead Consul's bastard son a lesson in manners. Scipio had sent out the word, from the baths to the forum, to the quays, to the basilica. Scipio of the Black Knives wanted a word. And he wanted it with Metellus Scaevola of the Left Hand.

'So,' Metellus sat down at the table opposite the younger man, 'how is this going to work?'

Scipio jerked his head to a servant who passed wine and jugs to Metellus. There were six men at his back. Metellus had nine. Nine because that was his lucky number and he never travelled far without them.

'Well,' Scipio said, pouring himself a cup of wine and smiling broadly, 'we can carry on as before. The Left Hand have north of the river up to the bishop's gate, the Black Knives the rest.'

'And south of the river?' Metellus waited until Scipio's men had sampled some of the wine before he took a sip himself.

'Marshes and sheepshit?' Scipio shrugged. 'You can have that too, if you like. I'm not a greedy man, Metellus.' He chuckled and his six stalwarts joined in.

'No,' Metellus grunted, 'but you're a dodgy one. What do you *really* want?'

Scipio's smile vanished and he slammed his cup down on the scarred oak of the table. 'Londinium,' he said, looking hard into Metellus' eyes. '*All* of it.'

Only the wind rattled the shutters now. All movement in the Hen's Tooth had stopped and it was as silent as the grave. Metellus leaned back, staring Scipio down. The leader of the Black Knives was only a boy; he hadn't finished shitting yellow yet. Metellus' flat face creased into a grin and he started laughing. His nine joined in.

'That's very good,' Metellus said, still laughing. 'I like a sense of humour. You don't often get that in flies just before you squash them.'

'Is that what I am to you, Metellus?' Scipio looked a little hurt. 'A fly?'

'You,' Metellus sat upright, 'are the shit on my shoes.'

There was a hiss and a thud and Metellus' eyes widened with shock and pain. He half stood, staring down at the hilt of a knife jutting out from his tunic. The blade had just bitten deep through his scrotum, half-severing his penis and slicing his bladder. Blood and urine spurted out over the table and the floor. Scipio leaned back, pleased with the throw. It had been quite awkward, what with the table and the chair legs, but he'd managed it.

'Not bad, eh?' he asked Metellus, who was still on his feet, swaying and about to pass out with shock and pain. 'And a left-handed throw, too. I thought you'd approve of that.'

Metellus slid sideways before crashing heavily to the floor, moaning in agony. From nowhere, men dashed from the darkness, swords and knives glittering in their hands. Even before Metellus' nine could decide what to do, they were stripped of their weapons and forced to kneel on the floor.

Scipio stood over them. 'I've never been a military man myself,' he said, 'but my papa was. In fact, before they made him Consul, he was a hero of the Wall, one of those great hearts that made it possible for us all to sleep safely in our beds. And one of the many things old Leocadius taught me was "Never go to a party without bringing a present".' He stooped and wrenched out his knife from the dying Metellus. 'He also said "Get the present back if you can". Now, gentlemen,' he wiped Metellus' blood onto the hair of the nearest Left Hand. 'You have a straight choice. You can work for me, following my orders to the letter. Or my boys here will take you for a short walk to the river. The fish will welcome you. So will the rats. Well?'

Nobody spoke, but eyes swivelled left and right. That sounded like a reasonable offer about now.

'I'm a reasonable man,' Scipio went on, sheathing the knife. 'Calatina and I have unfinished business upstairs,' he crossed the room, stepping over the body of Metellus and caught the girl's hand. 'When I come back, I'll expect an answer.'

He clicked his tongue at them and wrinkled his nose as the Hen's Tooth became a taverna again and cups clinked together and music struck up and men's nervous laughs turned to frivolity. Scipio and his love were just at the bottom of the stairs when he heard his name again.

'Scipio Honorius.'

The leader of the Black Knives, now leader of the Left Hand, now ruler of the city's underworld, sighed and looked across to the door where an officer of the Londinium garrison stood dripping in the porchway. Scipio patted Calatina's hand and kissed her forehead. 'Keep yourself warm, darling,' he murmured. 'Dear Mama wants a word with me.'

Verulamium

Justinus Coelius was Dux Britannorum, the military commander of the provinces that vicarius Chrysanthos governed. Under him, a succession of men with titles longer than his sword arm, jumped to attention at his arrival, trained and drilled their troops, barked orders and watched the horizon. But nobody kept watch better than Justinus Coelius himself. He had come up the hard way, as a grunting, sweating pedes with the VI Victrix at Eboracum and had reached the rank of circitor before hell had broken out along the Wall in the summer of Valentinus of the silver mask. Politics and the way of the world had done the rest.

He was a hero of the Wall, the gold and jet with its four helmet insignia still glinting on a finger of his left hand. He was a symbol of all that was fine, all that was Roman and he knew it. Other men let their guard fall, whored and drank through the long winter months in the high country. Others at least took wives for themselves and watched their children grow. But not Justinus Coelius. As he rode out of the gates of Verulamium that morning with his knot of hard riders of the II Augusta close behind, he was already counting the summers that he had done this, patrolling the edge of the Roman world and facing the darkness that lay beyond. And he was already losing count.

The horsemen clattered past the great theatre, its arena a rubbish dump now for the great and good of the town, its stone seats rank with weeds. Justinus had been born in this place and his father, old Flavius, had taken him to see his first gladiator fight when little Justinus barely reached the primus pilus' boot-top. He had never forgotten it, the roars and shouts of the crowd, the clash of iron and that strange smell he could not place at first; the smell of blood. And now, half-starved dogs scavenged the rotting pile, barking and snarling at the crows that flapped black just out of reach of the bared teeth.

Justinus hated this place now. He hated all the south, with its softness and its red, tilled soil. And he was on his way to the place he hated most of all, Londinium, the city along the Thamesis that old Theodosius had fortified and where Magnus Maximus had pitched his tents before sailing to his destiny. And he still had Maximus in his mind as he saw the lone rider galloping from the south-east, lashing his horse's flanks with a whip. Justinus recognised the uniform of the Londinium garrison and saw from the foam on the horse's sides that the message was urgent.

The horseman hauled rein and saluted as Justinus halted his little column.

'Salve, Dux Britannorum.' The rider sounded as winded as his horse.

'Circitor,' Justinus nodded.

'The vicarius Crysanthos,' the rider said, drawing a ragged breath. 'From him.'

'What's the news?'

'Er … Magnus Maximus …' the messenger who had ridden so far so fast now found himself, suddenly, lost for words.

'Magnus Maximus is dead, circitor.'

'I know, sir, but …'

Justinus waved to the man and they both dismounted, one of the commander's escort holding the dangling reins. The hero of the Wall had been this way before. He had seen men fall apart in the heat of battle, watched them cry like babies and scream in the darkness of a long night along the Wall. 'How old are you, boy?' he asked, softly.

'I'm … I'm twenty-two,' sir,' the circitor said, stung a little by whatever it was the commander was implying by the question.

'Well,' Justinus said, 'if you want to reach twenty-three, perhaps you'll tell me what the hell you're gabbling about?'

The circitor took a deep breath. 'The head,' he said, 'the embalmed head of the Caesar … er … Magnus Maximus. It's here. In Londinium.'

Justinus stood up to his full height. What more indignities would they pour on the man he had once counted as a friend? 'Who brought it?' he asked.

'The emperor's man, Quintus Phillipus.'

The name meant nothing to Justinus. 'Why?' he asked.

'As a warning,' the circitor said, 'to all of us in Britannia.'

'A warning?'

'Not to follow him,' the circitor was surprised he had to spell it out. 'Not to send any more usurpers against Theodosius.'

'I see,' Justinus nodded. 'All very fascinating, but did you have to half-kill your horse to tell me something I would have found out by nightfall anyway?'

'That's just it, sir. The vicarius is concerned.'

'He is? Why?' Justinus rarely crossed paths with the man who governed Britannia in Theodosius' name, and when he had, he had felt a chill creep over him, as though someone had walked over his grave.

'Phillipus wants to show the head, to exhibit it in the Forum. There'll be a riot.'

Justinus nodded. He knew how popular Magnus Maximus had been. 'Very likely,' he said, 'but the vicarius has a garrison, of which you yourself are a member. Won't that do?'

'He fears a mutiny, sir.'

'What of Lucius Porca?'

The circitor swallowed hard. 'The garrison commander doesn't confide in me, sir.'

Justinus chuckled. 'I'm glad to hear it, circitor. Oh, and … um … very politic answers, by the way. I'm guessing that your commanding officer might *lead* the riots the vicarius is worried about.'

'That's not all, sir,' the circitor said, almost afraid to raise another issue.

'Oh?'

'The head,' the circitor almost whispered. 'Men say it opens its eyes. And talks.' He swallowed hard.

'Men,' Justinus repeated, with a smile on his face. 'Tell me, circitor, are you among the men?'

'No, sir.'

'So, you haven't seen it yourself?'

'No, sir.'

'Well, until you do,' the commander said, 'I'd take it all with a very large pinch of salt.'

'The vicarius was hoping you'd have troops with you, sir,' the circitor glanced to the few horsemen on the hill's slope to his right.

'The vicarius knows I travel light,' Justinus said, 'and whatever he told you, he wants me for an altogether different purpose. Let's find out what, shall we?'

Londinium

'I hope you're ready for this,' Conchessa's eyes were bright with pride as she held the little girl under her armpits. She was struggling already.

'Go on, Tullia,' she trilled, kneeling by the hearth. 'Go to Uncle Vit. You can do it.'

Vitalis knelt on the other side of the fireplace, his arms outstretched. 'Come on then, Tullia,' he smiled. 'Your mama's got every confidence in you.'

For the briefest of moments, the little one wobbled. She felt her mother's hands, so warm, so strong, so loving, leave her sides. She felt her world tremble and she focussed ahead. Across those

Roman miles of flagstones her uncle Vit was waiting, her big brother Patricius looking over his shoulder. Baby though she was, she wasn't sure about big brother Patricius; sometimes, as he looked at her with his crooked smile, she wasn't sure he loved her as much as she loved him. She looked back to her mother, and her eyes were smiling, her hands were outstretched to catch her little daughter, her mouth open to accommodate her heart. She saw the love in those clear blue eyes as she turned to face the greatest challenge of her young life. Uncle Vit's eyes were blue, too, and his hair a dark, shorter thatch of brown than Conchessa's gold. His hands were bigger, stronger; if anybody could catch her, and hold her safe, it was Uncle Vit.

Patricius Succatus, to all intents and purposes the son of the decurion of Londinium, watched his sister as she tottered across the floor. He loved her, of course, but missed those quiet times he had once shared alone with his mother. Now it was all 'watch the baby' or 'Tullia's sleeping' or 'Mama is tired – play outside'. But now she was walking; perhaps, with luck, she might one day walk away, with her golden hair and her dimpling smile. She had her father in the palm of her little hand and now, it seemed, she had Uncle Vit there too.

One step, two, her head too big for this, her body too uncoordinated. Three, four. She was falling forward, the flagstones hurtling up to meet her. Then she was whisked up into the sky, with strong hands holding her and Uncle Vit was rubbing noses with her, as she gurgled with joy and pride.

'Well done, Tullia,' Vitalis laughed.

'You see,' Conchessa said. 'I told you she could do it.'

Patricius leaned on his uncle's shoulder. 'Mama said I could walk when I was younger than Tullia,' he said, gruffly. 'Mama said I was the best baby in the world. Mama said …'

Vitalis was a big brother too, and he remembered how he had both loved and hated the little golden thing that Conchessa had been as a baby. Handing the little girl back to her mother, he grabbed Patricius in a mock wrestling hold and held him tight. The boy yelled with pleasure, back at the centre of the Universe. He feinted and grabbed Vitalis arm, fighting him off and yet wanting to be held, to feel as little as Tullia, just for a while. He collapsed onto Vitalis' chest, laughing.

'He's getting strong,' his uncle said. 'He'll be running Londinium before you know it.' Vitalis kissed the boy and made him shriek by tickling his neck.

'No.' Conchessa was serious suddenly, the smile gone, the eyes cold. 'Not that.'

Vitalis let the boy slide down onto his lap. 'And he won't carry the shield either,' he said, with equal seriousness.

'One soldier in the family is enough,' she agreed, looking deep into her brother's eyes.

Vitalis glanced down to the ring on his left hand, the one studded with four helmets in gold on a field as black as death. 'More than enough,' he said. Then he suddenly grabbed the boy, who had relaxed back against him, tired with laughing and relief, blowing raspberries on the lad's belly. Patricius shouted with laughter, shouting 'Again' whenever Uncle Vit seemed to tire of the game. Big brother though he was, sometimes it was good to be little again. Tullia watched him wide eyed from her mother's lap. That looked like fun and she reached out plump arms to her brother.

'However,' Vitalis said, sitting the boy upright on his lap and calming him down with an arm around him, holding him tight, 'when the time is right, we'll make a basket weaver of him. He'll never starve. His father must be pleased ...' His voice trailed away as he said it. Nobody had ever given the soldier-turned-basket-maker a medal for diplomacy.

'I'm sure he would be,' Conchessa said, her face half-averted, 'if he knew. Calpurnius is delighted.'

For a while, there was silence between them, broken only by Tullia's babble.

'You know they've brought Magnus Maximus' head to the city?' Conchessa murmured. Even though her boy could not possibly understand the significance of her words, it seemed wrong that he should even hear them.

Vitalis nodded. 'It's all everybody talks about.'

'There's talk of an army, too,' she said, holding out her arms to her son. She suddenly needed him near. 'An army from Theodosius, to punish us for our sins.'

'Our sins?' Vitalis laughed, short and brittle. 'Let him who is without sin cast the first stone.'

'We weren't here,' she reminded him, 'when Magnus threw his cap into the ring against Gratian. We were at Augusta ...'

'I don't think Theodosius will give a damn about that,' he said. 'What does Calpurnius think?'

Conchessa kissed the top of her boy's head as she held him

close. 'We don't talk politics,' she said. 'Come to think of it, we don't talk much at all.'

Calpurnius Succatus was one of those workhorses of the Roman Empire. A man drowning in paperwork, buried every day in scrolls of vellum, listening to the endless grievances of the citizens of Londinium, from the Ordo who ran the council to the humblest eel-catcher who made a soggy living in the reeds of the Thamesis. That morning, Calpurnius was at his post as usual, high in an office in the basilica as the city clashed and carried in the streets and squares below him. A dozen clerks got to their feet as the vicarius strode in.

'No ceremony,' Chrysanthos waved them back to work. 'A word, Calpurnius. On the balcony?'

The pair walked onto the walkway that ran the length of the building that was the symbol of Londinium's greatness. The sun of Septembris gilded the great walls and danced off the river, as though a late summer had come to Britannia. The vicarius turned to the man who had served, as he had, two emperors. 'You've heard about the head?' he murmured.

'I have,' Calpurnius nodded. 'Bad business.'

'It could be. You know Theodosius. What's he doing?'

Calpurnius knew Theodosius. He had known his father too and had played a part in the old man's downfall and execution. He was not proud of that, but a man has to live with himself and in the corridors of power, many was the skeleton that rattled, the ghost that whispered. 'It's a hint,' he said, 'and a pretty clumsy one at that. We're all supposed to be afraid, to behave ourselves. He's sent what's left of Magnus Maximus to discourage the others.'

'You think there'll be others?' Chrysanthos asked.

'Men who will try for the purple?' Calpurnius chuckled. 'Britannia is infamous for it. Magnus himself opened the floodgates. And the great Constantine long before him. The eagle is falling, Chrysanthos. We both know it. The world is too big, too ambitious. Perhaps Rome has had her time. Anybody who can swing a sword can make a grab for the purple.' He looked at the ant-people scurrying along the crowded streets, crying their wares and filling their market stalls. 'Any of them could be next.' He looked sideways at the vicarius. 'I can see you in a laurel wreath, Chrysanthos.'

For a moment, the vicarius looked surprised. Then he laughed. 'Can you now?' he said. He looked down at the teeming streets too. 'What is it about this little island?' he was asking himself really, 'that it breeds men of such ambition?'

'Where is the head now?' Calpurnius asked.

'In the garrison's chapel. I suggested to Phillipus it might be wise to show it some respect.'

'How did he take that?'

'Badly. But I can't keep him waiting for ever. I've given him various 'technical' reasons, all of it hogwash, of course, why he can't display it in the forum until tomorrow.'

'And then?'

'Then, God help us. I've put Porca's garrison on standby. There'll be some broken heads, that's for sure. And Justinus Coelius is on his way, if my messenger has found him.'

'The Dux Britannorum?' Calpurnius frowned. 'I'd heard he'd retired, curled up with the queen of the Votadini. Some say he's married her.'

'Some say the moon's made of cheese, Calpurnius; that doesn't make it right. I know Coelius; he's married to his job and the Wall. He'll die in harness.'

'Isn't that how we'd all like to go?'

'Is it?' Chrysanthos chortled. 'Speak for yourself. Tell me,' the vicarius led his man along the balcony. 'How well do you know Severianus?'

'The bishop? Tolerably well.'

'Go and see him, will you? Find out what his take is on the head of Magnus Maximus.'

'He's a yes man,' Calpurnius muttered. 'If Theodosius says "jump", he'll just ask "how high?"'

'Well, then, perhaps he can keep his rabble in order. We're all Christians now, Calpurnius; it's just that some of us are more muscular than others. Give the bishop my best.'

Justinus Coelius didn't like to be kept waiting. He had spurred hard from Verulamium at the messenger's insistence, only to be told that the vicarius was busy and could the Dux bear with him and stay at the Mansio. The vicarius could grant him an audience at first light.

Before first light, Justinus had gone to the chapel. The Chi-Rho of the Christian God gleamed here, its gilt and bronze shining in the candlelight. There was no sign of Jupiter Highest and best, no dying bull of Mithras, the soldier's god. Just the hooped cross of the Galilean carpenter. Well, it was the way of the world now; the Roman world at least. But it was none of these trappings that the

Dux Britannorum had come to see. He had looked, long and hard, at the head of his old master, his comrade-in-arms, the Caesar Magnus Maximus. It stood on a short pole, clipped to a platform, the eyes gone from the sockets, the dark skin mere leather, taut across the cheekbones. There would be no more commands from that tongue, no more belting out the lewd words of *The Girl from Clusium* on the march. The hound Bruno at his heels, the faithful Andragathius at his elbow, the legions that tramped in his wake; all gone, like fleeting echoes on the night wind.

Now, Justinus was back in the basilica, pacing backwards and forwards. This wasn't an army camp pitched on the heather and the only winds that blew here were likely to blow him no good.

'Justinus, dear friend,' Chrysanthos hurried in through a side door. 'A thousand apologies.' He shook the man's hand. 'Have you had breakfast yet?'

'I have, Chrysanthos,' the commander said.

'Wine, then?' The vicarius poured for them both.

Justinus nodded and took the cup.

'Britannia,' Chrysanthos toasted. 'May she flourish despite her enemies.'

'Enemies?' Justinus echoed.

'Barbarians.' The vicarius sat on his couch and Justinus sat opposite. 'The painted ones, the Scotti, Germani. You know them better than I.'

'I do,' Justinus nodded, his body scarred from his meetings with all of them. 'But it all seems quiet at the moment. You know I keep on the move.'

'Very commendable,' Chrysanthos smiled, rather as a man does who prefers the luxury of his couch and his bed.

'You sent for me,' Justinus reminded him.

'Did I?'

'In some urgency, I understood, judging by the lather on the messenger's mount.'

'Really? Well, you know how it is. I asked Lucius Porca to send his best rider and … well, you know what an old woman Porca can be. He obviously misunderstood.'

'So there's no emergency?'

'No,' Chrysanthos smiled. 'None.'

'The head?'

'Oh, that.' The vicarius topped up their wine. 'That's taken care of. You've seen it, of course.'

'I have,' Justinus nodded. 'I paid my respects.'

'Yes, I hope there's not *too* much of that in the Forum tomorrow. I mean, respect is one thing, but I hope it won't get out of hand.'

'Which is why you sent for me?'

'Well, always good to have the Dux Britannorum himself in such situations, I always say. First soldier of Britannia and so on. Come to think of it, there was something else. As I say, it wasn't urgent, but I was hoping to pick your brains.'

'Oh?'

'Do you know Terentius Marcus?'

'No,' Justinus said.

'Well, he's an officer here, in Porca's garrison. Junior Tribune at the moment. I think he'd make an excellent Count of the Saxon Shore – you know old Lucinius went … that nasty business with the young horse.'

'Never much of a rider,' Justinus nodded.

'Quite. So, there's a vacancy, at the Saxon Shore, I mean. Now, ordinarily, I'd leave military promotions to you, but …'

'But?'

'Let's just say, there are political considerations. I'll be blunt, Justinus, we need to build fences, with the emperor, I mean. He's sent this man Phillipus to threaten us and there are hints of rather more coercion if we don't knuckle under. An army, Phillipus says.'

'Does he?' Justinus had been this way before. Ever since he had thrown his standard behind Magnus Maximus, he knew that such a time would come.

'Terentius Marcus is somebody's cousin, if you get my meaning.'

'A friend of the Emperor?'

'Exactly. If Phillipus were to go home with that news, promotion for an old family friend … Well, it wouldn't do us any harm, would it?'

'Where can I find this Marcus?' Justinus asked.

'Now?' Chrysanthos leaned sideways to see the angle of the sun. 'He'll be at prayer. A more devout man I've never come across.'

CHAPTER III

They writhed in the shadows, the thud of the legs of the bed against the floor keeping time. First her sighs, then his, built to a crescendo, ragged, collapsing, until his long groan told the world their lovemaking was over. He rolled off her and lay still for a while, watching as she uncoiled her nakedness from the bed and reached for her robe.

He fumbled for the jug of wine at the bedside and took a swig, propped up on one arm. He liked the brunette. She was little but she matched him stroke for stroke and he couldn't complain about that. But the redhead now, the girl from Narbonensis; she was an artist, pure genius in bed. And she was waiting for him now, behind the curtain and along the corridor in this garden of delights just off the waterfront. Tonight, when he had more time, he'd take them both together.

'Next!' he called when no girl appeared.

'That would be me,' a male voice said in the half light. He sat upright, his lust momentarily forgotten.

'Who…?'

The intruder closed to the bed and peered into his face. 'I assume you are Terentius Marcus?' he said.

Marcus felt his heart leap and a sudden chill ran up his spine. 'Dux Britannorum,' he gulped, hurling the covers back and standing to attention, naked as he was.

Justinus turned and ripped the shutters back so that the sunlight streamed in, highlighting the tribune's attributes, but not in a good way. 'I'm sorry if I disappoint you,' he said, noticing how the tribune had wilted. 'There was a girl outside a moment ago, but she seems to have gone now.'

The brunette saw her moment and scuttled across the room. For a moment, Justinus blocked her retreat, then he chuckled and let her go.

'I was told you'd be at prayer,' the commander said.

'Well, I ...'

'So naturally I went to the garrison chapel.'

'I ...'

Justinus smiled at the man, enjoying his confusion. There were senior officers he knew who would break Terentius Marcus to the ranks for frequenting a brothel when duty called. The Dux Britannorum wasn't one of them and that was Marcus' luck. Even so, it didn't bode well.

Justinus crossed the room again and lifted the tribune's sword from the chair where he had flung it. He drew the blade slowly, both men listening to the ring and slide of iron. He weighted it in his hand. 'Nice,' he murmured. 'Expensive.'

'It was my father's, sir,' Marcus said. He wanted to reach for his subigaculum, his tunic, *anything* to cover his nakedness. Justinus had other ideas.

'Make him proud of you,' he said and tossed the sword to Marcus before drawing his own.

The tribune blinked. This was going from bad to worse. He'd just been caught with his subligaculum down and now a man wanted to kill him. 'You expect me to fight you?' he asked, wide-eyed.

'No,' Justinus smiled. 'I expect you to redeem what little honour you can from this situation.'

'But ... I'm naked.'

'If it was good enough for a few thousand Gauls in the good old days, it's good enough for you. Show me what you're made of ... again, I mean.'

Marcus didn't move. This was all so ridiculous. 'Sir ...' he began, 'why...?'

'Why have I paid you this little visit? Oh, it's just a whimsy of mine, testing my junior officers. Today, it's the turn of the Londinium garrison; or, more precisely, today, it's you.'

He thrust suddenly and Marcus scythed to the left, a spark flying from the iron as the blades clashed. Justinus smiled. Then he swung again, faster this time and Marcus half-stumbled against the bed before banging the blade away. He sprang backwards, standing on the bed now, giving himself the advantage of height. He'd forgotten that that also left him *very* exposed, his groin at Justinus' head height.

'Oh, I wouldn't do that,' the commander laughed and flicked his blade forward so that the tip grazed Marcus' thigh. The tribune hissed with pain and jumped down again, blocking Justinus' next blow and the next. All the time, he was retreating, edging around the furniture, looking for a way out. But the only way out was the door and between that and the tribune stood the Dux Britannorum with a sword in his hand.

'Your defence is fine,' Justinus said, 'but have you no attack, man?' He grabbed the jug and threw it, wine and all, at the tribune. Marcus banged the metal aside with his blade but couldn't save himself from the wine and he stood there, the juice of the grape trickling into his eyes and mouth. He launched himself, roaring, slicing through the air and carrying Justinus back to the wall. The door was available now, but Marcus had forgotten all thought of retreat. His sword ripped Justinus' tunic sleeve and he felt the Dux Britannorum sag against the brickwork. The wine had mixed with the red mist in Marcus' eyes and he lunged, but Justinus was faster. He flipped his sword from his right hand to the left and jabbed its hilt into the pit of his opponent's stomach before twisting him round and forcing him to his knees, with the sword of the Dux Britannorum lying horizontal and razor-sharp across his throat.

Terentius Marcus' life flashed before his eyes. His mother. His father. His little sisters. The old dog, Tiberius. And women … God, no, don't think of them at a moment like this. Not when he was about to meet that very God … He felt Justinus' knee in the back of his head and was jolted forward onto his hands and knees. His own sword bounced past his head to land on the bed and there was never a man more relieved to hear another man's sword slide home.

'Not bad,' Justinus said, smiling, 'but keep this …' he waved to the room with its silken drapes and thick incense, 'in its place. Remember, you're first and foremost a soldier of Britannia.' He half-turned in the doorway. 'And you might even make a half-decent one in ten or twenty years.'

The Dux Britannorum paced along the passageway. Wide-eyed girls watched him go, whispering to each other from their cubicles. The brothel-keeper saluted as he reached the stairwell. He had been a soldier once, but he hadn't liked it. Making money from the beast with two backs was much more to his taste. Justinus shook his head. Young Marcus could handle himself in bed; that much was clear. And he wasn't half bad with a sword. But … Count of the Saxon Shore? Never in a million years. He'd report his findings to the vicarius.

Bishop Severianus was not a man who liked conflict, but he *was* bishop of Londinium and there *were* standards. His sacristan had brought him the news from the basilica. And the vicarius' people had been shouting it from the street corners for two days now. A messenger had arrived from Rome; the Emperor Theodosius' right hand man, no less, and he had brought a message for the rebellious people of Britannia. It was a message stuffed into the dead mouth of the Caesar, Magnus Maximus.

'Don't misunderstand me,' Severianus said to Quintus Phillipus as the Septembris sun died over Londinium's rooftops, 'I had no love for Maximus. In fact, I spoke against him in the pulpit …'

'Once he'd gone.' Phillipus sat in a chair borrowed from the vicarius, watching the prelate closely. Nominal Christian though Phillipus was, he distrusted churchmen. He'd never met one he didn't want to knock into the middle of next week.

'Pardon me?'

'I said, you spoke against Maximus once he had left these shores.'

'That's an outrageous slur.' Severianus stood on his dignity, trusting the sacristan at his elbow not to let him down.

'Calm yourself, Lord Bishop,' Phillipus smiled. 'I fought against Maximus. He wasn't a man to cross lightly. If you didn't, as you say, support him, what's your objection to displaying his severed head?'

'It's not the head,' Severianus persisted. 'It's the day. Tomorrow is, after all, the Sabbath. It would be sacrilege on the Lord's Day.'

Phillipus got to his feet. The bishop had dressed up for this little interview, complete with cope, mitre and crozier. He needn't have bothered. 'Your vicarius,' the emperor's man said, 'has been playing me like a puppet since I arrived, keeping me dangling. What are you, his latest ploy?'

'I am nobody's ploy,' Severianus smouldered, his eyes narrowed in the half-light. The sacristan was impressed. He had never seen the bishop so annoyed. 'I am asking you, as one Christian to another, not to defile the Lord's Day.'

'And I am asking you to stick your head up your horse's arse. The exhibition goes ahead.'

'There will be blood!' Severianus shouted, the veins throbbing in his temples under the mitre's rim.

'Out there,' Phillipus said, pointing out of the basilica's windows to the east, 'Suebians, Alans, Vandals, every colour of barbarian you care to name, are massing on our frontiers. How long we can hold them, I don't know. Of course there will be blood. It's the way of the world and it always will be. What matters,' he closed to Severianus, 'is how well we cope with the rising tide.'

For a brief moment, Severianus felt his famous composure slipping. His eyebrows danced in his vision and his mouth twisted. Then he spun on his heel, the sacristan billowing in his wake. 'On your head be it!' the bishop shouted and strode for the passageway and the fresh air, muttering. 'Something must be done about that man. And quickly.'

'State your business!' The guard barked the order from his niche at the garrison gate.

'Vitalis Celatius, tribune of the Schola Palatinae,' the call came back. The guard stood to attention, spear at the upright as soon as he saw the emperor's eagle insignia. He wasn't to know the man in the uniform was now a civilian, who eked a living making baskets from the reeds of the Thamesis. He wasn't to know the man was a hero of the Wall, the subject of those tall tales they still told in the tavernas along the waterfront, the tales that mothers used to quieten their fractious children.

'I've come to pay my respects to the late Caesar,' Vitalis said.

'Of course, sir,' the guard said. 'You take the first …'

'I know my way,' Vitalis told him. He had never served with this garrison, but one army headquarters was very like another. The chapel would lie to the left of the principia, the quarters of Lucius Porca, the commanding officer. Here stood, proud bearers of memories of fights past and glorious, the standards with their wreaths, their hands, their moons. Here stood the Chi-Rho of the Christ, crowning them all. And here, on its pole and platform in the centre, the head of Magnus Maximus.

Vitalis unbuckled his helmet and placed it in the crook of his arm. His footfalls echoed on the flagstones and the candles guttered in a sudden wind that came from nowhere. To be honest, Vitalis didn't quite know why he had come. He had not followed Maximus, as so many had, to Gallia and beyond. He had not been with the Caesar's entourage when he had smashed the army of the emperor Gratian and he had not been with him when his own force was destroyed in Aquileia's lagoons. He had known Maximus in the old days, when they had ridden together to defend the Wall. Vitalis did not owe the man anything. And Magnus Maximus owed nothing to Vitalis. But *something* had made the man come to this place, on this night. He knew that Vitalis the basket-maker would never get past the guard so he dusted down the old uniform and put it on. That mere strips of leather and iron could open doors never ceased to amaze him. Vitalis looked at the head, shrivelled and unreal. He had turned his back on the army, on all that the dead man stood for, not once, but twice. He suddenly hated what he wore, what Maximus stood for. He hated the killing. And the blood. Always the blood.

Even so, this was not right. You don't show a man's hacked corpse to the mob and spit on it in your triumph. And he knew, in his heart, that that was what Quintus Phillipus had in mind. And it wouldn't do. Vitalis owed nothing to Magnus Maximus, but he owed him common humanity. The basket-maker saluted with the straight arm due to emperors and turned away. Whatever was planned for tomorrow, he must stop it.

The city was silent that night in the basilica's precincts. Phillipus had turned down Chrysanthos' offer to stay at the old governor's palace. The gesture was no doubt made genuinely enough, but the vicarius had aided and abetted the coup carried out by Maximus; at the very least, he had stood idly by and let it happen. Best not to get too close to the man. Mud stuck; you lie with dogs, you get up with fleas. Phillipus took in the night air. From where he stood on the walkway he could see the garrison's watchmen patrolling the walls. Beyond them the street ran straight and true to the bridge where more of Porca's men lolled on their spears, chewing the fat and swapping insults as old soldiers had done for ever. The squat merchant ships rode at anchor along the wharves, their masts and furled sails black against the silver of the river.

The river actually depressed Phillipus. He knew that this city was the best Britannia had to offer. Wherever he chose to take

Maximus' head, it would not be as grand as this. Damn Theodosius! Why had he sent him on this thankless mission? Well, it was late and time he turned in. The emperor's man padded down the steps into the courtyard. Torches guttered around the walls here, throwing twisted shadows across the uneven stones. He crossed the flagstones, pale under the moon and reached the door to his staircase. There would be wine waiting for him and a little bread and cheese, even though it couldn't compare with the fare at home. A sudden creak on the stair made him stop. Shit! He'd left his dagger in his apartment. Still, what harm could there be here? The basilica was crawling with guards. They couldn't *all* be asleep; he knew that – he'd just watched them going about their duties. Then, a phrase crept into the suspicious mind of Quintus Phillipus – Quis custodes ipsos custodiet? Who guards the guards?

'Who's there?' His hand was still on the door latch, the stairs curving ahead of him, following the circle of the tower wall. There was a window ahead, a slit of light that let the moonlight filter onto the stairs. There was no-one there. He shook himself free of his fears. Get a grip, man, he told himself. It's this damn climate. The wet. The chill. Let's get to bed and forget all about it, at least until morning. Phillipus found himself smiling at the thought of tomorrow. He was going to enjoy that. He was going to enjoy looking at the awestruck faces of the rabble and the Ordo and everyone else who had believed that Magnus Maximus had been a match for the divine Theodosius, the god-given. Here, in this shrunken face, those dead eyes, was the tangible proof that he was not.

He was still relishing these thoughts, walking up the wooden stairs when he heard the noise again. What had been ahead of him was now behind and he turned sharply.

'What do you want?' he asked.

'You, Quintus Phillipus,' a voice came back. 'I want you.'

Lucius Porca was not a happy man. He had been snapping at his orderlies and his servants since before dawn. His troops were on high alert, every man armed to the teeth. From the garrison's ramparts he had watched the trickle of people grow to a torrent, like ants on the march. Their noise was like thunder, rumbling in the mountains under the leaden sky. There would be no sun today, as the old month turned, but the weather was the least of Porca's worries.

It was bad enough that the Dux Britannorum was in the

city; worse that he had turned down Porca's invitation of quarters in the principia. Porca liked Justinus Coelius as a man. But as Dux Britannorum he could be a pain in the arse; forever inspecting weapons, putting men through their paces, questioning officers on theoretical military situations. And add to that this nonsense of the vicarius'. Porca had not known Magnus Maximus. The man had sailed to his destiny before Porca had been appointed to the Londinium job. But Porca was a man who didn't like surprises. And today, with the head of Magnus Maximus about to be displayed, there were likely to be a lot of surprises.

The people of Londinium, their children scampering alongside their fathers, holding their mothers' hands, keeping close, swarmed from the Land Gate and the Bishop's Gate and the Old Gate. Others had got the word and had come from the forests to the north and the marshes to the east. Porca's men manned the gates and let them in ten at a time, grunting at the odd complaint from families who insisted on staying together. It was like a circus. Was *no-one* working today?

Bishop Severianus kissed the stole before placing it over his shoulders. He bowed before the altar and looked at the gaunt, carved figure of the Christ nailed to his cross. At least his Lord had not suffered the indignity that was Magnus Maximus' lot today. The sacristan opened the door for his bishop.

'You did as I told you, Gallius?'

'I did, my Lord.'

'Come on, then. Let's get this over with.'

Vitalis was not wearing his uniform today. Today he was the basket-maker, jostled by the mob from his own waterfront, swept by the tide of humanity along the narrow streets, jammed almost solid with people. The young ones didn't understand what was happening.

'Are we going to see a head, Mama?' one little girl asked. 'A *real* head?'

'Good riddance, I say,' Vitalis heard an old man say. 'Maximus was a bloody tyrant, if you ask me.'

'Nobody's asking you, you old git,' a younger man at his elbow grunted.

Vitalis sighed. It was going to be one of those days.

Scipio Honorius had got himself a prime position overlooking the forum. There was a dais in the centre which the vicarius' carpenters had been working on for much of the night, with two of the vicarius' thrones hung with crimson velvet to the rear. At the front, a post stood upright with a small platform at the top. But Scipio wasn't interested in that. He was watching his people, scions of the Black Knives and the Left Hand, working the crowd with an expertise that was terrifying.

Julia was circling the area by the well, smiling at the men and whispering in their ears. She singled out the singletons. No point in getting into a punch-up with a man's woman today. Simpler if she chose the young, the impressionable. But not *too* young that they didn't have money on them. Julia of the Two Hands was a past mistress, in every sense of the phrase. While she was stroking a man's manhood with her right, she was helping herself to his purse with her left. It worked every time.

Little Veronica was different. She had eyes a man could drown in and although no doubt in time she would learn Julia's tricks, at the age of nine she let her knees do the talking. She could click them in and out of their sockets at will and hobbled through the crowd now on a well-worn crutch, holding out her hand in the desperation of the streets. Today those streets were full of people from beyond the city wall, mothers whose hearts broke at the sight of the motherless waif stumbling in front of them.

Placidus was the clumsiest drunk in Londinium. He was never looking where he was going and was forever barging into people, mostly well-dressed men with bulging purses. And every time Placidus collided with someone, complete with the humblest and most grovelling of apologies, he came away the heavier by that very purse.

These three, along with a dozen others were joining the crowds making their way to the forum's edge. Scipio smiled. It was going to be a good day.

Conchessa took her place with the ladies of the Ordo on their cushioned seats overlooking the forum. Calpurnius had told her that little Patricius must be there too, because it was important that a decurion show solidarity with the vicarius. Conchessa had ignored him. Her boy would, no doubt, have enough horror in his life without seeing the hacked head of a man displayed like a trophy of war. She had left both her babies with their nanny.

There was a flutter among the ladies, a tossing of heads and a pursing of lips. It was *her.* How dare she, the ladies muttered to each other. She wasn't the vicarius' wife. The vicarius had no wife. She was his mistress. Worse, she was riff-raff from the street, a whore who had made her living on her back. Honoria swept onto the steps, surrounded by her people. Her fingers glittered with gold under the iron of the sky and her purple cloak shimmered with the richest silk and fur. She ignored the ladies entirely but smiled briefly at Conchessa before scanning the balcony to her left. Yes, there he was, her Scipio.

The king of London's underworld saw his mama and bowed to her. What a team!

Lucius Porca urged his horse into the space his men had won for him by their muscles and the push of their spears. They turned their backs on the crowd and presented their shields to the front. A centurion barked orders and his gnarled stick whirled through the air. The cornicines of the garrison brayed their announcement and the crowd fell silent.

Crysanthos the vicarius, wearing the pallium of his office under the purple cloak, swept down the steps past Honoria and crossed the square alone. Porca drew his sword and saluted him, kissing the hilt of the spatha and resting the blade on his shoulder. Any minute now …

Another blast on the trumpets and a small retinue of Phillipus' Heruli cavalry, dismounted, squeezed their way past the garrison's shields to reach the dais. Two of them carried something on a litter between them, something wrapped in scarlet cloth.

Justinus Coelius blinked. That cloth was the vexillum of the II Augusta, one of his own legions. He would know that gilt lettering anywhere. What kind of bastard was Theodosius that he had mopped Maximus' blood with the flag of the II? He had not taken his place on the steps with the vicarius' entourage, as was his right. Instead, he stood near the basilica's door, not far from where Bishop Severianus had positioned himself with his people.

The Heruli guards lifted their burden and placed it on the pole on the dais. A sudden gust of wind caught a corner of the cloth and the crowd nearest to it stirred. Porca's men felt pressure at their backs and the commander himself sat upright in the saddle, trying to guess where the trouble would start. Because there was going to be trouble, that was certain. He bent to murmur orders into the ear of a centurion to his right, pointing with his sword to a knot of wharfmen who were jostling behind the screen of soldiers. The centurion beckoned a dozen soldiers and they clattered along the edge of the square, to be ready; just in case.

Crysanthos sat on one of the vacant chairs. He heard the crowd's murmurs growing, sensed the mood. Things could get ugly here and it wouldn't be long now. Where the hell was Phillipus? Chrysanthos barely knew the man. Was this his moment, a chance to make a grand entrance before he made his grand speech? If so, he was milking it for all it was worth. He fidgeted. Porca's men were everywhere. The Dux Britannorum was watching intently, his eyes scanning the crowd. To his left and below him, a little girl was hobbling to get a better view, her grey eyes huge with wonder. Her hand was held out in front of her.

There was a sudden shout to Chrysanthos' left and rear. The wharfmen hadn't moved but a knot of men were shouting, whistling and stomping with impatience. Someone threw a clod of earth that bounced off a garrison helmet and the line bulged as the people swayed.

'Hold that line steady!' Porca yelled, although he wasn't sure his men could hear him.

'Maximus!' somebody yelled and the crowd took up the chant. 'Maximus! Maximus! Maximus!' To Porca's horror, even his own troops were joining in, not with their voices but with their shields and the butts of their spears, thudding them onto the cobbles in time to the hypnotic rhythm of the mob.

'Now, vicarius,' Porca muttered against the cheekplate of his helmet. 'For God's sake, get it over with.'

He saw Chrysanthos, as though for all the world he had heard his rumblings, jump from his throne and cross to the flag draped over the pole. As though someone had shut a door, cutting out all sound, all light, the chanting stopped and an eerie silence descended on the forum. Even Julia of the Two Hands had stopped her secret fumblings and Placidus wasn't bumping into anybody. Everyone's eyes were fixed on Chrysanthos and his hand on the red flag.

Then he whisked it away and a human head sat there, impaled on a spike, the chestnut hair dabbled in blood that still looked fresh.

'Behold the head …' Chrysanthos began and his voice trailed away.

'It's a miracle.' The sacristan crossed himself. 'The head; look, it's uncorrupted!'

The cry was taken up by others around him and people fell to their knees. The Lord was in the city as never before. Severianus licked his lips in a valiant attempt to keep his heart in his mouth. For him the Lord was always in the city. But this was not a sign from Him.

'Is that him, Papa?' a little boy shouted, perched on his father's shoulders for a better view. 'Is that Maximus the monster?'

Justinus couldn't believe it. Neither could Vitalis. Surely, that was …

Chrysanthos pulled himself together and finished his sentence '… of Quintus Phillipus.'

The Heruli looked at each other in astonishment. No one had checked the head under the red flag. It had been brought up from the garrison chapel the night before and kept in the basilica. This wasn't possible. It wasn't happening.

The crowd that moments before had been about to burst with indignation at the insult to their hero now burst out laughing. People slapped each other's backs and Severianus' people started to sing until he stopped them with a very unchurchly reprimand.

Porca blew a sigh of relief. The wharfmen were dancing as far as the mass of humanity gave them room and people were pressing coins into the outstretched hand of the little crippled girl.

Chrysanthos threw the flag over the severed head of the emperor's man and turned to face the Heruli. 'You people,' he snarled, 'will come with me.'

Honoria swept the ranks of the Ordo with the imperious glance she had cultivated over the years. She loved the look of horror and confusion on their faces. They'd still be talking about this years from now. But she wouldn't. She looked across to the far balcony where Scipio winked at her and bowed again.

CHAPTER IV

'You wanted to see me, vicarius?' Bishop Severianus didn't like being summoned to the imperium. He was happy to serve his earthly master, the emperor and, by extension, the vicarius, the emperor's right hand here in Britannia. But he served his God first. And increasingly his God and his emperor stood on opposite sides of the coin.

'What do you know of this business?' Chrysanthos was lounging on his couch in the basilica, jerking his thumb in the direction of the severed head of Quintus Phillipus.

'Nothing.' Severianus was astonished to be asked the question.

Chrysanthos leapt to his feet, looking the man in the face. 'Nothing,' he repeated. 'I happen to know,' and he crossed to a table and poured wine for himself, 'that you visited this man yesterday and warned him not to go through with his ceremony, not to display the head of Maximus.'

Severianus blinked. 'You are well informed, sir,' he said.

'That's why I'm the vicarius, Lord Bishop,' Chrysanthos said. 'I also happen to know that you told your sacristan you would have to do something about him.'

This time the bishop's mouth just hung open. Chrysanthos grabbed the man's hands, the episcopal ring glinting in the half-light of his office. 'Oh, not personally, of course. I wouldn't expect the bishop of Londinium to soil these pretty little fingers. But you have people ...'

'I am a man of God!' Severianus was beside himself, the eyebrows twitching like a man possessed. 'I tried to talk Phillipus out of displaying the head, but that failed.'

'So you had him killed.' It was a statement, not a question.

'So I gave up!' Severianus shouted, suddenly embarrassed by so loud and so public an admission of failure.

Chrysanthos looked at the man, a man without the stomach necessary for his job, a shepherd as lost and confused as his flock. Then the vicarius smiled.

'I don't know whether you are aware of it, Bishop,' he said, 'but whatever happened to Phillipus, the emperor will want answers. He'll want another head, the head of the man who killed him.'

Severianus was lost for words. He knew the vicarius' justice. It was swift and terrible and there was no chance of reprieve. 'Don't worry,' Chrysanthos patted the trembling prelate on the shoulder. 'I've never hanged a bishop.' He crossed the room and hauled back the heavy curtain that hung there. 'Basket makers now; that's a different matter.'

Vitalis stood in the atrium. He had been summoned by Chrysanthos' guards from his workshop near the river and he guessed what it was about. He nodded at Severianus who made the sign of the cross over him and left as fast as his dignity would let him down.

The vicarius circled his new visitor, sipping his wine as he did so. 'You knew the late Caesar,' he said before returning to his couch again.

'You know I did,' Vitalis said. There had been a time when he had served in the emperor Gratian's personal escort at Augusta Treverorum. The machinations of a mere vicarius meant nothing to him. Chrysanthos lifted the man's hands, as he had with the bishop's. '*These* hands,' he said, 'have killed.'

'Yes,' Vitalis pulled away, 'and it's not something I'm proud of.'

Chrysanthos leaned back, smiling. 'Old soldiers,' he said, 'when they retire, usually settle for a bottomless wine cellar and a little plot of land. A hero of the Wall like you, I would have thought, would have wanted a villa or two, within a walk of the sea perhaps. Nice.'

'Why am I here?' Vitalis asked him.

Chrysanthos sighed, 'You may be a basket maker now, Vitalis, but you have the heart and mind of a soldier; no, a politician. What's happened to Phillipus over there is going to bring the wrath of Theodosius down on us. Severianus is more afraid of his God than the emperor, but some of us live in the real world.'

'I repeat,' Vitalis hadn't moved. 'Why am I here?'

Chrysanthos got up slowly and faced the basket maker as he had faced the bishop. 'Because you know Magnus Maximus. More, you were a comrade in arms. What was this?' he jerked his living head in the direction of the dead one of Quintus Phillipus. 'Pay-back?'

'While I was waiting outside,' Vitalis murmured. 'I thought I heard Severianus tell you that he was a man of God.'

'He did,' the vicarius nodded.

'Well, in a different way, so am I. Murder is not my style. I have hung up my sword for ever.'

'Have you?' Chrysanthos smiled. 'Have you really?'

'Was there anything else?' Vitalis asked.

'For now, no,' the vicarius said, 'but you won't be leaving Londinium, will you?'

'Where would I go?'

When his footfalls had died away along the passage, Chrysanthos hauled back another curtain. 'Well?' he said and this time he poured a second cup of wine.

'Well, what?' Calpurnius took it, sliding the curtain back behind him.

'In your opinion …'

The decurion looked at the vicarius. 'In my opinion, neither.'

'Really?'

'I don't know Severianus. He looks like a hare caught between two fires.'

'Yes, he's afraid of his shadow. But he's also the most powerful churchman in Britannia. Men would fall over each other at a casual hint from him, anxious to find their place in Heaven.'

'Then your list could be very long indeed.'

'It could.' Chrysanthos sipped the wine. 'What about the other one?'

'No,' Calpurnius said. 'Not in a thousand years.'

'Just because he's your brother-in-law …'

'*Precisely* because he's my brother-in-law. I know him, Chrysanthos. Vitalis Celatius is a tortured soul. He is a good man, more of a Christian than any I know …'

'I hear he follows Pelagius,' the vicarius interrupted. 'The renegade.'

'Well ... yes, but ...'

'But that's close to heresy, decurion.'

'Technically, yes, but ...'

Chrysanthos laughed, amused by the man's embarrassment. 'Look,' he said. 'I've got better things to do than watch Christians squabbling among themselves. I'm playing magistrate today – solely, you realise, because the real ones are such a bunch of idiots – and I'm looking for a murderer. Could Vitalis the basket-maker have killed Phillipus?'

'No,' Calpurnius said. 'Emphatically, no.'

There was a pause. 'What about Justinus Coelius?' he asked.

'The Dux Britannorum?' Calpurnius blinked. 'You can't be serious.'

'Oh, I'm deadly serious,' the vicarius said. 'He too was a comrade of Maximus. Got his present job because of him.'

'Agreed,' Calpurnius said, 'and I can't pretend to know the man as well as you do. But I don't think it's Justinus' style. If he had a grievance with Phillipus, he would have called him out into the open in broad daylight, gone toe to toe with the man with sword and shield. That's Justinus' way.'

'Yes,' Chrysanthos sighed. 'I thought you'd say that.' He poured another cup for them both. 'Tell me,' he said, 'about Andros Procopius.'

'What's to tell?' Calpurnius shrugged. 'The man's efficient. Capable.'

'Runs the drains, doesn't he?'

'He is a valued member of my staff.' The decurion stood his ground.

'Unstable, though?'

Calpurnius frowned. 'I don't know what you've heard,' he said. 'Andros has not been well.'

'I heard he was a madman.'

'You heard wrong.'

Chrysanthos shrugged. 'Clearly I did,' he said.

'Why this sudden interest in Procopius?' Calpurnius wanted to know.

'Oh, I'm just looking for a bit of a shake-up, you know, ring a few changes. He's not, for example, the kind of man I should send to the emperor, with news of Phillipus, I mean?'

'Er ... no. I'm not sure diplomacy is Andros' forte.'

'Well, there it is. Calpurnius … you will keep your eyes and ears open, won't you?'

'What for, vicarius?'

'For the murderer of Phillipus. Stands to reason it was an inside job. The mad died just out there, across the courtyard. They found his body stuffed under the stairs. God, the blood …' and he took a long swig of wine.

Calpurnius got up. 'Yes,' he said. 'I'll keep my eyes and ears open.'

Britannia Prima

Justinus Coelius, the Dux Britannorum, set out two days later, clattering over the cobbles of Lucius Porca's camp and leading a spare horse. He left his cavalry escort behind, temporarily under Porca's command and rode north-west, across Britannia Prima, with the wind at his back. As usual, he rode without ceremony and without fuss, a plain fur soldier's cap on his head and a rough cloak of fustian over his leather tunic. A legionary's shield hung from the saddle bow of his spare horse along with three days' rations and the head of Magnus Maximus. To say that the Dux Britannorum had stolen it would be technically true, but he had done it openly, in the full light of day, daring any of Phillipus' Heruli to stop him. He would not display the head of Maximus at every way station and make rousing speeches on behalf of Theodosius at each one. There was only one place the head belonged and he was going there now.

The first night brought him to Verulamium and he left his horses with a patrolling guard at the Londinium gate before visiting the little shrine deep in the earth. In these uncertain times when the God of the Christians was worshipped in churches across the empire, a temple to Mithras was increasingly a rarity. Justinus had been raised with this god and had washed his little hands in the blood of the blood when his father had served with the VI Victrix far to the north of here. The Dux Britannorum unbuckled his sword belt and knelt before the great bull, carved in stone, its horns a rich crimson. Justinus nicked his forearm with the sacrificial blade that hung there and smeared his blood over the left horn, then the right. 'Mithras,' he murmured, 'also a soldier, keep me pure 'til the dawn.'

And as that dawn broke, he was trotting north-west again, along the old legions' road that led to Deva, the old base of the XX Valeria Victrix. Magnus Maximus had depleted the place, taking men with him into the rolling wastes of the German Sea, never to return. Justinus felt the wind on his face and saw the trees, naked now in the coming autumn, bow in the wind. Their leaves fluttered before him, in a cascade of colour, reds, browns and golds. It would be winter soon enough and he wanted to be home by then, as far as a man like him had a home at all.

That night, under a frost of stars, the Dux Britannorum slept in the open, wrapped in his cloak and warming his hands by a crackling fire. Then he came to Viroconium of the Cornovii and made straight for its baths. The XX had built this base long ago, when the eagles were first flying over the wild heathlands of this island and the whole of Britannia was a battlefield. A vexillation of the XX kept this place now and duly turned out the guard for the Dux Britannorum. Justinus wanted no ceremony. He would pass on the inspection, if the tribune didn't mind. All he wanted to do was soak his tired muscles in the water of the tepidarium. The basilica may have been abandoned and little boys made mud pies in the forum, but whenever there were soldiers, there would still be a bath-house. He leaned back and let the steam swirl before him, visions of dragons coiling and writhing in the darkness. Tomorrow, he would leave the legions' road and ride across the heather to the south of Deva. The limitanei of the XX there could relax; the Dux Britannorum would not be inspecting them tomorrow.

Deceangli Territory

The rain had set in before he reached the high country, a drifting drizzle that came from the west, bouncing off the dead brown of the bracken. He heard them before he saw them, the bray of the hunting horn and the yelping of the dogs. His horse pricked up its ears and whinnied. Justinus had pulled the hood of his cloak over his head and the water droplets were splashing onto his hands tight around the reins. They were Deceangli horns, he was sure of that. He had not ridden this way for nearly six years, and he smiled to himself as he noted the welcome the weather gave him. It always rained in these mountains, whatever the season.

He urged the horse on, following an old path worn smooth and wide over the centuries by shepherds and their flocks. A sudden crash through the bracken brought his horse up short. The animal snorted, jinking backwards and shaking its head. A boar had crossed his path, large and brown and terrified. He steadied the horse, waiting for what would follow. What followed were hounds, long-legged, bristly animals, their tongues flopping from their yelping mouths. And after them the horsemen, rough men on little shaggy ponies, doing their damnedest to keep up with the dogs.

Justinus didn't speak these men's language well, but he knew the gist.

'Henwen,' one of them roared, 'the ancient one. We're onto him. Want to join in?'

The Dux Britannorum had hunted boar before. Cornered, they were vicious bastards that could rip a man's leg to the bone with their tusks. At full tilt, a male could topple a horse. He waved in decline and rode on, ducking under the birch branches that edged the path. The thud of the hunters' hooves and the braying of their horns died away and he found himself in a wood that had become a forest. What little light there was from the rain-filled sky was gone now and the pine trees outnumbered the birch. The wind sighed here, like the raven-women the Deceangli believed haunted the fields of battle, pecking the souls of the dead from their breasts. His horses didn't like this place, their hooves padding almost silently on the thick carpet of pine needles.

'Did you see him?' a voice croaked from the darkness. In an instant, Justinus' sword was in his hand and he swung the horse to face the trees to his right. He saw nothing at first. Then he made out a small hand clutching a tree branch. Then another. Her eyes darted fire out of a cherub's face and her long dark hair swayed as she crept out from her hiding place. She couldn't have been much more than seven years old.

In an instant, another figure broke from the cover of the pines and he half hid the child behind him. The man was old, white-haired and he hobbled on a stick. 'I said,' he croaked again, 'did you see him?'

'See who?' Justinus answered as well as he could in the old man's dialect.

'Henwen. The ancient one.'

'What are you talking about, old man?'

The old man had been watching Justinus for some time. He recognized the fur cap under the hood, the shield, the four-pronged saddle. 'You're a Roman,' he said.

'Forgive me,' said Justinus. He had not sheathed his sword yet because he had just run into a madman.

'The boar,' the old man explained. 'He crossed your path.'

'Yes,' Justinus humoured him. 'I saw him.'

'What colour was he?'

'Er … brown.'

A reedy laugh, more like a death rattle, rose from the old man's throat. 'Brown today, was he?' He shook his head. He led the girl out onto the path. Certain they were alone, Justinus sheathed his sword, but stayed in the saddle. The old man squinted up at him through rheumy eyes. 'He can be black,' he said. 'His name, "wen", means white.'

'A pig that changes colour?' Justinus chuckled, but the old man and the girl did not.

'You can scoff, Roman,' he said, 'but I have seen Henwen kill. His score is fifty men and fifty hounds. Blue-black he is at night, merging with the darkness. In the dawn, he is grey, like the mountain mist. He has no ears, no tail and his bollocks have been trampled by his iron-shod hooves. His mane stands tall on his back, tough bristles that skewer men. See?' He hauled up his sleeve and showed an arm raked with the livid white of an old scar. 'And his teeth! Roman, if you had ever seen his teeth …'

'I am looking for Elen of the Armies.' Justinus had wasted enough time with this old fool. 'Is this the right way?'

The old man clutched the little girl to him, holding her close. 'What business have you with Elen Llyddog?'

'My own,' Justinus told him.

The little girl wriggled free of the old man's grasp and stood defiantly, hands on hips, looking up at Justinus. 'Are you my Papa?' she asked him. In Latin.

Caer Llyn

Elen of the Armies had not changed. It had been years since Justinus had seen her but it was almost as though they had never been. She sat that night in front of a roaring fire. The air was chill this far north and winter was on the wind. The Dux Britannorum had eaten his fill and had talked over old times; about what he knew of Magnus Maximus whose bed Elen had shared and whose little girl Justinus had met in the forest. Elen had heard the news already that the man she called Macsen Wledig was dead. She had known long before the messengers came to her. When his letters stopped, she knew. Little Sevira was a different matter. She had never known her father, the great general who had driven the Hiberni and the painted ones from her mother's land. But she was seven and every stranger who came to her mountains held a fascination for her. Her papa was dead, her mother had told her, but that couldn't be right. He had thrown his sword into the holy waters of Llyn Tegid. Surely he would come back to get that, one day.

The little girl had gone to sleep on her mother's lap before the fire that crackled and crumbled on the hearth. Elen looked into Justinus' dark eyes, the flames reflected in her own. 'There's something you're not telling me,' she said.

He looked at her. For days now he had been wondering how to broach it, wondering how she would respond. 'Theodosius sent his head back,' he murmured, not wanting to wake the girl, 'as a warning.'

Elen blinked, swallowing hard. All her life she had been a warrior. She had killed her first man when she wasn't that much older than her baby curled on her lap now. Her people, like all natives of Britannia, had taken heads as trophies of war for centuries. They hung them from their saddle-bows and placed them on poles outside their huts. She licked her lips and chose her words. 'How very Celtic of him,' she said.

Justinus let go the breath he had been holding, it seemed, for days. How typical, he thought. And how brave. Other widows would have cried, screamed. Roman matrons he knew would have reached for their smelling salts, torn at their breasts with their fingernails. But this was the queen of the Deceangli. More, it was Elen of the Armies, the woman of Magnus Maximus. What other response could she have given?

'You've brought it, haven't you?' she asked. 'That's why you've come.'

He nodded, pointing to the leather bag that lay in the corner with his sword and cap.

'Tomorrow,' she said, 'we'll go to Llyn Tegid and Macsen can rejoin his sword.'

And so it was. They caught the boar that day and it was quite clearly brown. When they showed its body, ripped and torn by the dogs, to the old man, he shook his head. No, that wasn't Henwen. Nothing about the dead creature was right; first and foremost, *be-*

cause he was dead. No one could kill Henwen. He was out there still, in his mountains. He would be there forever.

Elen had insisted on no fuss. Most ceremonies involving the Deceangli would see the priests with their mistletoe and their fire, the rattle of their drums and the chanting of their warriors. Not today. While the hunters clustered around the old man and listened again to his tall tales and he sent shivers up the spine of Sevira and the other children around him, Elen and Justinus slipped unnoticed out of the palisade and rode south.

She wore her armour today, as befitted the burial of a soldier. Her long golden hair was swept up under the spangenhelm, its iron, silver-chased nasal obscuring most of her face. Her arms and legs shimmered with mail in the morning light and her chestnut easily kept pace with Justinus' saddle-horse.

Llyn Tegid lay like a slab of silver under the cold light of the sky. A heron flapped from the reeds, disturbed in its morning fishing and took to the sky, head held back and wings outstretched. Elen remembered exactly where it had happened, the place along the bank where she and Maximus, with his strange Egyptian prophetess muttering incantations, had thrown his sword. She reined in and dismounted. Justinus did too and he unhooked the leather bag from the saddle.

'No,' she said as he tightened the fastenings. 'I want to see.'

'Lady …' he began but the flash of fire from her eyes silenced him. Dux Britannorum he may be but he could not come between a woman and her love. He suddenly felt embarrassed, ashamed even and he passed her the bag before wandering away.

On a spur of rock that jutted into the lake, Justinus stood and waited. He hauled off his cap in respect and watched as Elen sank to her knees in Llyn Tegid's mud. She cradled the head of Macsen Wledig in her hands, smoothing the matted, dry hair from the leather of the face. She looked into the dry ghosts of his eyes, shrunk in their sockets. She heard his voice, felt the touch of him against her. No one had known the great Maximus as she had. Justinus had ridden into battle alongside the man. So had she. But only she had held him in the darkness of a Deceangli night, listening to the little popping noises he made as he slept. Only she had felt his seed pumping into her. Only she had gritted her teeth as Macsen's child, the baby Sevira, had wriggled into the world. She lifted the head to the sky, then brought it down and kissed the withered lips.

As Justinus watched, Elen of the Armies placed the head back into the bag. Then she threw it out across the waters of the lake and it seemed to hang in the air forever. Then, it hit the surface with a splash that sent the moorhens screeching to safety. It bubbled once or twice. And was gone.

Elen of the Armies turned to her horse, she took her helmet off for the first time that day and let her hair fly free. Her eyes were dry, her face composed. Elen of the Armies had said her goodbye. She would do her crying later.

CHAPTER V

Valentia

They crouched in the heather listening to the lowing of the cattle. The painted ones were excellent warriors but what they did for a living was to steal. Cattle, sheep, horses, women, it didn't matter much. It had always been like this, the wild men of the north swooping down on the rolling hills of the lowlands, burning villages, raping, helping themselves.

'How many do you count, little brother?' Taran had a number in his head but this, he was determined, was going to be Edern's day.

'Fifteen,' the boy said. Edern was five years younger than Taran and, in the way of things, he always would be. His father had been the tribune Paternus Priscus, a hero of the Wall, and the man had died long ago, defending this unforgiving wilderness against the kind of men who were stealing the cattle now. Edern was small for his age, so that he didn't look his eighteen summers. And all his life he had lived in the shadow of the half-brother who crouched alongside him now, watching the valley and the ponderous progress of the herd.

Taran was not just older than little Edern, he was bigger, harder, a king in all but name. His father was a prince of the Gododdin, but he barely remembered him. The gulf of cultures separated these two and only their mother, Brenna, held them together.

'Go and win your laurels, then,' Taran smiled. 'Isn't that what your friends the Romans give each other for bravery? Anyway, it's your turn.'

It was. This was a game that the brothers had played since they were not much taller than the grass in the meadows of Din Paladyr. They fought each other constantly, but when they banded together, they were formidable and they swapped the roles at will. When that had been backyard fights, with fists and feet and wooden swords, that was fine. Bruised faces and egos was as bad as it got. But those men leading off the Gododdin cattle were Picts. They played for real. And they didn't know about the game.

Edern looked beyond his brother to where their men sat their ponies, waiting for the word. They outnumbered the painted ones two to one, so the outcome was assured.

'Of course,' Taran said, sensing the younger lad's hesitation, 'if you'd rather not …'

All his life Edern had been goaded this way. He thought that by now he would have got over it and learned to ride out the jibes, the mockery, the raised eyebrow. He hadn't. He hauled himself upright and ran to his horse, swinging into the saddle. As he trotted past Taran, still crouching in the heather, he murmured, 'Your best support, now.'

'Count on it, dear brother,' Taran smiled. As the younger man crested the hill, the horsemen at Taran's back prepared to mount. 'Hold,' their prince barked. '*I'll* tell you when.' The Gododdin looked at each other, suspicion in their eyes. Suspicion turned to a shrug. This was Taran, prince of the Gododdin and their future king. What, in the scheme of things, did they know? The man was protected by the shining one himself – and Belatucadros knew best.

Edern shouted something in Pictish as he cantered down the slope. The nearest painted ones wheeled their horses and readied their spears. The cowherds whose cattle these were lay dead three or four miles back, but no Pict imagined a raid like this could be that easy. Even so, this was one man. They let the beasts wander the valley, slowing now and munching the sweet grass. Edern reined in his horse and faced the thieves, who had drawn themselves up into a tight formation, bristling with spears.

'Thank you for collecting my cattle,' he said, in the best Pictish he could muster.

There was laughter. '*Your* cattle?' the leader threw back.

'Mine,' Edern nodded. 'I am Edern, prince of the Gododdin.'

More laughter. Whoops and whistles. 'Good for you.'

'Ride away,' Edern sat his horse impassively, 'and we'll say no more about it.'

'*You* ride away,' the leader said. Suddenly he braced himself and threw his spear. The shaft hissed through the air and the broad iron bit deep into the shoulder of Edern's horse. The animal reared, whinnying in pain, then rolled to the ground, throwing her rider. 'Oh,' said the leader, above the roar of his men. 'You can't, can you?'

Edern scrambled to his feet. Only his pride was hurt, but his horse was dying, blood spurting in gouts from the spear wound. He drew his sword, the Roman spatha his father had given him. 'You shouldn't have done that,' he said, scowling up at the Pict from under his brows.

'Really?' The Pict lifted his reins, ready to ride forward and finish the job. 'Why not?'

'Well,' Edern smiled, 'you didn't think I'd come alone, did you?' His smile was beginning to fade. Where was Taran? He must have seen what had happened, must have seen Edern's horse go down. This wasn't the game. Not at all.

'So where's your army, prince of the Gododdin?' the Pict wanted to know.

Edern looked behind him. Nothing. Just the line of the purple hills at his back. The only sound was the lowing of the cattle and the shiver of the wind in the heather. He was alone. He planted his legs firmly, sword raised to take the impact of the charge he knew would come. But there was no charge. He looked into the eyes of the Pictish leader. Into the eyes of all of them. But they weren't looking at him. They were looking at the far horizon. Taran! At last! Edern spun to watch his brother come galloping over the ridge. But there was no Taran, no little army. Instead, a single horseman was cantering through the heather, a fur cap on his head and a legionary's shield bouncing from his saddle bow.

Edern couldn't believe it. It couldn't be …

'My lord.' The rider bowed in the saddle as he reached the boy.

'Dux Britannorum,' Edern returned the compliment.

'Is there a problem here?' Justinus spoke Gododdin as well as Edern spoke Latin. They spoke now in the mother tongue of Rome.

'So that's it!' the Pict shouted. 'You've got a bloody Roman army at your back.'

'Army?' Justinus had enough Pictish to cope with this conversation. He chuckled. 'You don't think I'd bother my defenders of the Wall to sort out a few cattle thieves, do you? No, it's just me.'

'Just us,' Edern reminded him, raising his sword.

'Oh, now, you're not being fair, my lord.' Justinus frowned, like the fond uncle he virtually was. 'Two of us against fifteen? What would people say?' This in Pictish.

'They'd say,' the Pict leader said, drawing his sword, 'that it was a good day for Drust mac Talorg when he killed the biggest Roman bastard of them all.' He rammed home his heels and the pony darted forward, throwing its head back and chewing the iron bit. Justinus stooped in his saddle to murmur in Edern's ear, 'Next one's yours.' He straightened, steadying his horse and waiting for exactly the right moment. Edern had seen the Roman use his darts before but he was never ready for the speed. Justinus' left hand lunged out ahead of him, as though he was saluting his emperor and there was an unearthly scream from the Pict. The horse galloped on, but its rider was dead, a Roman dart protruding from his eye socket. The sword slipped from his grasp and the reins fell away as he pitched forward and hit the ground with a thud.

The Picts looked thunder-struck. Most of them had never seen a Roman soldier before. None of them had seen the Dux Britannorum. And now he had killed their chief and they had not seen how he had done it.

'Next?' he called, adjusting his cloak.

Two or three of the Picts edged forward, but hesitantly. Which of them was going to make the first move? Justinus looked up from fussing with his cloak, fixing them with his gaze.

'The cattle,' Edern called. 'You will leave them where they are. And … we are generous men. You can still ride away.'

There was a roar from the hillside and Taran's horsemen were thundering over the ridge, pouring down the rivulets where the streams ran and splashed. That was enough for the Picts. Their leader dead and their nerve gone, they turned their horses and galloped away, past the cattle they had won and lost, the Gododdin at their heels.

Taran reined in his horse alongside his brother. 'Dux Britannorum,' he nodded, not exactly pleased to see the man.

Justinus saluted. 'My lord,' he said.

'Brother.' Taran looked down at the boy. 'Timing a bit off

there. Sorry.'

Edern had sheathed his sword but suddenly launched himself at Taran, grabbing his cloak and dragging him out of the saddle. The horse shied and wandered away while the brothers thumped and kicked each other, sprawling on the ground. Justinus swung out of the saddle and hauled the younger one up by the hair, steadying the arm of the other as he was reaching to draw his sword.

'Boys, boys,' he tutted. 'This is no way to behave before a vanquished enemy. What would your Mama say?'

Din Paladyr

'I don't know what to say,' Brenna murmured. She lay in Justinus' arms in the warmth of the furs. Outside the winds of winter roared in from the estuary, flattening the tall grass in the meadows and bending the boughs on the hill. But in here, in the firelight's glow, the lovers lay together in peace and quiet. 'They've always been like it. You know that.'

Justinus did. Brenna turned over to lie on her back, looking up at the herbs hanging from the rafters, listening to the occasional crackle of the logs in the grate. Brenna had been the wife of Paternus, his old friend from the VI Victrix, from the days when they patrolled the Wall together. Edern was his; in some lights he could *be* Pat, back from the dead. And yes, he and Taran had been squabbling since the younger boy could stand. But now they were men. They had their own households, their own armies and although neither of the lovers said as much under their furs, Brenna would not be there for ever.

She sat up, resting her head on her knees. Brenna was queen of the Gododdin, the tribe the Romans called the Votadini, a woman twice widowed. Justinus was the second Roman she had loved, but theirs was a strange, fleeting relationship. She wore no ring but Paternus' Wall ring with its four helmets. And Justinus wore his. In their different ways, they were both married to the Wall and all it stood for, the woman whose lands lay to its north and the man who would lay down his life to defend it.

'You were telling me about Elen of the Armies,' Brenna said. 'Would I like her?'

'No,' Justinus chuckled. 'Nor she you. You're like peas in a pod, you two. Oh, she's blonde and gorgeous …'

He waited patiently until her pillow bounced off his head. He defended himself weakly, still laughing. 'But apart from that, you could be sisters. Queens, generals, wives, mothers.'

'Widows,' Brenna reminded him.

'Widows,' Justinus nodded.

'She has a child by Maximus?'

'Yes.' He patted the pillow back and she lay back on it. 'A girl, Sevira. It's funny. I can see Maximus in her. Let's hope she doesn't grow up to swear like him!'

'Let's hope she doesn't grow up to have her head on a pole,' Brenna said, ruefully.

Justinus teased a lock of hair away from the face of the woman he loved. Brenna had lost Din Paladyr twice, driven from it by war and treachery. She had lost two husbands and now her boys, who she loved more than either of them, were at each other's throats. She was right. Taran and Edern had always fought. But now it was about kingdoms. Now it was for real. She snuggled close. If she had no solution to her warring sons, the Dux Britannorum would find one. Brenna was sure of that.

Maxima Caesariensis

The island called Vectis wobbled on the rolling horizon. The Hibernian ships rose and fell with the current, making for the narrows. They had sailed across the western sea that men said marked the edge of the world and the great white rocks lay off their starboard hulls like needles in the sun.

Niall Mugmedon knew this land well. His mother, the fair Cairenn, had been born at the legionary base at Isca where her father had served as aquilifer of the II Augusta. She told him, in the watchfires of the villages, the stories of Rome; the iron men in their tight formations, shoulder to shoulder under the eagle – the eagle her own father carried. They were invincible, these men, and they ate babies for breakfast, carrying their little corpses on their spears for the days' rations.

That was long ago, when he was one of four brothers, each jostling with the others for their mother's attention, like piglets at the teats of a sow. Now, his brothers had long gone and he was a high king, Niall of the Five Hostages. Five men were his permanent guests, shackled to the ground with iron, one each from the wild provinces, from Laigin, Ulaid, Connacht, Mumu and Mide. And now, as Niall's warships prowled the south coast of Maxima Caesariensis, he was looking for another to add to his collection.

Londinium

'We have a problem, Marcus,' the vicarius was sitting in his office as the snow began to flutter outside, dusting the roofs of his capital and turning to water as it hit the river.

'Do we, sir?' Terentius Marcus had become quite used to attending to Chrysanthos' needs. He found himself invited to cenae, hobnobbing with the great and the good of Maxima Caesariensis, sampling the best wine off the finest plate. The vicarius introduced him to the loveliest girls, all of them from good families but, Marcus was delighted to discover, with the morals of alley cats, Marcus was not an idiot. He knew there would be a price; men like Chrysanthos the vicarius always came at a cost.

'Raids,' the vicarius said, stamping a handful of documents with his signet ring before passing them to his clerks, 'along the south coast.'

'I'd heard,' Marcus said. He had long ago stopped much of the ceremony with the vicarius. He unbuckled his helmet and sat down on a couch. Chrysanthos clicked his fingers and a slave bought a silver ewer and cups. He poured for them both.

'What had you heard?' the vicarius asked.

'As far east as Vectis.' Marcus sipped appreciatively. Good. The vicarius' taste was impeccable.

'Who?'

'The Picti,' Marcus said, 'the painted ones.'

'That didn't strike you as odd?'

'Well, yes, it did, actually. They're a long way from home.'

'That's because it's not the Picti. It's the Hiberni.'

'Really?'

'Their leader is … ah, Calpurnius; perfect timing. You received the panic from the south.'

'Panic, indeed.' Calpurnius nodded, still shaking the snow off his cloak. 'Raids along the coast are nothing new. But, look at the season. Who raids in winter?'

'Niall of the Five Hostages,' Chrysanthos said.

'Who?' Marcus was losing track of this conversation.

'Niall Mugmedon,' the vicarius explained, 'he's a high king of the Hiberni.'

'Which is a polite way of saying he's a cattle thief,' Calpurnius reminded everybody.

'Don't write him off so easily,' Chrysanthos poured a cup of wine for his subordinate. 'He's conquered five provinces in his God-forsaken island.'

'So what's he doing here?' Marcus wanted to know.

Chrysanthos smiled. 'There was once a chieftain of Britannia Prima, Calpurnius,' he said. 'His name was Caratacus and he fought us to a standstill. Oh, this was back in the good old days of course; you know, when men were men.'

The others chuckled.

'Anyway, this Caratacus was finally beaten and taken in chains to Rome. He was rightly astonished at the finery and power he saw there and he said, "Why, when you have all this, do you want our poor huts too?"'

'And what was the answer?' Marcus asked.

'The answer, Marcus, was that we just did. Do you question Rome's God-given right to forge an empire?'

'Er … no.'

'Then don't question Niall Mugmedon. He's just trying to do what we used to do so well.'

'Conquer us?' Marcus blinked.

'The deified Julius came ashore with a raiding party,' Chrysanthos reminded him. 'It wasn't until a year later he came back to stay.'

'You think that's what this Niall is doing?' Calpurnius asked.

'Read that description, Calpurnius,' Crysanthos said. 'It's on your table somewhere.'

Calpurnius rummaged among the parchment littering every surface in the room. He picked a sheet out. '"The man I saw was nearly nine foot tall,"' he read, '"with wild red hair and nails like eagles' talons. He burned our village and killed the priest at his own altar. Eight hundred cattle were slaughtered and he put out the eyes of all the old people …" Do you want me to go on?'

'No,' Chrysanthos sighed, 'but if those bastards have eight hundred cattle in their fields, we aren't taxing them hard enough.'

'I don't see how I fit in.' Marcus sipped his wine.

'I want you to beard this red-headed giant in wherever he's holed up,' Chrysanthos said. 'Win a few laurels for yourself.'

'Me, vicarius?' Marcus was taken aback. 'I'm a tribune. I don't have …'

'No, you're not,' Chrysanthos interrupted him. 'You are the Comes Litoris Saxonici, Count of the Saxon shore.' The vicarius opened a cupboard at his knee and hauled out gilt insignia, hung with eagles and bolts of lightning. Sea-serpents coiled around anchors at its centre.

Marcus was on his feet, mouth open, as Chrysanthos laid the chain of office across his shoulders. The ex-tribune looked down at the eagle and serpents, the gilt flashing in his eyes. Then he frowned. 'I assume, sir, that this ... unexpected ... and wholly undeserved ... promotion has the blessing of the Dux Britannorum.'

'Oh, absolutely,' Chrysanthos beamed. 'He suggested it.'

'Then, what can I say?' Marcus held out his right hand.

Chrysanthos shook it Roman style, forearm to forearm. 'Congratulations, Count.'

Thank you. Thank you, vicarius.'

'We'll have the ceremony when you get back.'

'Back?'

'From the south coast, man. Your first command. Take a vexillation from the garrison here and collect the Second Augusta on your way. Niall won't be expecting a full-blown response knee-deep in snow.'

'Sir!' Marcus saluted, clutching the hilt of his sword before turning on his heel and making for the door.

'And, Marcus ...' Chrysanthos stopped him.

'Sir?'

'Make sure you don't become Niall's sixth hostage, won't you?'

He raised his wine cup and the man was gone.

Chrysanthos looked at his decurion and saw misgivings in the man's face. 'You don't approve,' he said.

'I just hope it was a wise move,' Calpurnius said. He had once served Theodosius and Gratian, emperors at the pinnacle of the empire's politics. He had seen men over-promoted before.

'Time will tell,' Chrysanthos said.

'And that business about Justinus?' Calpurnius wouldn't let it go. 'Was that true?'

'Of course not. If I waited for the approval of the Dux Britannorum, I'd be rotting in my grave.'

'He's sending you where?' Scipio Honorius lay back in the steam of the baths. Normally he'd have a few of the Black Knives with him, just in case; a man in Scipio's position couldn't be too careful. Today, he was alone.

'God knows,' Terentius Marcus wiped the water from his face and shook his hair like a dog coming out of a river. 'Wherever this bastard of the Hiberni chooses to strike.' He paused and looked at Scipio. 'Do you think I'll catch him?'

Scipio laughed. 'You're the bloody soldier,' he said. 'You tell me.'

'Your father was a Hero of the Wall.' Marcus sank back to his chin again. 'I thought some of it might have rubbed off.'

'My father,' Scipio said, 'was a master at staying alive, whether he served the eagles or not. And, in the end, even that skill deserted him.' He reached across for the cup of wine on the marble surface. 'A little bird told me you've been promoted.'

The little bird, of course, was his mother, Honoria, but there was no reason for Marcus to know that.

'Well, you know how it is,' the Count of the Saxon Shore said. 'Some have greatness thrust upon them.'

'When do you march out?'

'The day after tomorrow. Porca's not best pleased.'

'Garrison commanders are never pleased,' Scipio winced as the wine hit his tonsils.

Marcus laughed. 'That's what I like about you, Scip,' he said.

'What?'

'How old are you?'

Scipio was a little surprised at the question but didn't show it. 'Eighteen,' he said.

'Eighteen going on forty-three,' Marcus said. 'You're wise beyond your years, Rex Inferni.'

It was Scipio's turn to laugh. 'Rex Inferni. King of the Underworld. Yes, I like that. Coming to the Hen's Tooth tonight? I've got a new blonde for you. A tongue to die for.'

'Not tonight, Scip,' Marcus sighed. 'Military duties.'

'Bugger military duties, Tere; you're Count of the Saxon Shore now.'

'Exactly,' Marcus nodded, remembering the little visit that the Dux Britannorum had paid him not so long ago. 'And I'd like to stay that way.'

He slipped past the basilica in the darkness, his breath smoking out on the crisp night air. The guard had saluted him in the broad thoroughfare but none of them patrolled these alleyways, slippery with the forming frost. A dog barked somewhere in the distance and he heard laughter and a lute wafting from a far street, from a tavern known only to a few.

He took the stone steps two at a time and knocked on the door at the top. A slave opened it and bowed. Marcus threw his hood back. 'The mistress is expecting me,' he said.

The slave bowed and showed him in. He took the visitor's cloak and led him through a passageway into a chamber lit with soft candles, couches and a wide bed. She sat here, waiting for him, a black robe over her nakedness and she got up as he arrived.

'Count of the Saxon Shore,' she bowed deeply and he laughed as he helped her up and kissed her hand.

'Madame,' he bowed in turn. 'You are too kind.'

'Not really,' she said. 'It's just that I never sleep with anyone below that rank these days.' She poured wine for them both. 'The vicarius has his standards.'

'Of course he does,' Marcus sipped from the cup.

'How's that boy of mine?' she asked.

'Scip?' Marcus began to unbuckle his shoulder straps and slid off his breastplate. 'He's well, as far as I know. I haven't seen him in a while.' He sat on a couch, helping himself to the grapes that lay there. 'But I haven't come to talk politics tonight. I passed up a gorgeous blonde at the Hen's Tooth to be here,' he said.

'Did you?' She stood up. 'Well, let's hope you won't be disappointed, then.' She unfastened her gold brooch and let the robe fall.

Marcus smiled, letting his eyes wander over her flawless body. The woman's son provided him with girls. The woman's husband in all but name had just promoted him. It was only right that all this should be kept in the family, even if neither of the men in the family knew anything about it. 'Disappointed, Lady Honoria?' he said, running appreciative fingers down her neck and onto her breasts. 'How could I be?'

CHAPTER VI

The II Augusta still carried that name in Chrysanthos' Britannia. The official ledgers of the emperor, at Augusta Treverorum, Rome and Constantinople, called them something else, Secunda Britannica and various others, bound up in the endless reorganization that stylus pushers the world over do to make themselves seem important. In Britannia, they were still the old legion of the deified Vespasian who had conquered the south country of the Atrebates and Dumnonii when the eagles first flew over the lands at the edge of the world.

Today they were marching south, their shields and impedimenta slung over their backs, their boots crunching on the frosty bracken. The Count of the Saxon Shore took the centre, his horse slithering on the cobbles of the legionary road, the standards of the II dancing behind him in the mist of the morning. Ahead of Marcus, his cavalry trotted, spears at the rest, scanning the heathland and the silver twist of the river. Behind him stretched his long-suffering foot sloggers of the legion and his auxiliaries behind that.

Marcus had brought no artillery with him. This Hibernian chieftain who called himself a high king was leading a raiding party. He would either run his ships up the sandy beaches of the south coast, burn a village and sail away again or he would steal horses and move fast from one huddle of huts to another. Either way, it would all be about speed and the II could not slow themselves down with the lumbering wild asses that threw rocks against walls. The Hibernian would have no walls except his own shields and the II would knock those down soon enough.

A semisallis of cavalry was galloping across the heathland,

riding hard for the column. It was mid-morning and Marcus was already freezing his arse off in the four-pronged saddle. He raised his right hand and the column halted.

'Shit!' Locicero grunted in the ranks. 'What is it now?' Locicero had served with the II for more years than he cared to remember. And his father had before him. And his father. He had been born to the lancea, the infantry spear, the sword and the shield. He had worn boots in his cradle, or so he told the new recruits whether they asked him or not. And he cut his teeth on a sword blade.

'That's the trouble with soldiering.' Quintillius slid his spear to the upright and waited. 'Here you are, enjoying a nice little walk in the country and some bastard spoils it. Pissing cavalryman. He should have my bunions.'

'Nobody should have your bunions, Quint,' Locicero observed.

Quintillis looked at his old comrade in arms. The two of them went way back, to that time in old soldiers' lives when men were men and all was right with the world. If they were honest, there had never actually been such a time and they had been grumbling about it ever since.

The foot-sloggers looked ahead to the knot of horsemen at the head of the column. The scout was talking to the commander, pointing behind him.

'Smoke,' Locicero grunted. 'He's telling the kid he's seen smoke.'

They all had. A black plume was drifting over the horizon, darker than the sea mist rolling from the south.

'That's what I love about the cavalry,' Quintillis said, leaning on his spear to give his back a rest. 'Their perspicacity. Don't miss a thing, do they?'

'Don't look a gift horse in the mouth, Quint. With a bit of luck, we can put our feet up for a while.'

The scout had reported a burning village, a Roman mile ahead. There were dead everywhere and the raiders had horses. Their leader? He was a giant of a man, black and with eyes that glowed like hot coals in the dark. The II had come too late, but there would be other chances. Marcus left his column on the road, much to the relief of Locicero and Quintillis and rode ahead with the cavalry.

They fanned out as they reached the slope at the trot, spears probing the sky and their dragon banner snapping in the breeze. The mist had lifted and the river lay clear below them. The odd fishing boat bobbed here, moored to a spot on the bank and the mallards flapped and called in their harsh voices as the horsemen approached. A man lay dead on a wooden jetty, dark blood pooling under his body and dripping between the planks into the water. Marcus halted his horsemen and followed the path with his eyes, from the jetty to the village. Three huts still burned, the smoke belching from the cracking timbers of the roofs. The raiders would have hit at dawn, the Count guessed, giving no warning. Another corpse lay near the huts. Another. And another.

Constantine, his Alamani cavalry commander was at his side. 'They'll have moved on, sir,' he said.

'Go into the village, Constantine.' Marcus unbuckled his helmet and took it off, scratching his cheek where the leather chafed. 'See if anybody's alive. If so, find out which way they went.'

'And burials, sir?' Constantine asked.

Marcus shook his head. 'No time for that,' he said. 'Besides, they're peasants. They're expendable.'

So they were. And they were again at the next village they came across. And the next. The raiders were moving north-west, following the river towards Clausentum. They had taken no cattle to slow them up, no women to amuse them. As for the children, they lay with their parents, as battered and dead as they were.

Quintillis and Locicero marched past their little bodies, lying in heaps where they had fallen. For once, the grumblers were silent. Both men had kids, somewhere in the provinces of Britannia. Both men had buried their own. They would have been happy to bury somebody else's, if only for the humanity of the thing. But the boy at the column's head had said no, so they marched on.

All that day Marcus trailed the river as it narrowed and split into half a dozen tributaries to the north. He had no experience of this sort of thing. Constantine knew it. Locicero and Quintillis knew it. Everybody in the II knew it. This upstart from Londinium must be somebody's son and heir. As sure as Mithras was in his heaven, he was no soldier. Count of the Saxon Shore? Jupiter, highest and best!

'All right, Constantine.' Marcus wasn't too proud to ask for help when he needed it. 'What now? Which way will they have gone?'

The words had not left his mouth when Constantine pointed ahead. Men were emerging from the woods that ran down to the river, wild-haired men in rough cloaks of wolfskin with iron shining dully at their throats. As the II's cavalry watched, they spread out into formation, an infantry unit no more than thirty strong.

'Is that it?' Marcus chuckled. 'Are they our raiders?'

'No horses,' Constantine mumbled. 'This is a false front, sir. They're taunting us.'

They were. The raiders were leaping and dancing, waving queer banners in the air and shrieking with outlandish cries. One after the other, they turned their backs on the II and threw their cloaks over their heads to shake their naked arses at them. Then they turned round and lifted their tunics again, flashing their manhoods in defiance.

Marcus' hand was in the air. 'The Ala will advance, cornifer.'

'No, sir.' Constantine stayed his hand. 'That's just what they want. We should wait. We don't know what's in those trees.'

'Bugger the trees, Constantine,' Marcus snapped. Chrysanthos the vicarius had given him a job to do. It was a test; that much was clear. He wasn't about to let this slaughterer of children get away with any more murder and he had laurels to win. 'Cornicen. Now.'

The trumpet blasted the morning and the horses' ears pricked up. Marcus had buckled his helmet back on and drew his sword, listening to the sound of steel sliding into the air. To his left and his right, his horsemen of the II Ala Augusta sat ready. 'The Ala will advance,' Marcus shouted. 'Walk. March.'

He nudged his horse forward and the first rank followed. The dragon standard streamed overhead, the breeze of the heathland rattling the wooden tongue in its throat. Marcus kept them steady. The cornicen's horn signalled the march speed and the lines held. The ground was firm here away from the river and there was no risk of the horses squelching into the mud. One or two raiders hurled their spears but they were still out of range and fell short. They thudded into the coarse grass tufts as the horsemen swept past.

Constantine waited at the head of the second turma, watching the woods ahead. He saw the wild raiders give one last whooped shriek, then vanish into the darkness. The Count of the Saxon Shore would have seen that and read it as a triumph. In the lad's mind, all his cavalry had to do was to pick off the rabble one by one and hack them down. That wasn't how Constantine saw it. He whirled his chestnut across the turma's front and back again, to get a clear view of what was happening on Marcus' flanks. If the bastards had really panicked at the sight of the ala moving, all well and good, but if they hadn't, it was an almost perfect trap.

Marcus' horsemen slowed to a walk as they reached the trees, then to a crawl. The oaks stood naked above them in the winter morning but the ground as high as a man was thick with decayed brambles and dead bracken. Beyond this the conifers stood like sentinels against the darkness of the night. The turma was broken now, before any iron had clashed at all. The difficulty of the ground meant that Marcus' cavalry was reduced to individual horsemen, their formation gone and it would be every man for himself.

No one spoke. The cornicen was silent and the dragon standard hung limp under the spreading oaks. Horses snorted and champed their bits. They had been trained to move to the sound of the trumpet, to the touch of their riders' heels and hands. Without that, they were confused and tossed their heads in their annoyance.

Constantine heard it before Marcus did, even though it was happening half a mile ahead. A scream, echoing, wild, followed by another and another. The noise shattered the morning, bouncing off oak and pine and it sounded as though Hell itself was unleashed. The cavalry commander checked himself, growling at the cornicen to wait for his command. That idiot Marcus might want to charge everything in sight, but Constantine was a realist. No point in wasting his precious horsemen on cattle thieves and child killers. A time would come and a better time than this.

In the woods, all hell had indeed broken loose. Wild men leapt from trees, throwing themselves onto Marcus' men and dragging them out of the saddle. Iron flashed in the bracken and blood sprayed wide, spattering the Count of the Saxon Shore as his cornicen went down, his head split open like an apple. Marcus hacked to his right, slicing through an attacker's arm, but the bastards were springing up everywhere out of the bracken, from behind the gnarled trunks. For a moment, only Marcus saw him, a giant of a man directing operations, pointing with his sword and watching how the slaughter went. He was standing on the raised ground, black with dead pine needles, his eyes bright and glittering under the helmet rim. And the helmet had a bright twist of gold around it

– the crown of a king. The next instant, Marcus was parrying for his life as two men grabbed his bridle and tried to drag his horse down. He saw the dragon standard fall beside him and the draconarius lurch forward onto his face. He did not move again.

Constantine had no choice but to act now. His infantry column was too far behind. Those foot sloggers would have rooted the raiders out, tramped their way through the bloodied bracken and driven them back. But all he had to hand was the second turma and he had no reserve. He drew his sword and held it high. 'The ala will advance,' he roared. 'Cornicen, sound the charge.'

The spears shot skyward and the ground shook briefly as the horses gathered speed. No time for the steady walk, march of the parade ground. The Count was in difficulty and Constantine had no idea how many raiders there were. If this was really the high king called Niall of the Five Hostages, would he really travel so light with only thirty men?

Niall of the Five Hostages had not heard a Roman cavalry charge sounded before, but he saw the horsemen coming on at the gallop and knew they would crash through anything in their path at that speed. He hadn't crossed the Hibernian Sea to burn himself out as early as this. He was a man who played a cat and mouse game very well and he intended it should last a little longer. He watched for a while, until it was obvious that his men would be ridden down, undergrowth or no undergrowth; then he waved his great sword in a circle over his head and the fighting broke off. Those raiders who could, fell back to the pines, to form a circle around their king. Others, still hacking and stabbing against Marcus' fractured line, finished their business and hauled themselves away. Some dabbed at bloody heads and ripped arms but Niall was delighted to see they were all there. He had not lost a single man. Then, as one, they turned into the blackness of the forest and were gone.

Londinium

Conchessa patted the shoulder of the little girl who was Calpurnius' daughter. She looked across in the candlelight to the boy curled up on the other bed. Patricius was not Calpurnius' son, she was sure of that. He had the crooked smile of the man she had met at the western capital of Augusta Treverorum, the man she had come to love while searching for her lost husband. And now her husband had been found and was here with her in freezing Londinium, while the man she had loved was gone; and she had no idea where.

She got up and crossed the room to the boy, bending over him and teasing the curls from his face. She smiled; then she looked up and saw Calpurnius standing there. She moved out into the passageway and half closed the door to the nursery. Calpurnius looked tired. All day he had been closeted away with Chrysanthos, high in the secret rooms of the basilica. No member of the Ordo, the council; no clerks with styli and abaci to record the minutes of meetings and to make copies for posterity. No messages sent across the capital of Maxima Caesariensis to oil the creaking wheels of government. No messages? No, that wasn't quite true. There had been one.

'He's sending Andros Procopius,' Calpurnius muttered, still not believing it.

'Who?' Conchessa's voice had long ago become chill, her emotions stifled, wrapped deep under the furs she wore as Februarius worked his icy fingers over the city. They shared a bed because that was her duty as a wife. They shared a cena, especially in the morning before the public day began. And of course, once that day was under way and the decurion and his wife were the acceptable face of Chrysanthos' Britannia, they seemed the perfect couple, blessed with two gorgeous children. And Conchessa thought it best if their conversation in private remained apolitical, matter-of-fact, everyday. That, she could handle.

'Procopius,' Calpurnius repeated, 'runs the drains.'

'He's sending a plumber to the emperor?' This made no sense at all.

'Worse.' Calpurnius threw himself down on the couch in the atrium. 'He's sending him with the head.'

'Quintus Phillipus' head?'

Calpurnius nodded. A slave was pouring the warm mulled wine for them, laying out the olives imported from the East and the hard, rough cheese of Britannia Secunda. 'He's up to something.'

'Surely,' Conchessa reasoned, 'he has to tell the emperor what's happened … to Phillipus, I mean.'

'Yes, of course,' Calpurnius said, 'but he's had months to do it: he doesn't actually need to send the head, which will be like a red rag to a bull and there are surely more persuasive men than Procopius. It's almost as though …'

'What?' Conchessa did not love Calpurnius, not like she

had. Those days at Carthago would never come back. But she still cared for him, in the way you do for an old friend, the way you do for the family dog who has become part of the household. She knew that Calpurnius had fallen foul of emperors before. It was always a delicate balancing act in the imperial court, being so close to the purple. Calpurnius had not always got it right. And Conchessa didn't want to see that happening again.

'Almost as though he's challenging the man, throwing down a spear into the arena.'

'He wants to be Magnus Maximus,' Conchessa said. She had been in and out of the imperial circle all her life; she knew how these things worked. Calpurnius looked at her. The darling wife who was his darling no more still had that extraordinary skill, that innate ability to cut to the chase and reach the heart of any matter, however dark that heart may be.

'He wouldn't dare,' Calpurnius said. 'Chrysanthos knows what happened last time. He's not a man to risk his head.'

'What if he doesn't have to?' Conchessa asked. 'What if he's risking somebody else's?'

Britannia Prime; the Coast

The II Augusta licked their wounds that night along the broad river's banks. Marcus' clerks had counted heads and he lost fourteen men killed with another twenty three unfit for purpose. Those invalids could rest until they felt well enough to move; then they could make their way back to Clausentum.

Marcus slammed his goblet down on the table and made the candles jump. It wasn't the men he minded losing, it was the horses. If this Hibernian cattle thief was using cavalry, he could keep this up all winter and into the spring, his hit and run tactics making a wasteland of the south; making a mockery of the Count of the Saxon Shore.

He looked at Constantine sitting across the table from him; at Octavius Gerontius, his senior tribune. Both men had been overlooked when the title of Comes Litoris Saxonici had been handed out and both men could have had Marcus for breakfast.

'Well,' the Count said, 'what's next?'

Gerontius shrugged. 'Depends on which way the bastards run,' he said.

'Thank you for that blinding glimpse of the obvious, tribune,' Marcus snapped. 'What's your best guess?'

'West,' Constantine cut in. 'He'll go west.'

'Why?'

'We don't know where his ships are, but from the numbers we saw he must have at least three.'

'I didn't see that many.' Marcus whined like a petulant schoolboy, which, by comparison with the others, he was.

'It's what we didn't see that matters,' Gerontius agreed. 'What do you think, Constantine? He's trailing the coast with his ships following?'

'That would be my guess. He came inland up the Icena, but he doesn't know the size of our force. He won't move further east in case we cut him off. He'd be too far from home.'

'So, if we keep moving west …' Marcus took up the thread.

'Not too fast, sir, or we'll outflank him.'

'Is that bad?'

Gerontius smiled. 'If we were fighting the Suebi or the Alans, it would be good, but this bastard is slippery. He's not interested in tangling with us. He'd rather keep one step ahead. If we extend our march, he'll just double back.'

'So what do we do?'

'Go home,' Gerontius said.

Marcus sat upright and wiped the wine from his lips. 'Go home, you lazy shit? You might be winding down, Gerontius, biding your time to retirement, but I'm the Count of the Saxon Shore. I'm going places.'

'We just need to keep our scouts on the alert, sir,' Constantine said. 'He'll slip up one day soon, tip his hand; give us a clear account of his numbers.'

'And how many villages will be smoking holes in the ground by then?' Gerontius asked.

'Damn the villages!' Marcus snapped. 'I've seen no sign of them even trying to defend themselves.'

'That's what we're for,' Constantine said. 'They've been relying on us now for three hundred years. We owe them something.'

'We owe them nothing,' Marcus corrected him. 'Tomorrow, we're marching on. Send your scouts west, Constantine – and you'd better be right. Gerontius, I expect double speed from your foot sloggers,'

The tribune scowled. 'We can't keep that up for long, sir. Men on foot chasing men on horses – it doesn't work that way.'

'Send your optios in among them,' Marcus ordered. 'I want to see their sticks coming down on the head of anyone lagging behind. At each halt on the road, the last five men will have loss of pay and privileges.'

'You intend to halt on the road?' Gerontius grunted, his contempt for Marcus now fully in the open.

'No,' the Count said, grateful for the idea his senior tribune had just thrown him. 'No, you're right. There will be no halts tomorrow. Or the next day. Or the next.' He snatched up his cup and raised it in a toast. 'No more rest until Niall of the Five Hostages is taken or dead.'

Constantine and Gerontius looked at each other. Slowly and without enthusiasm, they raised their cups. 'Until Niall of the Five Hostages is taken or dead,' they muttered.

Livia looked out over the frozen lake. There was still free water in the centre, but the rim was ice and broken bulrushes sprouted from it. She loved these moments when the first light crept over the downs and the hills and the forests lay white with frost. She had heard the first clatterings of the slaves moving below her in the great house and she watched the little knot of woodsmen padding silently over the silvered grass, axes over their shoulders, dragging their sledges and chains. A house like that of Domitius did not heat itself. There were fires to be lit, flues to be cleared, the whole labyrinth of tunnels that lay below the mosaics had to be maintained. And that meant feeding the fire. And that meant chopping wood.

Livia turned from the window and looked at herself in the bronze of the mirror. She was twenty-two; old some of the matrons said; past it, some of her mother's friends muttered behind her back. What *was* the problem, they asked each other, over the endless cenae where the wine flowed free and the air was thick with gossip? Livia was pretty enough. And intelligent. And that *was* probably the problem. Gnaeus Domitius was a politician, long retired from the rat race run at Augusta Treverorum and Rome; but he remained a scholar, one wing of his villa nestling into a fold of the downs devoted to his books. All the greats were there – Cato and Cicero, Varro and Seneca; Plutarch and the deified Julius. Livia had read them all. She had also read the secret books that Domitius thought he had hidden away from the women of his household – the love poems of Ovid and the naughty bits of Juvenal. *That* was Livia's problem, her mama's friends said. The girl was just too clever. And nothing was guaranteed to frighten a man more.

So there was no man in Livia's life. There was Tullius, that stupid spotty oaf from the house of Loricus near the river. Antonius, who couldn't dance or ride without his mother's permission. The others were all old men, widowers who leered at her; especially old Plautus for whom leering was merely the gustatio. Many was the time Livia had had to rap the old lecher's knuckles as his fingers strayed up her thigh. As a girl she had seen the Caesar, Magnus Maximus, once. He had been leading his mighty army across the downs on his way to his ships and Livia had never forgotten the sight.

A sound made her turn. She wrapped her furs around her naked body and looked out at the lake. That was a bark. More than that, it was Simco's bark. Her father's favourite hound had a distinctive bay. Moments ago Livia had watched him padding silently along with the woodsmen, his snout whiffling through the frozen bracken, his tail carried high. Livia felt suddenly afraid. It wasn't the bark that had frightened her. It was that the bark had snapped off suddenly, as if …

Niall of the Five Hostages wiped his sword blade on the pelt of the dog he had just killed. Four men lay nearby, their axes unblooded, their lives over.

'This is more like it,' Eochaid said, peering through the birches at the great house of Domitius. 'But it'll be defended, like as not.'

'Well, if these four are anything to go by,' Laidcenn muttered at his elbow, 'they shouldn't give us much trouble.'

'It's a villa,' Niall murmured, sheathing his sword, 'not a fort. Do you see any walls? Ditches? Ramparts?'

They didn't. The raiders from the land the Romans called Hibernia had sailed along the south coast from Clausentum to Durnovaria. They had seen the fort of the II Augusta at Isca Dumnoniorum and they had wisely left it alone. Niall Mugmedon had forty three men and he already knew there was half a legion after him. Niall knew how to wage war. That was why he was high king of Tara; that was why he had taken five hostages and earned a king's ransom from each one. The man struck like a ghost, out of the darkness, out of the mist. And no man could tell where.

'Papa!' Livia was running along the passageway that led to her father's rooms. Gnaeus Domitius was a light sleeper and he was already halfway into his tunic. 'There are …'

'Men,' he muttered. 'I know. I saw them too. Get your mother. I'll send Germanicus to you. Once he's there, lock the door.'

Livia had no time to say anything else to him. The old man she had known all her life, the one who had taught her to read and write, the one who had told her stories until she fell asleep, was suddenly a soldier. She didn't even know he owned a sword yet her last clear sight of him was of her father strapping it around his waist and preparing for an attack.

Livia's mother slept the sleep of the dead and the girl had to shake her awake. Lavinia blinked up at her daughter's face and read the fear there. 'What's happened?'

'Raiders, Mama. They're at the door.'

In her own way, Lavinia was as doughty a warrior as her husband. She had learned to be hard as Domitius' wife and learned when to think fast. Now was one of those times. There was an unceremonious rap on the door and without waiting for a reply, Germanicus barged in. He nodded briefly to them, then locked the door and dragged furniture in front of it. Germanicus was armed to the teeth. Domitius' man had been at his master's side, it seemed, for ever, watching the crowd, guarding the alleyways. He had the instincts of a street fighter and this morning, with the light not yet full, his task was to lay his life on the line for his mistress and her child. Lavinia ignored the niceties and pulled on her day clothes. God knew where her maidservant was but the girl would be no use in this situation. She was an expert with powder and rouge but her bow-arm was weak and Lavinia was not sure she could stand the screaming.

And that was what they all heard now, a shriek that chilled the blood. Three faces peered out of the window as Lavinia threw her shutters back. The morning air rushed in, taking Livia's breath away for a moment. Germanicus was all for closing them again, but none of the trio could look away. Beyond the front gates, an armed rabble stood staring up at the house. Their leader stood in the centre, a giant of a man with a twisted gold crown riveted to his helmet. His left hand rested jauntily on his hip and his right was thrust out in front of him, his fingers entwined in the hair of a woman kneeling at his feet and facing the house.

'That's Amelia,' Lavinia whispered, as if the shutters were not allowed to hear her.

It was. The old washerwoman who lived on the estate was no doubt ruing the fact that her hovel lay beyond the villa's walls. It was obvious what had happened. Whoever these barbarians were they had struck the outbuildings first. Germanicus could not see the other side of the house but he guessed the villa was surrounded. He had no idea what had happened to the woodsmen, but assuming they were already dead, there were six able-bodied men in the house, including himself and the master. The boys would do their bit and the old men would desperately try to remember the moves of the parade ground, old soldiers as they were. But, all in all, it would be no contest.

'Whose house is this?'

The three looked at each other. It was the barbarian leader who spoke; they knew that from the breath curling out from his beard in the cold of the morning. But it was Latin. A little rough and ready perhaps and with a strange accent, but Latin nonetheless.

For a while there was silence, as though the villa itself was not daring to draw breath.

'I am Gnaeus Domitius,' Livia heard her father's voice, loud and clear and strong. 'This is my house. Who are you?'

'Niall Mugmedon,' came the answer. 'High king of Tara.'

'What do you want?'

'I am a collector,' Niall shouted.

'Of what?' Domitius wanted to know.

'Heirs and heiresses,' the Hibernian told him, still holding the old woman by the hair. 'Do you have children, Gnaeus Domitius?'

There was a pause. 'I have no children,' came the answer.

The high king laughed. 'You're a liar, Gnaeus Domitius,' he said. 'It's a fine house you have here, but it'll burn like this old crone's hut. Is that what you want, Gnaeus Domitius? Or will you send out your children?'

Another silence.

'But where are my manners?' Niall went on. 'You'll think me greedy. I'll settle for your eldest child.'

Instinctively, Livia pulled back from the window and the child-taker saw it. 'A daughter, eh?' he called. 'Lovely.' Domitius had the same view that his family did, but he had sent his people to every wall, every facet of the building. And they all reported the same thing, scurrying along passageways, hurtling up and down stairs; the house was surrounded.

'Send her out, Gnaeus Domitius,' Niall shouted. 'Or this old girl dies.'

Livia's heart thumped under her furs. She couldn't let Amelia die. She had known her all her life and here she was, terrified and kneeling on the hard, cold earth, staring at the house she had served all her life. She could see the master's face in one window, the mistress and little Livia in another. She wasn't little any more, but to Amelia she would always be the little tomboy, trailing along behind her father, riding with him to the hunt, fishing in the lake, fighting with the boys on the neighbouring estates.

'Livia,' her mother growled at her. 'Don't even think about it. Stay where you are.'

'I'm not giving you long, Roman,' Niall shouted. 'I'm not known for my patience.'

Gnaeus Domitius braced himself for the inevitable. He had seen women die before. He had seen his own people die before. He cursed the Count of the Saxon Shore. He'd never met the man, but it was his job to guard the coast – and that included all the villas along it. Where the hell was he?

Terentius Marcus was not at one with himself today. He had hit the wine too heavily the night before and his head was still singing, every movement of his eyes a nightmare. Even so, he was on the road soon after dawn, the II Augusta marching west. There had been no sign of the raiders for days, but Marcus believed that Chrysanthos was paying the bastards to keep him on his mettle. He half turned in the saddle, watching the legion trudging behind him. A more experienced man would have read the faces, the sullen scowls and grim jaws, the scores of Lociceros and Quintilli who hated him. A more experienced man would have jollied them along, cracking filthy jokes and leading the singing. But then, a more experienced man would not have been wasting his time chasing shadows.

'That's it, Roman!' Niall had had enough. 'This woman's blood is on your hands, not mine!'

And he drew his sword blade across Amelia's throat, her eyes rolling skyward.

CHAPTER VII

Livia couldn't believe what she had just seen. Blinking back the tears she called out, more an involuntary scream than anything anybody could understand. The raiders responded instantly, releasing a shower of arrows that clattered on the villa's walls or bit deep into the shutters. Germanicus had seen them hissing across the courtyard but he turned too slowly and the next thing Livia and Lavinia saw was the man thrown sideways by the impact of a barbarian's shaft through his neck. His throat had been skewered and the iron tip had torn his spinal cord. He fell heavily and the women rushed to him.

Livia was on her feet again in an instant. She couldn't help Germanicus; only God could help him now.

'Niall of the Five Hostages,' she called out in a firm, clear voice.

'Who's that?' the high king scanned the villa's windows to see where the sound had come from.

'I am Livia, the daughter of Gnaeus Domitius.'

'Livia!' she heard her father roar. 'What are you doing?'

She ignored her father for the first time in her life. 'If I surrender myself to you, do you give me your word that the rest of the house will be spared?'

'Mother of God!' Domitius muttered, drawing his sword and rushing from his quarters. It wasn't far to his wife's room but it seemed a Roman mile this morning.

'You have my word,' Niall shouted back, but Domitius didn't hear that. All he heard was the rushing of blood in his ears and the pounding of his heart. He knew his daughter was headstrong but this was madness.

The girl was dragging the furniture aside, clawing her way to the door. Lavinia grabbed her daughter's arm and shook her. 'What do you think you're doing, you little fool?'

Livia shook herself free and Lavinia, beside herself, slapped her hard across the face. Tears welled again in the girl's eyes. They welled in Lavinia's too and she hugged her daughter to her, as she had hugged her all her life. When her pets had died and her old nanny; when she had grazed a knee in the courtyard or had fallen from a tree; for all those times and more, her mama had been there, soothing, stroking, making things all right.

The women of Gnaeus Domitius looked into each other's eyes and they both knew the truth. It was a moment they both knew would come one day; and here it was. Livia's mama could not help her now, any more than either of them could help Germanicus.

Livia dragged the last of the furniture away and hauled open the door. She had to get down the far stairs before her father reached her. She knew he was on the way and she knew he would stop her, even if he had to tie her down. She poked her head out of the door – there he was, face ashen, sword drawn, thudding up the stairs to her right. She spun left, knowing she could outrun him any day and she ignored his tortured shouts, begging her to stop.

She had gathered up her cloak and jumped the stairs three at a time, landing with a jolt in the courtyard.

'Hold that gate, Alfridius!' Domitius shouted, skidding to a halt on the balcony outside his wife's room. But Alfridius had always been putty in Livia's hands. He had carried a torch for her since she was a little girl and if he was ever faced with an order from her that countered an order from the master … well … He wrenched back the heavy bolts as she looked at him, her cheeks streaked with tears and one of them still red from her mother's loving slap.

'Thank you,' she mouthed and was gone, the gate slammed shut behind her and the bolts slid back with a finality that Livia almost felt draining the life out of her.

Domitius on his balcony just stood there, the sword dangling uselessly in his hand. His own and only daughter condemned to die by a slave. Domitius had always treated his people well. But from this morning that would be different. He would personally flay Alfridius alive.

Niall of the Five Hostages rammed his sword tip into the frozen ground, inches from the body of old Amelia, still bleeding into the frost. A sylph of a girl was walking towards him, her feet bare, a fur cloak wrapped tightly around her. Her tawny hair lay strewn over her shoulders in the manner of Hibernian women, not Roman. Ten paces from him she stopped, ignoring the carnage at his feet and stared into his eyes. His men shifted, half of them still watching the villa's walls, half of them on her. Each of them wondered when it would be their turn with her. Whenever it was, it would be after the high king had grown bored.

'You gave me your word,' she reminded him, her voice still firm and she hoped she wasn't trembling too much with the fear and the cold. 'The house and its inhabitants will remain untouched.'

Niall laughed. He lifted his sword and sheathed it. 'You don't understand how this works, lady,' he said. 'I could take you and your house and its inhabitants. Cut a few more throats just to while away a morning. But there's more value in ransoms. Before I leave today, your sorrowing father will pay me a handsome sum – gold, silver, whatever he has. In exchange, I will return his daughter to him. Except that I won't, of course. I'll take you with me.' He grinned at his men. 'With all of us. Then I'll contact your papa again and the same business will be repeated over again. Predictable, but effective nonetheless.' For a long moment, they looked at each other. 'I assume you can write, Livia Domitia,' he said.

She nodded.

'I have some writing material with my ships. You will make an inventory of your father's valuables.'

'You can go to Hell,' she said, suddenly not willing to play this bastard's game.

Niall looked crestfallen. 'Oh, that is a shame,' he said, stepping forward. He held out a hand and stroked her cheek. 'I had hoped that you and I could get along.'

She half smiled, then suddenly grabbed the high king's hand and bit it savagely, sinking her teeth into his palm. He roared with pain and pulled it free, slapping the girl to the ground with his good hand. Livia found herself lying alongside the dead body of Amelia and waited to join her.

'You shouldn't have done that,' Niall growled, sucking the blood from his hand. 'Eoganmac. Burn it. Burn the house.' He looked down at the stricken girl and added, 'and the inhabitants.'

'Niall! Niall! High king!' the musical lilt of the Hibernian dialect broke from the woods to the raiders' right. 'Cavalry.' One of Mugmedon's men was crashing through the frozen bracken, whirling his sword above his head.

'How many?' Niall shouted.

'More than we can handle,' he man grunted as he reached him.

The high king took in the situation. This would be the cavalry he had faced before, the Ala of the II Augusta, but the last time he had carefully staged the moment, chosen the field himself. Now his little command was scattered and they were in the open. It would be slaughter. He hauled Livia up by the hair and dragged her away.

'Until the next time, Gnaeus Domitius!' he roared and as silently as they had come, the raiders were gone.

The Count of the Saxon Shore clattered into the courtyard of Gnaeus Domitius at the head of his staff. Around him, the standards shifted in the morning breeze and the horses stamped. Frightened people huddled in corners, Domitius' people, not relieved by the sight of the standards, not reassured by the coming of the cavalry.

A purposeful old man was striding out of the villa, his servants in his wake. 'I am Gnaeus Domitius,' he said curtly, 'and in normal times, I would welcome you to my villa.'

Marcus dismounted and gave the old Roman salute. 'Terentius Marcus,' he said, unbuckling his helmet. 'Comes Litoris Saxonici.'

Nobody was ready for what happened next. Lavinia, her eyes still red from crying, hurled herself at him, slapping him around the head with both hands before Domitius pulled her away.

'You bastard!' she screamed at Marcus. 'Those animals have taken my daughter and you ride in like some idler late to a dance.'

'Lavinia,' Domitius growled at her and the woman subsided. Lavinia Domitia was a feisty woman, but she *was* a woman and this was a man's world. Her father had always had the last word; now her husband did – it was the way of things.

'I'm sorry,' muttered Marcus, but he was too embarrassed to mean it and his knowledge of hysterical mothers was, to say the least, limited. 'My men are scouring the area. They'll find her.'

The girl's body lay half in, half out of the hut. The raiders had not torched it, nor the others nestling on the slope of the hill. Constantine knew that the sea lay beyond those woods and that somewhere along the shore the raiders must have run their ships onto the shingle. If only the II Ala could find that fleet, Constantine would stop Niall of the Five Hostages in his tracks.

The Alaman dismounted and knelt beside the body. What was she? Nineteen? Twenty? She was naked, her skin bruised by rough fingers, her flesh torn and bloody. Her eyes bulged and her lips were open in an eerie half-smile above the tell-tale purple lines around her throat. She had been strangled and how many men had had her before she died was anybody's guess.

Constantine unbuckled his cloak and wrapped her in it, lifting the frail body up onto his saddle and tying it there with the harness straps. Was this her home, he wondered? Or had she been dragged here, raped and butchered somewhere dry and warm, for convenience? There were no other bodies, no sign of a fight. Whoever had lived here once had gone, running to the woods, to the river, to the high ground, *anywhere* they knew that could save their lives. The purple clouds gathering over the treetops told their own story. Night was coming. Cavalry in the night were like so many blind worms groping in the dark. Constantine would wear out his horses and exhaust his men just like Terentius Marcus expected him to do. Well, Constantine was too old a soldier to play that game.

'Back to the villa,' he ordered and he walked beside the dead girl all the way.

Lavinia sat rocking in her room that night. She had watched the night creeping in after a sunless day, watched the fires being lit and the torches guttering in the courtyard. Beyond her window and beyond the walls, the II Augusta had erected their camp, leather and earth and timber. She could hear the whinnying of the horses and the earthy laugh of rough men, cracking jokes and throwing dice. The wine, she knew, would be passed around and no one would be thinking of a little girl, now grown, who had left her home that morning and had not come back.

That little girl lay before her mother now. A portrait on glass, painted a long time ago, of a baby with curls and huge eyes. And Lavinia sat and cried, humming to herself the lullabies of the years. She barely heard the tap on the door, but her heart froze as her husband's head popped round it.

'The cavalry are back,' he said, grim-faced. 'They've found a body.'

Constantine would have preferred it if they had had time to clean the girl up. The daughter of the house had gone, taken by the raiders. Then she was bright and alive, with laughter and the radiance of youth. And now ...?

'Sir,' Constantine blocked the entrance to the room, where they had laid her, with his bulk. 'This is not going to be easy.'

Gnaeus Domitius drew himself up to his full height, his wife beside him, her knuckles white as she gripped his hand. 'We have buried children before,' the old man said.

His wife closed her eyes. But not like this; she had buried her sons when they were still in swaddling bands. No day went by that she did not mourn them, but she had no memories of them to come and haunt her dreams. No first steps. No first word. In the case of her first born, not even a first breath. She felt as if the room had moved far away and her grip on her husband's hand grew stronger.

Constantine had no children. No wife. He couldn't imagine the pain this pair were going through. But he stepped aside.

The medicus waited until Domitius and his wife were ready, staring down at Constantine's cloak that still lay like a Christian shroud around the dead girl. Domitius nodded and the medicus slid back the hood. There was an audible gasp in that half-lit room, the dead eyes staring upwards to the low ceiling and the blue lips still with their wistful smile. Lavinia slumped against her husband, a sob convulsing her throat. He caught her and held her with both arms before shepherding her towards the door.

Here he turned to Constantine. 'It's not her,' Domitus said. 'It's not Livia.'

It was barely dawn the next morning when Alfridius stood in his master's atrium. Ever since he had slid the bolts back and let Livia go, he had wondered why he had done it, what idiot impulse had driven him. But it had been the work of an instant and once done, could not be undone. From that moment on, the slave who had been born on the estate had expected the worst. He could not look his master in the face. Nor his mistress. He had given their only daughter to the devil.

Gnaeus Domitius crossed the floor. He carried a chain in his hand and he swung it to and fro. Alfridius knew what this meant. He had seen men beaten to death before. His heart racing, he stripped the tunic over his head in the half light of the atrium and knelt down. With luck, the chain would strike his bare head first and he would lose consciousness before the links cracked his clavicles and bounced his shoulders out of their sockets. Punishment like this could last all day, in the right hands.

'Get up, Alfridius,' Domitius murmured, 'and get dressed.'

'Master?' the slave blinked up at the man he had always thought of as a father. Domitius raised the chain and Alfridius could see there was a break in a link. The master slid one piece of iron out of the other and let both pieces fall with a rattling thud to the mosaics.

'You are a free man, Alfridius,' he said.

The slave who was no longer a slave did not understand. 'Master, I …'

'Master no more,' Domitius stopped him. 'Now you are a free man in a world of free men. You may have dreamed of this all your life; I don't know. But freedom is a two-edged sword, Alfridius. Now you must earn it. You and I between us have consigned my little girl to hell. It's up to you to get her back.'

'How?' Alfridius was hauling on his tunic, desperate to help.

'Get ready for the road,' Domitius said, turning to parchment scrolls on the table nearby. 'Take this letter to Justinus Coelius. You know him, by sight, I mean?'

'The Dux Britannorum,' Alfridius nodded. 'Yes, I do.'

'Take three of my best horses and ride them into the ground if you must. Your best bet is the Wall, far to the north. Coelius rarely leaves it these days. I don't trust these men, Alfridius.' Domitius turned to the window to watch the camp lights beyond his walls twinkling in the morning. 'That popinjay Marcus and the oafs who follow him. If there is one man in all Britannia who can find my girl, it's Justinus Coelius.'

Alfridius took the letter and took the gift of life that Domitius had given him.

'As a free man,' Domitius slipped off his ring and slid it onto Alfridius' finger, 'you will get further than as a slave. If anyone queries you and your purpose, show them that.'

The freeman's eyes were wet with tears.

'And. Alfridius,' Domitius said, 'if you don't find the Dux

Britannorum, don't come back.'

Londinium

In the old days, it had been the feast of Lupercalia, the ceremony of the wolves. Goats were killed and their blood smeared on the foreheads of young men who laughed and ran away. The priests of the wolf ran naked, lashing all they met with thongs made from the skin of the goats. Girls ran and laughed with them, knowing that the flying lash would ease the pain of childbirth.

But that was in the old days. Today, it was dies Jovis and Calpurnius Succatus sat at the southern end of Londinium's bridge as the carts rolled north. Chalk from the forest of Anderida, timber from the forests that clothed the Downs, the first bleating lambs of the season, shrill and confused and missing their mothers, driven along the road by careless drovers, huddled in cloaks against the weather. Calpurnius counted each one and his clerks wrote them down, a catalogue of the produce coming into the great city along the Thamesis.

The decurion poured himself more wine. There had to be a way to get through the boredom of a day like this and wine was the quickest solution he knew. He barely noticed the rider lashing his horse hard for the bridge, trailing two other mounts behind him. He saw the garrison guard stop him at the bridgehead, then wave him on. He had shown them his ring and some papers; a young man in a hurry. Calpurnius wished him luck, whatever his purpose and went back to counting sheep, wide awake though he was.

Vitalis saw the rider too. He was waist-deep in the brackish waters of the dark Thamesis, half under the wooden jetty that jutted from one of Theodosius' towers. He had been here for the best part of the morning and couldn't feel his legs. He only knew he still had feet because he heard them sucking through the mud each time he moved. It was a wet, cold and thankless task, but this stretch of the river yielded the best reeds he knew and a basket-maker needs reeds like other men need air. He watched the rider clatter his way under the arch, then bent his back to his work again, hacking with his knife under the water's surface.

'This is hard, Mama,' Patricius complained. The boy wrote his name well enough and could count on his father's abacus, but this book was not his friend.

Conchessa smiled at him. If she was determined that her boy would not become a politician and if his uncle Vitalis was equally determined he should not be a soldier, what *would* he become? A scholar? Not on today's showing. 'Eusebius didn't write for children,' she said, squeezing onto the couch next to him and looping her arm across his shoulder. 'He was bishop of Caesarea in Judea, not far away from the birthplace of Lord Jesus.'

'Did he know Lord Jesus, Mama?'

'We all know Him in a way, don't we, Pat? But no, Eusebius lived a long time after Jesus went back to Heaven.'

Patricius may not have been a potential politician or a soldier, but that he had a mind like a strigil's edge was certain. 'So the Lord Jesus didn't have to read him, then?'

Conchessa laughed. 'No,' she said. 'But you do. Cheer up.' She squeezed him to her. 'Eusebius only wrote ten books on Church History. You've only got nine and a half to go!'

A horseman, wet and cold from his ride, clattered under the basilica window, looking for a hot meal, a drink and shelter for the night.

Alfridius had intended to move on that same day, but his first horse had pulled up lame south of the river and he had to soak away the cold numbness of his muscles, crouched over the saddle as he had been for so long. Dawn would be soon enough to take the road again, striking north into Flavia Caesariensis on the next leg of his journey. Alfridius had never been to Londinium before; had never been a free man before. He stabled his horses and found lodgings for the night. There was something going on, some count of heads – he had faced that at the bridge and Londinium was bursting at the seams. There was only one room at the Hen's Tooth, they told him, at the back by the sty. And he'd have to share. Alfridius was too tired to argue. He paid in advance and before it was truly dark, his head had crashed to the straw and he was dead to the world.

He didn't know what woke him; whether it was the first rays of dawn's light or the rustling of the straw. His travelling companion had not moved. Since he had burst in long after cock-shut time and collapsed in a drunken stupor, he had done nothing but snore. He was still snoring now. But what caught Alfridius' attention was the dark figure crouched over his cloak and tunic, riffling through the precious papers Domitius had given him. In an instant he had leapt up from the straw and grabbed a skinny wrist. A girl screamed.

'Let me go, you bastard!'

She was struggling and the two of them stumbled over the still-sleeping snorer out into the yard. She drove her foot into Alfridius' balls, but he clung on. Then she twisted so that her teeth were about to sink into his arm. Still Alfridius held on. If the contents of his purse were his own, he might have let them go, but they were not. In his limited, fevered brain, the life of Livia depended on his keeping those papers safe and he was prepared to die for that.

As they wrestled against the pig-sty wall, the alarmed beasts grunting and squealing in terror, Alfridius felt a stinging slap around the head that sent him reeling. When he whirled upright again, a man stood there. He was dark, with a dazzling smile. And the smiler carried a knife.

'You're slipping, Julia,' he said. 'Time was, you'd have had this peasant for jentaculum.'

'He cheated,' Julia of the Two Heads whined. 'Pretended to be asleep.'

The man clicked his tongue. 'Whatever next?' His eyes darted quickly over the letter that Julia had held onto during the fight. He looked at Alfridius. 'You are the freeman of Gnaeus Domitius?' he asked.

'I am,' Alfridius said. 'Do you know him?'

'No,' the man said. 'But I know the man this letter is addressed to. I can see from this that Domitius' daughter has been taken.'

'She has.'

'Well then.' The man sheathed his knife with a deft movement and handed the parchment scroll back to Alfridius. 'Don't let us keep you. Julia, give the man his money back.'

Alfridius' hand flew to his side. He would never be so stupid as to leave it with his clothes, but this girl of the fast and furious fingers had relieved him of it anyway.

'Now!' the man growled. Julia scowled and threw the bag to Alfridius. 'The road north lies that way.'

Alfridius grabbed his clothes and stumbled for the gate. There, he stopped. 'Who are you?' he asked.

'Me?' the smiler said. 'Just think of me as a helping hand for a poor traveller on the road.'

'You'll get your reward in Heaven, sir,' Alfridius said and he left.

'Heaven!' Julia scoffed, pulling her dress straight. 'That's no place for the king of the underworld.'

Scipio laughed.

Before he left Londinium, Alfridius checked at the basilica, with the outer offices of the vicarius Britannorum. No, the Dux Britannorum was not in Londinium. Try Lindum, five days north.

Flavia Caesariensis

The weather closed in again as Alfridius followed the old legionary road through the days ahead. His second horse plodded on as the rain soaked through his cloak and water dripped from his sodden boots. He took shelter where he could, in the boles of dead trees or under the lee of rocky outcrops. On the fourth night, it was too wet to light a fire and Alfridius went to sleep hungry. Lindum was a paradise after days on the road, but the Dux Britannorum was not there. Perhaps Eboracum, an unconcerned official had suggested.

Britannia Secunda

'No.' The centurion of the VI Victrix at Eboracum shook his head. 'We haven't seen the Dux Britannorum in weeks. I can show you his dad's grave if you like? No? Well, then, the Wall it is. Now, move along there; I'm a busy man.'

Vindolanda, on the Wall

Night had long ago spread black over the moorlands of the north. There were no forests here to drip their wetness on the traveller from the south. He was down to his last horse, the dogged bay with the hard mouth, the least reliable of all Domitius' horses. Alfridius had lost count of the days since he had raced away from the villa which had been his only home. Since then, he had ruined two horses, nearly been robbed, even killed. He had been ignored, fobbed off, growled at by strange men on the road who spoke a language he didn't understand.

Justinus Coelius, he had heard, had hung up his sword. He had thrown away his insignia and his title. He had gone to bed with the queen of the Votadini and had become her lapdog. Then he had heard that none of that was true. That was because Justinus Coelius was dead, cut down by a Pictish sheep-shagger – an arrow in his coward's back as he ran. Then again …

'Who goes?' A barked question brought Alfridius up sharp. He reined in his horse and blinked through the rain at the torches flickering on the stone turrets of Vindolanda.

'I am the freeman Alfridius,' he called back, making out the helmets of the guard under the torches, 'from the house of Gnaeus Domitius, in Britannia Prima.'

'What do you want?'

'I am looking for the Dux Britannorum,' Alfridius shouted.

There was a silence. Then a shuffling and sounds of movement on the Wall. A cloaked figure emerged.

'You've found him.' Justinus said.

Mediolanum

'Your name is Procopius?' The Emperor Theodosius looked up from the papers the man had brought him from far Britannia.

'It is, Sire.' Andros Procopius had served the vicarius Chrysanthos all his adult life. There was nothing he could not tell you about the drains of Londinium. Visits to the great Theodosius' capital at Mediolanum now … that was a different matter. He stood in the emperor's atrium alongside the great palace in his full dress uniform and felt like shitting himself. Had he known what was in the letters he had carried all the way from Londinium, he would have.

Theodosius passed the letter to a lackey, whose mouth hung slack in disbelief. The emperor cleared his throat. 'You have brought me the head of Quintus Phillipus?' he asked, as though enquiring about the prices in the fish market.

'Yes, Sire.' Procopius flapped his hands to summon his people forward with the lacquered box.

'No!' Theodosius snapped. 'No, thank you; I don't need to see it. Tell me, Procopius, do you know what this letter contains, the one from Terentius Marcus?'

'From …?' It was Procopius' turn to look bemused. 'I was given those papers by Chrysanthos, the vicarius …'

'Of course you were,' Theodosius said. 'That's how we do things. This letter tells me that Terentius Marcus has raised his standard against me, thrown down a challenge. The head, he says, is merely the start. What have you to say to that?'

'I … er …' Procopius clearly had nothing to say – to that or anything else.

'Well, er, Procopius, is it? Yes, you must be tired after your long journey. My house is your house. Refresh yourself. We'll talk later.'

'Sire.' Procopius saluted.

'Leave the head,' Theodosius said. 'I'll see to its proper burial, inform the family, you know.'

'Very good, Sire.' Procopius bowed and made his exit. All in all, that had gone rather well and he breathed a sigh of relief. All that talk he had heard of emperors cutting the throats of messengers. What nonsense! Yesterday, the drains of Londinium; tomorrow … who knew?

'What do you make of it, Tertullius?' Theodosius asked.

'This Marcus,' the emperor's aide crossed to the lacquered box that Procopius' men had left behind. 'Isn't he old Gracchus' nephew?'

'He is,' sighed Theodosius. 'I had him down for a well-meaning idiot. Just goes to show, you can't be too careful. Er … I suppose that is …?'

Tertullius had opened the box and lifted the grisly head out of the bag inside. 'Oh, yes,' he muttered. 'No doubt about it.'

Theodosius got to his feet. 'So, what's going on?' He was half talking to himself. 'This Marcus sees himself as another Magnus Maximus, does he? I thought sending the usurper's head to Britannia would be enough to deter anybody else. Obviously, I was wrong.'

'What do you propose to do, Sire?' Tertullius asked.

Theodosius crossed the room to the maps of his empire that hung there. They were never likely to be accurate, but it was the sheer scale of the territory they covered that sent a chill up the emperor's spine. Even split into East and West as it had been, it was ungovernable. 'I intend to unleash the wrath of God onto Britannia,' he said softly. 'Tertullius, get word to Flavius Stilicho. I think we need his special talents for this one. I'll make Terentius Marcus wish he'd never been born.'

'And this idiot?' Tertullius asked. 'Procopius?'

'Oh, don't bother me with trivia, Tertullius,' Theodosius tutted. 'Just kill the stupid bastard.'

LIBER II
CHAPTER VIII

Britannia Secunda

Justinus Coelius travelled light as always, his horse's hooves thudding over the heather as he rode south. Spring had come to Britannia and the lambs clung to their mothers, dotted over the moorlands of the north. In the old calendar, the Nones fell on the fifth day. The day gave its light for thirteen hours and the sun was in the sign of Aries, the ram. This, when Rome was new and the eagles first flew, was the month that lay under the special protection of Venus. They cut the throats of ewes on the altars of Isis and prayed to Serapis. And if the Christian God smiled over the land now, he who had sacrificed the man men called his son, what was that to a soldier of Mithras, a follower of Jupiter Highest and Best?

He reached Cataractonium on its broad river sweep and changed horses there. Then he rode on through a night of driving rain, the droplets cold on his face and hands, the cloak heavy and dripping as he followed the legions' road. He would have liked to have swung east to Eboracum, to visit his old friends of the VI Victrix and to pay his respects at his father's grave. But time was pressing. A girl had been abducted far to the south and not just any girl. She was the prisoner of Niall of the Five Hostages, one of the many minnows nibbling at the fins of the great pike that was Rome. He had to be stopped. Old Flavius would understand.

He slept under a rocky outcrop the next night and washed his grimy face in the clear rising waters of the high country above the Fosse. On the third day, cold and exhausted, he clattered into Verulamium where he had been born four tempestuous decades ago. Here he received news that trouble was threatened from across the German Sea. Something had happened. Something, the garrison commander at Verulamium told him, that had displeased the emperor. Terentius Marcus, it was whispered, had thrown down a challenge to Theodosius. He, Marcus, ran Britannia now. It was only a matter of time until the legions elected him Caesar. Justinus laughed it off. He was cold and tired and back in the alien south again. The Terentius Marcus he remembered, rolling around on a bed with a harlot, could not run a bath, still less the provinces that made up Britannia. He noticed, though, that the commander wasn't laughing. Rumours had a habit of crawling through Britannia like a plague. Each piece of nonsense grew with the telling, every demon had its shadow and soon, unless sanity intervened, darkness would cover the land. Justinus swapped horses and rode on.

Londinium

'The rumour is,' Chrysanthos the vicarius rolled off Honoria and reached for his wine, 'that the emperor is going to unleash Stilicho against us.'

'Stilicho?' Honoria had to go and wash, but she had heard that name somewhere and, she didn't know why, it frightened her.

'Half Vandal, half bastard.' Chrysanthos refreshed her cup. 'He's Theodosius' Commander of Cavalry, maybe even Magister Militum by now. About the only man I'd trust to have stood against Magnus Maximus. If he's on his way here, we'll have our work cut out.'

'We?' Honoria sipped her wine.

Chrysanthos laughed. 'I'm never going to make an honest woman of you, Honoria,' he said. 'What would the ladies of the Ordo say? The ladies of the court?'

'Who gives a shit about them?' she felt obliged to ask.

'Who indeed? My point is, that, wedded bliss or not – and I'm sure that crawler Severianus would pronounce us man and wife if we asked him – wedded bliss or not, we are a family, you and I.'

'And Scip,' she smiled, 'don't forget little Scip.'

Chrysanthos chuckled. 'Ah, yes,' he said. 'Rex Inferni. Cuts off a good head, does Scipio.'

She sat up. 'You knew about that?'

'A hint from me,' he said, plumping the pillows under him, 'a nod from you. He's an ambitious little sod, though, isn't he? Today, Londinium. Tomorrow, the world.'

'He's a good boy, Chrysanthos,' Honoria said. 'And his father's son. You owe him.'

Chrysanthos remembered Scipio's father, Leocadius, hero of the Wall. The man was as slippery as an eel and Scipio was just like him. The boy would cut his mother's enemies' throats as good as look at them; but Chrysanthos had a sneaky feeling that might apply to his mother's lover as well. 'Oh, yes,' he nodded. 'I owe him.'

Bishop Severianus lay face down on the cold stones of his church floor. The tall candle-flames danced in the draughts and the sickliness of incense filled his nose. His arms were outstretched and the candle-light shone bright on the rings that adorned his chubby little fingers. His whispered words to his God over, he knelt up, hearing his joints click and he crossed himself.

His sacristan, Gallius, hovered in the shadows, waiting for the bishop's prayers to finish and for his daily contemplation to begin. Instead, Severianus stood up and crossed to the altar. He fondled the parchment lying there, still twisted with the purple ribbon of the emperor. He unrolled it, holding it up to the light and he chuckled. The chuckle grew to a laugh, then a guffaw and soon his cheeks were running with tears, his infectious laugh echoing and re-echoing around the great church. The sacristan was confused. The Lord Bishop wasn't known for his sense of humour and the sound of laughter in this hallowed place was almost sacrilege.

'Good news, my lord?' the man felt he had to ask, if only to stop Severianus from turning purple.

'What?' The bishop had barely realised that he was there. 'News? The best, Gallius, the best. Do you know who's coming, bringing the wrath of the Lord with him?'

'No, my lord,' the sacristan shook his head, assuming it must be the Lord's second coming that the bishop was talking about.

'Stilicho,' Severianus pounded the altar, waving the emperor's proclamation up to the agonized carved face of the wooden Christ. 'Stilicho himself.'

'Stilicho?' The sacristan was not a man of the world.

'The emperor's Master of Horse or Master of the Army, I don't know. All I know is that he's half Vandal, half saint. He's a servant of the Lord, Gallius and he's coming for Chrysanthos.'

'He is?' The sacristan's eyes widened. He had, unbeknownst to the Lord Bishop, always got on rather well with the vicarius.

'He is,' Severianus assured him. 'For him and all the Godless bastards who take the Lord's name in vain.' The bishop grabbed the sacristan and held him to him. 'Oh, there'll be changes, Gallius, such changes. But for now,' he glanced frantically around him, 'Not a word, understand? The emperor won't have shared this little fact with the vicarius or for that matter the Dux Britannorum. Let's keep it that way, shall we? Our little secret?'

'Secrets,' Calpurnius finished his drink and looked at his wife. 'I don't like secrets.'

Conchessa looked at her husband in the lamplight. The servants had gone to bed at her request and the children were asleep, lying in each other's arms in the centre of the great bed.

'Who does?' she asked him. She still had a little of her wine left, but it tasted bitter, old, like what lay between them. For a long time now, a ghost had lived in the house of Calpurnius and Conchessa Succatus. It was the ghost of a lover, a tall man with a twisted smile who had passed that peculiarity on to his son, the boy Patricius.

'You know he's dead, don't you?' he asked her.

'Who?' Conchessa's expression had not changed. It was cold as the snow that coated Londinium's rooftops in the depths of winter; a cold that the spring sunshine could not warm.

'Who?' he snarled. 'You know perfectly well who!'

Conchessa slammed her cup down. 'I thought *you* were dead, Calpurnius,' she said.

'And it's what widows do, isn't it?' he said. 'As soon as their husbands are cold, they leap into bed with the nearest man.'

'It wasn't like that,' she said, her eyes burning with an intensity he rarely saw these days.

'Oh,' he said. 'What *was* it like?'

For a moment, she wanted to tell him, then wisdom intervened and she was calm again. 'Why are you bringing this up now? It was years ago.'

'Nearly seven,' he said, 'Using Patric's age as a yardstick.'

'What ...' Conchessa was choosing her words carefully, 'what if he's not yours? Just for sake of argument. Would that make such a difference? Come upstairs with me and look at our babies. Alike as two peas in a pod, a brother and sister, every bit as close and loving as Vitalis and me.'

'Vitalis,' Calpurnius hissed. He admired the man who was his brother-in-law; liked him, even. But Vitalis belonged to that terrible time, to the desperate years when Calpurnius had been on the run in the sewers of Augusta Treverorum, with a price on his head and without a friend in the world.

Without warning, Conchessa flew across the room and slapped him hard across the face. 'If you can't live with this, decurion,' she said, smouldering with rage, 'then perhaps you'd better get back to the sewers we found you hiding in, Vitalis and I. Perhaps that's where you belong.'

Calpurnius didn't strike back. He didn't lash out, although he wanted to. Instead, he strode out into the chill of the night, away from the ghosts. Away from the secrets. Until the next time.

Clausentum

Terentius Marcus lay in the shadows. The girl with the long, dark hair lay on top of him, moving slowly in the darkness and moaning softly. She had had several men in her time but none as high-ranking as this. The Count of the Saxon Shore had seen her in the forum that day and had asked for her specially. There had been the usual haggling over price and a happy pimp had gone away with a bulging purse. Marcus didn't begrudge the man his money. The girl was good, very good. The way she ground her hips was something very special and the Count of the Saxon Shore was coming to the boil nicely.

Suddenly, there was cold iron on the girl's back. She screamed and lost her rhythm, scrabbling to her knees and causing Marcus to scream along with her. He doubled up in pain and flopped to his side.

'Take your hand off that, Count,' a voice said. 'You'll go blind.'

The girl had gone, grabbing some of her clothes as she ran, trembling and crying.

'You know,' said the voice, 'we mustn't make a habit of this. At least I didn't waste my time trying to find you in a chapel this time.'

'Dux Britannorum,' Marcus gasped, trying to fight the clawing ache rising below his waist. 'I didn't …'

'Think it was possible to be caught in such an indelicate position twice? No, neither did I.' Justinus sheathed his sword. He'd had no intention of using it on the girl – the cold of the blade had done the trick there. And he wasn't going to use it on the Count of the Saxon Shore either. At least, not yet.

'The girl,' Justinus said. 'Not the one you've just been stoating, but the one you're supposed to be rescuing, Livia Domitia. What news?'

The II Augusta had had no news of Livia Domitia for nearly a month. For a while, Marcus assumed that Niall of the Five Hostages had gone home, butting through the wild Hibernian Sea and taking his prize with him. Then the raids had begun again and Constantine's cavalry had found burned out villages and slaughtered men. Women and children lay dead too, so the Hiberni weren't taking slaves. That would only have slowed them down and they knew there was half a legion still on their backs.

Justinus knew Constantine and knew him for the good soldier he was.

'We're getting nowhere, sir,' the man told him under the leather awning of his tent. Around him the watch fires of the night guttered in the stiffening breeze and the horses whinnied in their lines. 'Every day, we go out and every day the bastards are a step ahead of us.'

'Show me,' Justinus said. He had thrown his cloak and cap onto a chair and unbuckled his mail. The ride from Verulamium had been longer than he remembered and the wind was in his face all the way. Constantine unrolled the parchment in the candlelight and his fingers flew over the lines sketched there.

'We're here. The raiders have struck wherever I've marked a cross. With respect, sir,' Constantine looked up at the Dux Britannorum, 'shouldn't the Count be here, to discuss all this?'

'How far west have you gone?' Justinus' ignoring of the question told Constantine all he needed to know.

'The villages beyond Durnovaria. He hasn't hit the town.'

'No,' Justinus nodded, reacquainting himself with the lie of the land. 'That's because this Niall isn't strong enough. If you're right about his count of men, he'll avoid the towns and camps.

You've put all the camps in the area on alert?'

Constantine nodded.

'And he's still here.' Justinus was thinking aloud. 'He came in the winter and it's my guess he'll make a summer of it; won't stop until we've driven him back to his ships. Right, Constantine. This is what we'll do. Tell me, has the Count made any promises to Gnaeus Domitius?'

'He told him he would get his daughter back,' Constantine said.

'Hmm,' Justinus nodded. 'That may have been a little rash of him. Get me a scribe, Constantine. And two of your best riders. They're going to Isca Dumnoniorum. Let's see if we can't squeeze this Hibernian sheep-shagger like grapes in a press.'

Locicero was buckling on his mail as Quintilius clattered into the tent of his contubernium. The others were still in bed, Antoninus farting for Britannia, as usual. Quintilius threw his helmet at him.

'That's what you miss,' he grunted, reaching for the remains of last night's bread, 'when you've been out on the bloody ramparts all night. That indefinable waft that can empty a room.'

'Sorry,' Antoninus had the humility to apologise. 'Figs.'

'What's the news, then, Quint?' Locicero asked him. 'I heard movement this morning.'

'Cavalry's gone out,' Quintilius told him. 'For quite a while, judging by their rations. Constantine and the Dux.'

'So, it *was* him, then.' Antoninus, now fully awake thanks to Quintilius' helmet having landed on his shoulder with some force, was sitting up. 'I thought I recognised him last night; quite late it was. And as soon as I saw him, I thought, "Hello, this isn't going to end well." I said to you, didn't I, Sen?'

He probably did, but Seniacus hadn't stirred yet and was still dreaming of the little plot of land he'd get when he retired. *If* he retired.

'The rumour is,' said Quintilius through a mouthful of food, 'the cavalry's going forward to flush the Hiberni out. The lads from Isca Dumnoniorum are coming from the west. And we're going to roll everybody up from the east, crush the thieving bastards between us.'

'Well, why couldn't we have done that in the first place?' Antoninus asked. 'It's bleeding obvious. I don't know what Constantine and the Dux are pulling down between them, salary-wise, but it's a damn sight more than I'm getting. I told the circitor the other day, but would he listen? Would he buggery!'

'Look,' Quintilius interrupted. 'It may have escaped you boys' notice, but I've been freezing my bollocks off for the past six hours. Any chance of some breakfast? This bread's older than I am.'

With only a small force against him, Justinus Coelius took the risk of splitting his command. He sent Constantine to the north, leading the right wing, his Ala riding in column over the slopes of the downs. The earth was not so dry as to send out dust clouds and his men moved at walking pace so that the only sound was the plodding of the hooves and the jingle of harness. The dragon standard flapped in the wind and eyes swivelled right and left, the flankmen checking behind them every thirty paces. They had been chasing this Hibernian will o' the wisp for weeks now and had only caught up with him once. Then he had chosen ground with woods at his back and he had vanished into them. Now, the trick was to catch him in the open. And the end then would be swift.

Justinus himself led the cavalry to the south. His Ala trotted through marshland that led to the sea and splashed across rivers yet unbridged. Terentius Marcus could bring his engineers into play if he wanted to but he was far back and Justinus wanted no impedimenta to slow him down. He didn't have the open country here on the left flank and he knew that Constantine would have outpaced him. Even so, he knew that the gap between them was not wide enough for a Hibernian war band to slip through and he was content with that. For a whole day they advanced, the riders on the flanks of both Alae keeping each other in sight. At night, they built no camp but slept in the open, their horses saddled and bridled, the sentries walking their animals in huge circles. Food was cold. Wine forbidden. The only item of clothing that could be removed was a helmet. Otherwise, men slept on the unforgiving ground in their mail, with their swords beside them.

It was on the second day, a little after noon, that Justinus saw a semisallis lashing his horse from the north-west. He raised his hand and the column halted, horses snorting and shaking their heads, eager for action.

'We've spotted them, sir,' the semisallis saluted. 'To the north.'

'How many?'

'The commander counted thirty, sir. Could be more.'

'Horses?'

'Yes, sir.'

'All right.' Justinus checked the lie of the land. Ahead of him, the ground fell away to a broad valley floor, thick with trees. At other times, in other campaigns, it would be a perfect place for an ambush, but Niall of the Five Hostages didn't have enough men for that. 'My compliments to the commander, semisallis and could he drive the enemy south. I assume you're ahead of us.'

'I'd say so, sir.' The man turned to scan the hills he had just ridden over. 'About two miles.'

'Perfect. Try to drive the bastards due south of you. I'll wait here so that they can't see us and will think they have a clear run to the sea. Remember, if there are women with them, they are not to be harmed in any way.'

'Very good, sir,' and the man was gone, galloping north.

If Livia Domitia was still alive, Justinus reasoned, she would not be raiding with the high king of Tara. She would be held prisoner on board ship. And there must *be* ships. It was just a matter of where. Justinus' Ala had seen no sign of them yet, so logic dictated they must be ahead. It could only be a matter of time now.

'The Ala will advance,' Constantine bellowed and the cornicen blasted out the notes. The dragon standard came to the upright, the draconarius walking his horse to the right of his commander and a little behind. This afternoon was all about power. Constantine had no intention of engaging the enemy unless he had to. The Dux Britannorum wanted the thieving rabble driven south and Constantine would oblige. It would be like driving sheep to slaughter. He had never seen a Hiberni until this campaign, if anybody could dignify what was happening as a campaign. He had seen Niall of the Five Hostages before and he saw him again now, straddling a bay in the shallows of a brook. It was clear that he and his men had been watering their horses and they had no idea that Nemesis rode against them, lance points piercing the lead-grey of the sky.

'Walk, march!' Constantine roared and the Ala picked up the pace. At the blast of the cornicen, horses' ears pricked and the amble became a march that rose without further orders into a trot. The officers had drawn their swords and carried them at the slope against their shoulders. To Niall and his riff-raff, it must look as though this was no pointless mime, but the real thing.

The commander felt the ground thunder under him and heard the final blast of the cornicen. Two hundred men were cantering over the crazy angle of the hill, the circitors yelling at their men to keep steady and mend their pace. The lance points came down and men hunched in the saddle, ready for the impact of a charging horse or ready to skewer men on the ground. Ahead, Constantine saw the little knot of men on their stolen ponies panic and swerve away. One man dithered, looked for a moment as though he was about to stand alone against the wave of horseflesh coming at him; then, he broke and ran with the others.

Constantine's right flank had swung wide, riding in an arc which drove the raiders away from the river. The Roman horses were blown now, because the going had been tough, but it was vital that Niall's men didn't get away merely by riding further west. The Dux might never find their ships.

From his vantage point in the trees, Justinus watched the skyline. Behind him, his men had dismounted, eased girths and adjusted saddles, stroking their mounts' noses to keep them calm and quiet. The wind had dropped, so the rustling of leaves no longer disturbed them and there was daylight enough to finish this job. The first rider thundered over the hill, then another and another, until the pale green of the downland grass was black with the knot of riders. Beside him, an eager tribune was reaching for his saddle bow.

'Stand fast,' Justinus hissed at him. 'The object of this exercise is to let them ride past us. We don't want to tip our hand too soon.'

Annoyed and embarrassed in equal proportions, the tribune did as he was told. Justinus counted thirty four riders. His own command outnumbered them four to one; Constantine's would double that. And Constantine, he knew, would not be far behind. But Constantine knew his commander's mind and would not be hurried. He slowed the charge to a trot and then to a walk, the horses snorting and frisking with the exhilaration of the run. He heard the ripple of curses under men's breath; men geared up for a fight were more difficult to rein in than the horses they rode. Everybody's blood was up. By the time they topped the rise, the Hiberni had all but disappeared, but Constantine could see the little woods to his left come alive with horsemen and he knew he had found Justinus' command. He could see the Dux waving at him, pointing to the far hills and Constantine understood.

'Ala!' he roared so that the front rank at least could hear him. 'Right front!' And the horsemen on the left kicked their horses forward while those on the right held their mounts steady, hauling back on the rein. Within seconds, the entire formation was trotting south-west, to outflank the Hiberni and funnel them into the trap.

It was now that Justinus had to hope that what Marcus had told him and what Constantine had told him was right, that the raiders were only a small war band. If this was another lure, a ploy to draw the Romans on into some defile, then it could get very bloody indeed. There was a strip of silver birch trees ahead, stretching to right and left. Their trunks shone dully in the afternoon light and their branches were fluttering green against the grey of the sky. It was raining in the west and those clouds, angry and spiteful, were rumbling ever eastwards, threatening to empty themselves on Roman and Hiberni alike. Unless Jupiter Highest and Best ordered it, the weather was on no man's side.

Justinus turned in the saddle. Constantine was nearly a mile behind him, too far away to be of immediate assistance if things got ugly, yet in a perfect position if Justinus' plan was to work. He saw them first and halted the column, ordering his horsemen to move by hand signals. There must be no clash and hurry now, no brazen warhorns and yelled orders. At last, he could see the raiders' ships.

They were half-hidden under brushwood in a little inlet sheltered from the crash of the sea. The Hiberni were there already, hauling away branches and tossing them onto the shingle beach. They slapped their horses' rumps and the animals scattered, alarmed by the lack of weight on their backs and the sudden freedom. There were shouts and there was panic. Niall Mugmedon ripped off his fierce helmet and scanned the line of birch that screened the makeshift harbour. The cavalry he had seen would take a time to reach the inlet and by then, he and his three ships would be gone, like the thieves in the night that they were.

He hadn't seen the second Ala, though, the one that was cantering down the slope, batting the birch branches aside with their lances. He swore in his incomprehensible language and grabbed a rope, tugging an anchor free and climbing onto the deck. Behind him, men frantically hauled the sail upwards, the spar sliding and scraping, timber on timber, oak on oak, until it engaged near the mast-head. But there was no time to catch the wind and the raiders bent to their oars, the helmsman leaning hard on the tiller to bring the ship around.

Only one vessel was moving, the others lay fast in the cloying mud.

'Arrows!' Justinus bellowed. He had reined in on a hillock above the flying foam of the sea and watched as his men cantered down onto the shingle and cut down the raiders, one by one. Behind him, his horse archers, who had done nothing but ride so far this day, let loose their goose-shafts from their short bows. Cat-gut thudded from yew wood and the air was alive with arrows, sailing through the sky to rip the dangling, useless sail and thud into the deck of Niall's ship. There were too many men on board and the vessel was unstable. The oarsmen's backs cracked and strained as they bent every sinew in their mad race for the sea. Others knelt on the oak planks, trying to defend the rowers with their shields. The arrows bit deep, the second volley and the third, sliding off iron helmets and thudding into mail.

Soon the deck was awash with the dead or dying and the stricken ship, free from its inlet mooring, slid helplessly onto the shingle and lodged there, swaying and surging with each increasing rush of the tide.

By the time Constantine's Ala arrived, it was all over and the Dux Britannorum had accomplished what he had set out to do. Well, perhaps not quite …

CHAPTER IX

They took no prisoners at the water's edge. The rabble who had slaughtered women and children lay where they fell, to roll in and out with the tide. No one buried them and they became food for the gulls and the cormorants, wheeling and diving from the high air currents to rip and peck the corpses.

Niall of the Five Hostages was not among them. There was no helmet with a king's crown riveted to it, no one resembling the figure that Constantine had seen weeks before, directing his men in the skirmish at the forest's edge. Neither were there any captives and certainly not a feisty girl of the house of Gnaeus Domitius. The three ships were laden with stolen wine, silver trinkets and coins, carelessly lifted from people who no longer had any use for them because they were dead.

Justinus had sent a rider back to Marcus; the pursuit was over but the quarry was not found. For the rest of his life, the Count of the Saxon Shore would claim the victory over Niall Mugmedon as his. The loss of the high king and the girl? Well, that he laid at the door of Justinus Coelius, the Dux Britannorum.

'Well, that's it,' Locicero mouthed to Quintillius as they trudged along the ridge, marching east. 'All very pointful, wasn't it?'

'It was,' Quintillius agreed. 'I've got bunions on my bunions tramping all over the south of Britannia Prima, admiring the sheer beauty of it all.'

'Remember old Severus? Semisallis, bloke with a stutter?'

'I do. What about him?'

Locicero shifted the weight of the impedimenta dangling

from his lancea. 'He had a thing about grasses.'

'Did he?' Quintillius asked. 'I did not know that.'

'Made a collection of them on the march, pressed them into a book.'

'Get away.' Quintillius gave the information more thought. 'Went mad in the end, didn't he?'

'Yes, he did,' Locicero said. 'I'm just saying. He'd have enjoyed this; all this pointful marching about.'

'Lovely.'

At the head of the column, where the silver eagle of the II Augusta flashed in the spring sun, Justinus reined in his horse, pulling out of the line and taking his senior officers with him.

'I can't leave it like this,' he said to Marcus.

'Sir?' the Count of the Saxon Shore was already planning this chapter in his memoirs and he would keep his scribe up until the early hours to get it set down.

'The reason I'm here,' Justinus murmured, watching the half legion rumble past, spears at the slope, impedimenta stowed, 'is that I had a letter from a man whose daughter had been taken. Do you have children, Marcus?'

'No, sir,' the Count said. 'None that I know of.'

'Nor do I,' Justinus said. 'Somehow, I've never had the time. I've never met Gnaeus Domitius, but the fact that he reached out to *me*. A personal request from a man consumed, no doubt, with grief.'

'She's dead, sir.' Marcus thought it was time for some straight talking. Ahead of him stretched a glittering future; he was sure of that. But if the Dux Britannorum had his way, he'd spend most of it chasing a ghost.

Justinus looked at him levelly. 'We don't know that,' he said. 'And even if she is, Niall of the Five Hostages is still very much alive. How he got away from us on the coast I don't know, but he did.'

Constantine leaned forward to murmur in Marcus' ear. 'Until Niall of the Five Hostages is taken or dead,' he said.

'What?' Marcus snapped. Irritating cavalry commanders he could do without.

'Our pledge,' Constantine reminded him. 'What we swore as we drank at the start of this little dance. Didn't we, Gerontius?'

'We did,' the tribune nodded, looking at Marcus with the same contempt.

Marcus hadn't moved. 'We haven't killed him,' Constantine said. 'We haven't even taken him.'

'Unfinished business,' Gerontius underlined it.

'Well, I'm going to finish it,' Justinus said, wheeling his horse. 'Constantine, I'd like twenty of your best men, please. Hard riders.'

'Very good, sir.' And the cavalry commander kicked his animal's flanks and trotted over to join the Alae.

Marcus was furious. 'It is customary,' he said, 'for such a request to be made to the commanding officer of a unit. That would be me.'

'Well, it would be if we had flying pigs,' Justinus said. 'You've won no laurels today, Marcus. Remember that.' And he rode away.

'Hear that?' Quintillius grunted as he marched past the knot of officers.

'I did,' Locicero said, finding it difficult to keep the smirk off his face. 'Makes you believe in a Christian Heaven, don't it?'

'No,' Quinitillius said. 'I'll stick to Mithras, thanks. You know where you are with Mithras.'

Gnaeus Domitius had taken to wandering the lakeside most evenings since Livia had gone. Lavinia of course had been distraught for the days that followed, but somehow, perhaps because of the God she prayed to every day, she had found an inner strength, a purpose. Somehow, she *knew* that not only was Livia still alive, but she was well. Her husband had no such strength, no such belief. Wherever he looked, wherever he went around the estate, he saw her, the daughter he loved. She smiled at him from her loom, she was riding at his side as he patrolled the bounds. Her laughter rippled with the waters where the brook crossed the stones and her sighing mingled with the wind in the trees. Lavinia watched him and worried. She was suffering as he was. She had given birth to the girl, brought her into the world twenty three summers ago; but Livia had always been her papa's girl – there was no doubt of that. In the end, all that Lavinia could do was to smile and hold her husband close. And that had to be enough.

'Gnaeus Domitius?'

He turned at the sound of his name. He had been staring into the still waters of the lake, watching the sun-rimmed clouds reflected there and, as always, he had been far away. A tall soldier stood there, in fur cap and rough cloak and there were others sitting their horses under the trees. How had he not heard them?

'I am Justinus Coelius, Dux Britannorum. You sent for me.'

Mediolanum

The emperor fell ill that summer. His medici fussed around him, prescribing potions and applying leeches but nothing seemed to work. And all the time he had an empire to run, the vast and, men said increasingly, the ungovernable empire that stretched from Asia to Britannia. He lay on his bed propped by pillows and trying to concentrate on the matter in hand. The matter in hand was Stilicho.

'Great Theodosius,' the man who was half Vandal, half bastard, half saint – he always added up to more than the whole – bowed low. 'You are looking well, Sire.'

'Liar,' Theodosius wheezed. He looked at the man before him, his hair combed forward in the style of an emperor of the old days. All that was missing was the laurel wreath of the gods. The face was strong and difficult to read, the eyes cold and grey. There was no love there; that was certain. But the great Theodosius did not want Flavius Stilicho for a lover.

'You sent for me, Sire?'

'Did I?' For the briefest of moments, Theodosius' sight clouded and his army commander blurred almost to invisibility. 'Yes, yes, of course.'

'Britannia?' Stilicho felt it necessary to remind the man.

'There's no change there,' Theodosius said, his voice like gravel. 'I'm dying, Stilicho.'

'Never, Sire,' the half Vandal said, shaking his head. In the scheme of things, it was rather an optimistic thing to say.

'Honorius,' the emperor scrabbled at his side for the picture of the boy, 'my dearest, my best.'

'He will make a fine emperor, Sire,' Stilicho said, 'when that dread day comes.'

'He will,' Theodosius smiled. 'He will. But the day is coming, Stilicho, and sooner than any of us expected. And he is still a boy.'

'You can count on my loyalty, Sire,' Stilicho said.

'I know I can,' the emperor said, 'but there has to be more. Will you stand as the boy's guardian? Will you keep this tottering empire of mine together?'

For a moment, Stilicho was stunned. 'Sire,' he said, 'it seems only yesterday I commanded your cavalry. Today I command your army. Would you have me be emperor in all but name?'

'I would, Stilicho,' Theodosius rasped. 'You're the one man in the empire I would trust with my son's life. You will act in his name and then – and this is the most difficult part – then, when the time comes, you will stand aside and let him assume the purple.' Theodosius reached up and grabbed the man's cloak. 'Can I ask that of you?' he murmured, out of breath and almost out of hope. 'Is it too much?'

Stilicho smiled, the grey eyes sparkling. 'You can, Sire,' he said, 'and it isn't.'

Theodosius sank back on his pillows, exhausted. 'Thank God,' he mumbled, 'and thank you, Stilicho.'

Britannia Prima

'Jesus and Mary!' the old man stumbled backwards from his rod and line. They weren't biting this morning, but that wasn't the point. What was the point was that a large man had just had a word in his ear and had caught the fisherman unawares. 'I didn't hear you.'

'That's to the good,' the man said. 'I am Justinus Coelius, Dux Britannorum.'

The old man gulped. He was used to seeing soldiers, from the camp and along the roads. He often sold his fish to the II Augusta and knew some of them by name. The Dux Britannorum he did not know; only the man's reputation.

'You live near here, old man?' Justinus asked.

'I do, sir,' the fisherman was on his feet, touching his forelock and suddenly feeling very inferior and very alone.

'I'm looking for a stranger,' the Dux Britannorum went on. 'Tall, red hair. He may have a slave with him, a girl.'

'A slave, sir?'

There was something in the man's tone that made Justinus look at him hard. 'Yes. She may be tied, beaten; I don't know.'

'Well …'

'Yes? Out with it, man.'

'Well, I did see such a man, sir. He asked directions. He had red hair and a girl with him.'

'What language did he speak?'

'Oh, Latin, sir, but not Durotriges Latin. He wasn't local.'

'Tell me about the girl.'

'Well, she was no slave like any I've seen, sir,' the fisherman said. 'If you'd asked me, I'd have said they were man and wife.'

The old man had given the pair directions to Sorviodunum, with its ramparts and ridges. That was the extent of the old man's knowledge. Who knew what lay beyond that? Justinus Coelius knew, because he had ridden or marched every Roman mile of it. He and his riders cantered over the springy turf of the broad plain. Yes, a couple had passed that way, they told them at Sorviodunum. They had asked directions to Portus Abonae, but the odd thing was, it was the woman who was asking; the man didn't seem to know the place existed.

Justinus and the Ala of the II rode past the strange, silent mounds to the dead and the curious circle of standing stones, the wind moaning over the plain and the crows circling in the high clouds, tumbling and falling on the air currents. Portus Abonae would provide a ship for Niall Mugmedon to get home. But it was also the western base for the classis Britannica, the fleet, and he'd see more Romans there than he had ever seen before in his life.

As he rode in grim silence, nothing was making sense to the Dux Britannorum. If the pair he was chasing were really Niall of the Five Hostages and his prize, why was she unbound? And why was she the one asking directions? Was she so afraid of him that she would do his bidding? Had he held a knife to her back while she had asked? This simpering, shrinking violet was not the girl that Gnaeus Domitius had described. The Livia Domitia her father had talked of would have taken the first opportunity, if not to slit the throat of the high king of Tara, at least to slip away from him when she could.

They slept that night on the slopes of the ridge that led to Aquae Sulis. Common sense told Justinus that a foreigner on the run would not go near a town, however tempting its baths and waters. There would be too many eyebrows raised, too many questions asked. He would seek a hollow somewhere, a shelter where he didn't have to burn and destroy. Somehow, a raiding party of one man held few terrors for anyone. The tables had been turned on the high king of Tara and his homeland was far away.

They found them shortly before dawn, huddled together under a rocky outcrop near a stand of oaks. Silently, Justinus' men slipped the tethers of their ponies as they cropped the sweet grass and led them away.

Justinus looked down at them, letting his shadow fall on the still-sleeping pair. If this was the great raider, the man who had put the south of Britannia Prima to the sword, he appeared to have shrunk several feet. No fire flashed from his mouth, no sparks from his arse. He was just a man.

'Get up, sheep-shagger.'

Niall was halfway to that position, knife in his hand when two of Justinus' men grabbed him from behind, forcing him to his knees and knocking the weapon from his grasp. A third man coiled a noose of rough hemp around the man's neck, pulling his beard upwards so that it fitted tightly around his throat.

Justinus looked at him. 'Just for the record,' he said, 'just so I'm sure I'm hanging the right man; you *are* Niall of the Five Hostages?'

As well as he could, the Hibernian straightened. 'I am Niall Mugmedon, high king of Tara,' he said in perfect Latin.

'Whatever,' Justinus muttered. 'Well, you're Niall of the Four Hostages, now.' He held out his hand to the girl. 'Come, child.'

Until now, the girl had not moved, except to get out of the way of the struggling men. Now, she stood like an ox in the furrow. 'No,' she said.

Justinus frowned. 'Are you not Livia Domitia, daughter of Gnaeus Domitius?'

'What if I am?' she asked defiantly.

'Your father's worried about you.' Justinus' hand was still outstretched.

'Tell him I'm dead,' she said.

Justinus let his hand fall. He looked at the Hibernian on his knees, head held high. 'Hang him,' he said. 'That oak over there looks strong enough.'

'No.' Livia hurled herself at Justinus, a knife suddenly in her hand, the blade tip biting deep into his chest. He stumbled backwards, carrying her with him. He used his weight and threw her to the ground. Niall saw his chance and swung the man to his right across him, driving his knee into his face as he went down. The second man still gripped him but the Hibernian knocked him away, driving both fists into his chest and grabbing his sword as he went down.

Bleeding heavily as he was, Justinus drew his weapon and swung to the attack. From all directions, Constantine's horsemen were leaping out of their saddles, coming to his aid, but Justinus waved them aside. He tossed his sword to his left hand because his right arm was hanging useless, the muscles ruptured and torn by Livia's knife.

'What's this, Roman?' Niall faced him. 'The high king of Tara doesn't fight cripples.'

'That's all right,' Justinus said, wincing. 'I don't usually fight sheep-shaggers either. But I'm prepared to make an exception in your case.'

He hacked against the Hibernian's blade and the man jerked backwards. Livia was being held by two men and she wasn't about to wriggle away from that. The horses tossed their heads and their riders pulled them back from the tight circle they had created. Niall was circling too, testing the ground, checking his footing. He was taller than Justinus and so far, it was only his pride that was hurt, at being caught napping.

'For the record,' he said, smiling. 'Who is it I am about to kill?'

'You're not going to kill anybody,' Justinus said, but every word cost him dear. 'But I am Justinus Coelius, Dux Britannorum.'

'Well, well,' the Hibernian laughed. 'It's an honour. Men told me you lived in the north, hiding behind some woman's skirts. And yet, here you are, with a hole in your side, made by – guess what? Another woman.' He lunged, but Justinus was faster, banging down the blade and turning to face him again. He could fight with either hand, but he was far better with his right. Except that today the muscles in his right arm just weren't working. His blood dripped from his fingers and his legs felt like lead. He squinted across to Livia. How could her little blade have done so much damage and so quickly?

Now he brought the play to the Hibernian. He swung sideways, driving him back up the slope and his blade licked under the man's guard and gashed his hip. Niall grunted with the sudden pain and jumped backwards, regretting it instantly. The blades clashed together again, a spark flying in the morning and iron slid along iron.

'Feeling tired yet, Dux Britannorum?' Niall taunted. 'About

now, you'd like nothing better than to fold up and go to sleep, eh? Eyes a little heavy? Can you still see me? I've been invisible for quite a while, haven't I? No reason why I shouldn't disappear altogether.'

Justinus didn't see where the next attack came from. All he saw was a blade hissing down from the sky. All he could do was parry for his life and he sank to his knees. Suddenly there were Constantine's men swarming to the attack. Niall of the Five Hostages was beaten to the ground, his sword, streaming red, flung out to the side of the melee.

'No!' Livia and Justinus were both calling out, but for very different reasons.

'Don't,' she screamed. 'Don't hurt him!'

'She's right,' Justinus muttered, leaning with both hands on his sword hilt and fighting for breath. 'The man's a king. And he's worth a king's ransom.' He tried to focus on the Hibernian, held at sword point by a circitor with a short temper and a mean disposition. 'What'll they call me after this, sheep-shagger? Justinus of the One Hostage?'

And he plummeted forward onto his face.

'They say your mind stays clear to the end.'

It was a female voice, the Latin impeccable. Justinus couldn't see her. She was just a shape at the end of a long passage and the shape kept shifting. He looked down. There were vomit stains on his tunic; and his arm, when he tried to move it, felt like lead. Both his hands were huge, filling his vision as he raised them. He was aware of straps across his shoulder and linen bandages through which his blood still oozed. His head felt enormous and, lying though he was, it was too heavy for him. Sitting up was impossible.

'Who are you?' he asked the shape at the end of the tunnel.

'You know who I am,' she told him. 'You have come from the far north to find me.'

'Livia Domitia,' he nodded and the slight movement sent the room spinning wildly on an off kilter axis.

'I told you your mind would stay clear.'

Justinus had been stabbed before. In battles and skirmishes and fights without number, he had felt the bite of iron, the searing pain as his skin broke and his blood spurted free. He had had fever before too, in the icy heather beyond the Wall, in the teeming, rat-infested streets of Londinium. Always, he had seen the same thing – a stairway that edged a wall, the wall of a tower. And the stairway led to a high window, impossibly bright, impossibly small. In his delirium he climbed the stairs, each step agony. But there was always another flight of steps twisting ahead, another facet to the square of the tower. And the window stayed out of reach, far, far away.

But this was different. Justinus had never felt like this.

'The blade,' he reasoned, speaking slowly and deliberately to make sure the words came out right. 'Your blade tip was poisoned. With what?'

'What does it matter?' she asked. 'There's no cure. It will be in your blood by now.'

'For the record,' he said, his voice, it seemed to him, booming like the surf along the shore. 'Mithras will want to know.'

'Mithras!' she taunted him. 'Mithras is a myth, a fairy story. You should have worshipped the one, true God, Dux Britannorum.'

'As you do?' he asked her, but his voice was now blown away on a wild sea wind and wasn't booming now, but a whisper on the breeze.

'I do,' she said. 'I haven't lost that.'

He struggled up on his one good elbow; he knew the other wouldn't bear his weight. He kept his eyes shut, so the room wouldn't spin round. 'But you've lost everything else,' he said. 'Your home. Your father and mother. Your virginity, I've no doubt.'

'Yes,' she yelled at him, proud, defiant. 'Yes, I've lost my virginity. I have lain with the high king of Tara and I hope there's a warrior prince in my belly. You Romans! You've had it all your own way for so long. Well, the end is coming, Roman, for you sooner than the rest, but it *is* coming.'

Justinus thought he was laughing, but only a gurgling sound came out. '*You* Romans?' he said, 'You're more of a Roman than I am. We were both born in Britannia, you and I. Your father told me, how he would tell you the stories of Romulus and Remus and the she-wolf, of the early days of the Volsci and the Sabines. That's your heritage as much as it's mine. This sheep-shagger who has lain with you, what does he know?'

Suddenly, her face, so far away, was very close, her eyes burning into his. 'His way of life is as old as yours,' she said. 'His culture is as rich, his people as proud.'

'Livia,' he said softly so that she could barely hear him. 'You went with Niall Mugmedon against your will, to save your parents' lives. That was only weeks ago. You can't have forgotten. You can't have turned against them.'

He saw her eyes drop, her lip tremble. 'No,' she said. 'I haven't forgotten. I owe them everything, I know that. But Niall has opened my eyes, shown me a different world. He comes from a place where no Roman has set foot. Can you imagine that, Dux Britannorum?'

Justinus shook his head. 'No, he said. 'No, I can't.' Everywhere, in his world, the eagles had flown and flew still. Life without all that was unthinkable.

'How are they?' Livia asked him, after a silence. 'My parents. How are they?'

'Your mama is strong,' he told her. 'She'll mend, in time. But your papa. He's lost, Livia, going slowly to Hell in his grief. I was supposed to bring you back to him.'

'I am your prisoner,' she said, holding up her tethered wrists. He could see the blood where she had twisted against the bonds. 'I can't stop you from taking me back.'

'Will they want you?' he asked her, 'now?'

She blinked back her tears.

'Their little girl has gone. They're half convinced of it already. If I take you back, they will know. They will have the worst of all worlds. Your body will be there, but your soul?' He smiled, bitterly. 'Your soul is in the Christian limbo, halfway between this world and the realm of the devil. Every time they looked at you, they would see a shell, empty and cold as a tomb. In spirit, you would be riding with a slaughterer of women and a kidnapper of children. You would never be theirs again.'

'So,' she sniffed. 'What happens now?'

Justinus lay back on the pillows, trying to garner his strength. This was exhausting him, probably hastening his end, he knew. But he had made a promise and he had to let this wayward girl know what ill she had done. Finally, he could speak. 'To you, I don't know. The high king of Tara will be taken first to Clausentum, then to Londinium. He'll be displayed in a cage for the crowd to spit at.'

'As a warning to the others.' Livia knew how these things worked.

'We'll give him the honour due to his rank and offer him in exchange.'

'In exchange for what?'

'For each of the hostages he has taken in Hibernia. As you say, no Roman has ever set foot there, but it's fitting nevertheless. I like the neatness of the thing.'

'And if Niall's people won't agree?'

Justinus shrugged but it felt as if he were rolling an elephant uphill. 'Then they will have consigned their king to death.'

'Whatever,' she snapped, her voice harsh again, as it had been when she had stabbed the Dux Britannorum, as it had been when this conversation had begun. 'You won't be here to see it.'

'No.' He sank back onto his pillows, watching her face fade. Only by an enormous effort of will could he bring her into focus and he decided it wasn't worth it. Let the darkness come; he was ready. 'Rome isn't about me,' he murmured. 'It's never about one man, not even the emperor. There are millions of us. And we'll always be here.'

She watched him shudder and shiver and, despite herself, she ran a cool hand over his sweating forehead, the one that to him felt so cold. 'Wolfsbane,' she whispered, suddenly, desperately, sorry. 'The poison on the knife-blade. You can tell your Mithras it was wolfsbane.'

CHAPTER X

Clausentum

Clausentum stood on its rocky promontory along the broad sweep of the river. The gulls wheeled here, watching the fishing boats as they came home from the wild winds and the sea. The soldiers had been here now for some weeks and summer had come to the south lands. The men of the II Augusta had made their home under leather beyond the new walls and made a nuisance of themselves every night in the tabernae.

On such a night, the Dux Britannorum came to Clausentum. For weeks, Justinus Coelius had lain, half in, half out of delirium. When he wasn't vomiting, he was fighting the thirst raging in his throat and shivering as though he lay in the ice fields north of the Wall. He had the best medici in all Britannia, but they were at a loss. Whatever that mad Roman girl, the one who had gone native, had smeared on her blade, the medici had not seen it before. Wolfsbane, had she called it? They looked mystified, checked their learned books, consulted with one another and looked mystified all over again. There was no cure; of that, they were certain. Only rest and care. And time, perhaps.

But the Dux Britannorum did not have time for time. He had four sub-provinces to defend, legions to put through their paces, frontiers to watch. The rumours had been coming in for months now. The Suebi, the Alans, the whole of Germania, was on the march. And if they were all a long way from Britannia, that was little comfort. Every emperor since the great Constantine had helped himself to troops from Britannia, the hereditary limitanei who guarded the Wall and its outposts, whenever the need arose; for whatever mad-brained scheme he had in mind.

'Jupiter, highest and best!' Locicero hissed through his teeth. 'Dead man riding, Quint.'

Quintillius looked up from leaning on his spear in the flickering torchlight. Then both men snapped to attention. Locicero was right. Justinus Coelius looked like a living ghost. His cloak hung on him like so many blankets and his face was a fungal grey. He barely acknowledged their presence as he walked his horse under the arch of Clausentum's main gate. They heard his voice, a croaking shadow of itself, as he reached the guard-port.

'The Count of the Saxon Shore,' he said. 'Where will I find him?'

'In the basilica, sir,' the circitor of the watch told him. 'I'll show you.'

'No need, circitor.' Justinus climbed slowly out of the saddle. 'See to my horse, will you? Sponge his nostrils first, then water, then feed.'

'Very good, sir.' The circitor was a little put out to be told how to suck eggs by his granny, but he could see granny wasn't well and let it go.

The steps seemed tall and many to the Dux Britannorum, but he made it to the top. Guards jumped to attention at the door to the chamber and one of them swung it open for him. Terentius Marcus sat with Constantine and Gerontius at their cena, clinking cups and tasting grapes. Servants scurried backwards and forwards, carrying dishes and tureens. The officers stood to attention at Justinus' arrival.

'Gentlemen,' he half-whispered. 'Glad to see you upright, Count.'

Marcus blushed, despite his status and his arrogance. The last twice the Dux Britannorum had caught him in compromising positions. At least this time he was only having a meal, not a girl.

'Welcome, sir,' the Count said. 'Vallius, wine.'

A servant hurried over and Justinus was grateful to sit on a couch. Constantine and Gerontius looked at each other. The man looked appalling, a cobwebbed grey in the dancing candles and the reflecting silver. He had lost weight and seemed half-buried in his cloak.

'Where is Niall of the Five Hostages?' Justinus asked.

Marcus had been dreading this moment. He waved the

slave away but kept the ewer, pouring a cup for his master and a larger one for himself. 'There has been … a complication, sir,' he said.

Justinus paused, the cup halfway to his lips. 'A complication?'

'He's gone,' Constantine said, realizing that Marcus wasn't going to.

'Gone?' Justinus frowned at them both. Gerontius sat bolt upright, like a naughty schoolboy caught with his hand in the apple barrel.

'Escaped,' Constantine said. He glowered at Marcus. 'As in, got away.'

'And the girl?' Justinus wanted to know. 'Livia?'

'With him,' Gerontius added, feeling strangely relieved now that the cat was well and truly out of the bag.

'When?'

'Two weeks ago.' Marcus had found his voice at last.

'Two weeks …?' Justinus sat up sharply and the sudden movement cost him. He slammed the cup down, the wine untouched. 'Why wasn't I told?'

'You weren't well, sir.' Marcus slickly assumed the disguise of the concerned subordinate. 'The advice from the medici was that you were not to be disturbed.'

'Bollocks!' Justinus grunted. 'This Hibernian brigand ran rings around you in the spring, Marcus. Now he's made a fool of you again. What steps have you taken?'

'I've sent patrols out, every day,' the Count of the Saxon Shore was desperate to build bridges.

'And?'

'Nothing,' Constantine said. 'The man's a will o' the wisp; but you knew that.'

Justinus nodded. 'I did,' he said. He got to his feet with difficulty, regretting his ride through the night, the climb up the stairs, leaving such a critical command to a first class idiot. 'Stand up, Terentius Marcus.'

The man did as he was told, blinking. He glanced down briefly. The Dux Britannorum was armed to the teeth. He could see the sword and knew what he could do with that. He could see the dagger and guessed he was equally proficient with that. The darts he could not see, but he'd heard the stories. No one threw a Roman dart like Justinus Coelius, ex-circitor of the VI Victrix.

Death could come to Terentius Marcus in so many ways. As he stood there, swallowing hard, he just wondered which.

'Terentius Marcus,' he heard Justinus say in the firmest voice he had heard from him all night, 'by the authority vested in me by the emperor, I hereby strip you of the rank of Comes Litoris Saxonici,' and he ripped the insignia from the man's shoulder. 'You will revert to your former rank of tribune in the garrison of Londinium – if they'll take you back.'

He spun on his heel.

'Sir.' Constantine stopped him. 'Where are you going? You're not well.'

Justinus was swaying in the doorway, Constantine's voice far away as though calling with the gulls out to sea. 'I have to pay a call,' he said. 'I have to tell a man who deserves better news that his daughter is dead.' And he crashed to the floor.

While Constantine and Gerontius eased the fallen man's clothing and checked for a heartbeat, Terentius Marcus picked up his insignia from where it had fallen with Justinus and repinned it to his tunic. He stood over the huddle in the doorway. 'Is he dead, Constantine?'

The cavalry commander looked up at him with contempt. 'No. But he's not the man he was, that's for certain.'

'No,' Marcus smiled, half to himself. 'But I am. This,' he raised his voice and waited until Gerontius was on his feet, 'this stage-play tonight never happened; do you understand?' He tapped the insignia. 'The Count of the Saxon Shore is still in business. Is that clear?'

Rutupiae

The mighty walls of Rutupiae frowned down on the ships plying their way upriver. The sails came down and the ropes shortened and the oarsmen hauled their timber upright, letting the tide carry them. From the masthead of the leading vessel, the great eagle of the emperor flapped on its leather field and the Chi-Rho of the risen Christ alongside it. Sailors dashed along footrails and splashed into the shallows, wallowing up to their waists as the ropes flew and the anchors bit deep. Soldiers followed them, clapping on their helmets and hauling their shields clear of the water. They formed a double column on either side of the stone ramp that ran green and weed-covered into the sea.

Above them the gulls shrieked at each other in the sun. Rome had come to Britannia in the form of six ships of the great Theodosius and that meant food and a bountiful harvest from the scraps that armies always left behind.

A hard-pressed garrison commander was running along the harbour wall, an entourage of yes-men in his wake. He was late and he knew it. The double line of soldiers clicked to attention as their officers began to wade ashore. At the back of the gaggle of them, bareheaded and unarmed, Flavius Stilicho kicked his booted way through the shallows, impervious to the chill of the autumn waters. Behind him, another man, tall, unkempt and wearing a rough, wild cloak looked up at the great towers and smiled.

'So, Pelagius,' Stilicho turned to him. 'Britannia at last. Is it much as you remembered it? Or do one set of Roman walls look very much like another to you?'

'Rome builds them,' Pelagius smiled, breathing in the salt tang of the air. 'God watches over them.'

'Indeed he does,' Stilicho said. 'Gentlemen,' he turned to his officers, plumed and ready for ceremony. 'In front of you stands the great fortress of the deified Claudius, when the eagles first flew over this land. They built a triumphal arch to the deified Agricola.' He turned and saw nothing and shrugged. 'Then, I suppose, they pulled it down. Well, they had their reasons, no doubt. We are gazing, gentlemen, on three hundred years of history. We are here to ensure that there is another three hundred.'

'Salve, Flavius Stilicho Maximus,' the garrison commander gave the old salute, striking his armoured chest with his fist. 'Welcome to Britannia.'

'Thank you, commander,' Stilicho nodded, and he closed to him. 'You're late.'

Londinium

'Do try to look vaguely interested, darling,' Chrysanthos murmured, his grin frozen, his mind clouding.

Honoria lifted her chin from her hand. 'I feel as if I've been watching this tosh for the last three hundred years,' she said, flashing a smile at the youngest tribune in the Londinium garrison, sitting across the stage from her.

'We all do,' Chrysanthos yawned. 'It's Greek culture. And you know how grateful we all are to the Greeks.'

She looked at him, the smile gone, the pout more prominent. 'Bollocks,' she grunted. 'That's a Greek word, I suppose.'

'They had a word for them, yes.' Chrysanthos flicked his fingers and a slave was at his elbow. The vicarius had decided that copious amounts of wine were all that would help him get through the evening. This was one of the one hundred and two *ludi dies* given over to the theatre in every provincial capital and it seemed that he had officiated at every one of them. 'Actually, that girl's quite good.'

The youngest cast member was flirting coyly in the stage-street below them, the pretty, painted mask covering and uncovering her pretty, painted face.

Honoria was not impressed. 'As arses go, she's all right,' she shrugged. 'The *adulescens* has it for me every time.'

'I thought he might,' Chrysanthos nodded, glancing at the handsome young lead. 'I should have thought the *miles gloriosus* was more your type.' He nodded to the large actor in armour who was standing drinking with his cronies to the side of the set.

'Oh, no,' Honoria grinned. 'Too hairy. Besides, it looks as though I've got a braggart soldier already.' She inclined her head towards the tribune who bowed in return.

'God, you're insatiable.' Chrysanthos took a swig of his wine. 'Why don't you go down and give the *meretrix* a few pointers? She doesn't seem to know how to handle her clients.'

She didn't. The woman playing the prostitute seemed decidedly ill at ease with the men on stage and was only too glad to hide behind her mask.

'Oh, look, Chrysanthos,' Honoria said, eyes bright with mischief. 'The *senex* is making his move on the girl. Watch carefully now and you'll see how it's done.'

A doddery old man was wobbling his way towards the lovely girl, who looked suitably horrified and shied away from him. The vicarius sighed. 'All this and Stilicho too,' he said.

'Ah, Stilicho.' Honoria looked her escort in the face. 'The elephant in the theatre. I wondered when you'd get around to mentioning him.'

'It's not going to be easy,' Chrysanthos smiled and nodded at one of the Ordo who caught his eye. 'We'll need to be at the top of our game.'

'Tell me about him, again.'

'What's to tell?' Chrysanthos shrugged. 'He's Theodosius'

hatchet man, his troubleshooter. He was commander of the Schola Palatinae by the age of eighteen.'

Honoria raised an eyebrow. The Schola Palatinae were the emperor's bodyguard, the elite. 'So he had something on Theodosius?' she asked.

'It's possible,' Chrysanthos said. 'But then, we've all got *something* on Theodosius. Rumour has it that the emperor has made Stilicho guardian of his heir.'

'Honorius?'

Chrysanthos nodded. 'His favourite, his best, apparently. If he's half the bastard his father is, we can all kiss our prospects goodbye.'

'You must have known this day would come, darling heart,' she said, calling over a maidservant to tease her hair into place, just *so*, 'when you sent Phillipus' head back to Theodosius. From what you've told me, the emperor is not the forgiving kind. I thought it was all part of your plan.'

'Oh, it was, it was.' Chrysanthos sipped his wine again, 'but the timing is all wrong. I'll be honest with you; young Marcus has proved a huge disappointment. I may have to help him along a little. And I didn't reckon on Stilicho. Anybody else, yes. But Stilicho …'

She reached across and stroked his manhood under his robes of office. 'We've faced problems before,' she said. 'Would you like me to meet this half-Vandal for you?' She raised an eyebrow and quickened her pace with her fingers.

He stopped her. 'That's enough of that,' he murmured reluctantly. 'I shall be helping along a young actress's career later. And you've got to make a man of a boy.' He nodded across to the tribune.

'All right,' she laughed. 'When are you expecting Stilicho?'

He looked at her. 'Stilicho arrives when you expect him least.'

A rising breeze rattled the shutters of the Hen's Tooth that night. Scipio Honorius lay on his bed, snoring gently. It had been a good night. All over the sleeping city his people had been busy. Julia of the Two Hands had come up trumps once again. Placidus had stumbled into more purse-carrying pedestrians than most people saw from one month's end to the next. Little Veronica was hobbling more than ever, what with the weight of the coins kind sympathisers had given her. More importantly, the grain ships had finally arrived from Aegyptus and the wine amphorae from Hispania. Scipio's people had been on hand to take their cut before the merchants could get their hands on it, the soldiers of Lucius Porca's garrison standing by and turning blind eyes in all directions.

Yes, it had been a good day. And to cap it all, he had the delectable Amelia lying beside him. She was a new actress at the theatre and rumour had it that the vicarius himself was interested in her. Well, that was all well and good, but the vicarius already slept with Scipio's mother and that was as far as Scipio's generosity ran. Chrysanthos could have Amelia certainly, but only after Scipio had. And he had had her once tonight already. She'd been agonising earlier over her performance, worrying about her motivation. Scipio wasn't an insensitive man. He listened, nodded, made all the right noises, then solemnly took her virginity.

She was all right for a beginner; she was quite good, in fact. But that was all of an hour ago and Scipio Honorius was ready again. He'd teach her a few tricks this time and he reached out a lazy hand. Suddenly he was sitting bolt upright in his bed. Where he had expected to feel the girl's warm, soft flesh, he felt coarse, curly wool, matted with blood that stuck to his fingers.

As his eyes focussed, he found himself looking at a tall man, with a full beard and his hair combed forward in the style of an emperor. And the man was sitting on his bed, looking back at him. Instinctively, Scipio rolled sideways to grab for the knife he kept on the bedside table. But it wasn't there. Instead, he felt the razor-tip of a spearpoint against his throat, forcing him back so that his head crunched on the wall. Oil lamps lit the room; first one, then two and his eyes widened in horror. Next to him on the bed, where Amelia had lain purring softly as he had fallen asleep, a dead sheep bled into the mattress.

The man sitting on the bed was surrounded by soldiers, all armed to the teeth and looking down at the bed. 'I'm sorry,' he said, sensing Scipio's unease. 'I thought you'd be pleased. Before I got here, anybody who was anybody told me Britannia was full of sheep shaggers. It's not for me, I must admit, so I wasn't quite sure whether the sheep was supposed to be dead or alive; I took a chance. All done on the toss of a solidus, really.'

'Who the bloody Hell are you?' Scipio shouted as soon as the spear point had left his throat.

'Oh, I'm sorry again,' the man said. 'Where *are* my manners? I am Flavius Stilicho. I'm the new boy.'

Scipio blinked. If this was a nightmare, he was taking forever to wake up. 'What do you want?' he asked.

Stilicho frowned and looked at the faces of his guards. 'Gentlemen,' he said. 'I think we've been misinformed.' He turned back to Scipio. 'I'm looking for the man who runs Londinium,' he said.

'Oh, no,' Scipio answered, before realization dawned. 'You want Chrysanthos … oh, I see.'

'You *are* Scipio Honorius?' Stilicho asked, 'leader of the Black Knives, the Left Hand, Rex Inferni?'

Scipio nodded.

'Then you're the man I want,' Stilicho said.

Vitalis was back in the river early the next morning watching the mallards flap and squawk, water droplets flying from their orange feet. He loved this time in the autumn, before the ice of winter froze his legs and made reed cutting impossible. He was up to his knees, hacking with his sickle as the day's visitors assembled at the bridge to have their papers and their business checked by Porca's men.

'Are you the tribune Vitalis Celatius of the Schola Palatinae?' a voice called to him from the bank.

'No, I …'

'Then you must be Vitalis the basket-maker.'

Vitalis nearly dropped his sickle. In front of him stood a man he thought he would never see again, a face from his past, the preacher Pelagius. The man had put on some weight since they had last met, but he was still the scruffy vagabond, with matted hair and patched clothes. He looked as if he hadn't shaved in years.

Vitalis splashed his way out of the river and gripped both of Pelagius' arms before hugging him and slapping his back. 'I don't believe it,' he laughed. 'I'd heard you were dead.'

'Ah, the rumour mill is still grinding, then?'

'What are you doing here?' Vitalis asked the preacher. 'When I saw you last, you were going to Rome.'

'When I saw you last, you were coming with me.'

Vitalis shrugged. 'Sorry,' he said. 'I had things to do.'

Pelagius nodded. He had always sensed that Vitalis Celatius was a man cast in his own mould, driven by his own demons. He had heard rumours about him too; that he had served the late emperor, Honorius; that he had saved the renegade decurion

Calpurnius Succatus from death in the sewers of Augusta Treverorum; that he had been made a tribune in the most elite of the emperor's cohorts. Could a basket-maker have done all this? And whenever he had thought of it, Pelagius had found himself smiling – the man from Nazareth was the son of a carpenter and he had done *much* more.

'Did you go to Rome?' Vitalis asked.

'Rome,' Pelagius nodded. 'Hierosolyma, Alexandria; wherever God guides my way.'

'And now you're here. With Stilicho? I hear he's on his way.'

'Oh, Stilicho's been here for days. It's his way. You probably sold him a basket yesterday. He'll have tried out the tabernae, sampled your Thamesis fish. Then he'll slip out again and ride in in triumph to be greeted by the authorities.'

'Chrysanthos,' Vitalis nodded.

'Yes, of course. He's vicarius now, isn't he? What about your friend, Justinus? Dux Britannorum now, I've heard.'

'He is,' Vitalis said. 'I haven't seen him for a while.' He took the man gently by the arm. 'Pelagius, this Stilicho; what's going on? Why has the emperor sent him and with troops at his back? Is it that business with the head of Quintus Phillipus?'

'When the Magister Militum confides in me, Vitalis, old friend, I'll be happy to tell you.'

'Good,' Vitalis smiled. 'Until then, how about the tabernae you mentioned?'

'Not for me.' Pelagius held up his hand. 'But the Thamesis fish, now; that's a different matter.'

All Londinium turned out three days later for the arrival of the emperor's army commander. Stilicho dismounted from his grey at the southern end of the bridge, unbuckled his plumed helmet and threw his sword to an attendant. To wildly cheering crowds, he thudded across the oak planking as the river hurtled, grey and greasy, below him.

At the gate itself, Lucius Porca's garrison had turned out in force, their arms polished and gleaming, a pale sun flashing on their helmets and shields. Porca gave Stilicho the imperial salute which the general acknowledged and then the new boy threw himself face down to lie on the rough ground. Julia of the Two Hands took advantage of the moment by lifting the purse of one of the

Ordo who was too excited at the prospect of shaking the hand of the great Stilicho to notice. All along the ramparts, heads craned to watch the spectacle as the drums thundered on both sides of the river and the cornicines blasted.

Chrysanthos, dressed in his finery as the vicarius of Britannia, stood squarely in the centre of the arch. 'Do you come in peace, stranger?' he asked, his voice loud and clear as the drums stopped abruptly.

Stilicho rose to his knees and kept his head bowed. 'I do, Vicarius Britannorum.'

'What is your name and business?' Chrysanthos asked.

'My name is Flavius Stilicho and my business is the emperor's.'

Chrysanthos held out both hands and Stilicho stood up, clasping the vicarius in a brotherly grasp. Porca's band struck up again and the watching crowd roared and cheered; not however before several of them had given a little crippled girl their small change and almost been bowled over by a careless, drunken and very apologetic lout.

'God be praised,' Scipio Honorius murmured to himself, 'for high days and holidays.'

There was feasting that night at the governor's palace and no expense had been spared. Chrysanthos liked his entertainments intimate as a rule and his cooks had become lax and lazy, but the chance of preparing a meal for the great Stilicho had spurred them on to create wonders. Tables and benches had been dusted off by the household slaves, regilded on every surface. Silk cushions had been recovered, stuffed with more goose-down so they were plump and inviting. The geese from which the down had been plucked featured widely in the feast, from their fatty livers seethed in wine and herbs to their roasted bodies stuffed with larks. Candied fruits were scattered over the tables, in case any of the guests could find a spare corner in their loaded stomachs. Wine flowed like water and for the lower orders at the tables in the anterooms, water was the main ingredient. If some of it was on the verge of vinegar, after a while no one noticed.

Chrysanthos liked his wine and loved his women but he wasn't that bothered about food. He looked out over the room, at his guzzling guests and shook his head slightly. All that money spent on so many delicacies; the way some were shoving them down their throats, the food might have just as well been fodder for the cattle. The poets would be starting soon, heaven help him. But a man must keep up appearances. He turned, at a touch on his arm.

'The emperor has very fond memories of this place,' Stilicho said. Chrysanthos had counted the cups the man had downed and he seemed impervious to it. If the vicarius was looking for weaknesses, which he was, he wouldn't find it in Stilicho's ability to hold his drink. 'Good to see his old papa's walls still standing.'

'You knew the older Theodosius?' the vicarius asked.

'Before my time.' Stilicho tore at a goose and sucked the grease from his fingers.

'Shall we leave our business until tomorrow?' Chrysanthos didn't want to be rushed. On the surface, the Vandal was all sweetness and light but the vicarius had been in politics too long to go by appearances.

'Never put off; tomorrow is another day; procrastination is the thief of time – there are a dozen other platitudes I could use. I can always mix business with pleasure, Chrysanthos; I don't know about you.'

The vicarius caught Stilicho's glance across to where Honoria sat. She looked particularly alluring tonight as the candlelight danced in her eyes and her golden hair hung wild and free over her bare shoulders. The matrons of the Ordo wore theirs in fierce ringlets, piled high and pinned as befitted their status. 'So be it.' Chrysanthos clicked his fingers for their cups to be refilled. 'Contrary to appearances, I can't believe that this is a social call.'

'You cut off the head of Quintus Phillipus.' Stilicho believed in cutting to the chase.

Chrysanthos barely blinked. 'It happened here, under my watch, yes.'

'The emperor was displeased.'

'Of course he was.' The vicarius sipped, smiling and nodding at the great and good of Londinium, all of whom were anxious to catch his eye or Stilicho's. Vicarial preferment was good; imperial preferment even better. And not a few of them had eligible daughters.

'By the way, whatever happened to Andros Procopius?'

'Who?' Stilicho was smiling too, nodding to total strangers. It was the way of Roman courts the world over.

'The messenger sent by Terentius Marcus.'

'He died,' Stilicho said and that line of conversation died too. 'And talking of Terentius Marcus, what can you tell me about him?'

'He's the nephew of Marcellus Gracchus.'

Stilicho nodded. 'Now, tell me something I don't know.'

'He's Count of the Saxon Shore.'

'Still waiting,' the Vandal said.

Chrysanthos closed to the man. 'There are rumours,' he said.

'Always,' Stilicho nodded.

'That he intends to rise rather higher.'

'To your exalted rank, vicarius?' Stilicho raised an eyebrow.

Chrysanthos laughed. 'I am just a humble cog, General,' he said, 'as are you. No, they say Terentius Marcus aims at the purple.'

Stilicho flicked a piece of meat from between his teeth. 'Which means the army will have to elect him Caesar first.'

'It's been done before,' Chrysanthos said. 'The deified Constantine, Magnus Maximus.'

The general nodded. 'Yes,' he said. 'Britannia is famous for it. Didn't turn out too well for Maximus, though, did it?'

'The fortunes of war,' Chrysanthos shrugged.

'Tell me,' Stilicho said. 'Who appointed Marcus to his current command?'

'Justinus Coelius, the Dux Britannorum.'

'Ah, yes,' the Vandal said. 'A good man, I hear. Loyal, true. I was surprised not to see him here tonight. Heroes of the Wall are in short supply.'

'He *was* invited,' Chrysanthos said, apologetically.

'Other commitments?' Stilicho asked.

'I'm afraid, General – and this is very embarrassing – he said he didn't get out of bed for foreigners.'

Stilicho laughed. 'Well, that's the kind of thing that made us great. Today, though … well, times change, don't they? Who would have thought that a Vandal would be the emperor's Magister Militum?'

'Who indeed?' Chrysanthos smiled, wide-eyed. 'So, your business, General? You'll start with Terentius Marcus, I suppose.'

'No.' Stilicho leaned back, savouring his wine. 'No, the emperor is concerned about the state of religion at this arse-end of his empire, Chrysanthos. He hasn't been well of late and his thoughts turn increasingly to God.'

'Oh, dear.'

'Quite. But we are all the emperor's servants, just as we are God's.'

'Oh, quite. Quite.'

'Tomorrow I shall pay a call on the bishop of Londinium – Severianus, isn't it?'

The vicarius nodded.

'There are pockets of Godlessness in this city, vicarius; indeed, in the province as a whole. Mithras is still worshipped. Jupiter. Even Isis, I'm told.'

'Change takes time, General,' Chrysanthos reminded him.

'The great Constantine declared the Empire Christian three generations ago, vicarius. These idolators have had long enough. With your permission, I'll start with them.'

'With my permission?' Chrysanthos raised an eyebrow.

'Or without it.'

The torchlight threw strange shadows on the grey stones of the stairwell. The feasting was over and tired slaves were dragging away the trestle tables and sweeping the straw. He hadn't heard her padding softly along the passageway but he couldn't miss the scent of her. Honoria, at her sensuous best, was on the prowl. She had slept with fishermen, taberna keepers, soldiers, consuls and now the vicarius of Britannia. A mere general she would take in her stride.

Her hand was on his arm as he turned the corner to his chambers. 'I didn't have a chance to say goodnight,' she said.

'Forgive me, madam,' Stilicho smiled. 'It's been a long day.'

'And it could be a longer night,' she said.

He looked at her, the smouldering eyes, the smooth curves of her breasts and hips. 'And what would the vicarius say?' he asked her.

Honoria laughed, that musical sound that had enchanted so many men. 'The vicarius will never know,' she said.

Stilicho laughed too. 'Oh, I doubt that, madam,' he said. He closed to her and kissed her, their tongues entwining as the torchlight flickered on her gold and her hair. 'Let's see,' he said, tracing a finger over her shoulder and teasing the gown downwards so that her breasts were naked. 'Chrysanthos has tried copious amounts of wine. Now he's trying his whore.' He traced the finger around her left nipple and it rose under his caress. Then he pulled sharply away. 'And, seriously tempted though I am, that hasn't worked either.'

Honoria was furious. She hauled her gown up and slapped the man hard across the face.

'Thank you,' he smiled, when his vision stopped reeling. 'That was a goodnight to remember.'

CHAPTER XI

'You *hit* the Magister Militum?' Chrysanthos was looking at Honoria, open-mouthed.

'No,' she snarled. 'I hit an arrogant bastard who's got to go.'

Chrysanthos found himself chuckling despite the situation. 'He's only just arrived, heart,' he said.

She flashed a scowl at him. Her pride was hurt. *Nobody* turned down Honoria Honorius. Ever. 'I mean "go",' she said, 'as in disappear. I'll talk to Scip.'

Scipio Honorius had been helpfulness itself to the Magister Militum. He knew Londinium like the back of his hand, its alleys, its backwaters. He knew where bodies were buried and not just those who lay mouldering in the necropolis beyond the eastern walls. And if the Magister Militum had enough gold on him to pay for that local knowledge, well, that was to the good.

The Mithraeum itself had been destroyed years ago, burnt by zealous Christians when Scipio was a boy. Now that he was a man, the worshippers of the bull still met, in secret after dark, as was the way of Mithras. Scipio knew where that was and who they were. And there were still the shrines of Jupiter that some still called the Highest and Best. And the niches devoted to Sol Invictus, the unconquered sun. And there were the paps of Isis.

'God will reward you, my son,' Severianus was at his most unctuous that morning. He had warmed to Stilicho at once because Stilicho was his saviour. It was as if the Lord Jesus himself had come to Londinium. That might be blasphemy, but that was the way of it. There were temples to be cleared, right here in Londinium.

'I'm sure He will,' Stilicho said. He was standing in the bishop's robing room as Gallius the sacristan bobbed and weaved, providing wine and cakes for their celebrated guest. 'This is your diocese, Bishop. Where would the Lord have us strike first?'

On the table in front of them, a plan of the city lay on parchment. The sites of the unbelievers had been circled in red by Scipio; and the Rex Inferni had not missed one.

'Here.' Severianus stabbed a circle with his chubby finger. 'It's near the old Mithraeum, along the Walbrook. The unbelievers have not moved far away.'

Stilicho shook his head. 'I am Magister Militum, Lord Bishop,' he said, 'and I have to tread softly there. It's my guess that half the soldiers in the empire worship Mithras and I have no reason to doubt that Britannia is any different. Can't take the risk of offending my own right arm. Not yet. What's this?' He pointed to another circle.

'Ah,' Severianus was almost salivating. 'That's the Old Gate. There used to be a temple to Isis there.'

'This far West?' Stilicho was surprised. Isis was an Eastern deity, from Aegyptus in Africa.

'The devil is everywhere, General,' Severianus warned, as if his own walls were eavesdropping. 'The late Magnus Maximus had an Egyptian whore he carted everywhere with him. She prophesied the future.'

'Bad news for everybody,' Stilicho said. 'But … and here's the problem, bishop; Isis is popular with the women. Oh, she has male adherents, certainly, but … well, women? Will that be a problem?' Stilicho looked hard at the man. He knew a zealot when he saw one, but he wanted confirmation of that. The fire of righteousness burned in Severianus' eyes and this man was far from the Galilean carpenter's son who had turned the other cheek. 'Severianus,' he said softly, knowing that his voice was music to the bishop's ears, 'the emperor is displeased with your Britannia. He has sent me to burn the devil out. And if the devil comes in the guise of women? Well, they burn as brightly as do men.'

'Oh, of course.' Severianus felt he had misread the man. Here was his brother in Christ and he felt a weight lifted from him. It was as though Stilicho had released the man's conscience and let it float wide out of the window. 'Yes, of course. Er … when will you begin?'

Stilicho rolled up the parchment. 'When I'm good and ready,' he said.

Britannia Prima

Justinus Coelius sat in the atrium of Gnaeus Domitius. It was winter now, with a raw wind blowing from the north, the north that Justinus counted as his home, the north he missed. Domitius' people were stoking the fires that fed the flues of the house and the room was warm despite the season. A puppy, newly-trained, lay on the mosaic floor, cracking a bone and rolling over, playing with his food with sharp yips and the occasional growl that had him startled and chasing his tail, looking for an invisible gruff-voiced enemy. It was a pleasant homely scene, which could be found in almost any country house, anywhere in the length and breadth of the empire. Except that this was different. A pall of loss lay over the villa that no amount of sweet woodsmoke could dispel.

'So she's dead.' The old man had aged years in the months since Niall of the Five Hostages had come calling. His voice was unsteady, his eyes misty and he sensed that he didn't have long.

Justinus nodded. It was a lie, of course, but he had lived with a lie for years. When Valentinus of the silver mask had raised his rebellion and all but destroyed the Wall, Justinus had been a mere circitor, manning a lonely outpost in the middle of nowhere. He had run south, with Paternus, Leocadius and Vitalis, in fear and desperation. And Leocadius, whose son, men said, now ruled Londinium's underworld, had invented the braggart lie. They were heroes, all four of them, even though, in reality, they had run. And heroes they became; the jet and gold ring on his finger still bore testimony to that. He was Dux Britannorum because of it. Paternus was long dead because of it. And Leocadius. As for Vitalis, only his God knew what had become of him.

So Justinus lived with a lie. And here was another. But it was better than the truth. The truth that the girl had gone native, betrayed all that her upbringing had taught her, abandoned the mother and father that gave her life. The truth that her knife had left a gaping wound in Justinus' shoulder that would not heal and left her poison mixing with his blood and dulling his brain.

'Thank you,' the old man said. 'I know that you did all you

could, Dux Britannorum.' He looked about him, at the darkened room and the emptiness. 'And my wife and I, we'll always have our memories.'

'Keep them fresh,' Justinus said and stood up.

'Forgive me, sir,' Gnaeus Domitius said. 'You don't look well. Won't you rest awhile? Take food and spend the night?'

'No,' Justinus said. 'No, it's time I went home.'

Londinium

It was raining three nights later when darkness fell over the capital of Maxima Caesariensis. Those who knelt at the feet of the goddess, her paps gleaming in the candlelight, had always clung to the old calendar and the old ways. The Nones had fallen on the fifth of Decembris and the day, cold and raw, had nine hours. The sun, on those rare days when it shone, was in the sign of Sagittarius, the archer. Archers like Lucius Porca's men manning the city wall to the east that night, testing their bowstrings and lining up their arrows. Decembris lay under the protection of Vesta, goddess of the hearth, but few of Isis' followers would see their hearths again after tonight. Ahead in the month lay Saturnalia, the wild and lawless time of merriment that the bishop's Christians had stolen for the birth of their false prophet.

The garrison sentries slammed and locked the Old Gate, bolting the wicket and standing guard alongside it. 'Anybody trying to get in tonight'll have a warm welcome,' one of them grunted.

'Commander on the wall.' They all heard the shout from overhead and the click of hobnailed boots and the rattle of spears on shields. Lucius Porca was wrapped in his cloak against the weather but under it he was fully armed. Ever since that day when all of Londinium had assembled to see the head of Magnus Maximus in the forum, the head that actually belonged to the emperor's man, Phillipus, Porca had known that this night had been coming. He had not expected Stilicho, but then, no one ever did. And yet he had turned up, like a bad solidus.

'Anything untoward, circitor?' he murmured to the man to his left.

'All correct, sir. Sir …' The man had a family somewhere in the dark maze of streets inside the wall. He couldn't stay silent.

'What is it, man?' Porca had wondered who would be the first to break silence.

'Well, sir, it's just …'

'Yes? Out with it, circitor.'

'Well, we all know that this is the emperor's order, sir, stamping out heresy and all that, but …'

Porca gave the man time to put his jumbled thoughts into words.

'Things can get out of hand, can't they? In the darkness, I mean.'

Porca nodded. 'Our target,' he said, 'is the temple of Isis. Does your family worship the goddess?'

'No, sir.' The circitor was outraged at the suggestion. 'Umm … the missus leaves all that to me. Mithras, you know.'

Porca knew. He had shed his own blood on the altar of the bull as a young soldier and he knew. He patted the circitor's shoulder. 'Let's hope it's not our turn next,' he said and swirled away to the steps to find his horse.

Across the city, Stilicho, dressed for battle, crashed through the great doors of Severianus' church. Candles guttered as the wind caught them and churchmen scurried out of the man's way. 'Ready, bishop?' Stilicho shouted, his voice echoing in the vaults.

'Er …' Severianus had been about to retire to his private quarters. 'Oh, no, there's some mistake. *I'm* not coming.'

Stilicho's laugh was hollow. He crossed the nave in a few strides and grabbed the churchman by his robes. 'Wrong again, bishop,' he said. 'What happens tonight is by the will of the emperor – Lucius Porca will carry his likeness – and the will of God. *You* will carry his.'

He clicked his fingers and a soldier tossed a standard to him. At its top, above the spread eagle in silver, the Chi Rho, symbol of the risen Christ, rose against the pale granite of the walls. Stilicho thrust the staff into Severianus' hand and held it there with his own. 'And you will stand at the front,' he said, quietly. 'And you will applaud each sinner who recants and seeks the one true God.'

'But that …'

'…isn't Christian?' Stilicho mocked. 'You're about as close to the Lord Jesus as black is to white, bishop, but it's a little late for a crisis of conscience now, isn't it? All of you,' he roared to the horrified priests, 'follow us. I want you to see just how muscular Christianity can be.'

Little Petronius was late. He had been south of the river on this day of Isis and had met some friends. The boys couldn't resist pushing the old boat out into the Thamesis and trying to catch some fish, icy though the wind was on the river. They had caught nothing and he had realized to his horror that night was falling and the rain getting heavier from the west. He had scrambled ashore and run as fast as his little legs could carry him along the bridge. A soldier had stopped him here and that was unusual. They stopped adults all the time, checking papers, snooping in carts and rummaging in bundles. But lads like Petronius weren't carrying anything. No valuables. No weapons. Why tonight? Tonight of all nights when he had to be at the temple of Isis near the Old Gate? He didn't scream too loudly when the guard pulled him up short by tugging his hair and he answered all his questions truthfully. Well, almost truthfully. 'Petronius Borro, sir,' he told him, 'of the house of Amianus Borro, the pot-maker.'

'Amianus Borro?' the guard frowned. 'Worships Isis, doesn't he?'

'No, sir,' Petronius said. There was the lie.

'Where do you live, young Borro?'

'Near the Old Gate, sir.'

'Not tonight,' the soldier said. 'You stay away from the Old Gate tonight.'

'Why … sir?'

The guard bent down to the boy. 'Never you mind why, lad. Just stay away.'

But there wasn't a guard in Londinium, in fact the whole of Britannia, who could outrun Petronius Borro in that rabbit warren of streets and he was gone, heart thumping, running east.

Lucius Porca was late too but that was because he had been checking the agreed perimeter to make sure his men were ready. He threw his reins to a soldier and swung out of the saddle. In front of him, in the huddle of streets with the rain bouncing off gable and roof-top, two lines of his own command stood to attention, shields at the carry, swords drawn. They had left their cloaks behind because in confined killing spaces, cloaks got in the way. He kept his on, if only to stop the Britannia weather from trickling down his neck.

'Nice of you to call, Commander,' Stilicho nodded to him. 'Is all set?'

'We're ready, sir,' Porca told him, nodding to a trembling Severianus alongside him. The man's knuckles shone white around his Chi-Rho staff. 'Every road is blocked and I've lined the walls with archers.'

Stilicho nodded.

Now it was Porca's turn to become a concerned circitor. He had no family in the city but he was a soldier and that was enough. 'We are about to commit murder, sir,' he said.

'That we are,' the general nodded, his face grim. He was looking ahead to the blackness of the nondescript building that housed in secret the temple of Isis. He glanced at Porca and read in the man's face all that was fine, all that was Roman. 'It's a messy business, Porca,' he said. 'Politics. And religion. But I have my orders. So have you.'

Porca thumped his clenched fist against his chest in the old salute and stepped back.

The ministrations of the priest were nearly over and the congregation mumbled their responses. 'Oh, mother Isis, friend of the friendless, saviour of sinners, give us your wisdom, give us your strength. Guide us in our darkness. Lead us to the light.'

As the last words died away, the candles were snuffed out one by one until finally, only one flame glowed in the vaulted chamber and the followers of Isis made their way up the steps to the street. No one knew, in the endless retelling of what happened, who screamed first. But everyone knew why. There was a line of soldiers, outlined black across the street ahead. And another to the left. And another to the right. At a signal from Porca, brands burst into flame, illuminating the helmets of the garrison, but not their faces. They stayed in darkness, as black and terrible as the Christian Hell itself.

Stilicho nudged Severianus hard in the ribs and the bishop called out, trying desperately to keep his voice steady. 'Followers of the damned Isis, you have sinned against your true Lord, Jesus Christ. Renounce your ways now and kneel before the symbol of the Lord … or …'

'Or you will die.' Stilicho, in the eerie stillness, finished the sentence for him.

For an instant no one moved; no one spoke. Then the priest of Isis, responding to the scream, forced his way to the front. 'What is this?' he asked.

'The day of judgement,' Severianus called back. He was warming to this now. When Stilicho had dragged him along, he had been terrified but now he could see it was the followers of Isis who were terrified. Christ had risen and Christ would be triumphant. From nowhere an arrow hissed through the rain to thud into the chest of the priest of Isis. He grunted, the impact driving him back. He looked down at the shaft, incredulous, then sank to his knees.

'Battle order!' Porca's harsh command rang out and his lines marched forward, breaking into a run as they reached the building. Panicking worshippers broke and ran but there was nowhere to run. To their left they collided with the swords of the garrison. To the right, the flaming brands drove them back into a tight huddle around their fallen priest. Severianus, his eyes bright with excitement, was wielding the Chi-Rho like a club, the rain bouncing off its bronze curls. As Porca's men reached the supplicants, all thoughts of their returning to the risen Christ were forgotten. Those at the back stumbled down the steps into the cellar, stumbled and ran to Isis' statue. The single candle flame blew out with a sudden gust of movement and they dashed from wall to wall in the darkness, falling over each other in their panic. Suddenly, the whole chamber flooded with light and Porca's torch bearers stood at the top of the steps. The screaming and the rushing about stopped; men tried to stand in front of their women, women tried to shield their children. The pot maker, Amianus Borro, didn't know where his son was. Little Petronius should have been here for the service, but he hadn't seen him. Until this moment, he'd been all set to thrash the boy, let him have a taste of leather. Now he thanked Isis that the boy had disobeyed him.

There was a commotion at the stairhead and bishop Severianus struggled to the front. His mitre had gone and his tonsured head gleamed with rainwater and sweat. The Chi-Rho in his hand was slick with blood from the slaughter in the street above. He looked at the huddled worshippers, eyes wide and hands raised to him in silent pleading. For the briefest of moments, his heart softened. Then he saw the gilded statue of Isis, her face calm and serene and mocking above her body, grotesquely carved with a dozen swollen paps.

'Finish it!' he roared and steadied himself as the garrison burst down the steps in a wave of death, hacking and thrusting with their swords at anything in their path. The noise was horrible and

Severianus steadied himself against the stone of the doorway watching the butchery take place. Unarmed civilians against a trained cohort of soldiers was no contest and it was all over quickly. When a circitor called a halt, the killers left off their ghastly work and shuffled back into line, shields high, swords bloody and ready again.

There was a pile of corpses at the foot of Isis and her breasts were spattered with blood. One or two of the dying twitched, trying to make sense of what had just happened to them. Amianus Borro lay nearest the wall, his knuckles raw from the blows he had rained down on a soldier, his throat gaping with a crimson wound from which the blood still spurted. Children lay dead under their mothers, smothered by the very breasts which had fed them, their faces blue and swollen as they had fought desperately to breathe in the crush.

The circitor gave the command, 'Sheath swords' and the blades slid home. The moaning and the sobbing had stopped now and the bishop of Londinium drew himself up to his full height.

'Burn it,' he said. 'Consign this abomination to Hell.'

In the driving rain on the street above, little Petronius stood, staring as the flames licked up from the temple of Isis. Today he had been just another happy little boy, playing with his friends in the river. Tonight, he was an orphan of the storm. The storm that was Stilicho.

Fog lay over the river the next morning, its grey coldness mingling with the smoke from the temple of Isis, a blackened husk on a desolate street. Those who had died on that street had been dragged away by Lucius Porca's men and dumped in a pit beyond the city wall where the locals threw their rubbish.

No one mourned them, at least, not in public. The wrath of the Lord had come to Londinium with the bishop himself as His messenger. And, as if to remind the people that God had had help, the garrison had doubled their guard, patrolling the streets as well as the wall-ramparts. A frightened people huddled in doorways and whispered behind shutters. Who would be next and where would it all end?

'It was that head,' some said, swivelling eyes left and right, 'the head of the emperor's man. I said no good would come of it.'

'It's the bishop I blame,' others hissed. 'He's been itching to do something like this for years.'

'What's to be done?' Calpurnius Succatus was not actually on duty at the basilica the next day after the burning but here he was anyway, standing four-square in the vicarius' office, looking down at the vicarius.

Chrysanthos didn't look up, engrossed in paperwork as he was. He had letters to write to the II Augusta at Clausentum and four armed messengers waited in the courtyard to gallop south with heavy, iron-rimmed coffers. 'About what?' he murmured.

It took a lot to rattle Chrysanthos, but even he jumped when Calpurnius slammed his fist down on the table and ink and parchment went everywhere.

'There are reports of sixty dead, Vicarius,' he said, 'and no wounded, funnily enough. Except that nobody's laughing, least of all me.'

N*ow* the man had the vicarius' attention and Chrysanthos sat back, calmly wiping the spilt ink from his fingers. 'When I last looked,' he said, 'I had five decurions on my staff. Why should I give a stuffed fig about what you think?'

Calpurnius straightened up, his jaw flexing.

'And also, the last time I looked, you were a Christian, Calpurnius Succatus. Don't tell me your heart bleeds for a bunch of heathens.'

'My heart bleeds for sixty people,' Calpurnius said. '*Our* people, Vicarius. Yours and mine.'

'Do you think I had a hand in this?'

'Did you?'

'No.'

'You'll swear it?'

Chrysanthos narrowed his eyes. 'Do I need to?' he asked.

'It would reassure the people,' Calpurnius said, ever the diplomat.

'That's not my job,' the vicarius said, reaching for his quill again and starting work on a clean piece of parchment. 'My job is to govern four provinces. If you have some sound advice on that, I'd be delighted to hear it. Until then, get the Hell out of my chambers.'

'No one left?' Pelagius was standing in the ruins of the charred temple. 'No one at all?'

Vitalis was squatting over the shattered, blackened image of

Isis, her glass eyes melted, her paps now powdered plaster. Everywhere he looked, there was destruction. 'We should be grateful, I suppose, that it was raining last night,' he said. 'It's nothing short of a miracle – no other houses torched.' He was right. The shop fronts, the stables, the tabernae, were all intact. Only the temple of Isis was missing in the shabby row, like a bad tooth knocked out. 'It's as though God's finger pointed,' he said, half to himself.

Pelagius frowned. 'You don't seriously imagine God had anything to do with this, do you?'

'No,' Vitalis stood up. 'No, this has Stilicho written all over it. You know the man, Pelagius; is he capable of such cold-blooded murder?'

'Magister Militum of the emperor?' Pelagius chuckled grimly. 'Undoubtedly. He'll have his orders in the context of Britannia – and, remember, I haven't a clue what they are. And he won't hesitate to exceed them if he feels the need. But they say the bishop was here as well, last night.'

'Severianus?' Vitalis hadn't heard that.

'You know I paid a call on the man last week. Or, at least, I tried to. Didn't get past his sacristan. Pretty church, though.'

'He wouldn't see you?'

'He would not have – and I quote – "that bastard heretic who denies original sin" across his portals. Epitome of brotherly love, isn't he, your bishop?'

Vitalis shook his head. 'He's not my bishop,' he said.

'Nevertheless,' Pelagius had a curious look on his face, 'it's dies Solis tomorrow, the Lord's day. There'll be a Mass.'

'There will.'

'What say we go along, you and I, and beard this iconoclast in his lair?'

'Confront him, you mean?'

'I think he owes Londinium an explanation, don't you?'

Vitalis smiled.

'You there!' a voice barked behind them. 'Move on!'

They turned to face a detachment of Porca's men.

'Why?' Pelagius asked them.

'You've no business here,' the semisallis told them.

'As much as you, child-killer,' Vitalis said flatly.

The semisallis' sword slid clear of its scabbard. Pelagius raised his hand. 'You are drawing iron on a tribune of the Schola Palatinae, semisallis. Is that wise?'

'About as wise as drawing iron on a member of General Stilicho's entourage,' Vitalis said.

The semisallis blinked. His men were looking at him, wondering which way he'd jump. In the end, he licked his lips and slammed the sword away. 'As a point of fact,' he muttered, 'I wasn't here last night. I've never killed a kid in my life.'

Pelagius patted the man's shoulder. 'I didn't think for a moment you had, my son,' he said.

The great and the good of Londinium made their way to Mass that dies Solis as the great bell clanged and bellowed over the city. The sky was a lurid pearl, heralding the cold of another winter. It was the third in Advent and the Christians of the city were eagerly awaiting the birth day of their Lord. The Ordo were there in numbers, rings on chubby fingers, fingers that made small donations at the church door. Their conversation, as they waited for the grand entrance of the bishop, turned, as it always did, to business and taxation. They nodded and smiled at the vicarius who sat on his dais to one side of the nave, the candles shimmering in his eyes and on the gold circlet on his head. The wives of the Ordo were there too and even though this was a church and a solemn occasion, they couldn't resist fluttering their collective eyelashes at the emperor's man, the general they called Stilicho. He was half Vandal, half satyr, they had heard and even those who had dined with the man at Chrysanthos' banquet, could never get enough of that delicious rumour. Each one of them, even those who would never see fifty again, swore that Stilicho smiled directly at them and that they saw something magnificent stirring in his lap.

Honoria wasn't there, of course. She would rather be seen dead than be seen in Severianus' church. And anyway, she had urgent business across the city, at the Hen's Tooth she had once called home. She was telling her Scipio of the outrage committed on her – or, to be more accurate, *not* committed on her, by Stilicho; and the Lord of the Underworld seemed particularly disinterested. That annoyed Honoria and she told him so, but it wasn't the end of the world. She had been sending enemies to meet their maker long before little Scipio had filled her belly. She could do it again.

There were soldiers patrolling outside the church, their cloaks wrapped around them and their faces pinched and blue with the cold. This was not normally the custom, but these were not normal times. A temple had been burned; its people butchered.

There may be reprisals. Lucius Porca was taking no chances. He sat near the side door. In accordance with tradition he had left his sword outside, but it was within easy reach should trouble break out; and he would be ready.

Severianus padded in from his robing room, his face calm and placid. The Kyrie rose from the singers hidden from view behind the screen and the congregation began to relax into its familiar cadences. Those who knew the bishop well noticed a certain smugness, a crease at the corner of his mouth, a dimple appearing in his cheek. He looked like a tall cupid under his mitre and he held the gilded crozier aloft.

'Oh, Lord,' he intoned as the censer swung and the green smoke coiled into the cold air, 'accept this, our worship of You. In this month of your blessed birth …'

'Lord Bishop!' A clear voice from the far end of the nave interrupted him.

Severianus looked as if he had been slapped. His colour drained, but he did not move, except to lower the crozier. Every head had turned to see who had dared disturb the Lord's Mass. A couple of muscular priests darted towards the culprit, but he was faster and a scruffy, wild-haired man stood there, looking, the children thought, like the Baptist they had been told about in the scriptures. He stood in the centre and the throng parted for him, just like the Red Sea did for Moses, the children thought. In their excitement, they longed to jabber to each other, but their parents held them fast. Their parents longed to whisper together as well, but decorum got the better of them and besides, they wanted to know what this upstart had to say.

'Who are you?' Severianus demanded to know, confident that his people outnumbered this wandering madman two hundred to one. But in his pounding heart he was afraid to hear the answer.

'Men call me Pelagius,' came the reply.

The name echoed in hissed whispers around the nave and Stilicho's eyes rolled heavenwards. He leaned across to Chrysanthos. 'Remind me again why I brought him,' he chuckled.

'Idolater!' Severianus shrieked. 'Apostate. Denier of the true Christ.'

'I am none of those things, Lord Bishop,' Pelagius said, striding forward.

'In the name of God,' Severianus held his ground, 'why have you come to this place, alone and friendless?'

'Not quite alone.' Another voice echoed through the granite space, bouncing off the marble-faced columns. This second man was nearly as scruffy as the first, with a rough peasant's cloak over his shoulders.

'Who are you?' Severianus wavered a little now. Were they all going to rise up against him, one by one?

The man swept off his cloak and stood there in the resplendent uniform of an army officer. 'I am Vitalis Celatius, tribune of the Schola Palatinae.'

More murmurs. Eyes widened, tongues wagged. The wife of the Aedile looked more confused than the others. She was sure that only the other day, she had told her slave to buy a basket from this man. He must be an imposter. Or, just perhaps, she was going the way her mother went and was losing her grip.

Stilicho leaned to Chrysanthos again, and he wasn't chuckling now. 'This is a *little* awkward,' he said. 'Puts rather a different complexion on things, hmm?'

'Lord Bishop,' Pelagius stood in front of the man, 'an outrage was committed on some citizens of Londinium a few days ago.'

Severianus stood tall, sure of his ground. 'The temple of a foreign idol was destroyed, I believe,' he said.

'You believe?' Pelagius' voice was hard with contempt. 'Weren't you there?'

For a moment, Severianus panicked. He looked at Stilicho but the man had not moved. He looked at Chrysanthos and he sat like stone. He looked across to the side door to where Lucius Porca sat. He had not reached for his sword, yet. What was the matter with everybody? In desperation he glanced around to find Gallius, but the little sacristan suddenly looked littler than ever and was creeping back into the shadows behind the altar. When the bishop turned back, Pelagius' nose was inches from his own.

'Did you have a hand in this, Severianus Londiniensis? Did you sanction this slaughter?'

Severianus had never felt so alone in his life. His heart pounded in his throat and he felt his lip tremble. He had never been a brave man and suddenly, now that his God was calling him to account, he didn't have a friend in the world.

'There is God's word, Lord Bishop,' Pelagius growled, pointing at the great chained Bible on the lectern to Severianus' left. 'Place your hand on it and swear before God and this congregation that you took no part in the slaughter of the innocents.'

'I ...' but rational argument had long ago deserted the bishop of Londinium, as surely as his friends had. He had no answer, neither 'Yea' nor 'Nay'. Pelagius' right hand snaked out and grabbed Severianus' wrist, wrenching the crozier from him which clattered on to the stones. The noise seemed to galvanize Porca, who got up soundlessly and lifted his sword from its hidden recess. He held it to him, still sheathed, watching the way things would go. The wild-haired preacher slammed the bishop's hand flat on the book. 'Swear it,' he grunted. 'Swear it in God's name, that you had no hand in the attack on the temple of Isis.'

'They are idolaters!' Severianus found his voice at last. 'Devil worshippers ...'

'Swear it!' Pelagius yelled.

'I swear!' Severianus' lie hung on the air, echoing and re-echoing around the old stones. No one in the congregation had moved and all eyes were riveted on him.

Pelagius relaxed his grip and knelt before the bishop, taking his chubby hand again, but this time to kiss his ring. Severianus, chest heaving and head reeling with the blasphemy he had just committed, snatched it away and Pelagius rose to return to his place.

'One moment.' Another voice carried clear in the now silent church. All eyes, including Pelagius', turned again. Calpurnius Succatus was standing alone with the light behind him. Alongside him, Conchessa's mouth opened, but no sound came out. Instead, she reached down to hush her children. Calpurnius strode into the aisle and nodded to Pelagius and Vitalius as he brushed past them.

'My lord Vicarius,' he said, standing now where Pelagius had stood a moment before, 'I ask the same question of you. Will you swear before God and this congregation that you took no part in the attack on the temple of Isis? And neither did you have a hand in its inception?'

Stilicho leaned across to Chrysanthos. He was smiling again. 'Now, this really *is* a day for awkwardness, isn't it?'

Chrysanthos glowered at him, then strode across to the lectern and slapped his hand onto the Bible there. 'I swear it,' he said loudly, looking straight into Calpurnius' eyes. The decurion bowed and returned to his place.

'I am a little hurt,' Stilicho said loudly. He was on his feet, 'that no one has so far asked me to swear.' He looked at the cowering, trembling Severianus, the cold, arrogant Chrysanthos. He looked at the tribune of the Schola Palatinae and the mad Christian he had himself brought from Rome. He looked at the retreating figure of the decurion and noted the strange look in the eyes of the woman with the children. It had to be a look of love, of admiration … and yet.

The general who was half Vandal, half anything else you'd care to name, sauntered across the altar front and placed his right hand firmly on the Bible. 'I swear,' he said, in a loud and purposeful voice, 'that I orchestrated the attack on the temple of Isis. I sanctioned the slaughter of the innocents as Pelagius here so poetically puts it. I did it in the name of the emperor. Oh, and let's not forget the Lord Jesus Christ.' He waited as his words sank home. 'And I would do it again.'

CHAPTER XII

Night had fallen again by the time Justinus Coelius' horse clattered under the archway north of the bridge. The guard there saluted him and he trotted north-west through the tangle of narrow streets that led to the river and on to the Walbrook. He saw lights glowing from the governor's palace and he wondered who was home. On his way from Clausentum where he had lain, weak and delirious, for days – or was it weeks? – he had heard at posting stations that General Flavius Stilicho, the emperor's man, had landed with two vexillations of Heruli cavalry at Rutupiae and had made his way to the capital. Was it Stilicho reclining on the gilded couches or Chrysanthos or both? How cosy would those two have been?

Justinus rode past the long abandoned temple of Mithras in the darkness. His breath smoked out ahead of him and the cold bit into the marrow of his bones. He trembled now and then, but whether that was because of the season or the poison that lived in his blood, he didn't know. He took the southern bridge over the Walbrook, the stream's upper reaches rimmed with ice at this time of year. Ahead of him the black silhouette of the amphitheatre jutted against the purple of the night. Scavenging dogs prowled its terraces now and squatters had set up their shanty hovels where the gods of the arena had swaggered when Justinus was a boy, living far to the north.

They still used the baths to the south, but those were allocated to Lucius Porca's garrison these days and the Ordo bathed in their own villas. Everything that had made Rome great – its games, its baths, its legions, everything seemed to be collapsing so fast. So it was with a sense of gratitude that Justinus saw the black bulk of Porca's fortress ahead, the fires of the watch burning bravely in the night. There would be dice around those fires, he knew, and games of Hand, filthy jokes and coarse songs. With the army, nothing changed. With the army, Justinus was home.

'Here,' Lucius Porca handed the Dux Britannorum a cup of mulled wine. 'Warm your cockles.'

'I haven't kept you up?' Justinus asked, easing himself down into a chair.

'I don't sleep much these days,' Porca said, raising his own cup in a silent toast. 'Nobody does.'

'Stilicho?' Justinus said. 'I hear he's in town.'

'Oh, he's that all right,' Porca nodded.

Justinus looked around the commander's principia. It was like thousands of others all over the Empire. Maps graced the walls, showing every camp in Britannia, every cavalry post and naval base. Was it Justinus' imagination or were there fewer of them than there had been? A bronze head of Theodosius looked haughtily at him as he sampled his wine. It stood between the sun of Sol Invictus and the Chi-Rho of the risen Christ.

'Hedging your bets, Porca?' Justinus asked.

The commander laughed. 'Can't be too careful,' he said, 'the way the wind's blowing at the moment. I've stashed the Mithras bull in a storeroom somewhere and I'm having the Jupiter statue regilded at the moment. From what I've heard, I may have to replace Theodosius one day soon.'

'Oh?' Justinus straightened. 'I've been out of touch a little recently. What have you heard?'

'The emperor's not well, apparently.'

Justinus was reasoning it out. 'So, that will leave us Honorius. What is he, eight?'

'No,' Porca shook his head and he wasn't smiling now. 'That will leave us Stilicho.'

'Ah.'

'Unless …'

'Unless?' Justinus was all ears. Britannia was his province, more than it was Chrysanthos'. Every rumour, every whisper, had to be checked and double-checked.

'They say the Count of the Saxon Shore intends to get himself elected Caesar.'

'Terentius Marcus?' Justinus couldn't help but laugh, but

the effort cost him and he winced as his muscles shook.

'Yes.' Porca topped up their cups. 'That was my reaction, too. The man's a popinjay, an idiot but he's good in the bragging department. Claims to have rid the south of Niall of the Five Hostages and that the II Augusta love him.'

'If the Second Augusta love him, they're not the legion I know. And the fact is he let the Hibernian sheep-shagger escape after *I* caught him. I thought I'd broken him to the ranks already.'

'Thinking of yourself as Caesar, sir?' Porca said. In different times, in different places, Justinus Coelius would have felled the man for a question like that. Instead, he just shook his head.

'If a man like Magnus Maximus failed, what possible chance would Marcus stand?'

'Oh, I agree.' Porca leaned back, breathing in the fumes of the wine. 'But even so, that's why Stilicho is here. You remember the head of Quintus Phillipus?'

Justinus did.

'What does the Hebrew testament say – "an eye for an eye"?'

'"And a tooth for a tooth",' Justinus added. 'Yes, I know.'

'He's started already,' Porca said grimly.

'How so?'

'Orchestrated the destruction of the temple of Isis, right here in the city.'

'When?'

'Two nights ago. And believe me, I'm not proud of the part my men and I played in it.'

'Why Isis?' Justinus asked.

'Why not?' Porca shrugged. 'Oh, it's got nothing to do with Isis. It's a message. A message that Stilicho wants sent to all Britannia. A message that says "Cross me at your peril". He's got Londinium in the palm of his hand now. He'll have no trouble here. Other cities will fall in line – Isca Dumnoniorum, Eboracum, Lindum, Deva – they'll all dance to his tune. That way, even if the south-east backs Marcus, they'll be outnumbered.'

'And even if the Second Augusta follow him, Stilicho will have the Sixth Victrix and the Twentieth Valeria.'

'They're your men, Dux,' Porca said. 'You know them. Will they follow Marcus or Stilicho?'

'Stilicho, without a doubt,' Justinus said. 'Oh, they threw in their lot with Magnus Maximus, but he could have had Marcus for breakfast. The legions know a good soldier when they see one. Stilicho speaks for the emperor and from what I hear, he's a man's man. I'll go and see him tomorrow.'

'Sir …' Porca changed tack, but he did it slowly, feeling his way. 'I hope you won't mind my saying this, but you look far from well.'

'Thank you for your concern,' Justinus smiled, 'but things are at a critical stage just now and the last thing I plan to do is to die. Tell me,' and he too changed tack, 'where does the vicarius stand in all this?'

Chrysanthos the vicarius kept Calpurnius the decurion waiting all morning while he attended to other business. Calpurnius had expected this. After the events in Severianus' church, he expected the summons from on high. And he expected to be made to wait. Men like Chrysanthos were, at rock bottom, so predictable.

'I won't beat about the bush, Calpurnius,' the vicarius leaned back in his chair, arms folded, face grim. 'That public show of petulance on your part in church the other day was inexcusable.'

'I felt it had to be said.' Calpurnius stood his ground.

Chrysanthos unfolded his arms and dragged a heavy ledger in front of him on the table. 'I took the trouble,' he said, 'to consult your file.' He looked up and saw the astonished look on his subordinate's face. 'Oh, don't worry,' he said. 'It's not all about you. In fact, very little of it is. No, this book contains all I need to know about all my minions. I even have a slave section. Know your enemy, Calpurnius, *that's* how I stay in office.'

'So I am your enemy?' The decurion needed to know where he stood.

'After what happened in church, you can't expect me to turn the other cheek and include you in my will, now, can you?'

Calpurnius shrugged. The man was right.

'Your career,' Chrysanthos consulted the ledger, 'is, to be polite, chequered. You served the emperor at Carthago with that business with the elder Theodosius who you hung out to dry.'

'It wasn't that simple.'

'No,' Chrysanthos sighed. 'It never is. Then you disappeared. Ran, I have it on good authority, to the sewers of Augusta Treverorum, where you lived with the Jews and other rats.'

'They were troubled times,' Calpurnius remembered, although he had no wish to remember.

'After which, your wife and brother-in-law brought you here and I took pity on you.'

'I *was* grateful,' Calpurnius said. 'I *am* grateful.'

'Yes,' Chrysanthos snapped. 'I saw the extent of your gratitude in church.'

'You swore on God's book, sir,' Calpurnius said, holding his head up. 'I accepted that. Let it be an end.'

Chrysanthos slammed shut the ledger and the dust and various attendants jumped. 'An end, you ingrate? *I'll* decide when things end. And when they start. As for you …' he got up and crossed to the far wall of the council chamber where a map of Britannia was bolted to the stonework, '… that start will be … here.'

He pointed to the north, above the tangle of roads and camps and towns to the bleak, desolate land north of the Wall.

'What?' Calpurnius blinked.

'Valentia, decurion,' Chrysanthos smiled. 'Even here in cosy, comfortable Londinium, you must have heard of it. It's a dire place, so I'm told, full of sheep shit and wind and rain. That will be your home for the foreseeable future.'

Calpurnius stood up to his full height. 'Is this exile?' he asked.

'No.' The vicarius shrugged. 'You will still be on the pay roll, albeit greatly reduced. You will be my man north of the Wall and I expect monthly reports. The Votadini aren't exactly civilized people but I believe they eat with the hand they haven't just wiped their arses with, so it can't be all bad.'

'And if I refuse?' Calpurnius said, stone-faced.

Chrysanthos turned to him and crossed the room in two strides. 'Oh, that *would* be unwise, decurion,' he said. 'I told you, the people of Londinium and God that I had no hand in the slaughter at the temple of Isis. That's because I don't make war on women and children. But in the case of your family now, I am prepared to make an exception.'

Calpurnius' mouth hung open. Then he recovered himself. 'You wouldn't dare,' he growled.

'Wouldn't I, Calpurnius? Wouldn't I? You …' he clicked his fingers at a clerk awaiting orders. 'Get me Lucius Porca. He is to send an escort to the house of Calpurnius Succatus and he is to arrest …'

'All right!' Calpurnius shouted, then, quieter, 'all right, you've made your point.'

'Make your preparations, decurion,' Chrysanthos said, 'and count yourself lucky I'm in a generous mood this morning.'

He stood in the doorway to her bedroom, silhouetted by the light of the Decembris day. Bishop Severianus had celebrated the birth of Christ with an unusual vehemence this year, certain that the old revels of Saturnalia would not take place in his city. Now, nearly at the turning of the year, flurries of snow blew in from the marshes south of the river.

She turned as she saw him and let the maid go. 'Do that later, Drusilla.' The girl bobbed and left.

'I'm sorry,' he said. 'I came as soon as I heard. He sniffed his ragged sleeve. 'I smell of the river.'

She smiled and reached up to kiss his cheek. 'Since when does a brother of mine have to dress up for a visit?' she asked.

Conchessa was folding robes into a chest and the whole house was in chaos. Vitalis had passed it all as he came in, slaves of the city hauling boxes and loading horses and mules in the courtyard below. 'So much stuff,' she sighed.

'How have the children taken it?'

'Oh, they're excited. Tullia doesn't understand it and Patricius, well, he'll miss his friends of course, but I've told him he'll make new ones. Calpurnius has said he'll teach him to ride. There never seemed to be much call for that here.'

'It was a brave thing that he did,' Vitalis said.

'Yes.' Conchessa stopped her folding, her hands resting quiet on the clean linen. 'Yes, it was. But you did the same.'

Vitalis laughed. 'What have I got to lose, Conchessa?' he asked her. 'A hovel near the river and a few bent bits of reed? Calpurnius … well, he's everything to lose. And he's lost it.'

'No.' She shook her head, frowning. 'No, he hasn't. Things between us … well, things best left unsaid …'

'Patricius,' Vitalis nodded.

'He knows.' Conchessa closed her eyes. 'He knows the boy is not his. Does he love him any the less? I don't know. As I told you, we don't talk about it. Anyway,' she sniffed defiantly, 'we're going north with him. Us. The Succati. We're a family, ordained by God. And it's going to stay that way.'

'Good for you,' he smiled.

'What's it like?' Conchessa was all too ready to change the subject. 'Valentia? You've been there.'

'I have,' Vitalis said. 'Back in the mists of time when I marched with the xth Victrix. It's beautiful, I suppose. I saw it then with a soldier's eye. Now, I might see it as God intended. The sky is … oh, I don't know … bigger than here, somehow. The clouds are lined with God's glory. Pat will love it, Tullia too. And you … you can be yourself there, Conchessa. Work things out.'

'Yes,' she said. 'I have a need to work things out.'

'And,' Vitalis beamed, 'you'll be able to meet Brenna of the Votadini. You'll like her, Conchessa. I know she worships Belatucadros and rides and fights like a man, but you and she will soon be sisters under the skin.'

Conchessa laughed, despite her misgivings. 'I can't wait,' she said.

'And, even better, you'll meet up with Justinus again. I hear he spends most of his time in the north these days.'

'I hear he's in Londinium,' Conchessa said, turning back to her folding.

'Really?'

'Calpurnius is still sorting things out at the basilica. That's the latest piece of gossip.' She looked around her, at the walls without hangings, the floor without straw. 'I shan't miss much about this place. But the gossip,' she winked at him, '*that* I'll miss. And you.' She smiled, but her mouth was crooked and her eyes were shiny with tears she daren't shed.

He held her and kissed her forehead. For a moment, they were children again, back in the tenderness of their years when they had wrestled and fought as often as they had hugged. Before Britannia had sunk their claws into them, the claws of duty and care.

Dubris

The fleet lay in its winter quarters in the harbour and the beacon from the farum burnt night and day, reflecting the sister tower that winked on the western heights to guide home the ships. This was the permanent base of the Roman fleet, the classis Britannia and, that Januarius, the temporary home of Terentius Marcus, still claiming to be the Count of the Saxon shore because no one had reminded him that he was not.

The point was that Terentius Marcus had friends in high places. Not only were the Gracchi, the man's family, well connected at the emperor's court, but the vicarius himself smiled on the man. That was evident that bitterly cold dies Veneris as the local garrison and three vexilla of the II Augusta paraded in hollow square. Constantine had refused point blank to officiate and sat grimly in his quarters, listening to the drums and the thudding feet wheeling in formation outside. So it was Gerontius who did the honours.

He crossed the parade ground under a leaden sky as the torches of the legion guttered in the wind. The dragon standards lifted and snarled as the air rushed through their open mouths. As one, the aquilifer and signifers raised their standards aloft, the eagle flashing silver and the battle honours that stretched back to the deified Vespasian rattling on their poles.

In the centre, on a dais draped in purple, Terentius Marcus sat like a cat that had got the cream. He was wearing the uniform of his rank but his cloak was the colour of emperors and his head was bare. Gerontius halted in front of him and gave the imperial salute, then he snapped his fingers and the youngest drummer in the legion, a lad of twelve wearing outsized boots, handed him a plain wreath of laurels. Gerontius held it aloft so that all could see. Then he stepped forward, holding it above Marcus' head.

'In the name of the Second Augusta, Count, we beg you to take the purple. Lead us under God as our Caesar.'

For the expected moment, there was silence on the parade ground at Dubris. Other men might have hesitated, gone through the charade that they were unworthy, or bowed humbly to the inevitable pressure of the army and submitted – Marcus did none of these things. He bowed his head slightly and said, 'Spiritus exercitus, I submit.' And Gerontius put the wreath around the man's brows. Then he stood back, unsheathed his sword and tossed it in his hand so that the pommel was extended to Marcus. The former Count of the Saxon Shore reached out to touch it and the legion bellowed along its lines, 'Caesar! Caesar! Caesar! Caesar!' like the roar of the surf along the shingle coast.

Quintillius turned to Locicero amidst all the cheering and row. 'Remind me again why we're doing this.'

'Because that slippery, useless bastard wearing that silly leaf hat has just increased your wages. And paid for your new boots.'

'Ah, yes, that would be it.' And they both re-joined the cohorts, clashing their sword blades on their shields. 'Caesar! Caesar!'

It meant nothing to them that their recent wage increase,

their new boots and the extra day's ration of wine was all paid for, not by the new caesar of Britannia, but by Chrysanthos the vicarius, who had in turn 'borrowed' the vast sum concerned from the coffers of Britannia herself. It also meant nothing; Tartarus would freeze over before they would have a single coin in their hands.

Londinium

They had warned Stilicho that the Dux Britannorum was not a well man. The half Vandal, half temple destroyer had heard impressive things about Justinus Coelius. Above all, he knew the man had risen in the ranks, a soldier's soldier who knew what it was like to feel a shield strap cut a groove in his shoulder and the incessant itch of lice in his tunic. And Stilicho instinctively knew that what stood before him in Chrysanthos' basilica that morning was a shadow of the man he had heard had cut his teeth on iron.

With the civilities over, Stilicho asked the man to sit. Chrysanthos was not here this morning. This was soldiers' talk, man to man.

'They told me,' Stilicho said, resting his elbows on the arms of his chair, 'that you appointed this Marcus to be Count of the Saxon Shore.'

'They told you wrong,' Justinus said. 'My advice was against it.'

'Chrysanthos, then?'

Justinus shrugged. He had never really liked the vicarius and trusted the man even less, but he wasn't prepared to throw him to the wolves either; and few wolves, he knew, had sharper teeth than Stilicho.

'Your silence does you credit, Dux,' the general said, 'but you must know that in Roman law, silence means assent. I have you either way.'

'Is that your intention, General?' Justinus asked. 'To have me? Has the emperor sent you to wipe us all out?'

'On the contrary, Justinus.' Stilicho was softer, reassuring. 'The emperor has sent me to bring this rebellious little province of yours to heel. If you didn't appoint Marcus Count of the Saxon Shore, I assume you don't condone his election to the purple, either?'

'Mithras, god of the morning!' Justinus threw his hands in the air. 'Has he done that?'

'He has,' Stilicho said. 'I heard only yesterday. The Second Augusta elected him at Dubris. But you've been here before.'

'I have?'

'Magnus Maximus. You rode with him.'

'I did,' Justinus admitted. 'He had a magic all his own, that man.'

'But you didn't follow him to the ends of the earth?' Stilicho reasoned.

Justinus shook his head. 'I didn't follow him beyond these shores,' he said. 'He was a great soldier. And I was proud to count him a friend. But his march on Rome? No, that was madness. Even the newest pedes knows you don't split your command; you don't give an army *two* emperors to follow.'

'It might come to that,' Stilicho said.

'How so?'

'Theodosius is dying, Justinus. Of what, I don't know. But I don't expect him to be there when I get back. The empire is tottering. It's too big for one man, God's anointed or not. The reality is,' he looked the man squarely in the face, 'Rome's days are numbered, Dux Britannorum. Our job, yours and mine, is to hold her together. Somehow. I don't know about you, but I'm starting here in Britannia. I'm starting with upstarts who've got too big for their boots. I'm starting with Terentius Marcus.'

'No,' Justinus said, grim-faced. 'No, he's my problem. I had my sword at his throat once and I should have used it. He has disobeyed orders. I stripped him of his rank.'

'Dux,' Stilicho said quietly, 'Justinus …' He looked into the man's eyes. 'I know what happened,' he said. 'The renegade girl, the knife, the poison. Take this winter. Regroup. Regain your strength. Marcus is my problem now. Where's your home?'

Justinus chuckled. 'A good question,' he said. 'I have no home other than the Wall.'

'Go there, then. Isn't there shelter for you there, with the queen of the Votadini?'

Justinus was surprised in spite of himself. 'You are well informed, General,' he said.

'That's why I am Magister Militum,' Stilicho said. He looked at Justinus again, the ox in the furrow, the stubbornest mule in the army. 'I could order it,' he said.

'You'll have to,' Justinus told him.

'Very well.' Stilicho stood up and Justinus did too, though

the room swayed in his vision as he did it. 'Justinus Coelius, Dux Britannorum, as Magister Militum, invested with the powers of the emperor, I order you to take leave. You will report for duty again, here in Londinium, on … well, let's let God decide that, shall we?'

Justinus blinked. Men took leave from the army all the time though he had taken none for years. But there was a finality about this, a sense that he was looking at Stilicho and this basilica and this city, for the last time. Well, perhaps it was for the best. 'If it's all the same to you, General,' he murmured, 'I'd rather let Mithras decide.'

Stilicho smiled. 'Yes, Justinus,' he said. 'It *is* all the same to me.

CHAPTER XIII

'Vitalis? Is that you?'

Justinus Coelius was propped on a pillow. Yesterday had been a bad day and he needed his rest. The day before had been better and he had walked the windy ramparts of Lucius Porca's fort.

'It is, Justinus.' Vitalis nodded to the guard and ducked in under the fringed canopy. 'How are you?'

'I've been better.' The Dux Britannorum managed a brittle laugh. Vitalis knew that. He had not seen him for months, but the pale shadow lying on his bed was not the warrior he remembered. Justinus had been *the* watchman on the Wall, the rock on which Britannia stood. He was made of the same granite. But now the granite was crumbling. 'Wine? Let me get you some wine.'

'No, no,' Vitalis sat on the bed and patted the man's arm. 'Don't trouble on my account. I'd heard you were unwell, but I didn't realise …'

'That I'm dying? Don't distress yourself, old friend. I'm going home.'

'Home to Heaven or home to Mithras?' Vitalis had to ask. The deified Constantine had found Christ on his deathbed. Miracles happened.

Justinus still had the strength to throw a pillow at him. 'Home to Valentia,' he said.

This was better. A Dux Britannorum with a streak of humour in him might yet make it through the day, through the night. 'Who said you're dying?' Vitalis asked.

'Nobody. The medici haven't got a clue. Only the girl who

gave me this.' He peeled back the dressing on his shoulder where the blood lay congealed and dark around an angry red slit. 'She said there was no cure.'

'All right,' Vitalis said, his voice firm and bright. 'So, you're dying. We all are, day by day. But I've got a job for you, if you don't mind, first.'

Justinus smiled. In front of him sat a basket maker who used to be a soldier, a brother who had stood shoulder to shoulder on the battlefield under the eagle. He had prayed to Jupiter, Highest and Best. He had bled with the bull under Mithras' cruel knife. Now he worshipped a carpenter's son from Judea. However long Mithras had given Justinus, he would never understand the man, the man who needed him now. 'If I can,' he said.

'Oh, you can,' Vitalis assured him. 'If you're the Justinus Coelius I remember. There's a dart under your other pillow, isn't there?'

'There is,' Justinus nodded.

Vitalis half-turned on the bed. 'See that glass jug over there?'

Justinus did.

'I've never liked that particular design. Do the honours for me, would you?'

He dodged aside and blinked as the deadly iron hissed past his head to shatter the glass which flew glittering in all directions. He swallowed. 'I'd hate to see you when you're fully recovered,' he said.

Justinus chuckled, his heart higher than it had been for days. 'They've put me out to pasture, Vit,' he said. 'Like my old man before me. Remember old Flavius?'

Vitalis did. Justinus' father had been the hastiliarius, the weapons trainer of the VI Victrix, who had made Vitalis curse him up hill and down dale on many an occasion. 'I can't think of a finer situation,' he smiled. 'You'll be able to growl at all the ham-fisted, lame-brained recruits in Britannia Secunda and turn them into men.'

'I'm not sure that's what Stilicho has in mind. Officially, I'm on leave.'

'And unofficially?'

Justinus' face darkened. 'Unofficially, I'm part of Stilicho's problem. I backed a rebel against the emperor. Stilicho is the emperor's man; he could have had me executed.'

'He can't kill us all,' Vitalis reasoned.

'I heard about the temple of Isis,' Justinus said. 'Bad business.'

'It was,' Vitalis nodded, 'which brings me to the little job I had in mind.'

Justinus sat up, waiting.

'You're going north, to Valentia?'

Justinus nodded.

'So is Conchessa. And Calpurnius and the kids.'

'So, it's true then. Chrysanthos has exiled him.'

'Not exactly. Calpurnius still has to report to the vicarius. Except he'll be doing it from north of the Wall.'

'You want me to escort them?' Justinus frowned.

'That's the idea.'

Justinus chuckled. 'I'm not sure who'll be nurse-maiding who,' he said. 'Little Patricius had better stand for me.'

Vitalis leaned nearer. 'Anybody who can still throw a dart like that doesn't need anyone to stand for them,' he said. 'Will you do it, Justinus? For old time's sake?'

The Dux Britannorum nodded. 'I'll do it,' he said, 'but what about you?'

'Oh,' Vitalis stood up. 'With the way things are going here, I think I'll be rather busy for a while.' He clasped the man's hand. 'Pax et Deus vobiscum, Dux Britannorum.'

'Too many chiefs, Mama dear.' Scipio Honorius was wallowing in the steam of his private baths as his mother handed him a cup of wine. 'That's how I see it.'

'Do you?' Honoria waved her women away and was vaguely surprised that her son seemed to be without any of his own.

'Well, I mean,' he held the cup resting on his chest and closed his eyes, 'we've got your better half representing the emperor as vicarius. We've got Justinus Coelius representing the emperor with his sword. Now we've got Terentius Marcus pretending to *be* the emperor. And the gods know where good old Stilicho stands in all this.'

'I notice,' she said archly, 'that that man is still walking around. I thought you and I had an agreement.'

'I'm afraid you thought wrong, mama. Oh, I was happy to oblige with Quintus Phillipus. Quite surprised me how easy it is to take off a head, actually. But Stilicho … well, that's different.'

A smile spread over Honoria's face. 'He's got to you, hasn't he?' she said. 'Bought you.'

'Body and soul,' Scipio confessed. 'For as long as it suits me.'

'I thought you were Terentius Marcus' friend,' she said. No one stirred a hornets' nest like Honoria Honorius.

'We drank and whored together, yes.' Scipio sipped his wine. 'But I wouldn't call him a friend. From what I hear, he's likely to be a dead friend before too long.'

Honoria stood up, her wine untouched and she clapped her hands for her ladies to return. 'My son,' she said softly, 'look after yourself, won't you?'

'Count on it, Mama,' he smiled.

'He said he was dying.' Vitalis was waiting while Conchessa checked her rooms for one last time. Tears were trickling down his face. She saw them and reached up to wipe them away, her face as pained as his.

'If it is God's plan, Vit,' she said softly.

Vitalis nodded. 'I was rough with him,' he said. 'Virtually told him to pull himself together. Me? That's rich. I could dither for Rome.'

'Justinus was always there, wasn't he?' she said. 'Standing like the Wall he served.'

'He was,' her brother nodded, drying the last tears himself. 'And he always will be. What about you, Con?' He looked into her sad, grey eyes. 'Are you ready for this?'

She looked down into the courtyard. Patricius and Tullia, who had been babbling with excitement for days, were strangely quiet today. Today it had dawned on them. They were leaving their house, the only home they'd known. Was there a world beyond these walls? They didn't know. And not knowing frightened them both. Calpurnius was saying his farewells to his steward and the servants; in a moment, Conchessa would have to do the same. But worse than that, she would have to say goodbye to Vit. They had said their goodbyes before, confident that God would reunite them one day. But that was then and Conchessa had never been to Valentia before. Did God live north of the Wall? And worse, so much worse than that, she would have no one near her who knew Septimus Pontus, Patric's real father. She didn't need that person to have liked him; just that they had been in the same room, had trodden the same streets, that was enough. Patricius' crooked smile made her heart clench whenever she saw it, but Vit … Vit was the last lifeline and it was being cut that day.

She swept out of the room. The only way she could do this, say her goodbyes, was to be as cold as Vitalis had been to Justinus. She had asked him a dozen times – why couldn't he come with them? He had no ties in Londinium, no family, no girl. But every time he had smiled at her; he had things to do and her way could not be his way.

Maxima Caesariensis

The vexillation of the XX Valeria Victrix had been summoned by Stilicho, his riders thrashing their mounts as they crossed Britannia Prima. The praeses there had not been a happy man. A Vandal general was asking for troops to put down a little local difficulty, but that difficulty, Stilicho's messengers admitted, involved the II Augusta. Hadn't Rome had enough of civil wars through its long and bloody history? Spring would not be far away and the raiding season would begin again. The XX had to be ready and the XX could only spare a vexillation; the rest of the legion nailed itself to its fortress at Deva and watched the weather.

The Vandal general would not send for reinforcements from the rump of the II Augusta at Isca; that would be brotherly slaughter too far. Neither would he ask Lucius Porca to commit his garrison. These men had loafed around Londinium for too long. They had turned into night watchmen, putting out fires and helping old ladies across the street. And Stilicho did not have time to turn them into a fighting field force. He would have to rely on the XX and his own Heruli cavalry for that.

By the time Calpurnius, Conchessa, Justinus and the children were plodding along the old legionary road through Flavia Caesariensis, Stilicho was marching due east, to Rutupiae. His scouts had told him that Terentius Marcus, the Caesar, could have been at any one of the forts of the Saxon shore, from Branodunum to Vectis, but the smart money was that he would be somewhere in the south, ready for a run to the German sea if things went badly.

Stilicho had left Marcus in no doubt where he stood. He had sent gallopers to all the forts the man commanded with the same message. The emperor's man would wait in Londinium until Good Friday, expecting the Count of the Saxon Shore to surrender himself and, crawling on his belly, beg forgiveness of the emperor over that nonsense with the laurel wreath. Marcus had sent back an equally haughty reply, from Rutupiae; if the general would care to join him there, he would happily accept the Vandal into his service – on certain conditions, of course. Stilicho had not waited for Easter. He had marched east.

The great walls of Rutupiae were daunting and Stilicho had no artillery with him. There were wild asses inside the fort and he helped himself to these almost as soon as the white flag fluttered over the ramparts. A decidedly nervous fort commander was sorry that the caesar … er … the Count of the Saxon shore wasn't there, but would the general like to stay at the mansio? There were baths waiting, the finest in the south-east. Or perhaps the general would like to see a play at the new theatre? The great Aelius was playing the senex and the meretrix, the commander had heard, offered off-stage services like no other.

Stilicho turned down the lady's finely-honed skills and, in a busy life, had to miss the great tragedian Aelius (in fact, he had seen him before, in Rome and wasn't very impressed) but he soaked in the tepidarium, a slave working on his muscles and he slept soundly in the mansio. In the morning, he took four wild asses along with their operators, all the commander's horses and enough food for three days' march. He was, of course, very polite about it, as was his way, but he had left Terentius Marcus nothing to fall back on should the events of the next four weeks bring him back that way. The commander of Rutupiae breathed a sigh of relief. Stilicho hanged men, he had heard; so the loss of a few basics affected him not at all.

The fog was thick along the Venta the next day as Stilicho's force followed its meandering banks. It was hardly an army in the true sense of the word and if it met Marcus on the road today, it would be seriously outnumbered. But in the centre of the grunting, marching column, boots crunching on the frost-rimed clumps of grass, the standard of the emperor danced alongside Stilicho's scarlet flag and that alone gave the Vandal the edge.

No one had eaten by the time they reached Regulbium. Whatever sun might have gleamed above the low clouds resolutely refused to shine and the rank and file were grateful for the watch-fires of the fort. This place had been scaled down years before and there was little comfort other than the warmth of the fires for Stilicho's men. They camped half in the open that night, huddled together under the stars that twinkled at them as the sea mists cleared and left the night raw.

At first light they were on the march again, the asses creaking and groaning as the artillerymen lashed the mules. Ahead, the screen of cavalry with their dragon standard and their painted shields, watched the land to the south; the eyes and ears of the little army. The Heruli had ridden with Stilicho before. They knew his ways and would ride through fire for him, but the XX were less convinced. It was not for a long-suffering pedes to reason why; it never had been. But it seemed to them they were chasing a ghost. They'd never heard of Terentius Marcus but already the rumours were flying. As they plodded over the iron-rutted roads, impedimenta dangling from their spear-shafts, their backs straining and their feet wrapped in linen against the cold, they muttered together, as soldiers will. Terentius Marcus was a giant. He could have Stilicho for breakfast. Then, all thoughts of that were dispelled by thoughts of *actual* breakfast and suddenly, all seemed right with the world.

Three marches later, they reached Dubris. The farum winked at them out to sea and another at the harbour wall. The mutterers of the XX took comfort from the sight there. They were a long way from home and the harbour was crowded with the spars and timbers of the fleet. The galleys of Rome lay locked and chained for the winter with their sails furled and their oars at rest, but there was no doubting their power. That power ruled the Roman world, from Mona to Palmyra. And that power was Stilicho's.

At Dubris, the general learned that the caesar had left two days earlier. He had told no one where he was going but he had ridden south, hugging the coast, so that meant, logically, Portus Lemanis. There were only a few merchant vessels riding the swell in the harbour here now, the fleet having gone south for the winter. Stilicho and his officers paid their respects at the altar dedicated by Admiral Gaius Pantera to Neptune. Of course, the Christian God ruled the waves now, but it paid to be careful. A half Vandal feeling his way through alien territory was bound to hedge his bets.

Here, while his men nursed their aching feet and sneezed their way through warm bread and hot broth, Stilicho took stock. It made sense for Marcus to hole up somewhere with stout walls and a good water supply. His troops may outnumber Stilicho's, but the general's reputation had gone before him. The last thing Marcus wanted was to be caught in the open by a soldier of Stilicho's experience. Behind walls, he could sweat it out, relying on the weather and reach his ships before Nemesis struck. Stilicho's scouts were well-informed and he trusted them. The largest of the Saxon Shore forts was Portus Adurni, but the garrison, Stilicho knew, had been moved to Clausentum. It was a vast shell, the scouts said, and if rumours of Marcus' numbers were true, they would be ricocheting around inside like a pea in a slingshot. There wouldn't be enough of them to man the walls. Beyond that lay Vectis. It was an island and in theory, an island was easy to defend. But again, it was a numbers game; Marcus couldn't guard its bays, inlets and river approaches. Besides, the deified Vespasian had taken Vectis centuries before and with a single legion. There'd be no safe haven for the caesar there. So that left Anderitum …

Anderitum

A solitary horseman rode out of the fog that morning, the hooves padding almost silently over the silvered grass, crisp with frost. Quintillius stirred himself. He'd drawn the short straw *again* and had been shivering on the fort's ramparts all night. Jupiter Highest and Best, but it was cold. Spring? Somebody – and it was probably Locicero – had told him that spring was on the way. You could almost hear the new born lambs bleating and smell the snowdrops, he'd said. There was definitely something wrong with Locicero. But none of that mattered a damn this morning. Quintillius called out as soon as he saw it. 'Semisallis; rider.'

The semisallis wandered along the wall walk. Quintillius was a surly old bastard, not given to panic or flights of fancy. So, there was no cause for alarm. He took one look at the horseman on the black and yelled to the courtyard below, 'Circitor of the Watch!'

The circitor of the Watch was halfway through his breakfast and he stuffed the bread up his tunic sleeve rather than leave it lying around in the circitors' mess, where he *knew* he'd never see it again. He clattered up the steps and followed the semisallis' pointing finger. 'Better get Constantine,' he muttered and the man was gone.

A second horseman cantered out of the wall of fog that cloaked the hillside. And then a third. The circitor licked his lips, chapped as they were already by the biting cold. Each horseman carried a battle standard. The man on the black held aloft the emperor's likeness, Theodosius by the grace of God, in lorica and laurel wreath. The second carried the plain scarlet flag of a general.

And the third the raging bull of the XX Valeria Victrix. Almost by the time the circitor had checked all three totems, the tribune Constantine was at his elbow.

'Well, well,' the cavalryman said. 'Looks like Stilicho has moved faster than we thought. Pedes.'

'Sir.' Quintillius clicked to attention.

'My compliments to the caesar. Tell him we have some guests for breakfast.'

And Quintillius was gone, clattering down the steps and making for Marcus' quarters, cloak flying behind him.

Constantine nodded to the bulge in the circitor's sleeve. 'Better eat that,' he said. 'It's going to be a long day.'

Terentius Marcus resented being woken so early. Especially by a scruffy pedes who looked as if he hadn't washed for a week.

'Guests?' Marcus sat up in bed. 'What are you talking about, man?'

'General Stilicho, Sire,' Quintillius remembered to add the final respectful 'e' to the title, just in time.

Marcus sat bolt upright in bed, his back, in every sense, to the wall.

'Oh, Tere,' whined the half-asleep girl beside him. 'What's the matter?'

'Shut up, you stupid tart, and get out!' He lashed out with his left foot and sent the girl sprawling. Quintillius enjoyed the view he got briefly, then stared straight ahead, ever the loyal soldier.

'Messenus!' Marcus roared as the girl scurried out, sobbing and swearing in equal measure. 'My armour. Now. Are they past the marsh?' He was talking to Quintillius, but the wall might have been better informed.

'I don't know, Sire.'

'How many?'

'I don't know, Sire.'

Marcus was on his feet now and he slapped Quintillius hard across the face, wincing as his fingers hit the cheek plate of the man's helmet. 'Well, you're no bloody use to me,' the caesar told him. 'Get on the ramparts where you might do some good. Massenus, where the bloody Hell is my armour?'

Flavius Stilicho sat his horse on the edge of the fog bank that hid his forces. If he'd prayed all night, he couldn't have wished for better. His army was invisible to the men behind the ramparts.

Marcus could have no idea how many men he had brought. Below their position, fanned out in battle order as they were with the cavalry on the wings, the marshes lay half frozen in their winter mud. Two of the wild asses had stuck there but their loaders had hauled them free with the minimum of blasphemy and all four were now dragged to Stilicho's front. Their mules were uncoupled and the machines loaded, men grunting with the effort of hauling stones into the leather buckets.

Stilicho walked his horse forward and called in a loud voice, 'Terentius Marcus, who calls himself Count of the Saxon Shore. I want a word with you.'

They were all on the ramparts now, Marcus, Constantine, Gerontius and the entire command.

'I think it's you he wants, sir,' Constantine said. No final 'e' niceties for him. He hadn't elected the buffoon caesar. And if Terentius Marcus had been on fire, Constantine wouldn't have pissed on him to put him out.

'Who wants him?' Marcus shouted back, although he knew the answer already.

'Flavius Stilicho, Magister Militum,' came the reply, echoing strangely over the marshes and the slope of the hill. 'In the name of the emperor. The real one, I mean.'

There were guffaws from the fog and one or two titters from the ramparts too. Marcus spun round but could pin the blame on no-one in particular. He turned back to the four horsemen he could see and the asses' frames jutting ominously from the mist. 'Go to Hell, Flavius Stilicho,' he shouted. 'You have been misinformed. I am caesar here.'

Stilicho laughed and the echo rippled in the shifting greyness behind him. 'Indeed you are,' he said, 'and I wish you the joy of your empire. What is it? Nine heredia? Ten? You've got the sea to your back, Marcus, and me to your front. If that isn't a classic case of being between the devil and the deep, I don't know what is. Surrender yourself to me and I'll let your command go; learn to be soldiers again, serving their rightful emperor.'

'Sounds fair to me,' Locicero grunted to Quintillius alongside him on the ramparts.

'It does,' Quintillius said. 'But I'll say this about the late caesar, he picks a good whore. Tits to die for.'

Locicero frowned. 'Let's hope not, Quint,' he said. 'I don't know about you, but I've got plans.'

'Oh?'

'Yes. I want to go on living.'

'This is your last chance, Marcus,' Stilicho's patience was wearing thin.

'You have your answer,' the caesar called back, cursing the fact that Stilicho was out of arrow-shot from the walls.

'So be it,' the Vandal wheeled his horse and the next thing the men on the ramparts heard was the command to shoot and the thud and whine of the asses as the stones sailed through the morning air. They bit deep into the earthworks of Anderitum, sending huge flitches of soil and grass high into the air. There were whoops and whistles from the ramparts. The artillery had not been made that could dent these walls. They were twenty feet thick and fifteen bastions commanded the perimeter, each of them capable of being defended one by one and to the death.

'Is that the best you can do?' Marcus shouted and swung his arm high. When he dropped it, his own wild asses crashed into action, the ropes flying free as the rocks hurtled out over the ramparts and disappeared into the fog. There was a scream as a horse went down, its forelegs smashed in an arc of blood and bone. Its rider rolled clear as the doomed animal slithered, struggling and snorting, into the freezing water of the marsh.

'We can keep this up all day,' Marcus said. 'Get one of your lackeys to count our ballistae. We outnumber you, Stilicho.'

That was true enough. And even though Marcus' artillerymen couldn't see what they were aiming at, their chances of claiming lives were high. At the moment, it was a single horse, but how long could Stilicho's men remain that lucky?

'Scorpion shot!' Stilicho ordered, wheeling his horse backwards and forwards between the asses. His artillerymen scrambled to reload, this time with smaller stones and pebbles. 'That skyline looks untidy, gentlemen,' he said to his men. 'Neaten it up for me, would you?'

The wild asses bucked again. This time the shot rained down like lightning bolts, clattering on helmets and quickly-raised shields.

'Baby coming!' Locicero shouted but he was almost too late. A jagged stone sliced through the crown of his helmet and broke his nose. He staggered back, his face a mask of blood and his eyes swimming with tears. Alongside him, Quintillius took a hit squarely on his shield and the impact forced him to his knees. 'Mother of

Mithras, these men are good. Remind me, Lo, next time I'm given the opportunity, to transfer to the Twentieth. Lo? Lo?'

But Locicero was lying with a heap of other men, moaning and crying in the courtyard below.

'Reload!' Marcus screamed, his sword drawn now and his blood up. In fact, he was spattered with blood, but it wasn't his own. It had spurted from the neck of a semisallis alongside him when a sharp flint had ripped his flesh.

'Give it up, Marcus,' Constantine snapped. The caesar had just collided with him on the ramparts.

'Scorpion shot!' Marcus shouted to his artillerymen, too furious and shocked to listen to his second in command.

Stilicho heard the order too and pulled his men back, out of the range of the sling-shot that peppered down harmlessly onto the abandoned wild asses, the stones clattering on the framework. The only other sound was the splashes as dozens of them landed in the freezing water of the marsh. Then it was his turn again and the scorpion stones swept the ramparts, thudding against the upright stakes of the parapet. Most of the garrison had their heads down now and the most they got was a chronic headache as the pebbles dented the iron and buckled the copper. One man was too slow though and he screamed as a razor-sharp missile took out his eye and he somersaulted backwards off the wall walk, stung by the scorpion.

'Reload!' Marcus was running back along the wall, slapping the crouching artillerymen with his sword blade.

'Stand fast!' Constantine's voice was louder and the artillerymen stopped in their tracks, ropes held taut in their fists.

Marcus whirled to the man. 'What the Hell do you think you're doing?' he shouted.

'What I should have done weeks, no, months ago. Army regulations state that in the event of a commander taking leave of his senses, his second-in-command has the right to relieve him of command.'

'You can go to Hell, Constantine,' Marcus spat and drove his sword forward. The cavalryman was faster and sliced the deadly blade aside. Iron scraped on iron as the men struggled on the ramparts.

'Baby coming!' somebody shouted and the thunder of the stones forced them apart. When Marcus next regained his footing, his sword was wrenched from his grasp and he was being held firmly between two very large soldiers. Constantine sheathed his sword, still unbloodied, and turned to the ramparts.

'Flavius Stilicho,' he called.

'Who's that?' Stilicho walked his horse forward, the animal's hooves slipping and sliding on the debris of the stones. He didn't recognize the voice, but he knew it wasn't Marcus.

'I am Flavius Constantine, commander of the Alae of the Second Augusta. I have just relieved the Count of the Saxon Shore of his command. The fort is yours, sir.'

Stilicho rested his hand on his hip and the horse shifted under his weight. 'If this is some sort of trick, Constantine …'

'No trick, sir,' the cavalry commander called and he beckoned Marcus' guards forward. He struggled on the palisades, scowling at Stilicho with the creeping fog at his back.

'Open your gates, Constantine, and bring that man out.'

Slowly, as if in a dream, the army of the Vandal emerged from the screen of mist, the infantry with their shields locked, spears level like a giant porcupine on the move. On either side of them, lances skyward, the cavalry of the Heruli checked their reins and advanced at a walk. At their head, Stilicho hauled rein to his right and walked the horse forward to the huge towers that flanked the great gate. When he saw that, he was grateful for Constantine's mutiny. He could never had taken that before the Tiber froze.

The heavy oak gates swung open with much squealing and groaning of timber and a knot of men came through it onto the open ground of the vallum, forcing Marcus to the shot-riddled earth, their knees against his back. Stilicho urged his horse forward and looked down at the man.

'You are Terentius Marcus?' he asked.

'I am,' the caesar may have been beaten, but he was unbowed.

'Lately Count of the Saxon Shore?'

'I *am* Count of the Saxon Shore,' Marcus insisted.

'No, you're not,' Stilicho chuckled. 'I have that on the authority of the Dux Britannorum himself. And as for caesar … well, we all have our daydreams, don't we?' He looked up at the mob of soldiery inside the courtyard. 'Where is Constantine?'

The cavalry commander came forward, his helmet in the crook of his arm.

'What are your terms?' Stilicho asked.

Constantine blinked. What was this? Commanders agreed

terms *before* a siege ended, not after the defenders had thrown open the gates. 'I have no terms, sir,' he said. 'Anderitum is yours.'

Stilicho let his eyes wander over the tired, frightened men behind Constantine. 'You, pedes,' he said, pointing to one. 'What's your name?'

'Er … Quintillius, Sire.'

'Don't "sire" me, soldier. I'm a general. We've all had enough false emperors for a while, haven't we? What do you want?'

'Sir?' Quintillius could barely speak. Here was the Vandal general, the Magister Militum, the emperor's right hand man and he was asking him, Quintillius, what he wanted. Quintillius was the shit on Stilicho's boots. He didn't have opinions. Not outside the safety of his contubernium.

'You're a soldier of Britannia, man. More, of the Second Augusta. My old tutor used to tell me stories about you men, how you crossed the German Sea when no man knew what lay beyond it. How, under Vespasian of blessed memory, you smashed tribes without number. Have you *really* slipped so far?'

'I want to go on serving, sir,' Quintillius blurted out. That was true, although the alternative didn't bear thinking about.

'Good. Where's your optio?' Stilicho looked into the mass of men. A thickset officer in a plumed helmet pushed his way to the front. 'You're this man's optio?'

'I am, sir.'

'Give him your stick.'

The optio hesitated. The only time he'd given Quintillius his stick was when he'd brought it down on his back because the old ne'er-do-well was shirking in field formation. He passed the oak baton over, knurled and studded with knots as it was.

Stilicho chuckled as he watched Quintillius handle it. 'Felt that often in your time, eh, soldier?' he asked.

'I have, sir,' Quintillius admitted.

'Optio, I assume you have more of these little persuaders in your quarters, you and the other optios?'

'Yes, sir.'

'Get them. Gentlemen,' he raised his voice so that all could hear him. 'I have one volunteer here. His name, as many of you will know, is Quintillius. Today, he is going to do his emperor a service. But he cannot do it alone. I need nineteen more of you. Here. Now.'

There was a murmur in the ranks. At first no one moved,

then Locicero shambled forward, his swollen nose covering most of his face, under the mask of dried blood. Then another. And another. Until, altogether, twenty pedes of the II Augusta stood in front of the general. He looked at them, their muscles, the power in their shoulders. 'Fustuarium,' he said quietly.

'No!' That was Marcus' voice as he realised what was going to happen to him. Stilicho ordered the II into hollow square outside the great gate of Anderitum and drew up his twenty men with their persuaders in a narrow column, ten facing ten. His sword and dagger gone, Marcus now had his armour ripped off and he stood there, still held by his guards, in tunic and boots.

'Caesar,' Stilicho had been handed the man's laurel wreath and he ordered it placed on his head now. 'Let no man say I didn't give you a chance. There, at the end of this tunnel of men, lies freedom. If you can get that far, I give you my word you will go free. I will give you a ship, a crew and enough provisions for you to cross the German sea. Well, don't look so worried, Marcus,' he raised his right foot and hooked it casually over the saddle bow, getting into a comfortable position to enjoy the show. 'There are only twenty of them and you *are* the caesar, after all. It'll be a piece of piss.'

Marcus stood there, his chest heaving. He wanted to be sick. He wanted to cry. He wanted to be anywhere that morning except under the walls of Anderitum, except under that leaden sky. He felt his bowels writhe and his bladder empty. The first stick caught his shoulder and he twisted away from it. The second hit him across the forehead and he fell like a stone. To the roars and whoops of the II Augusta, he was prodded upright again. He tried to run but they tripped him and the iron-hard oak bounced off a broken shoulder and shattered his teeth. He could see the end of the tunnel, a dim and wobbling light in the darkness that was closing around him. If only … if only. But Terentius Marcus never reached the light. Long, long before the last stick came down, spraying Locicero again with blood, Terentius Marcus was dead.

The shouting and the slaughter over, Stilicho dismounted and walked over to the battered body where Constantine stood. The man drew his sword and reversed it, offering the ivory hilt to the general, in the time-honoured symbol of surrender.

'Put that away,' he said. 'I've got a little job for you.'

CHAPTER XIV

'Dux Britannorum?' Constantine stared at the man.

'There's a vacancy at the moment,' Stilicho said.

'But, I thought Justinus Coelius ...'

'On borrowed time, that man,' the general assured him. 'I need someone up to the job.'

'Sir, I am a legionary tribune ...'

'And Justinus was a pedes once, Constantine, the shit on your boots. I'm not interested in lineage and family and all that crap. If I find a man I can trust, I promote him. I *can* trust you, can't I, Constantine?'

The tribune looked rather sheepish. 'I *have* just taken part in a rebellion, sir,' he said.

'Ah,' Stilicho chuckled. 'We've all done that. It's what we Romans do, isn't it? So, do you accept?'

Constantine hesitated. The events of the past weeks were still whirling in his brain. It was all so ... unreal. He looked at the Vandal general, the emperor's right hand man. 'I accept,' he said and Stilicho clasped his arm in the old Roman way.

Londinium

'Tell me again.' Chrysanthos sat, grim-faced, in his chambers at the basilica. Outside, the sun danced on the rippling waters of the Thamesis and the city went about its business.

'Beaten to death, sir.' The centurion was still standing to attention because the vicarius had not told him to do otherwise. Neither was he offering the man any refreshment after his long ride from Anderitum. 'The Fustuarium.'

Chrysanthos frowned. 'I thought that went out with chariots and the lorica segmentata.'

'The general has an affinity with the past, sir,' the centurion said.

It wasn't the past that bothered Chrysanthos; it was the present and beyond that, the future. Terentius Marcus, the man he had set up as a would-be emperor, a man whose strings he could have pulled with ease, was no more, smashed into the mud under the cudgels of a legion. 'Sic semper tyrannis,' he muttered. 'So it is always with tyrants.' He looked up at the centurion, noting suddenly his rank and unit. 'The Second Augusta, centurion,' he said. 'What does the general intend to do with you?'

'We have been pardoned, sir. All of us. The tribune Flavius Constantine is Dux Britannorum.'

Chrysanthos' eyelids flickered for a moment, the only outward sign of his inner fury. 'He has no right to make such an appointment,' he said, 'especially as Justinus Coelius is still in post.'

'Is he, sir?' the centurion frowned. 'We heard he was dead.'

Din Paladyr

'I heard you were dead,' she said, her eyes big with tears.

'A slight exaggeration,' he smiled. 'But only slight.'

She shook her head. 'I've lost two loves in my life,' she whispered. 'I won't lose another.'

He sank back on the wolfskins, grateful for the rest and the warmth of the hearth fire. It had taken Justinus nearly three weeks to get this far north, stopping at mansios, way stations and army camps on the way. He couldn't remember much of the journey, except that for most of the way north, the snow had lain thick. He had left Calpurnius and his family at Onnum on the Wall. It was not the most salubrious of forts, but it would do until the spring, when the decurion could establish himself further north and present his papers to Brenna, queen of the Votadini.

She wrapped her arms around Justinus in the glow of the embers. When she had first seen him, walking his horse up the low hills that led to her capital, she hadn't believed it. The man had aged years and his clothes hung on him. His skin had a grey pallor of its own and he dismounted with difficulty, glad to leave the saddle behind for a while. They had not been lying together long when she realised that he had fallen asleep. She eased herself off the bed and tenderly untied the thongs of his tunic. The dressing on his shoulder was old and bloody and he moaned in pain as she prised it loose. He had told her what had happened, the knife, the poison. She dipped fresh linen into a pot of the healing water from the pool of Coventina and wiped the jagged wound clean. Some clod of an army medicus had stitched it, but badly and the gut itself had become infected. Brenna, the queen, the mother, the wife and nurse, would do what she could. The rest was up to Belatucadros.

Londinium

Vitalis wandered the cold ashes of the temple of Isis. He had walked this way several times in the past weeks, never quite sure why. It was not on his way to anywhere, except perhaps the Bishop's Gate and the necropolis and Vitalis had no dead there. His only family, Conchessa and her children, had gone north as the last flurries of winter gripped the land. It was nearly dark now and he could see the moon glinting on the helmets of Lucius Porca's guard patrolling the walls.

Something made him look up and a boy stood there, in rags and with bare feet. 'Ave,' he said to the lad.

The boy nodded.

'I've seen you here before,' Vitalis said. 'What's your name, boy?'

'Petronius, sir; Petronius Borro.'

'Ave, Petronius,' Vitalis said. 'And you don't have to call me sir. I'm a basket maker. What does your father do?'

'Nothing, sir … um, nothing. He's dead.'

It suddenly dawned on Vitalis, the reason he had seen the boy here before. 'He was a worshipper of Isis?'

Petronius nodded.

'I'm sorry,' Vitalis closed to the boy. What was he? Ten? Eleven? 'Who looks after you now?'

'Papa Londinium.'

'Papa …? You mean you live by your wits, here on the streets?'

'I don't steal,' Petronius said, perhaps a little too quickly. 'I've never stolen.'

'I'm sure you haven't,' Vitalis smiled. He had never had a son, had never married. He had never even considered being somebody's father. And here was an urchin of the streets, with no father. No mother. Just the less than kindly old Papa Londinium.

'Tell me, Petronius Borro; do you like fish?'

Stilicho had been in the city for a little over two months when the galloper came. He wore the uniform of the Schola Palatinae and he had orders to talk to no one but the Magister Militum.

'Veronia,' Stilicho whispered to the girl who shared his bed these days, 'business, I'm afraid.'

She sighed and reached up from her slumbers to kiss him on the cheek, reaching for her robe.

'No, no,' he patted the pillow, still warm from her head. 'No need to leave. Just become unaccountably deaf for the next few minutes, will you? By the look of that man,' he watched him again through a slit in the curtain, 'he means trouble.'

'What?' she whispered, giggling.

He threw his pillow at her, then hauled on his robe and stepped into the antechamber, from lover to general in the swish of a curtain. 'Tribune,' he nodded to the messenger.

The man dropped to one knee, head bowed. He handed Stilicho a scroll, bound with purple ribbon and a seal. 'From Vienna, sire,' he said. 'The great Theodosius is dead.'

Stilicho was not surprised. The man hadn't looked well when he'd seen him last and that was months ago. He read the letter, a missive from the senate, asking for his return in accordance with the late emperor's wishes.

'You came via Rome?'

'Yes, Sire.'

'Drop the "sire" stuff, tribune and get up. It's been a long time since we invested our emperors with divine powers and I'm not even an emperor. Where are Theodosius' boys?'

'Honorius was with his father, sir, at Mediolanum.'

'And Arcadius?'

'Constantinople, I believe.'

'And Alaric?'

'Sir?' The tribune looked blank. As far as he knew, Theodosius only had two sons. Was this another, born the wrong side of the imperial blanket?

'The Goth, man. The uncouth oaf that Theodosius has been busy ignoring or underestimating for the last five years. You know, sort of works for us and commands an army twice the size of mine.'

'Er … I don't know, sir,' the tribune had to admit.

'Well,' Stilicho sighed. 'Nothing new there, then. Get yourself some sleep, tribune. And some food. You're going back with me. And you're doing it tomorrow.'

'Must you go?' Chrysanthos was concern itself.

Stilicho, distracted as he was, looked at him coldly. 'I don't flatter myself you'll miss me, Vicarius,' he said. 'Just promise me this – there'll be no more upstart warlords from this bloody island of yours.'

Chrysanthos chuckled. 'I'm afraid I've no control over that, General,' he said.

Stilicho closed to the man. 'We both know that's not exactly true, Chrysanthos, don't we? As the guardian of *both* new emperors, I shall be paying particularly careful attention to what's going on in Britannia. Flavius Constantine will keep me informed.'

'Excellent choice,' Chrysanthos beamed. 'God smile on your voyage, Magister Militum.'

'I'm sure He will, Vicarius,' Stilicho said. 'I'm sure He will.'

The wind from the river rattled the shutters of the governor's palace that night and Honoria turned over onto her back. 'It's not that I mind, of course,' she said. 'I would just like to have felt my knife slicing through Stilicho's throat.'

Chrysanthos burst out laughing. 'It's talk like that that so upsets the ladies of the Ordo,' he said. 'In the end, I suppose, it was a stand-off. As Magister Militum, let alone as the emperor's guardian, he could have had my head. As part-owner of a murderous mistress and her equally murderous son, I could have had his. Honours even, you might say.'

'Even so,' she said, tracing her fingers languidly over his arm. 'I'm sorry it didn't work out, with Marcus, I mean. Your plans.'

'Yes,' Chrysanthos sighed. 'I will admit I chose wrong there. He never measured up to expectations.'

'He got to be caesar,' she reasoned. 'Briefly.'

Chrysanthos laughed. 'It'll take more than that to stand up to Stilicho.'

She looked at him in the candlelight, his eyes bright, his face calm and composed. 'Do you have anyone in mind?' she asked.

He turned to her. 'Yes,' he said. 'Yes, I do. The next warlord I choose to groom for high office. And this one will work, I promise.'

'Should I pack my things?' she asked archly. 'Ready for the journey to Rome?'

'A *little* premature, darling heart,' he said with a smile. 'But I do have a pretty little place in mind for you, on the Palatine. Think you'll be able to manage with just the one thousand slaves?'

Din Paladyr

Lug, the old priest of the Gododdin, had died years ago, gone to the Otherworld of his ancestors. His successor that night was Gwydyr, born of the tempest, son of the raven. At first, Justinus could barely see him in the shadows of the oak. They had left Din Paladyr as the sun fell at the end of the short spring day. All that day, Brenna, as high priestess of her people, had knelt before the mystic shrine of Belatucadros, the bright, shining one, asking for the life of the man she loved. Although she never told Justinus, in the muttered imprecations of her ritual, she made a deal with Belatucudros; a life for a life. Hers for that of the Dux Britannorum. It was the most that the queen of the Votadini could do for her Roman conqueror.

Gwydyr officiated now, in the watches of the night. Justinus sat on a chair that Brenna's people had brought out over the wild heather and placed beneath the sacred oak. He looked up at the gnarled trunk, twisted with age and the weather, at the branches with their young buds shivering in the wind from the sea. It was all a far cry from the Mithras of his experience, with the horns of the bull for comfort and the warmth of its flanks. And a far cry, too, from the Jesus of the Christians, though hadn't they nailed him to a tree years ago? Perhaps, after all, everything came full circle. Perhaps, in the end, it was all the same.

'I turn to the East,' Gwydyr intoned, in a dialect that Justinus barely understood.

'To the East, to the East,' Brenna and her under-priests repeated.

Gwydyr's face was shining gold, like the god he worshipped and the antlers of a stag splayed out from his matted hair, hung with moss and ivy. 'There is sunlight on the sea,' he said, 'and the floating weed shall bind you. Breathe, Roman, as you've never breathed before.'

This Justinus understood. His vision was blurring and his arms and legs useless, but he could still hear and he did his best to obey.

'Again,' Gwydyr barked, his eyes blank and hard in the golden mask.

Brenna knelt beside Justinus and laid a hand on his chest. His skin felt cold and clammy and he was shivering in the night air. He raised himself up, arching his back and she placed her other hand under him. Now she was easing his movement, breathing with him as she would have worked a pair of bellows. Justinus grunted through the pain in his lungs, feeling his heart thump and pound with the exertion of it all.

Gwydyr raised the gnarled wand in his hand and swung his body from side to side, keening in an unearthly scream. The wolf pelts dangling from his shoulders swayed with him and he beckoned a priest forward from the tree's shadows. The man wore the mail shirt and helmet of the Gododdin warrior and in both hands he carried a sword that Justinus had never seen before. Its blade was dark and pitted with rust and its edges were nicked with the scars of battle. The hilt, cradled in the warrior's hands, was fashioned in the shape of a man, arms and legs outstretched and mouth wide in a silent battle cry; all of it gleaming in Gododdin silver.

'Lord of battles,' Gwydyr intoned, 'take your servant, Justinus, whose soul you have guarded so many times in the field. Lady …' the high priest nodded his antlered head to Brenna and she relaxed her grip on Justinus' body, taking instead both his hands in hers. She held him fast and he had no idea what was coming. Naked as he was, weak as he was, he couldn't break the woman's grip, even as the flat of the blade slapped the suppurating wound on his shoulder. His screams filled the night and the thud of a single drum took up his racing heartbeat. As the pain subsided and the drum slowed, he saw Brenna through a film of tears, his and hers. She still held him, silently repeating his name over and over through the pain, making it pass from him with the help of Belatucudros.

Gwydyr raised his wand again, piercing the clouds of dark and another priest came forward. In his hands he carried a silver cauldron, worked with serpents that writhed around its rim. Justinus had seen no fires, no sign of cooking yet here was a broth, steaming in the night air and smelling wonderful. Brenna let his hands slip to his sides and took a ladle from the priest, scooping the bowl's contents and passing it three times around Justinus' head before lowering it to his mouth.

'Eat, Roman,' Gwydyr said. 'Build your strength in Belatucudros' name.'

The broth may have smelt divine but it tasted hellish. Justinus could not help screwing up his face as the ladle reached his lips. Brenna's face had lost its agony now and she smiled indulgently, as she would with a petulant child; as she had with the four children she had borne. They had all been the same, determined to be difficult and to fight the wisdom of the ancient ones. For her sake, he persevered and even forced down two more mouthfuls before that part of the cycle was over.

'The stone,' Gwydyr moaned and the last of the priests brought it forward. 'The power of the shining one, the sword of battles, the cauldron of goodness; anchor them all with the weight of the stone.'

'Take it, Justinus,' Brenna whispered in the dialect he understood. 'Take it in both hands.'

He did.

'Now, lift,' she murmured. 'As high as you can.'

He licked his lips and steadied himself. The stone came up out of his lap and he felt the muscles stretch and scream as he took the weight.

'Stand up!' Gwydyr snapped suddenly, speaking the language that Justinus understood. When he didn't move, the high priest gave the command again; this time, to Justinus' surprise, in Latin. The Dux Britannorum who was no longer Dux Britannorum staggered to his feet. His legs felt like lead and he couldn't feel his feet at all.

'Lift!' Gwydyr roared, again in the Roman tongue.

Justinus' breathing was ragged with the sudden exertion but he managed it, his back arching, his legs trembling as he held the stone on high.

'Hold it there!' the high priest ordered. 'Let go, Justinus Coelius and you're a dead man.'

That was the last thing that Justinus heard. And Brenna's face was the last thing he saw, before he collapsed on the heather.

Din Eidyn

The high king of Tara had brought a small retinue with him. It had been over a year since he had fled the marshes of the south country with the hostage who was now his woman. Livia had not come with him this time. Despite her protests he had folded his arms against her entreaties. There were negotiations in the wind, business to be conducted, deals to be struck. If it all went wrong, he'd have to fight his way to the sea again, as he had last time. And besides, Livia, the Roman girl from the house of Gnaeus Domitius, was now called Mhaire and she sat at the right hand of Niall of the Six Hostages. And she was with child.

Taran of the Gododdin was wearing his crown that day. He was not king yet, not as long as his little brother had a say in the matter; and not as long as his mother lived. Even so, he held Din Eidyn on its desolate crags and the only thing higher than that were the ravens that screamed and wheeled in the mares' tails of the sky.

Niall strode in at the head of his men, the battle and raid-hardened warriors of the Danann who worshipped the red god. Their mail rattled in the vaulted chambers of the great hall and they didn't bow or prostrate themselves, as the Gododdin might have expected.

'Ave, Dux Votadini,' Niall said, in his rough Latin.

The Gododdin looked at each other and at Taran.

'I'm sorry,' Niall smiled his most charming smile. 'Have I said the wrong thing?' He was speaking Gododdin now, just as roughly.

'We are not the Votadini,' Taran told him, 'whatever you may have heard.'

Niall crossed to the line of Taran's guard. He tapped the javelin of the first man he reached. 'That's a spiculum,' he said, 'a Roman weapon. That,' he pointed to a dagger in another man's belt, 'is a pugio; made, where? Hispania?' He snatched a sword hilt and slid it free of the scabbard. Its owner jumped forward to retrieve it and weapons came to the level on both sides. 'Nice,' Niall smiled, tossing the sword from one hand to another. 'Greek, unless I miss my guess. From Achea probably.' He reversed the weapon and handed it back to the man who had just lost it, 'but I can see you've had it re-hilted.'

'What's your point, Hibernius?' Taran asked.

Niall laughed. 'Exactly that,' he said. 'The Romans call us Hiberni. Your boys here fight with Roman swords and no doubt draw Roman pay. Yet you say you want these all-conquering bastards out. How am I supposed to believe that?'

Taran stood up for the first time and came down from his

dais. He was half a head shorter than the high king and fifteen years his junior, but stories of giants and forked lightning had never frightened the man who was born to rule the Gododdin. He closed to Niall so that they stood almost toe to toe. 'We fight with Roman swords and we take Roman silver because it suits us. Those blades are the best in the world and a gold solidus buys comfort anywhere from here to Thracia and beyond. But Rome was then, Niall of the Six Hostages. We've kissed arse for long enough. It's time I took my birthright.'

'Take it,' Niall shrugged. 'What do you need us for?'

Taran held up his left hand, the palm towards Niall. 'The Wall,' he said, 'and beyond it four provinces of Britannia. Three legions – the Sixth Victrix, the Twentieth Valeria Victrix and the Second Augusta, not to mention more auxiliaries than you've butchered women and children.'

There were dark murmurs and mutterings from the Hiberni ranks, but Niall quieted them with a single wave of his hand. Taran held up his right hand. 'To the north – and to the west – the Painted Ones and the Scotti, godless bastards who live for slaughter. Add to that mix a certain high king of Tara who throws in his lot with the highest bidder – I know you're in bed with the Picti at the moment, Niall; that's why you're here.'

Niall nodded. 'My private life,' he said, smiling, 'would normally be my private life; but in this particular case, you're right. It's easier to join forces with the picturesque people than to batter our heads together each time I cross the sea. What's in the middle,' he asked, 'between the left hand and the right?'

Taran let his hands fall. 'Little old me,' he said. 'The territory the Romans call Valentia. *My* territory.'

Niall wandered to the huge round table laden with cups and food and wine. He helped himself to a cup, filled it and raised it to his lips. Here he paused, amused at the faces of his own men. Had the chief gone mad? Only Dagda himself knew what poisons lay in that cup. Niall drank from it anyway.

'I assume you have a proposal?' he asked, looking at Taran.

The prince of the Gododdin nodded and took another cup, pouring from the same ewer. 'I have,' he said. 'You, me, the Gododdin, the Picti and the Scotti. Against the Wall. Against Rome.'

Niall snorted. 'It's been tried,' he said. 'With a little Saxon involvement too, if memory serves.'

'It has,' Taran knew.

'It didn't work,' Niall reminded him.

'In the days of that old rogue Valentinus, no. But that was years ago, man. And the principle was right. Strength in numbers. One goal. One purpose.'

'Save the speeches to persuade your people,' Niall said. 'What's in it for us?'

Taran clapped his hands and there was a commotion in the soldiery behind him. A dark-haired young man in a richly embroidered cloak pushed his way through the crowd, with two others standing behind him, a large oak coffer between them.

'Niall, high king of Tara,' Taran said. 'I'd like to introduce you to Scipio Honorius, Rex Inferni.'

Niall laughed and translated for the benefit of his men, who guffawed and hooted. 'Lord of Hell,' he said. 'I am impressed.' But Scipio wasn't smiling.

Taran crossed to the Hibernius and murmured in his ear. 'Careful, Niall, this man's a stone-cold killer. And I'm not sure which way his sense of humour runs.'

The high king looked across at the dark-haired man. There was something about his eyes which was, he had to admit, unnerving. 'All right,' he said, pouring wine into a third cup. 'Lord of Hell, what do you bring to this round table, exactly?' He held the cup out but Scipio didn't take it.

'You sample that first, sheep-shagger,' he said in Latin. 'Then we'll talk.' Scipio had never been further north than Flavia Caesariensis in his life and he spoke none of the dialects of the Wall, north or south of it. Niall smiled, took a deep draught, wiped his mouth and waited. Scipio clapped his hands and the two lackeys were only too glad to put the coffer down. From nowhere, there was a knife in Scipio's hand and he flicked open the lock with it. This time, Niall was *genuinely* impressed but he didn't intend to show it. The lid crashed back on its hinges and the light of gold filled Taran's hall, more gold than anyone except Scipio had seen in one place in their lives. There were gasps and mutterings in half a dozen dialects.

'That,' Scipio said, sliding the blade away, 'is a mere fraction of the wealth of Londinium, my home town.'

'Really?' Niall said. 'And what's to stop me and my boys coming south and helping ourselves?'

'Three legions,' said Scipio, echoing what he had heard earlier, 'and more auxiliaries than the women and children you've butchered.'

Slowly, Niall's grin grew to a laugh and his men laughed with him; none of them had any idea why.

'With Scipio and his people in the south,' Taran said, refilling the man's cup now that Scipio could trust it. 'You, me and the Painted Ones in the north, we can stamp out Roman Britannia once and for all. Our hammer, Scipio's anvil and the Romans a twisted piece of dead metal between us.'

Niall nodded. 'Sounds intriguing,' he said. 'But across the sea we heard that Stilicho was on the march.'

'He is,' Scipio told him, 'to the east. The emperor is dead and the Vandal's been recalled. It's all going to hell in a handcart for them. Even the Dux Britannorum's been replaced.'

Niall looked up. 'Is that because the old one's dead?' he felt bound to ask. After all, it was his lover's knife that had found its mark in Justinus Coelius' shoulder.

'As good as,' Tara told him. 'My dear mama's got him tucked up in bed. Can't last the summer.'

'And, talking of your dear mama,' Niall went on, 'what's to be done about her? And that irritating little brother of yours?'

'*Half*-brother,' Taran corrected him. 'Don't worry. You can leave them to me.'

Londinium

'Have you met my new apprentice, Pelagius?' Vitalis was pouring the man a little light wine. 'Say hello to Petronius Borro; he'll make a good basket maker, in ten or twenty years.'

'Pleased to meet you, sir.' Petronius was carrying the reeds to the drying yards but he managed a half-bow anyway.

'Just Pelagius,' Pelagius said. 'And I'm pleased to meet you, Petronius Borro.'

When he'd gone, Pelagius sat himself down in a corner of Vitalis' workshop. 'A waif and stray, Vit?' he asked, nodding in the boy's direction.

'Aren't we all that, one way or another?' Vitalis asked. Then, he became more serious. 'Pelagius, I heard there was a price on your head.'

'Mine?' Pelagius laughed. 'You flatter me, Vit.'

'No, I mean it. It was the talk of the forum yesterday. Severianus wants your head. It'll be exile at least.'

'He doesn't have the power,' Pelagius said.

'You caught him in a lie,' Vitalis reminded him, 'and a public one at that. I don't know how the man shows his face in public these days.'

'No,' Pelagius sighed, 'neither do I. But God will judge him, Vit. It's not up to us.'

'I thought you'd leave with Stilicho.'

'No,' Pelagius said. 'No, I never had any intention of that. I will go back to Rome one day. And perhaps next time, you really will go with me.'

'Yes,' Vitalis smiled. 'Perhaps I really will.'

CHAPTER XV

Din Paladyr

Night lay deep over the bare rock above the estuary. The water ran silver under a fitful moon, hiding now and then behind sheltering clouds. In the Gododdin stronghold, fires were dying with the coming of the dawn, a pale light far to the east.

He made no sound as he slid the sword from its sheath, treading carefully on the steps that led to the queen's private quarters. At her door, he stopped and listened. She was breathing softly, sighing as she turned under the wolfskins. He smelt the herbs that dangled from her ceiling and ducked back into the darkness. He knew the way of old, knew the room he was looking for. And he reached it now. He licked his ash-dry lips and hoped that no one else could hear the thud of his heart. With his left hand he pressed the rough planks and the door swung inward. No sound. He waited until his eyes had grown accustomed to the dark, standing aside so that his silhouette did not fill the open doorway.

He could make out the bed now and the sleeping figure lying on it. In the corner, the sword of Justinus Coelius leaned against the wall. Even if the man in bed was wide awake, he could never reach that sword in time. He'd be sleepy, disoriented, his reflexes unsure.

Slowly, he edged forward, the sword point ahead of him, half feeling his way in the darkness. With his left hand he reached out, feeling the wolf pelt under his fingers, sliding over the fur. Then he yanked them back, yelling the old Gododdin war cry and raising the sword. He felt a sickening thud between his shoulder blades and hit the wolfskin, his nose in the fur. There was a dagger point tickling his ear and a body was straddling him, pinning him to the bed.

'They told me you were better,' he said through the fur. 'I had to see for myself.'

He felt someone hauling him up by the hair and he turned to see Justinus smiling down at him. 'You didn't think I'd forgotten the old game, Eddi?' he asked. 'My old papa taught me before he taught you, remember?'

Edern remembered. It was a game that the Dux Britannorum had played with his father since he was a boy when old Flavius was still primus pilus with the VI Victrix. And no matter how promoted Justinus was and how renowned he became, he could never *quite* get the better of the old man. Flavius had passed the trick onto Brenna's boys and now, history was repeating itself.

'Old age and cunning are always going to beat youth and brawn,' Justinus said, sheathing the knife.

'I thought you were going to kill me,' Edern laughed.

'No.' Justinus laughed with him. 'I only ever kill slaves this early in the morning.'

Edern looked at the man who had ridden all those years ago with his father. When he had last seen him, he thought it might be for the last time. His mother's affairs of state had taken him south, to the Wall, but on his way back, a messenger had reached him. Brenna's prayers had been answered. The Christians to the south would call it a miracle, but it was Belatucadros who had worked his wonders again. Edern's eyes were big with tears to see Justinus on his feet again. 'I've brought your Roman friends from Onnum,' he said. 'The decurion Calpurnius and his family.'

'You have?' Justinus helped the lad up off the bed. 'Good. Good. Now, how about some breakfast? I could eat a horse.'

Patricius was fascinated by them and couldn't look away. He was supposed to be watching his little sister, but when you're ten, little sisters are nothing but a nuisance. She couldn't run as fast as he could. She couldn't catch a ball. And as for wrestling, forget it! What are girls for, he had asked his father once. And Calpurnius had laughed and told the boy he would find out one day.

Tullia was fascinated too. It was exhausting trying to keep up with Patric, especially when he pulled her hair and ran away. And the idiot had no interest in dolls at all. She wasn't old enough yet to ask her mother what boys were for. But she already knew they weren't for fun.

The tiny insects buzzed and darted in the blue of the summer's day before circling with their curious flight patterns to cluster on the hive. Old Cran had been tending the queen's bees for as long as he could remember. He knew their seasons, their habits. He loved them and they loved him. And he never failed to love the look on the faces of little children the first time they saw the bees. The old man's face and hands were lumpy and disfigured, victim as he was of countless bee stings. That all happened when he was young and had not understood the creatures' ways. They never stung him now.

He smiled at the boy and girl watching him across the tall grass and he beckoned them over.

'What's your name?' he asked the girl, his Latin a little shaky.

'Tullia,' she said, uncertain of the old man's scarred face and standing unusually close to her big brother.

'Do you like sweet things, Tullia?' Cran asked.

She nodded.

'Try this, then.' The old man lifted a piece of honeycomb from the hive. There was a mild protest from the bees, and they took to the air briefly before forgiving him and circling back again.

'Take it,' Patricius told her, vaguely annoyed at his sister's cowardice. 'It's honeycomb. The bees make it.'

'How?' Tullia wanted to know.

Patricius' knowledge of bees had already come to an end.

'That's their secret,' Cran murmured, smiling. 'They have lots of secrets, bees. Well, do you like it?'

Tullia had almost forgotten the sticky slab in her hand, wondering what secrets the bees kept from the world and she sniffed it. Nice. She put her lips to it. Sweet. She bit into it. Delicious. Soon, she was chomping like a cow in a new pasture, trying to free her teeth from the stickiness and cram yet more in.

'What about you?' Cran looked at Patricius. The boy shook his head. He had tasted honeycomb before once, in a market in Londinium and he wasn't going to make a fool of himself like Tullia was doing at that very moment. Their father was a decurion, for God's sake, even up here at the edge of the world; there were standards.

'No, of course not.' Cran put the honeycomb back again, to a background of loud buzzing. He bent down and picked up a goatskin sack from the grass. 'A man should try something more befitting.'

This was better. A bit of recognition. This was more like it.

'What is it?' Patricius asked. If it was water, how boring! If it was wine, he'd had that before and he didn't really like it.

'A drink the bees make,' Cran told him. 'We call it mead.' He handed to goatskin to the boy, who took it cautiously.

'Go on,' Tullia goaded him, but Patricius hadn't moved. 'I'll have it if you won't.' Her mouth was still full of honeycomb. She made a grab for the goatskin but her brother was faster.

'No, you won't!' he shouted and took a swig. His eyes swivelled in all directions. His throat burned with a strange fire, a fire that was sickly sweet. It left him with a thirst for more and he took a hefty swig.

'Not too much,' Cran warned. 'The nectar of the bees takes a bit of getting used to.'

Tullia screamed. There was a bee on her hand and she shook it off, screaming again as one settled in her hair.

'No, no,' Cran said softly, taking the girl firmly by the shoulders. 'Don't do that. You'll frighten them. Look. They're just saying hello. Look.'

The old man's Latin was rusty but Tullia understood enough to calm down and she found herself peering intently as the bees swarmed around her, darting down for a closer look and taking to the sky again. 'See.' Cran knelt beside her in the grass. 'See how they work together, helping each other? You'll never find people doing that.'

'Do they have names?' she asked him.

'Don't be stupid,' Patricius sneered, but Cran interrupted him.

'Indeed they do. Their ruler, their queen, is called Claudia.'

'That's a Roman name,' Tullia said.

'Is it?' Cran asked. 'I think it's a very pretty name.'

'So do I,' the girl said, feeling increasingly at one with the hive.

Patricius took another swig of the mead. Funny how everything looked more rosy now. The sun was warmer, the flowers more fragrant. Old Cran of the hideous face was kindness itself. Even his little sister wasn't so annoying.

'The bees come,' Cran told them, 'from the world of the sun, from the realm of Belatucadros himself. They bring second sight. That one there, see him, on your arm?'

Tullia nodded. The little creature held no terrors for her

now.

'That's Bleddri, the wolf. He hunts for new places for the hive. And tells the queen. When she flies, oh, my children, you should see it. A thousand, thousand wings fluttering in the air, darkening the sky. They dance in the sun, telling of new pastures with the sweetest flowers. Even Gwydyr, our high priest, dances in their fashion, leaping the flames and crossing the water. And it's Gwydyr, who sees the future, who must tell the bees when someone dies; that's very important. Listen.'

Conchessa's children hardly dared breathe. This old man with his knotted face and his kindly eyes had hypnotised them as surely as the basilisk their old nanny had told them about. 'Hear that? Hear their hum? It's their song.'

'What are they singing about?' Tullia whispered, wide-eyed.

Cran smiled. 'About their loves,' he said, 'and the sights they have seen. Up there,' he pointed to the sky, 'where the winds play and where we humans will never go.'

'Never, old man?' A harsh Latin voice shattered the peaceful moment. All three of them looked up. So engrossed had they become with the bees, they hadn't heard the horsemen trotting through the grass, knee high to their horses. The riders of the Danann looked down at them. Cran staggered to his feet. He had never seen these men before, with their wild red hair and their bronze helmets. The man at their front was huge and heads, eyeless now and with leather skin, dangled by the hair from his saddle bow. Without warning, he threw a short axe that tumbled briefly through the air before thudding into Cran's chest. The old man gasped, the breath knocked out of him and he staggered backwards, blood bubbling from his nose and mouth. He crashed through the hive and the bees rose in a mighty swarm, buzzing madly and filling the air with their noise and fury.

'Run, Tullia!' Patricius threw away the goatskin and grabbed the girl's hand, still sticky as it was with honeycomb. They leapt over the grass tussocks, desperate to escape the horsemen. The ramparts of Din Paladyr lay dumb in the afternoon heat and seemed very, very far away. Neither of them cried out for help, they were too busy trying to keep their footing. Again and again Tullia stumbled, crying and again Patricius stopped to pick her up. In the end, it was pointless. In the end the horses were ahead of them, as well as behind, and they closed in.

The children of Conchessa knelt in the grass, clutching each other. Patricius cursed himself; he'd left his knife in their new quarters in the fortress and now all he had was his fists. The leader of the riders swung out of the saddle and stooped to force them apart. Little as he was, Patricius knew he had to do something. His father had not taught him to ride yet, but he had taught him to fight and Patricius smashed both fists into the horseman's face. There was a sickening crunch and blood trickled over the auburn beard. A sword flew clear of a scabbard behind him.

'No need for that,' he chuckled in his native tongue. 'We've got a little warrior here. Bring him along.'

'What about the girl?' somebody asked.

The chieftain looked at her tear-stained cheeks and silently moving lips. She wanted to cry again but she wasn't going to do that in front of this monster. 'Too little,' he said. 'She'll only slow us up.' And he made for his horse while someone grabbed Patricius and hauled him over his saddle bow, head, legs and arms dangling.

'Wait.' The chieftain stopped with his hands on the reins. 'What's your name, girl?' he asked in a tongue she understood.

'Tullia,' she said defiantly, hands on her hips.

'Well, Tullia, you run along now. And you tell your mama and papa that your brother has gone away.' He swung easily into the saddle. 'Gone with Niall of the Six Hostages … no, make that seven. And he's never coming back.'

Edern's patrol came back as night fell. His riders knew every inch of Valentia but even they could not see in the dark. He went straight to his mother, sitting with Conchessa alongside little Tullia's bed. The child had cried herself to sleep and lay peacefully now, except that a worried frown creased her forehead and her fingers flew now and then, as if she was still trying to catch Patric's hand and keep him safe. And all the time before sleep had claimed her, she feared for her big brother and knew that she must summon up the courage to go and tell the bees that he had gone.

Both women stood up at Edern's entrance, but there was no boy with him and nothing but disappointment etched in his face. He shook his head. 'We followed the tracks north,' he told them, 'as far as the Old Rocks. Nothing. We'll start again in the morning, try the west. Unless Justinus has struck lucky to the south.'

Justinus had not struck lucky. He wasn't as familiar as Edern with the wastes of Valentia that led to the old, ruined Wall of Antoninus

Pius, but he knew the sheep tracks to the south and that was the way he had ridden. Calpurnius rode with him. His grasp of the Gododdin tongue was not enough for him to lead a patrol of his own so he had stayed with Justinus. Another patrol had ridden north-west and yet another south-west. Gwydyr the high priest, seeing visions of the lost boy in his fire-smoke, had led his horsemen east, hugging the coast in case Niall of the Seven Hostages had run to a ship.

It had been dark for over an hour when Justinus reined in his horse.

'Why are you stopping?' Calpurnius wanted to know.

'The horses need rest, Calpurnius,' Justinus told him. 'So do we.'

'No,' the decurion said as the others eased themselves out of their saddles. 'I'm going on.'

'Good luck with that,' Justinus said. He had not ridden this far and this hard since his wound and it had taken its toll. 'It'll be all of an hour however you measure it before you're lost. You'll be lucky to find your arse by then.'

'We're talking about my son here, Justinus!' Calpurnius roared. Ever since Tullia had come scurrying into Din Paladyr, her legs ripped by brambles and her hair wild, Calpurnius had been in a turmoil. He knew that Patricius was not his by blood, but he loved him for all that. He had knelt down in front of the hysterical girl, calmed her down, got the story from her. He had held Conchessa to him for a brief moment and then dashed to find a horse. Nothing else mattered.

'And you're thinking like a father.' Justinus lifted the shield from his horse's back. 'Start thinking like a decurion of Rome.'

'Go to hell!' Calpurnius hauled at his rein. He didn't, in the darkness, see the nod from Justinus but the others did and they surrounded his horse, hemming him in so that the animal couldn't move. Calpurnius rammed his heels against the horse's flanks but the beast held firm, the Gododdin standing close and whispering to it. He drew his sword.

'I wouldn't do that,' Justinus warned him, but it was too late. Hands reached up and dragged the decurion from the saddle, sending him sprawling to the sheep-cropped grass and wrenching the sword out of his grip. He looked up at them. How many were there? Twenty? Thirty? They were his allies. They were Justinus' friends. But in this mad, dark world north of the Wall, none of that counted for very much.

'I haven't got to hobble you, have I, Calpurnius?' Justinus asked. 'Treat you like a jittery horse?'

'No,' the decurion said, getting up slowly as the men moved back. 'No, you haven't.' He looked at them all, trying his limited Gododdin on them. 'But at first light, I'm on the road again.'

He felt Justinus' hand on his shoulder. 'At first light,' he said, softly, 'we all are.'

Londinium

The Sanctus bell was sounding as Pelagius crossed the flagstones outside Severianus' church. Gallius the sacristan had watched him for some minutes. Was the man mad? he wondered to himself. Didn't he know that the bishop had banished him from Londinium? That he had no right to cross this threshold? Gallius scuttled along the cloister as fast as his legs could carry him, ducking past the old pagan columns that held up Christ's roof. He crashed into the nave, dashing down its dark length with robes flying.

'Lord Bishop! Lord Bishop!'

Severianus was in his counting house behind the altar and popped his head out at the commotion. 'Gallius!' he chided. 'This is God's house. What *is* the matter with you, man?'

'He's here!' Gallius gabbled, fighting for breath. 'It's him. He's here!'

Severianus was on his feet. He followed the man's trembling finger along the shadows of the nave and a man stood in the doorway, the Londinium sun at his back. The bishop checked himself. He knew who it was. Names were superfluous. There was only one man in Londinium, in the whole of Maxima Caesariensis who could put his sacristan in such a flutter. Clinging to what remained of his dignity, Severianus made the sign of the cross. 'Pelagius, my son; you are not welcome here.'

'Not welcome, my Lord Bishop?' Pelagius' voice boomed down into the crypt. 'This is a house of God. And I am a child of God.'

Severianus waited until the man had reached him. 'You are a son of the Devil,' he growled.

Pelagius smiled. 'Time will tell us that,' he said, 'when you and I stand before our Maker. Where will His finger point, Severianus?'

The bishop said nothing.

'I have come to surrender myself.' Pelagius got straight to the point.

'What?' Severianus blinked.

'You have accused me of blasphemy,' Pelagius said, 'because I made you swear on oath. Why did you do that, Severianus, if you told the truth? I would have thought you would have welcomed the chance to tell your congregation, to wash your hands of innocent blood, like Pilate.'

'Heretic!' Severianus screamed.

'Liar,' Pelagius said quietly. 'How much is the price you have placed on my head?'

'Twenty solidi,' the bishop told him.

Pelagius laughed. 'Well, I'm flattered. Twenty gold pieces outstrips thirty of silver, I suppose. Now who's the blasphemer, my Lord Bishop?'

Severianus was speechless. He had sworn on the Bible when he had Stilicho to back him. Now, Stilicho was gone and he had no one. Pelagius stood close to him, watching the bishop's eyes flicker and his jaw flex. 'You can keep your money,' he said. 'I've saved you the trouble.' He held out his hands. When Severianus didn't move, he stripped the tunic back and let it hang from his waist. 'I assume you have people to do the whipping,' he said.

'I want you gone,' Severianus hissed, beside himself with anger.

'I'm sure you do,' Pelagius smiled. 'But that would be too easy, wouldn't it? No, I'm going to stay, at least for a while. Lock me up, Lord Bishop. I won't give any trouble.'

For a moment, Severianus hesitated. He wanted to strike this renegade down, this dangerous maniac with his belief in the goodness of man. But he was a bishop of the church of Rome. More than that, he was a coward. Pelagius hauled his tunic back over his shoulders.

'You, sacristan,' he called to Gallius, lurking in the columns' shadows. 'You are witness, before us and before God. I offered my body to the bishop and he turned me down. That means that I am now a free man. Agreed, my lord?'

Severianus blinked again. This was the second time in months that Pelagius had humiliated him, on this very spot, in his own church. 'Oh,' Pelagius turned to go, 'and that twenty solidi. Why don't you use that to rebuild the temple of Isis? That would be a *real* act of Christian charity, don't you think?'

The basilica was all but deserted and the candles fluttered in the night air. Chrysanthos the vicarius was intrigued. In his dealings with Scipio Honorius, he had usually worked through Honoria, sure in the knowledge that she would relay his information accurately and to his advantage. If Honoria were elsewhere, he would meet the Rex Inferni on some street corner, under an arch where the harlots rutted away the night. It was beneath him, of course, but Chrysanthos had not got to run four provinces by being nice.

But tonight was different. Tonight, the King of the Underworld had asked to see him, as if he was some visiting dignitary. The hour, of course, was unusual, but Scipio Honorius always had something of the night about him. Chrysanthos hadn't expected the entourage either but there were four men with Scipio and they had not come to see Londinium's sights. The one on the far left he recognized. The name had slipped his mind but he was Scipio's right hand man in the Black Knives; he'd skin his granny for a solidus. The others were tall, auburn-haired and bristling with weapons. Chrysanthos' own guard had been disinclined to let them in, but the vicarius had waved them aside and they stood now in the basilica's great hall, arms folded, waiting. Their helmets hung from their studded belts and for all it was still high summer, their shoulders were hung with wolf-skins, coated with dust.

'To what do I owe the pleasure, little Scip?' Chrysanthos had not moved from his seat on the dais.

'I'll get to that,' Scipio said, ignoring the condescension, 'but first, some wine for my friends. We've had a long ride.'

The vicarius didn't signal to his slaves or make any move himself. 'Help yourself,' he said. Scipio crossed to a table and poured cups for the five of them. Chrysanthos' cup stayed empty, where it was.

'Allow me to introduce,' Scipio said and passed a cup to the tallest of the four. 'This is Nectan, of the painted ones. He doesn't speak Latin, but he speaks for his people.'

Chrysanthos nodded. The man had the build of an oak tree and wild designs swirled in blue over the skin of his shaved head and bare arms. The warrior knocked back his wine in one and belched.

'This is Eochaid, of the Hiberni. He speaks for Niall Mugmedon, high king of Tara.' Eochaid had not learned the Latin his master knew and he grunted something incomprehensible. The others laughed.

'Will you share the joke, Scipio?' Chrysanthos asked.

'He says this basilica will burn well,' the King of the Underworld explained. And Chrysanthos laughed too.

'Here,' Scipio led the man forward, 'is Modron – quaint name, isn't it, for one so clearly masculine. It means "mother".'

'Quaint indeed,' Chrysanthos agreed. 'And who does he speak for? Assuming he can speak, that is.'

Scipio ignored the sneering jibe. 'He speaks for Taran, King of the Votadini. Oh, and you know Caius, of course.'

'Of course.' Chrysanthos smiled and nodded to the man. 'Nice to see *someone* who speaks the language and comes from the civilized south.'

Caius broke wind and raised his cup in salutation.

'Well, well,' the vicarius left his chair and poured himself some wine of his own. 'Tell me, Scipio, did you run into these gentlemen in some brothel somewhere or have they come, hotfoot, from further afield?'

'We've come from the north,' Scipio told him, 'all of us – except Caius; you know what a homebody he is.'

'You can't even take the boy out of Londinium,' Chrysanthos said. 'Yes, I see. But tell me … er … Modron, is it?'

The sound of his name made the Gododdin stand taller.

'Brenna is ruler of the Votadini. Does he speak for her?'

'She's an irrelevance,' Scipio assured him, 'as is Justinus Coelius.'

'Dead?' Chrysanthos asked.

'As good as.'

'I see.' The vicarius sipped a little more. 'So, this deputation …'

Scipio put his cup down and crossed to the vicarius. 'Who did you have in mind,' he asked him, 'to replace Terentius Marcus?'

'Replace?' Chrysanthos could be as obtuse as the next man when it suited him. 'I don't understand.'

Scipio chuckled, 'Yes, you do,' he said. 'Did you really think that your idle pillow talk with my dear mama would go no further? I know your game, Chrysanthos. You're a puppeteer, aren't you? A puller of strings. It's more effective that way. You see, you're an ambitious bastard … not unlike me, in fact. You'd like to wear the purple yourself, sit on an emperor's throne. But there's a risk in that, isn't there? You've usually got to fight somebody for the privilege. And if even Magnus Maximus couldn't do that, what possible chance would you have? So you needed a soldier, someone bent who would do your bidding but someone who could nevertheless handle himself in the field. Pity you chose Marcus. I could have told you he wasn't worth wiping your arse with. Now, me now … well, that's a different proposition altogether.'

Chrysanthos was shocked and appalled, all at once, but tried not to show it. 'You?' he said. 'I never had you down for a warlord, Scipio.'

'Running the streets of Londinium as I do,' the man said, refilling his cup, 'is not a million miles away from ordering a legion or two. That's why these gentlemen are here. I've already got the Votadini, the Picti and the Hiberni at my back. The legions will just be the gilt on the gingerbread.'

'Fascinating.' Chrysanthos was chuckling and shaking his head. 'So what do you need me for?'

'That's funny,' Scipio joined in the joke, 'that's more or less what the high king of Tara said. Why not just take Londinium? He hasn't seen your walls, Chrysanthos and he hasn't faced a legion in the field. There's no point in breaking our balls with a little local difficulty, fighting each other, when there's no need.'

'I repeat,' Chrysanthos said, 'what do you need me for?'

'Your money.' Scipio came right out with it. 'The taxes and moveables of Britannia. It costs money to mount a campaign. And … I concede you *do* have a certain organizational flair. If you set your seal on my endeavours …'

'If I did that,' Chrysanthos said, 'I'd be a dead man. That's why I didn't back Terentius Marcus openly; any more than I backed Magnus Maximus. Talking of whom …' the vicarius looked from one man to another and all he saw was thuggery, 'are you *really* big enough to fill his boots, Scipio?'

'There's one way to find out,' the King of the Underworld said. 'First, I'm going to change my name. There's already one Honorius on the emperor's throne, for all he's still a snivelling brat. So, to avoid confusion across my empire … I thought perhaps Gratianus. I've always liked the name.'

'Gratian,' Chrysanthos repeated. 'That has a ring to it, certainly. You'll have to be elected caesar first, of course, win the army over.'

'I'm on my way south now,' Scipio told him. 'I'll start with the Second Augusta, at Rutupiae.'

Chrysanthos smiled. 'Well,' he said, 'good luck with that, Caesar Gratianus.'

Din Paladyr

Conchessa wandered the windy ramparts that night as she had every night since her boy had gone. There had been no sign of him and no word from Niall of the Seven Hostages. She had barely seen Calpurnius in the weeks that had passed. He had been out every day, often away for days, with Justinus' patrols, chasing a ghost, desperately clinging to a hope. And the autumn had come to Valentia and the shortening of the days. Conchessa rarely let little Tullia out of her sight these days and cuddled her to sleep every night. The girl knew, of course, what had happened to her big, bossy brother, but even so, she didn't really understand. He couldn't really be dead, because she still hadn't told the bees. And if she *never* told the bees, then everything would be all right, somehow. So, she asked mother nearly every night, 'Mama, when *is* Patric coming home?'

But her Mama didn't know.

LIBER III
CHAPTER XVI

Hadrianopolis

The fires blazed into the night, reflected in the rippling waters of the Hebros. Drums and warhorns thudded and brayed in that night's music, punctuated by the whoops and howls of the warriors. All of them had armour now, the mail coats and helmets of the Roman workshops. Their long hair flew in the chill wind and they danced and feinted with their swords, the iron clashing in the ritual of mock battle.

He had known that this night would come. For months he had known it. And when he heard of the death of Theodosius he had told his scribes to write letters to Honorius, the new emperor in the West; and to Arcadius, the new emperor in the East. Above all, he had written to Stilicho, the guardian of them both. He reminded the half Vandal, half emperor of what Rome owed to him. He and his people had served the empire faithfully for years now; had stood in the trenches of the army camps, ridden over the bloody miles, gained the hard yards. They had fallen without number under the eagle and now it was their turn for some balance, some reward. Gold and silver were mere trinkets. What he wanted for his people was land and a permanent home, they who had wandered for so long.

He had received no reply from Honorius, boy that he was. He had heard nothing from Arcadius, even though the boy had the first hairs on his chin now. Above all, he had heard nothing from Stilicho; and the silence said it all.

So, it had come to this night and to this place, along the Hebros where the emperor Valens had been destroyed, an arrow through his imperial head. The place was right. The time was right.

He strode from his quarters, resplendent in his gilded scale armour, the sword strapped to his hip and his face grim and hard behind the cheekplates of the spangenhelm. They cheered wildly, steading the huge coffin-shaped shield and he climbed onto it. They lifted him bodily, carrying him to the greatest of the bonfires. He stood like a rock on that shield, barely swaying with the movement, his legs planted apart and his arms folded.

'Where is Rome?' he roared over the noise.

'There!' The cry was taken up and spears and swords pointed to the west.

'No!' he yelled back at them, raising a hand. He opened the gloved fist and a handful of earth flew away on the right. 'I have it here, in the palm of my hand.' And the answering roar was the loudest that the city of Hadrian had ever heard.

He was Alaric, king of the Goths, and he was about to claim his birthright.

Rutupiae

'Scipio who?' Gerontius had had a long day. Now that Constantine was Dux Britannorum, travelling Britannia to check the legions to the west and north, he was praeses *and* commander of the II Augusta and he hadn't expected so much paperwork. The lamps were glowing in his principia and he was annoyed that some stranger had arrived just as he had been about to turn in.

The guard who had made the announcement was unceremoniously barged aside and a young man stood there, cloaked and tired from travel. 'Scipio Gratianus,' he said, his dark eyes smouldering at the tribune.

Gerontius was none the wiser. 'And?'

Scipio clicked his fingers and two lackeys emerged from the darkness, carrying a chest. They put it down, glad to lose the burden and Scipio flicked open the lid. The tribune who had risen to praeses blinked, the gold in the coffer shining into his face. 'That's for the Second,' Scipio said.

'It is?' Gerontius wasn't taking all this in.

Scipio crossed to a table and helped himself to Gerontius' wine. 'What about you?' he asked the man. 'What do you want?'

'Me?'

'Permanent command of the Second Augusta, of course,' Scipio went on. 'Double … no, *triple* salary, so you can afford some decent wine. After that … what shall we say? Dux Britannorum?'

'Are you serious?' Gerontius felt he had to ask.

'I took you for a soldier,' Scipio frowned, 'but perhaps administration is more to your taste …' he looked at the chaos of parchment on the man's table. 'Vicarius, then?'

'Unless I am completely out of touch,' Gerontius poured himself a cup too, 'we already have a Dux Britannorum and a vicarius.'

'Oh, yes,' Scipio smiled, 'but Constantine was appointed by Stilicho, wasn't he? And Stilicho's not here. And as for Chrysanthos, well, his days of lording it over us all are well and truly over.'

'Have they displeased the emperor?'

Scipio roared with laughter and clapped a patronising arm around the older man. 'Gerontius, Gerontius,' he said as the laugh subsided. 'If you're talking about Honorius, the boy is barely twelve. His closest friends are his chickens and his bollocks have yet to drop. Do you seriously think anyone gives a shit about what displeases him?'

'Stilicho, then.' Gerontius cut to the chase. 'Have the Dux and the vicarius offended *him*?'

'That's irrelevant.' Scipio refreshed his cup, average though the wine was.

'Irrelevant? Why?'

'Because,' Scipio said patiently, 'Stilicho is yesterday's man. And Honorius? It's as though he never sat on his papa's throne.'

'I'm missing something,' Gerontius confessed.

Scipio sighed. 'All right,' he said. 'Allow me to spell it out. You are looking at your new Caesar, Scipio Gratianus – the names of two great Romans rolled into one. If that isn't an omen, I don't know what is.'

'Believe in omens, do you?' the tribune asked.

Scipio closed to the man and stared into his eyes, cold and hard. 'I believe in reality,' he said. 'The reality that gold and power can buy me.'

'It's not just about the Second,' Gerontius reminded him. '*All* the legions must declare you Caesar; it's the way of it.'

'That won't be a problem,' Scipio smiled, wandering to a couch and sprawling on it. 'I saw the look on your face just now, the lure of the gold. Any one of your lice-ridden bastards in this camp would skin his own mother for a single coin of that. I know it. You know it. It'll be the same with the other legions.'

'It's been tried,' Gerontius said solemnly. 'Terentius Marcus. I can show you his grave if you like.'

'Terentius Marcus was a waste of space,' Scipio grunted. 'Couldn't find his arse with both hands, that man.'

Gerontius shook his head. 'Constantine will stop you,' he warned.

'No, he won't,' Scipio said, 'because, sooner than he realises, the new Dux will have his hands full elsewhere.'

'What do you mean?' Gerontius asked.

Scipio finished his wine and stood up. 'When you're officially Dux Britannorum,' he said, 'I'll tell you. Until then … You've got three days, Gerontius, to think over my offer, sort out the details of the Caesar ceremony. If you accept, I'll have myself measured for the laurel wreath. If you don't …' he snapped shut the gold chest, 'well, the end of another beautiful dream, eh?'

Din Paladyr

The summer had gone since Patricius Succatus was taken. The Gododdin had ridden hard and wide, over the purple of the moors, asking at Roman waystations and in native villages. No one had seen a boy in the company of tall men, a slave dragged along behind a horse. In his darkest moments, Justinus Coelius knew what had happened to Conchessa's boy and what would happen to him. Patricius would have sailed the wild Hibernian Sea to the hills of Tara, that godless region where the eagles had never flown. He would be learning the incomprehensible language of the Hiberni and would become, perhaps like the girl Livia, more than his slave. Perhaps little Patricius would become almost his son.

Conchessa thought that too, but she kept her thoughts to herself. She had come to like Brenna, as Vitalis said she would, but Brenna knew nothing of Conchessa's past, that Patricius was not Calpurnius' son. Did that matter? It was common in the scheme of things; there were bastards all over the empire. What mattered, to Conchessa, was that Patricius was the daily reminder of a love she had lost, a happiness she would never know again. Except that he was not a daily reminder now. Patricius had gone.

Tullia rarely left her mother's side. She played with her dolls, chattering to herself in the brightness of the day. But at night she cuddled close to Conchessa, murmuring and whimpering as the games in her head became dark and frightening. In all of them, her dolls fought each other, shouting and snarling, struggling in the recesses of the nursery. In all of them, the bees droned, buzzing in the darkness, searching from the sky for her lost brother.

Calpurnius had stopped looking. He would never give up, he told Conchessa. He would find Patric, he told Tullia and bring him home. Every now and then he took out a pointless patrol. Now that he knew Valentia nearly as well as the Votadini did, he followed the streams and the sheep-paths, his horses trudging through the snows of the high country, facing the vicious winds from the north. And he solemnly sent his reports by galloper to the Wall. The garrison there sent other riders south, bringing news of the frozen north to Chrysanthos the vicarius.

Londinium

Chrysanthos the vicarius rubbed his eyes. It was late. It was cold and the basilica had more draughts than the merchant ships that rocked at their wharves along the Thamesis. He was always vaguely surprised when another report came from Calpurnius. Yes, he was still paying the man but as far away as he was, it would have been easy for him to slip into the shadowland, put on the rough clothes of the Votadini and forget he was a Roman. On second thoughts, Chrysanthos mused, that was not Calpurnius' way. The man was a pain in the arse, but his past was shady and Calpurnius had ghosts to lay. Shame about the boy, but that sort of thing happened in Valentia. There was no God north of the Wall.

'All quiet on the northern front?' Honoria ran her eyes over Calpurnius' letter. There was a time when she didn't bother with such trivia, leaving the minutiae of politics to Chrysanthos. But now that Scipio had revealed ambitions of his own, she thought she ought to pay a little more attention.

'Hmm?' Chrysanthos was elsewhere, looking at another parchment scroll. 'Oh, yes. No change there.'

'What's that?' Honoria had lived with the vicarius for years now. She knew his moods, his inflection. A flick of the head, a hardening of the eyes; she could read the unreadable when most men could not.

'It's from Stilicho,' he said.

'Don't tell me the bastard's coming back.'

'No.' Chrysanthos half smiled. 'You can put your knife away, dearest. The Goths have declared Alaric their king.'

'Should I have heard of him?' Honoria poured them both a cup of wine.

'Perhaps not.' Chrysanthos thanked her with a nod. 'But you will. The Goths elect their leaders from a council of elders. And they don't call them kings. This is something new.'

'And worrying?' Honoria liked to know where she stood.

'Stilicho says Alaric is on the rampage across Graecia. He's taken Sparta, Argos and Corinth.'

Honoria shrugged. 'The far side of the moon,' she said.

'Maybe, maybe, but Alaric's a general, through and through. He can't take Constantinople and he knows it. The walls are too strong for him. But he's coming west, that's certain. He'll turn on Italia next and that means Rome.'

'And that means we can kiss goodbye to our villa on the Palatine.'

'We can,' Chrysanthos nodded, 'but more than that, darling heart. Without Rome, Britannia will be adrift. We'll be on our own. Which is why …' he reached over to tap Calpurnius' letter, 'I'm glad there is no news from the north.'

Honoria sipped her wine. 'Hate him with a passion though I do,' she said, 'I have every faith in Stilicho. He'll stop this Alaric.'

Pollentia

Stilicho stopped Alaric at Pollentia. It was Easter and the Goths had halted their advance on Italia to celebrate the Christian Mass. Incense hung heavy on the morning air and the smoke drifted across the barracks of Alaric's camp, high over the Tamaro.

In that dawn, celebrating the rising of the Christ from the dead, the Alpes peaks gleamed a pale purple in the haze. The snows had been slight that year and the spring rains had not turned the plains of Italia into the usual quagmire. The hard riding cavalry of the Goths had reached Hasta where the boy emperor Honorius huddled, surrounded by his nervous advisers and his chickens. The arrival of Stilicho had driven them back to Pollentia, but here Alaric would hold.

His priests had been kneeling in prayer when Stilicho's cavalry struck. Alaric could not believe that a Christian general would give battle on this sacred day and his scouts on the hills had let down their guard. While the Alans charged, hacking down the supplicants in the spring grass, the half Vandal ordered forward his infantry legions, marching in the dread silence they had employed for four hundred years, shields locked, spears ready, the boots thudding over the ground of north Italia. A hail of arrows hit them at the vallum, iron points biting into shields. This was war in the old style and no one waged it better than Stilicho. In the little scrap he had had with Terentius Marcus, both sides had used their wild asses to smash through men and level the field. Alaric had no such siege engines, just the desperate bodies of his men.

All day the battle raged as Stilicho's troops stormed the palisades and drove the Goths back. And by nightfall, as the fires proclaimed another Roman victory, a sorry little cohort was led into the general's presence. Stilicho sat with his legionary comrades, his warlords of the Numidians, the Sarmatians and the Alans who served under his scarlet flag. A slave was working on the man's muscles, the mail and tunic laid aside and the blood of others wiped away.

Stilicho looked up. 'Who are you?' He spoke the Gothic language well enough, but was surprised to hear the answer in Latin.

'I am Trajata,' the woman said.

'You are Alaric's woman?'

'No,' she held her head high, 'I am Alaric's wife.'

Stilicho brushed the slave's ministrations away and looked at her. She was beautiful, as arrogant as any Roman matron from Augusta Treverorum or Ravenna; nearly as arrogant, he smiled to himself, as his own Serena. 'And these,' he murmured, 'are Alaric's children.'

'They are.' Trajata held them to her, a girl perhaps six and two smaller boys.

'What kind of general,' Stilicho asked her, 'leaves his family to the tender mercies of an enemy?'

'What kind of general,' she countered, 'turns on a man who was once a comrade? What kind of man attacks fellow Christians on the Lord's Rising Day?'

The men around Stilicho straightened. At least one sword flew clear of its scabbard but today's victor held up his hand. 'No, no,' he chuckled, 'these are fair questions. Get a messenger through to Alaric, wherever he is hiding. If he wants to see his family again, he is to leave Italia. You, madam, will be my guest. Be assured, you will be well treated.' He summoned back the slave who proceeded to knead and twist the general's naked shoulders. 'At least,' Stilicho went on, 'until we go and see the emperor. He'll be pleased, of course, that the current danger is past and he is no longer under siege, so he may be generous to you.' He paused for effect. 'On the other hand, he is at a difficult age. Petty. Spiteful.' He glanced at the men around him, his staff and hangers-on. 'I mean no disrespect when I say that; it's just how it is. He may not be so inclined to wait until your husband has done the decent thing. If so,' he sat forward and his cold, grey eyes transfixed the wife of Alaric, 'you'll see your darlings here sold in a Roman forum to the highest bidder. Before he gives you to the legions.'

Londinium

That dies Solis, Pelagius the preacher was sitting in the workshop of his friend Vitalis, the basket maker. Vitalis had gone to the river with the coming of spring to inspect his lines and check the reeds. Papa Thamesis was in one of his more rebellious moods and the water ran high and cold. Both men had prayed as dawn crept over the low marshes to the south and thanked their God for the gift of His Son and His sacrifice. Now Pelagius was twisting his fingers in the workshop in the way that Petronius had shown him. It had to be said that the boy was better at this than the man, his fingers were more nimble and his reflexes quicker. Petronius had lost count of the months that he had been Vitalis' apprentice. He never went east of the city anymore, to the spot where the temple of Isis had stood. That terrible night, of rain and blood and fire, he had done his best to wipe from his mind. Now he was Petronius Borro, the basket maker and he would make his way in the world.

There was a crash in the little courtyard. 'Master?' the boy called. No answer. Pelagius only came to the workshop now and again and had no idea of the comings and goings of the place. But this was the Lord's day. In fact, it was *the* Lord's Day. No one came buying baskets on this day. Suddenly, three large soldiers filled the entrance way.

'Are you the man called Pelagius?' one of them grunted.

'I am.' Pelagius stood up.

'The Commander wants a word.'

'Lucius Porca?' Pelagius chuckled. 'Why?'

He felt his arms bent up behind his back and the rough kiss of the rope as they pinioned him. 'When the Commander confides in me,' the semisallis said, 'I'll kiss Mithras' arse. Have you got him, Carvo?'

'Good and tight, semisallis. I thought he'd put up some sort of struggle.'

'Not likely,' the semisallis muttered, helping himself to a couple of baskets. 'He's a Christian, ain't he?'

'No!' A boy's voice froze the moment. At the doorway, Petronius Borro stood, a reed cleaver in his hand. 'Let him go!'

The soldiers chuckled. 'Now, what are you going to do with that, little man?' the semisallis asked.

'Don't know about you boys,' Carvo grinned, 'but I'm shitting myself. You, semisallis?'

'Get rid of him, Carvo. We've wasted enough time this morning.'

The soldier drew his spatha, the blade twice the length of Petronius' weapon.

'No!' It was Pelagius' turn to shout. 'He's just a boy. There's no need for that. Petronius, put the cleaver down.' He stared hard at the boy, the stare he used on bishops and generals and would one day use on God himself. 'Now,' he said.

Petronius hesitated, his lip quivering. Then he let the blade fall and the soldiers barged their way out with their captive. The semisallis ruffled the boy's hair and the next instant the lad had gone, hurtling out of the workshop and running full pelt for the river.

Din Paladyr

That dies Solis, as darkness fell over the wooden ramparts of Brenna's stronghold, the queen of the Gododdin and the former Dux Britannorum lay under the wolfskins of her vast bed and watched the logs tumble and topple to red-veined dust in the hearth.

'You're going south again, aren't you?' she said, nestling her head into the crook of his neck.

'It's spring,' he told her. 'The day has thirteen and a half hours ...'

'... and the night ten and a half.' She laughed softly. 'Yes,

Roman, I know. What will you do?' She lifted herself up on her elbow.

He laughed too. 'Find out what happened to my life,' he said. 'Brenna,' he leaned forward and stroked her cheek, tucking the bright hair back behind her ear so he could see the curve of her neck swooping down to her shoulder, 'believe me when I say I could live with you forever, under this great sky with only the wild birds and the sea for company. But I had another mistress before you. She's called the army and I've a nagging feeling all is not well with her.'

She smiled and nodded. 'I know,' she said, 'and I know you won't be yourself until you find out.' She sat up suddenly and took his face in both hands, turning him so he had to look her in the eye. 'Promise me one thing. Promise me that, when you've found your first love; when you've proved to yourself that she's indestructible; when you've done that, you'll come back. Back to Din Paladyr. Back to me.'

He looked at her, the queen he had fought for, the woman he loved. 'Yes,' he said. 'I promise.'

CHAPTER XVII

Din Eidyn

Edirne was late. He was supposed to have joined his big brother on his rocky outcrop above the estuary for Imbolc, the festival that the Christians to the south had stolen. That hadn't happened – Belatucadros would understand; but he was here now, riding with his people over the heather, warm in the spring sunshine.

He saw them before they saw him; a warband of the painted ones, with their limewashed hair and their plaid cloaks. Against committed cavalry, their little, sure-footed ponies made little impression but as raiders and cattle-thieves, the Picti were second to none. Edern reined in his column. The Picti outnumbered him two to one and there would be no Justinus Coelius today to ride to his rescue over the brow of the hill. The man had left Din Paladyr three days ago and would, out of habit, be checking on the defences of the Wall and saying hello to the VI Victrix where he cut his teeth on iron all those years ago. Nor would there be a Taran, coming late to save the day as the brothers' battle plan usually had it. Today, Edern's little company was alone.

He drew his sword, half-turning to his men. 'Advance, walk,' he said. Edern had learned his battle-orders from his own father, the tribune Paternus, when the boy could barely straddle a horse; and more recently from Justinus Coelius and *his* father, soldiers to the core. The Picti had no shape on the battlefield, just wild lunatics thirsty for blood and riding for glory. The Gododdin urged their horses forward. No one carried a bow for this was a peaceful ride out in the spring sunshine; one brother paying his respects to another. No one expected trouble. Yet here it was.

The Picti began to stir themselves, unhooking their round shields from their saddles, shields that coiled with bronze serpents and hissed with mountain cats wrought in metal. Edern could hear their outlandish cries and whoops in the guttural harshness of Caledonia. They formed into one line, then two. This was the Roman way, a half turma in formation, like an Ala flanking a legion. Where the hell had they learned that?

Edern rammed his heels into his horse's flanks and the bay jolted into a gallop, hooves thudding over the rough, springy ground. He could see that the painted ones had no cattle with them, no women, no slaves. Whatever their target was, they clearly hadn't found it yet. He heard the Gododdin battle-roar to his right and left and his own warriors closed in so that their prince was not isolated at their head. He swerved his bay at the last moment and scythed with his sword, hacking into the body of the nearest Pict. Crimson flew in an arc before the man rolled out of the saddle and the bay collided with a black in the second line. Iron rang on iron as Edern steadied himself, clinging to the four-pronged saddle and his opponent hauled his horse away, screaming with pain.

Edern wheeled the bay. He had ridden right through the bastards and had come out the other side. So had his people. Their horses were blown but the only other result was scratches and bruises.

'Ready again!' he shouted. 'Form line.'

But the Picti were no longer playing that game. They rode straight on, galloping over the heather as though their tails were on fire. Even with their slight losses, they had ample men to finish the Gododdin off but they seemed to have no stomach for the fight. Edern's men hurled insults and laughed. Here was another tall tale to tell around the campfires of winter.

'A warband?' Taran passed the ale cup to his brother. 'Not a raiding party? Are you sure?'

'Twenty five, thirty of them,' Edern nodded, unslinging his sword and throwing it down on Taran's couch. For all he didn't really approve of Rome, the heir to Din Paladyr liked the conquerors' creature comforts. 'They weren't out for a picnic.'

'And where was this?'

'Ten, twelve miles south east.'

'In our territory,' Taran mused to himself.

'In yours, yes.'

Taran looked at the other prince of the Gododdin. The boy was a man now and that changed things in Valentia along the estuary. When Taran looked into the grey eyes and at the straw-coloured hair, he could see nothing of their mother, the patient Brenna. All he saw was Paternus, the Roman who had come, unwanted, into their lives all those years ago. But Taran was patient too and he was playing the long game.

'Yours. Mine,' he said. 'Brother, we are one. For convenience' sake I rule in Din Eidyn but when that grim day comes when Belatucadros calls mother to him, you and I will rule together.' He held the younger man by the shoulders. 'There is no "yours" and "mine", only ours. Now, I'm glad you're safe. There's food and wine in the great hall. Tell your boys to help themselves. I'll be along presently. Affairs of state,' he sighed. 'You know how it is.'

Edern knew. Brenna was shedding more of her responsibilities at Din Paladyr by the day, not because she was old or tired but because Edern would have to do it all one day. And she would not be there. He finished his ale, smiled and went to collect his riders waiting in the yard outside.

When he had gone, Taran slipped along a dark passageway to an anteroom Edern didn't even know existed. A scribe sat there in candlelight, scratching away with a reed pen at scrolls of parchment. 'Get a message,' Taran muttered, 'to Nectan of the Picti. He is to keep his lawless bastards north of the Boderia, until I tell him otherwise. If I find any of them this far south again, I'll send them back to him with their bollocks in their mouths.'

Londinium

'Where is he?' Vitalis stood in Lucius Porca's principia with minions of the man's garrison scuttling backwards and forwards in the daily business of the man who defended Londinium.

'Who?'

'Don't be obtuse, commander,' Vitalis said. 'I don't want to pull rank on you, but I am still a tribune of the Schola Palatinae – you know, the emperor's bodyguard.'

That was not strictly true. Vitalis still had the uniform, but he had actually resigned his commission and all it stood for. He was really just a basket maker now. Lucius Porca knew that, but he was a kind man and he liked Vitalis.

'You're talking about Pelagius,' he said.

'You know I am.'

The commander leaned back in his chair. 'I suppose the phrase "I'm only obeying orders" won't cut much ice with you, will it?'

'I cut reeds, commander,' Vitalis reminded him. 'For the last time, where is Pelagius?'

'I was acting on the orders of the Lord Bishop. You'll have to ask him.'

'I'm asking you,' Vitalis said, in level, deadly tones. 'You don't work for Severianus. And Severianus has no cells in which to keep the man. Try again.'

Porca stood up. Yes, he liked Vitalis, but there were limits. The man was all but calling him a liar. 'Then,' he said, 'I suggest you ask the vicarius.'

'Who?' Chrysanthos had been the guest of honour at one of the out-of-town villas the night before and, if truth were told, he had over-imbibed. His head hurt and his throat was on fire. What *was* in that wine? He'd either have his genial host flogged or at very least get the recipe; it could go either way.

Vitalis had not made merry the night before. He had been dragged from the riverbank by a hysterical Petronius to say that soldiers had come for Pelagius. He had been cold-shouldered by Lucius Porca and Bishop Severianus was unavailable, out of town on church business. He had been jerked around for long enough and he slammed his fist down on the vicarius' table.

'Tut, tut,' Chrysanthos scolded. 'You're beginning to become rather a nuisance, Vitalis. Allow me to remind you that your friends have gone. Calpurnius is rotting north of the Wall. Justinus is either dead or with him – I don't know which. And Augusta Treverorum was a long time ago, wasn't it? You're not the toast of the emperor's court now.'

'I never was,' Vitalis told him, 'and all I want is Pelagius.'

'Yes, but you see, Severianus "wanted" him too. As bishop, he takes precedence. And besides,' Chrysanthos flashed his most winning smile, 'he asked first.'

The vicarius looked at the man. With all the cares of state of his shoulders, these church vestry politics he could do without. 'He's here, Vitalis,' he said. 'Here, in my cells.' He raised a hand at the basket maker's protests. 'He's well treated, I assure you. And besides, Pelagius is no stranger to gaols.'

'What do you intend to do with him?'

'Well,' Chrysanthos yawned, 'you and I both know there's no actual law against upsetting bishops, but the church has him down as a heretic.'

'That's nonsense.'

'Yes, I know,' the vicarius nodded, 'but reason and the Roman church parted company long ago. Severianus wants the man hanged.'

'And you?'

Chrysanthos moaned, rubbing his temples. 'I want my headache to go away,' he said. He read the look on Vitalis' face and was not at all happy with what he saw there. 'I'll exile him,' he said. 'Banishment is nothing to men like Pelagius. He's been thrown out of more provinces than you and I have had hot dinners. It'll keep him alive, at least for the moment and get him out of Severianus' hair, what little he has of it.'

'When?' Vitalis asked. 'When will you banish Pelagius?'

Chrysanthos leaned back in his chair, spreading his arms. 'When the time is right,' he said.

Rutupiae

It was raining hard that night as the guards passed each other on the camp's ramparts. It was usually Quintillius who drew the short straw for night patrol, but there was an edginess about the Saxon Shore forts and Gerontius the praeses had decided to double the watch. Whether that was to keep trouble out or to keep trouble in, he wasn't saying. So Locicero was there too, the rain dripping off his helmet-rim and soaking into his cloak.

'Did I dream it, Lo?' Quintillis grunted as they trudged past each other on the wall walk, 'or did we elect another Caesar the other day?'

'You did not and we did,' Locicero told him. Ever since Stilicho's XX had broken his nose, the man had a nasal whine, but nobody commented. After all, like all battle scars, it was won in the line of duty. They walked on to the end of the wall and turned back.

'I've always looked up to you, Quint,' Locicero said when they were close enough to talk, 'admired your grasp of how things are done.'

'Good of you, Lo,' the senior man said.

'So, you'll know if anybody does. Isn't there a little prize money, whenever there's a new emperor, for us downtrodden servants of the empire, I mean?'

'There is, Lo,' Quintillius assured him. 'The donativum. It's a sort of golden "hello", a symbol of gratitude to us plebs who put the emperor where he is today. Why do you ask?'

Quintillius had to wait for the answer until they'd both returned from their respective towers.

'Well,' Locicero explained, 'we're owed, aren't we? We got bugger all from Terentius Marcus, whatever he promised us. Now, we've got two emperors, not one – Theodosius and Arcadius. That makes three donativi already.'

'Amazing how it builds up, ain't it?' Quintillius muttered. He couldn't feel his feet now.

'And that's before we get on to this new one – what's his name again?'

'Scipio Gratianus Maximus,' Quintillius reminded him. Hadn't Locicero *been* to the ceremony? They'd used the title more than enough that day.

'Yeah, but that's the official bollocks,' Locicero said. 'I mean, what's his *real* name?'

The tide of duty carried the pair apart and it was moment later when Locicero got his answer. 'Scipio Honorius, from Londinium. His papa was a soldier, bloody hero of the Wall, no less.'

'Get away!'

'It's as true as I'm standing here.'

'Anything else known?'

Again, Locicero had to wait. 'They do say,' Quintillius became confidential, doing his best to pat the side of his nose under the helmet's nasal, 'he runs a gang in the capital.'

'What, you mean he's a bloody criminal?' Locicero was aghast.

'Well, he's no bloody soldier, that's for sure. You've only got to look at his feet.'

'And we're supposed to follow him? Put him on the emperor's throne, that sort of thing?'

'Allegedly,' Quintillius shrugged.

'Well, I can't see it happening.'

'Nor can I.'

'I'll tell you what, though,' Locicero said, letting the butt of his spear hit the ground to shake some of the rainwater off it, '*I'm* not lifting a bloody finger until I get some of what's owed. *And* I want it from this low-life Caesar himself. Personally. I'll tell him straight. I'll say …'

'Oi!' A rough voice from below interrupted and brought the conversation to an end.

''Evening, circitor!' Quintillius called cheerily.

'I'll "evening" you, Quint, you sorry excuse for a soldier. Now, if the mothers' meeting's over, how about you two popping down here to pick up double pack. Then you can get on with your rampart duties, like what we pay you for.'

'Yes, circitor,' the rebels mumbled in unison.

Eboracum

Publius Dio had been the praeses of the VI Victrix for over a year. He was a competent soldier, with experience in the East. He found the lonely moors to the north a trifle cold in winter for his personal taste, but it was summer now and he walked that evening with Justinus Coelius, inspecting the cavalry lines at the edge of the colonia, where the river ran dark and deep. The stars looked down on this, the most northerly Roman outpost south of the Wall and Mithras was in his heaven and all was well in the world.

'I wasn't sure how welcome I'd be,' Justinus said. He had soaked in Eboracum's baths and changed his travel-stained clothes for a clean tunic.

'You're always welcome with the Sixth, Justinus,' Dio told him, reaching across to check the harness in the horse lines.

'As Justinus Coelius, perhaps,' Justinus smiled, 'but you must have met the new Dux Britannorum by now.'

'As a matter of fact, I have,' the praeses said. 'He was here only last week. He used to be a tribune of the Second, I understand.'

'Some have greatness thrust upon us,' Justinus laughed. 'I was a pedes once, on the Wall not far from here. And look where I am today.'

'Indeed,' Dio chuckled.

Justinus stopped walking, cradling the soft muzzle of the nearest horse in the lines. The man wasn't chuckling. Or even smiling. 'But that's just it, Publius; I don't know where I am today.'

The praeses looked at him. He was younger than Justinus and not from Britannia. He hated to presume … anything. And yet, for all his reputation, for all that Dio had heard about Justinus Coelius, he seemed lost, bewildered.

'The army,' Justinus said, rubbing the horse's nose and cradling its ears, 'it's the only life I know. I've been Dux Britannorum now for so long that I don't know how to be anything else.'

'You could always take it back,' Dio said.

'What?' Justinus let his hand fall from the horse's head.

'Constantine is just one man,' the praeses said. 'Appointed by a general as a matter of expediency because you were ill. Rumour had it you were likely to die.'

'That applies to us all,' Justinus muttered.

'He's unknown outside Maxima Caesariensis, Justinus. *You* have the respect of all Britannia's forces. Stilicho gave him the command and Stilicho's not here.'

'From what I hear,' Justinus said, 'Stilicho is emperor in all but name. I won't go against that.'

'Not even against Gratian?'

'Who?' Justinus had been languishing in Brenna's bed for longer than he thought.

'Gratianus Maximus, the new Caesar. The Second have elected him. He'll move on to receive the standards of the Twentieth next. Then it'll be our turn.'

'Jupiter Highest and Best!' Justinus roared. 'What is it about this island? What is it, more to the point, about the Second Augusta?'

Dio held up his hands. 'Not for me to pour scorn on my colleagues, Justinus. I'm sure Gerontius had his reasons.'

'Yes,' Justinus scowled. 'There are thousands of them and they're made of silver. Or gold, perhaps. I don't know Gerontius well; maybe the man doesn't come cheap. What do we know about the new usurper? This Gratian?'

'His real name is Scipio Honorius …'

Justinus grabbed Dio's tunic sleeve. 'From Londinium?'

'Yes, I believe so. Do you know him? He's not a soldier, they say.'

'Yes, I know him,' Justinus said, his eyes dark and hooded. 'I knew his father too. We were heroes of the Wall…' How empty the phrase sounded now, now that it had entered the language, not just of Rome, but of every tribe from Clausentum to Caledonia. 'And no, Gratianus Maximus is not a soldier. He is a murderous, heartless bastard who would skin his mother alive were it not for one thing.'

'What's that?'

'She'd skin him alive first. Publius, can I borrow a horse?'

Ravenna

The candles glowed golden on the mosaics that covered the walls of the emperor's palace. Below the huge Chi-Rho and the statues of emperors past, one sign stood out. '"In the Name of Christ,"' the boy read it out, '"you will always conquer." Will I, uncle Flavius? Is that true?'

Stilicho smiled and looked at the boy. He wasn't his blood relative. He had merely married the lad's aunt. And that was all about convenience, to establish a power base. How old was the little shit now? Thirteen? Fourteen? If so, he was thirteen, going on six. It astonished Stilicho that the little shit wasn't carrying a couple of pet chickens around with him; he usually did.

'Of course it is, Honorius,' the general who was half Vandal, half uncle smiled. The prospect of this little imbecile actually earning the purple he wore and commanding troops in battle filled Stilicho with dread. 'Look out here.'

He led the boy, stumbling in his wake over his long robes, to the basilica's windows. 'What do you see?'

The sun glinted on the salt marshes that shone like frost on this summer's day.

'Marshes, uncle,' Honorius said.

Stilicho smiled acidly. All that money on the finest tutors and that was the best the boy could manage.

'Swamps, nephew,' the general said. 'Mud that will drag down any enemy who tries to cross them down to Hell. And see there,' he pointed across the city, strangely silent in the heat of the noonday, 'Trajan's aqueduct. That will bring us all the fresh water we need, whatever the situation.'

'Is this place safer than Hasta, uncle?' Honorius asked.

'Far safer,' Stilicho assured him.

'Uncle Flavius ...'

'Yes, Honorius?'

'I have dreams about him, you know. Nightmares, really.'

'Nightmares?' Stilicho frowned. He couldn't remember

when his own children had talked like this. What a misfortune that Theodosius' brightest and best was such a ninny. 'About whom?'

'Alaric,' Honorius whispered the name, barely able to force himself to say it. 'Alaric the Goth.'

Stilicho laughed. 'Didn't I clear that man out of Italia?' he said. 'Haven't I got his family here with us? Shall we put them on show for the mob, Honorius? Let them tear them apart, just to make a point?'

'No, no,' tears were forming in the boy's large, dark eyes. 'No, we mustn't hurt them.'

'No,' Stilicho said, through a clenched smile. 'No, of course not. What *was* I thinking? The point, Honorius, is that Alaric is just a man. More than that, he's a beaten man. He can't hurt us. Either of us.'

'No.' Honorius took a deep breath. 'No, you're right. He can't. Can I go and play with my chickens now?'

Rutupiae

'Full pack, praeses. Double speed.'

The command was clear enough, carrying as it did across the parade ground.

'Sir …' Gerontius saw the appalled look on the faces of the men and thought it best to step in.

'Well?' Scipio raised an eyebrow. He was sitting on a dais under a purple awning and the entire legion was paraded in front of him in hollow square. If truth be told, the new Caesar was bored already with all this heel-clicking and wheeling about. He missed the draughts of the Hen's Tooth and the haggling with the city merchants. Hell, he even missed Julia of the Two Hands, irritating woman though she was and the father in him who had a soft spot for little crippled Veronica. When all this nonsense was over, he would send for them all, his people of the Underworld and they could carry on their furtive duties in the brave new world he would win, in Rome or Ravenna or wherever else the emperor was supposed to live these days. Come to think of it, once he *was* emperor, he could make his capital wherever he liked. What was wrong with Londinium? It was the finest city Scipio knew. And come to think of that, it was the *only* city he knew. But first he had to teach these over-indulged foot-sloggers who was master. Then he'd do the same with the XX Valeria Victrix and the VI. Then he'd weld them all together with his allies of the north, making sure of course that Taran of the Votadini and Niall of the Seven Hostages knew their place under him. Together, they would be more than a match for Stilicho and he, Scipio, would have great delight in snapping the man's neck as surely as he would snap the necks of Honorius' chickens.

'They've been marching all day, sir,' Gerontius, the professional soldier, reminded him.

'I think you'll find, according to the laws of protocol,' Scipio snapped waspishly, 'that a subordinate addresses his Caesar as "sire".'

'Yes … sire, of course. But that doesn't change the fact …'

'Caesars change facts, praeses. They also change commanding officers of legions. Now, for the last time, I want to see these men marching in full pack around the camp perimeter at double speed. No.' Scipio smiled. 'No, make that *run*. I want to see what my fighting forces are made of.'

While Scipio lounged on the couches under the awnings, drank wine, ate grapes and groped the two girls that Caius had provided for him from the town, the II Augusta ran themselves into the ground. Boots crunched on earth and boardwalk, men who tried to sing to keep their spirits up were beaten with the optiones' vine canes and oak cudgels. One by one, the weakest faltered, the unfit floundered, dropping first their packs, then their weapons. They lay panting in the unseasonable heat, their bodies drenched in sweat, their limbs cramping with dehydration. The water-carriers hurried to them but on the Caesar's orders they were driven back. When the man finally called a halt, the sun was setting over the walls of Rutupiae and an exhausted legion tried to stand to attention in front of him.

Scipio Gratianus Maximus mounted his horse with its gilded saddlery and walked it over to the lines. He flicked the flies away with his horse-tail whip and looked along the ragged lines of tired men.

'You!' The whip pointed to someone in the second line. 'You with the broken nose. Where's your shield?'

Locicero realised to his horror that the Caesar was talking to him. 'Er … I don't know, sir.'

'You don't know?' Scipio's voice was the only sound on that deathly parade ground. 'Praeses.'

'Sire?' Gerontius marched to the Caesar's side.

'What is the punishment for a man who throws away an item of equipment?'

'Loss of privileges, sire,' Gerontius told him.

'Specifically?'

'Reduced rations. Barley rather than corn. Loss of pay until the item is paid for.'

Scipio looked down at the commander. 'Call that a punishment?' he said. 'Optio, bring that man to me. I'll make him wish he'd never been born.'

CHAPTER XVIII

All that night, Locicero stood to attention in full battle-gear, his shield strapped to his arm, his spear off the ground. His belt he had been ordered to leave behind so that the full weight of his armour and weapons hung on him. As the watch changed around him, three men he vaguely knew from the Second Cohort marched across the earthworks, Caius, the Caesar's lackey from Londinium at their head.

When they reached him, they took away his weapons, his helmet and his shirt of mail until he stood naked to the night.

'You know what Scipio … er, the Caesar … thinks of you, don't you?'

'I can guess,' Locicero muttered.

His sentence was abruptly halted by a slap around the head that drew blood from his temple.

'That's what we call in Londinium a rhetorical question,' Caius growled. 'That means *you* don't answer it. *I* do. And the answer is "Shit", that's what he thinks of you. Latrines, now!'

Locicero felt himself being lifted off the ground and carried bodily to the lower courtyard. The privies stood here, trenches open to the sky with a wooden lattice stretched over them. Most camps had better facilities than this, but the cloaca at Rutupiae was a work in progress. While two men held Locicero, Caius and the spare man hauled away the trellis work and Caius aimed a deft kick at the pedes' groin, so that he jerked backwards and landed in the squelching bottom of the trench.

'See what I mean?' Caius laughed. 'Turns out the Caesar was right, wasn't he?' He squatted over the trellis as soon as it was back in place. He grunted and heaved but to no avail. 'No,' he said. 'It's no good. My bowels just aren't working tonight. I can piss all right, though.' He stood up and let a stream of urine cascade through the lattice, to splash on Locicero's head. The man looked up, steaming and smelling. There was nothing in the emperor's regulations like this. Never in the long and brutal history of the Roman army had there been an example of punishment of this kind. This was something grotesque imported by those upstart civilians.

'Your turn,' Caius grunted to the nearest pedes.

'What?'

'Piss on him.'

'Go to hell.' The soldier half-turned.

Caius gripped his arm. 'The Caesar shall hear of this,' he hissed. 'That's what we call in Londinium treason; to refuse a command of the Caesar's. That's a death sentence, that is. And rest assured, he won't hesitate to carry it out.'

'Oh, I'm sure he won't.' The soldier knocked Caius' arm away. 'But that man down there's one of ours. I've gone along with this nonsense up to this point, but if you think I'm going any further, you can stick the Caesar's staff of office up your arse.'

Caius' eyes flashed fire. For a moment, he toyed with burying his knife into this insubordinate's neck. But there were two more of them, all armed better than he was and those were odds he didn't like. Besides, the stench from the latrine was beginning to get to him.

'Dawn,' he snapped at the soldiers. 'Fish this bastard out and scrub him down then. He is to appear in subligaculum only before the Caesar on the parade ground. Make sure you're there. You've got something coming to you, too,'

'Oh,' the pedes grinned. 'I wouldn't miss it for the world.'

The entire legion was there because the Caesar had ordered it. The eagle stood tall, highest of the standards in the grey light of morning and the dragon banners below it. The shields of the II Augusta had been brightly painted on the Caesar's orders and for most of the hours of darkness, the whetstone wheels had been turning, bringing a new, keener edge to the legion's blades.

The II's Alae were drawn up beyond the camp perimeter, shields slung over the riders' backs, helmets buckled and plumes fitted. It was a field day, a Roman spectacle; and all to see one man die.

Before he had left Londinium, Scipio had had a uniform made for himself, one that befitted a Caesar, one worn by the second usurper to set himself up as a demigod in Britannia in the space of a year. There were mutterings in the ranks when he appeared. Under the purple of his cloak, edged with gold, he wore the muscled cuirass of the old Republic and the red sash around his waist, as though the deified Augustus himself had come back from the dead. Not even the oldest of the old sweats had seen an officer dressed like that. The beardless boys found it funny. Wiser men saw it as an omen of doom.

To muffled drums, Locicero was led into the hollow square formed by the vexillations, his wrists cut by tight, unforgiving ropes and a halter around his neck. He was naked, except for the subligaculum tied at his hips and his eyes were dull with exhaustion and humiliation. The drums stopped abruptly and the condemned man stood there, head bowed before the dais on which the Caesar sat.

Scipio Gratianus Maximus stood up so that all could hear him. He had been preparing for this moment for quite a while. 'Men of the Second Augusta,' he roared. 'I am Scipio Gratianus, whom you have elected Caesar. You will now do me another honour. You will march, when I have mustered the Sixth Victrix and the Twentieth Valeria Victrix, to the ships that will take us over the German Sea. We will march through Gallia and win support on the way. Then we will turn on Rome and take it. And I promise you, there will be riches beyond your wildest dreams.'

There was no cheer, no thud of spear butts on the ground, but Scipio had expected this. The streets of Londinium had taught him that applause was something that had to be won.

'The present emperor,' he went on, 'is a snivelling boy, in love with his chickens. He runs from city to city, afraid of his shadow. Will you serve such a nonentity? Is it right that such a waste of space should command a legion like the Second?'

There was a murmur now that ran like the ripples on the shore through the younger ranks. The Caesar had appealed to their honour. More, he had put into clear words the rumour that they had all heard for months now.

'What about Stilicho?' someone shouted from the ranks.

Scipio scanned the lines, the expressionless faces under the helmet rims. To the end of his life, he would never know who had

had the nerve to ask that. But he turned it to his advantage. 'Let me tell you a story about the half Vandal,' he said. 'Something you don't know. I met the man in Londinium months back. I caught him at a bad moment, though, because he was in bed. With a sheep.'

There was a stunned silence, then a series of giggles that broke into guffaws.

'Oh, don't worry,' Scipio went on. 'It *was* a female sheep. Nothing funny about Stilicho!'

The guffaws spread now so that even the grizzled old centurions were smiling.

'Stilicho,' Scipio said when the noise had died down, 'will not be a problem.' He half-turned to the roped man in the square and he held up his hand. 'But first, we have a disease in the legion, a cancer right here in the Second Augusta. And it must be cut out.' He drew his sword with a flourish, enjoying the sound of the scraping iron in the morning. 'If,' he sauntered down the steps and stood in front of Locicero, 'we are to drag down this whelp of an emperor and the sheep-shagger who protects him, we must do it together, as one man.' The blade flashed to the level, the razor-sharp point tickling Locicero's throat above the rope halter. 'Anyone,' he stressed the word, '*anyone* who doesn't follow the Caesar, who cannot be relied upon, must be removed.'

Although Scipio couldn't see it, the men of Locicero's contubernium stiffened. They stood shoulder to shoulder in the ranks of the I Cohors, Quintillius, Antoninus, Seniacus and the rest, their knuckles white around their spear shafts, each of them wondering what they would do when the Caesar made his move.

Suddenly, without warning, Scipio twirled away from the man facing death and slashed horizontally, the blade neatly slicing through the rank scarf of Gerontius the praeses. There was a gasp, not least from Gerontius himself as he felt the blood trickle from the nick in his throat. Scipio jerked his head and two guards broke forward, one taking the praeses' sword from its scabbard, the other his dagger. Now the Caesar's blade tip was at Gerontius' throat and another man of the legion was staring death in the face.

'Anyone,' Scipio said again, 'who doesn't follow the Caesar shall be removed.'

There were more murmurs now, in the ranks behind the pair. The officers looked haunted, in agonies of indecision. As was the custom, they had taken an oath to serve the Caesar; Gerontius had too. But this …

Scipio looked at them with contempt. He could read their minds, understood their dilemma. This would be the first test. It would be interesting to see how many of them passed it.

'Praeses …' His voice rang to the edge of the waiting lines. Every man there knew Gerontius. Some had come up through the ranks with him, all had served under him. There were those, as there were in any legion, who had grumbled about the man and damned him to all kinds of hell as they slogged up to their ankles in the clinging mud of Britannia or put their aching shoulders to the wheel of a soldier's daily grind. But what exactly did the Caesar have in mind?'

'… praeses no more. You will kneel and take your punishment. That man,' Scipio swept his sword blade behind him to point with the blade at Locicero, 'the vilest, slowest, most incompetent man in the Second. Whose fault is that?'

Gerontius looked hard into those dark, killer's eyes. 'Mine,' he nodded, 'as commander of the legion.'

'Yours.' Scipio's smile was pure ice. 'Strip him.'

At first the guards hesitated, but Gerontius himself gave the command.

'Do it,' he snapped. He dropped to his knees and waited while his helmet, cloak, mail and shirt were ripped from his body.

'Flagrum,' Scipio ordered. 'Twenty lashes.'

Another silence. One of the guards said, 'Sire, army regulations …'

Scipio stopped the man with a sword blade pointing between his eyes. The guard's pupils crossed and he gulped, 'You're right,' Scipio smiled. 'Make that thirty.'

For a moment, nobody moved. Then Gerontius broke the silence. 'Lay on; the Caesar has commanded it.'

The two men coiled the leather cats around their fists and took their positions on either side of Gerontius, feet planted apart.

'Now!' the demoted praeses said and the first thongs flew through the air, the metal tips flashing like fire sparks in the growing light. They slapped across Gerontius' shoulders and the impact threw him forward.

There were mutinous grumblings from the lines and the vexillations began to move.

'Stand fast in the ranks!' Gerontius shouted. And they obeyed.

The second guard flung back his arm and the leather did its work, painting another arc of blood across Gerontius' shoulder blades. He winced but kept his body upright. No one was holding him. His arms were unpinioned and there was no leather pad rammed into his mouth so that he couldn't bite his tongue in his agony. The third whip fell. And the fourth and the fifth. Gerontius' back was red raw now, a patchwork of ripped skin and bloody pulp, but he was still kneeling upright and his head was still high. The sixth slap hit high, tearing his left earlobe and the seventh sliced too low, bouncing harmlessly off his belt.

'Miss again,' Scipio roared at the guard, 'and it's your turn next.'

The Caesar began counting as each whiplash left its mark. Tears ran the length of Gerontius' face and his nose dripped with the effort of withstanding the pain. The officers behind him could barely look at their commander's back and the youngest of them flopped forward in a dead faint. Scipio saw it happen and made a mental note not to take that man across the German Sea with him. When he reached the number twenty nine, the Caesar held up his hand and the whipping stopped. He sheathed his sword and ignoring Gerontius entirely, snatched the cat from the nearest man. He turned to Locicero, still standing roped in front of the beaten praeses. He reversed the whip and held it out to the soldier. 'Have the last one on me,' he grinned. Locicero did not move. 'Go on,' Scipio said. 'All you endured yesterday and last night – it was because of him. Here's your chance. A spot of revenge.'

Locicero stood up to his full height. 'I am a soldier,' he said. There was no 'sire' now; there wasn't even a 'sir'.

Scipio chuckled, a chill, foreboding sound. 'No,' he said softly. 'No, you're not.' From nowhere there was a knife in his hand and the blade of that knife was thudding into Locicero's right arm. The man's good fist came up but too late and Scipio twisted the blade before wrenching it free and kicking the soldier to the dust. He stood with his blade gleaming crimson and the air was thick with the smell of blood.

'I want both these sorry excuses for men out of the camp. That,' he kicked Locicero, 'in the nearest dog ditch. That,' he pointed the knife blade at Gerontius, 'out of my sight.' He saw two anxious-looking men darting across the parade ground. 'No medici!' he roared and the men stopped in their tracks. 'We'll let Jupiter Highest and best decide whether they live or die.' He sheathed the weapon and returned to the dais, raising both fists in the air.

'Well?' he bellowed to the legion. 'You still think Stilicho can stand against me?'

There was no answer.

'Mithras was looking out for you, son, that's for sure.' Quintillius sat alongside Locicero's bed in the valetudinarium.

'To Hell with Mithras,' the medicus ordinarius said, 'God may have had a hand in it but the real work is down to me.'

'Oh, of course, sir.' Quintillius was not about to tangle with the man. He not only carried the rank of centurion but he had treated Quintillius' piles over the years and had made him the man he was. 'I didn't meant to imply ...'

'Keep that arm clean, pedes,' the medicus muttered. 'The muscle's ruptured and I'm not sure how much use you're ever going to be in the field again.'

'I think that's what the Caesar had in mind,' Locicero winced. The stitches hurt more than Scipio's blade but he told himself it was all in a good cause.

'Don't expect any political comment about that from me,' the medicus said. 'I just put you people back together again.'

'The Caesar wants him out of the camp, sir,' Quintillius told him.

'Right, well, this is where I *do* get political,' the medicus nodded. '*My* hospital, *my* patient. He doesn't leave that bed until I say so. Is that clear, gentlemen?'

When he had gone, Quintillius sat back down, helping himself to the grapes the lads of the contubernium had sent to Locicero for his well-being. He also slipped the leather ale bottle from under his cloak and passed it to the invalid.

'You shouldn't be doing this, Quint,' Locicero moaned, fighting the pain that shook his whole body. 'The medicus is taking a chance too. If the Caesar finds out ...'

'Don't you worry about the Caesar, Lo. He won't be in a position to find anything out soon.'

A raw wind had risen from nowhere in the night and it rattled the shutters of the principia. Scipio Gratianus had taken over this building at the heart of the Rutupiae camp even before he had stripped Gerontius of his rank. His harlots slept in an ante-room and Caius of the Black Hand lay snoring in another. The praeses' soldier servants, who were now the Caesar's, had finished their duties and had gone to bed.

Scipio sat at Gerontius' table, dipping the reed pen into the ink and thinking. He needed no scribe for this work and he wrote quickly with hurried strokes. Tomorrow he would send his gallopers for the north, to the Picti and the Scotti north of the Wall. If that mad Hibernian bastard who collected hostages like Julia of the Two Hands collected purses, was with them, all to the good. He'd order them all south, once he'd got his clutches on the XX and they could meet at Eboracum or some such uncivilized place to plan the march to the sea. The plan was coming together nicely.

In the watch fires of the night, the men of Locicero's contubernium moved silently. Each of them had a knife. Each of them had a purpose. They looked at each other in the fires' glow and they knew. Quintillius carried the rope, the rough hemp halter the Caesar's guards had thrown around Locicero's neck the day before.

The guards at the principia gate saw them and *they* knew. In the silence, they went through the motions, presenting their spears as though to challenge strangers. But they made no sound at all. There was no 'Who goes?' as a warning to the principia, no answering cry of 'Friend'. Tonight, this particular contubernium were not friends. Tonight, the Caesar had no friends at all. Neither was there any 'advance friend and be recognized'. The rope in Quintillius' hand and the look on Quintillius' face said it all and the guard stood aside, whistling in the dark and looking in another direction.

Something made Scipio look up. He was halfway through his final letter now, the one, as yet unaddressed, to Taran of the Votadini. He was fumbling around for the wax to make the seal. All his life, Scipio Honorius had kept his back to the wall. The night was made for drinking and whoring, but the night, too, was made for murder. Any sound that he could not instantly account for gave Scipio pause for thought. He slid the parchment clear of the knife that lay inches from him on the table. He couldn't make out the sound at first. It was a rasping noise, like iron on wire that led to a gasp and a whine. He slid the blade clear, keeping an eye on the only door. And he waited.

'Caius!' he laughed, sliding the blade home. 'What are you creeping around for, like a virgin at an orgy? Caius?'

The big man in the doorway wasn't creeping now. He was

standing there, gripping the doorframe with one hand and his throat with the other. Blood was spurting in crimson gouts over his knuckles and over his tunic. His eyes were wild and glazed and he tried to speak. Instead, the only sound he could make was the rasping gasp that Scipio had heard moments before. He gurgled, drowning in his own blood, and pitched forward on his face. There were half a dozen men in the room, one of them carrying a rope; all of them carrying knives.

Scipio stood up. His instinct was to throw his own blade at the nearest man, to bring him down before turning on the next. But that would deprive him of his knife and his sword hung from a pole at the far side of the room. He would never reach it in time. 'I won't bother asking,' he said, 'what you boys want. And I won't ask where my guards are, either.'

'I hope that,' Quintillius pointed to the parchment, 'is your last will and testament, whoremonger. Because you've got no time to write another.'

It was dawn before Justinus Coelius galloped into Rutupiae. The great walls looked as they always had, huge and powerful and reassuring. His professional eyes missed nothing. He knew the circitor of the watch would have seen him, but whether he recognized him or not was another matter. He was riding a borrowed horse and wore no insignia of the Dux Britannorum. Another man had that and the world had moved on. Justinus saw the dawn patrol clattering out as always, as happened at this time from every major camp in Britannia, the cavalry checking the roads and the smoky settlements that ringed the vallum and the walls. He saw the farum winking through the early mist. But then something else caught his eye.

Above the narrow gate in the east wall, where the stonework ran down to the harbour and the sea, the body of a man twirled at the end of a rope. Justinus hauled on his rein and the mare obeyed, trotting obediently to the ramparts. He had seen hanged men before, the broken neck, the purple puffing around the rope where it had all but cut the flesh. The eyes were closed and it looked for all the world as if the man had fallen asleep; were it not for the fact that his head lay at such a ridiculous angle. The wind from the sea lifted and the body swung from its unforgiving tether, the rope creaking in the cold of the morning.

'Mithras, god of the morning,' Justinus whispered, 'Teach

me to die aright.' He wheeled the horse away and clattered around the tower making for the main gate. 'Circitor of the watch! Get your head over the ramparts, you dozy bastard!'

A head popped up. 'Who goes?'

'Justinus Coelius,' he rapped out. 'Sometime Dux Britannorum.'

'Jupiter Highest and Best,' the circitor muttered before yelling orders in every direction. The gates swung back with much clattering and squealing of timbers. The circitor had hit the ground running and he stood before Justinus now, presenting arms and waiting for what would follow.

'Is Marcellus Gerontius the praeses here?' Justinus asked.

'He is, sir.'

'Get him.' Justinus rammed his booted heels into his horse's flanks. 'And cut that man down.'

'Very good, sir.'

The last time that Gerontius and Justinus had met, Terentius Marcus was still Count of the Saxon Shore and Justinus could barely stand, weak with poison as he was. All that seemed eternity ago and things were very different now. It was Gerontius' turn to find standing difficult and he was all too glad when Justinus let him sit down.

'Hurts like hell, doesn't it?' Justinus asked.

Gerontius had got his principia back, but he wasn't able to enjoy its comforts yet. He looked surprised at Justinus' observation. Were his wounds *so* obvious?

'You have a very talkative circitor of the watch on duty this morning,' Justinus explained. 'Or at least he was with my sword at his throat. I know what happened.'

'What do you know?' Gerontius asked.

'The new Caesar. What did he call himself – Scipio Gratianus Maximus? Has a certain ring to it. Why did you take the beating?'

Gerontius tried to shrug but thought better of it. The medicus ordinarius had done his best with honey and stitches, but he had made no bones about it. Infection might still set in and on no account was Gerontius to exert himself. 'What's fine, what's Roman,' he said. 'As praeses I was expected to do just that. If my men can take it, so can I.'

'We don't flog officers,' Justinus murmured, appalled anew by the reality of what had actually happened.

'We don't appoint Caesars from the gutter either. This Gratian, they tell me, is a whoremaster and thief from Londinium.'

'Is?' Justinus sat down on one of Gerontius' couches. 'Don't you mean "was"?'

'As God is my judge,' Gerontius said, 'I have no idea what happened to him.'

'He was hanged, Gerontius,' Justinus shouted, 'from your own walls. I've just had his body taken to the valetudinarium.'

'Yes,' Gerontius said. 'I mean, I don't know who is responsible. I was about to have him cut down when you arrived.'

'By your logic,' Justinus said, 'and by all that's fine and Roman, you are responsible. If your men did it, so did you. What's the punishment for murder, praeses?'

'Death.' Gerontius sat as straight as his tortured back would let him.

'Death,' Justinus nodded. 'Assemble the legion. All of them. Full arms. Hollow square.'

Gerontius took a deep breath. 'May I remind you that you are no longer Dux Britannorum? You have no jurisdiction here at all.'

Justinus crossed the room in two strides and hauled the man upright, watching him wince as the spasms caught his back. 'And may I remind you that the Second Augusta has backed not one usurper but two in the last year. You and I are too young to remember the generals of the old days – Caesar and Crassus and Corbulo. They knew how to teach legions a lesson, Gerontius. They used decimation – the death of one man in ten at the cudgels of the other nine.'

'You wouldn't dare!' Gerontius blinked, his voice a whisper.

'Well,' and a grim smile spread over Justinus' face, 'there's only one way to find out, isn't there?'

He lay in the valetudinarium at Rutupiae, the son of Leocadius Honorius, sometime consul of Londinium and Honoria, a street woman now elevated to the gods. For all his neck was broken and his skin was turning blue, the lad was still handsome, a smaller, more malevolent shadow of his father.

For a while, Justinus let his memory wander. He saw four men out hunting in the wild moors of Valentia, carrying dead deer back to their army post. Except that there was no post. It had gone, destroyed by the barbarians from the north, slaughtering their comrades like sheep. He saw the faces of the men with him; his friend Paternus of the calm countenance and sure tread; Vitalis, the Christian who was never cut out to be a soldier and who worried he would be unable to find his way in the world; and there was Leocadius, the joker, the lover, the killer. How, Justinus asked himself again, as he had so often in the years that had passed since then, how could one man be all those things?

He looked down at the naked body, laid out now for burial. He had not been beaten, not been abused. It was just that his neck had broken. The weight of his body had caused the rest. Then he saw it, the gleam of gold on the dead man's finger. The ring. Leo's ring. The one given to him by the older Theodosius all those years ago because Leo, like Paternus and Vitalis and Justinus Coelius himself, were all heroes of the Wall. They had stood like oxen in the furrow against the wave of extinction that had threatened to topple Rome when the four were little more than boys. Now, Paternus was dead and his son was a prince of the Gododdin the Romans called the Votadini. Vitalis was a basket maker these days – perhaps he had found his way after all. Leocadius was dead too, the victim, men said, of his own woman, Honoria. And now, here was his son. But the ring was still there; whatever else they were, the murderers of the II Augusta were not thieves. Justinus worked the ring loose, with its four helmets in gold and jet and held it against his own. He toyed for a moment with putting it back, to consign it to the grave with this over-reacher who had reached far too far. Then he tucked it inside his tunic and left the corpse to await the fire.

The wind had risen along the walls and ramparts of Rutupiae as the II Augusta took their places on the parade ground. This was becoming something of a habit. In the past days they had stood to attention to proclaim their new Caesar. Then they had stood while their praeses was flogged. What would it be now?

'Decimation, I heard,' Quintillius grunted, adjusting his helmet as the ranks formed up.

'Never,' Seniacus said. 'Nobody does that any more; there aren't enough of us left.'

'Nobody orders the fustuarium either,' Locicero muttered, 'but Quint and I were part of it. Remember Marcus?'

Seniacus spat into the mud.

'Are you sure you're up to this, Lo?' Quintillius asked.

'There's not much call in the army for a one-armed man these days.'

'I'm more of a soldier with my left arm than anybody in the Second Cohor is with both.'

'You got that right,' Quintillius grinned at him. 'Jupiter Highest and Best, it's the Dux Britannorum. I mean the old one. I mean …'

'I think you mean the *real* one,' Seniacus murmured, watching Justinus take up his position on the praeses' dais. They all looked at him, the men of his contubernium. Say what you like about old Seniacus, he had flashes of pure genius at times.

'Men of the Second Augusta,' Justinus roared when the only other sound was the wind snapping the wooden tongues of the dragon standards. 'You know me. I was Dux Britannorum and in the absence of Constantine, who holds that rank now, I have one question to ask. I expect it to be answered.'

He waited until the moment was right and held up Scipio's ring, flashing in the sunlight. 'Who killed the Caesar?' he asked.

Silence. Then a shuffle and Quintillius took a step out of the ranks. 'I did, sir,' he said.

All eyes swivelled to look at him. 'So did I,' another voice called. That was Locicero.

'Actually,' Seniacus lifted his shield and moved out of line, 'it was me.'

'And me.'

'And me,'

'You're all talking bollocks. I did it.'

As Justinus watched, the entire legion had taken three steps forward, all shouting their guilt at the tops of their voices. He half turned to Gerontius and his officers.

'Will you cut us all down?' the praeses asked.

'Promise me one thing, Marcellus Gerontius,' Justinus said.

'If I can, sir.'

'That the Second Augusta will leave politics alone and go back to soldiering again.'

Gerontius smiled. 'We'll do our very best,' he said.

CHAPTER XIX

Londinium

'I have no words, lady.' The circitor stood to attention in the consul's palace watching Honoria read Justinus' letter. Her son was dead, the victim of legionary violence. Justinus was sorry, but Honoria must understand that a legion was like a slave – loyal and brave; but push that slave too far and who knew what the consequences might be.

Honoria had always known, in her heart of hearts, that this day would come. She was a street girl from the east of the city who had got to the basilica and the consul's palace by lying on her back. Death, swift and sudden, had been around her always. She neither welcomed it nor feared it. Death was just something that she had always known, like the Thamesis that glided dark and deep past her door. But this was different. This was her Scipio, her boy. She could still see him, tripping over his outsize robes when Leocadius had been consul, watching his face wrinkle in disgust when he had taken his first sip of wine. She had other memories too, memories of the dark and the night. Her son killed people. But then, so did she.

'Has Justinus found the culprits?' she asked the messenger. She felt sure there had to be more than one.

The circitor shifted uneasily.

'Out with it,' she snapped, her face a mask of hatred.

'The whole legion confessed to it, lady,' the messenger said.

'I see.' She drew herself up to her full height and swept across the room towards her private quarters. Her ladies waited here, as stunned by the news as she was. Suddenly, a thought occurred to Honoria and she turned back to the messenger. 'My son's ring,' she said imperiously, 'the Wall ring that was his father's. Where is it?'

'Er … I have no knowledge of that, lady'

'No,' she shook her head sadly, 'no, of course not.' She sniffed, defying the world to mock her grief and let the letter fall. Then she smiled at the messenger. 'You've ridden from Rutupiae,' she said. 'Come here. I have a little something for you.'

The circitor breathed a sigh of relief. He couldn't understand why he had been chosen with this most delicate, most personal task. He could think of a dozen men of the II better suited to it than he was. He stood near the grieving mother, not yet in her funeral weeds.

'Closer,' she whispered.

He obliged, watching as she fumbled in her purse for the coins he expected to come his way. He saw the gleam of gold, more of the same that this woman's son, the rumour ran, had brought with him to Rutupiae to buy himself a legion. What the circitor did not see, because it came too fast and too silently, was the knife blade that took his breath away. It slashed across his throat, the blood pumping as he gurgled and writhed, using both hands to try to staunch it, both hands to stay alive. He failed.

Only now, as the blood dripped from the blade tip, did Honoria Honorius let her tears flow. They ran the length of her cheek and dropped onto her night-robe.

'A circitor,' she growled, looking down at the body still twitching at her feet. 'My only son is dead and Justinus Coelius sends a circitor to tell me.' She looked up suddenly to where her women crouched, terrified in the half-dark beyond the curtain. 'Look to yourself, Justinus Coelius,' she hissed, like the Medusa she was. 'You there,' she snapped at the women. 'Clean this mess up.'

Rutupiae

The Dux Britannorum had heard the rumours in Flavia Caesariensis, that the Caesar, Scipio Gratianus, was dead; murdered, it was said by the II Augusta. It was not the first time that a legion had turned on an unpopular commander and it gave him no comfort at all to think that it would not be the last.

He swung out of his saddle, throwing the reins to an orderly and took the steps to the principia two at a time. The place was a hive of activity, officers circled around maps, everybody talking at once. Gerontius, Constantine had expected to see. When he had ridden north to inspect his troops, he had left the man in charge, after all. The man he did not expect to see was Justinus Coelius, like a ghost at the feast.

It had been months since these two had last met and Constantine had to admit that Justinus looked a lot better today.

'Dux.' Justinus put the man at his ease by according him the rank many believed that Justinus still held. 'Welcome.' They shook hands in the old soldiers' way and Justinus stepped aside.

'No,' Constantine said. 'Stay where you are. I've been away from all this. What's happening?'

Gerontius seemed disinclined to tell him so Justinus took up the tale. 'You've heard about Scipio – the Caesar?'

'I have,' Constantine nodded. 'A friend of yours, Justinus, wasn't he?'

'In another life,' Justinus said solemnly, 'his father was. Loyalties change.'

'They do that,' Constantine acknowledged.

'We've more pressing matters,' Justinus passed him a bundle of parchment scrolls. 'We found these on Scipio's table on the night he died. I think you should read them.'

Constantine did. No one moved while he read. All eyes were on him, waiting. 'A conspiracy,' he said, looking from man to man, 'He was a traitor.' He looked at Justinus. 'You've been here before,' he said, 'in the rebellion of Valentinus; the attack on the Wall. Tell me, is it all going to happen all over again?'

Justinus had been here before, a long, grim time ago, it seemed to him now. 'There's a difference,' he said, sitting down and folding his arms. 'Valentinus was a barbarian; cleverer than most, I'll grant you that. And a general. But this is different. Scipio wrote to the leaders of the painted ones, of the Scotti and the high king of Tara – with whom, incidentally, I have a score to settle. But he also intended to bring in the Second here and the Twentieth and the Sixth. If he'd done that, he'd have achieved the impossible. And had Britannia in his purse.'

'He aimed for the purple,' Gerontius spoke for the first time, 'talked of a march on Rome.'

'He'll have to join the queue,' Justinus chuckled. 'Valentinus started it all those years ago.' He looked around the room. 'It was when most of you were still shitting yellow. He proved what could be done if the barbarians banded together. We've had five hundred years of the power and the glory, gentlemen. Is it somebody else's turn now?'

'But now we know what's going on,' Gerontius said, 'we can nip it in the bud. Strike first and strike fast. Scipio's given us all the ammunition we need.'

'Not quite,' Constantine said. 'What's this?' He held up a parchment scroll, unfinished, unheaded.

Justinus nodded. 'The Caesar was interrupted,' he said, 'before he could finish that. And we don't know who it was to be sent to. You'll see, it carries the same message as the others. And yet …'

'It's the Saxons,' Gerontius said. 'Those flaxen-haired bastards have been raiding our coasts for years. Scipio will have been kissing arses across the German Sea.'

'No,' Justinus said. 'No, I don't think it's that simple.'

The German Sea

The white horses roared and thundered in the waves as the little ship rose to each crest and wallowed in the hollows. Pelagius, for all his travels, had never been much of a sailor and now he just wanted to die. He had been released from Chrysanthos' custody and given a day to leave Britannia. The vicarius made it abundantly clear that there would be no more chances. Intercessions had been made on his behalf by an interested party – Chrysanthos had not told him that that was Vitalis the basket-maker – and so he had gained his freedom.

So Pelagius could breathe the air again, as long as it was not the air of Britannia. This time Pelagius had persuaded Vitalis. The pair had long ago planned to go to Rome, the fabled city of the seven hills that had governed both their lives since they came kicking and screaming into the world; the city that governed them still. And now, at last, Vitalis was ready. He had always felt that *something* was keeping him in Britannia but he never knew quite what. Now, suddenly, Pelagius' honeyed words made sense. They needed baskets in Rome too and the Tiber's reeds were likely to be as handy in that respect as those of the Thamesis.

As for Pelagius, he went wherever God sent him. And today, at the mercy of this wild sea, he felt that God wanted him in the east. Even so, did the journey have to be *so* awful? The rain drove hard, bouncing off the sail and the rigging, the decks awash with every surge and roll of the tide. Pelagius lay under an awning, praying, contemplating, *anything* to take his mind off the churning in his stomach.

Vitalis had no such problem. He stood on the prow, the wind whipping his cloak behind him and watching the grey-green horizon twist and shift. The lad Petronius stood beside him. Unlike his master, he had never left Britannia before and the world seemed huge and not a little terrifying. But he smiled up at Vitalis because he would follow his master anywhere and he heard that the fish in the Tiber were twice as big as the minnows he caught at home. That was enough for him.

'Sail ho!'

Vitalis turned at the sailor's shout. In their wake, another ship was butting its way through the white horses, disappearing momentarily below the wave-tops before leaping clear again. Petronius was excited. This was a race. The ship behind them was going to take them on. Then he saw another ship and another.

'Who are they?' he asked Vitalis above the roar of the wind. His master's face was grim and there was no light of excitement in his eyes.

'Stay here,' Vitalis told him and he staggered along the heaving deck to the helmsman wrestling with the tiller at the stern.

'Saxons?' he shouted to the man.

The helmsman nodded. 'Pirates,' he said, 'and they outnumber us three to one.'

Vitalis didn't need to be told the odds. The Saxon ships were war vessels, long and low and sleek and he could see their oar blades smashing through the water. They were in full sail too so that their speed was twice that of the Roman tub that Vitalis sailed.

'Can we outrun them?' he asked.

The helmsman spat onto the deck and wiped his mouth with a sodden sleeve. 'If Neptune wills it,' he muttered. This was no time for a doctrinal conversation. If this man was putting his faith in a myth who ruled the deep, that was up to him. Vitalis put his trust in God. And he hoped God was listening. The only oars on board were used for manoeuvring in harbours and shallow waters. They were useless in rough seas like this and there weren't enough of them. Vitalis the basket-maker became Vitalis the soldier again in that instant. He took stock. There were eight crewmen, four passengers including a seasick Christian and a boy. Only the sailors carried weapons and at long range had nothing at all.

The helmsman narrowed his eyes at Vitalis. The man wore a cross around his neck – that couldn't be good. His lads were superstitious, like all sailors and half of them thought the cross on board ship was bad luck. Then his scowl turned to a smile and he started laughing. Vitalis stared at him; had the man gone mad? The Saxons were gaining fast. He could see the rain and spray bouncing off their bright shields, buckled to their ships' hulls and he could hear the occasional guttural shout carried on the wind. The helmsman pointed ahead. Beyond the carved prow, the dragon head dipping and rising on the savage swell, a great blackness was spreading over the sea, so that the spray flashed silver against it.

'What's that?' Vitalis asked.

'That's old Neptune, laddie,' the helmsman laughed. 'Oh, you of little faith. To landsmen like you, it's a storm. The wind does strange things out here. It's running us north at the moment and it's driving us towards the Sands.'

'The sands?'

'Many a sailor's grave, laddie.' The helmsman gripped harder as the ship bucked and shuddered, hit broadside by a sudden wave. 'For the unwary, that is. But me, well I can navigate them in my sleep. I'll lay you any odds you like that our Saxon friends don't know them like I do. Herminius, grab this bloody helm or we'll all go over.'

Another saturated sailor scuttled along the treacherous planking and both men bent their backs to holding the rudder steady. 'You'd better get below and take the lad with you. It's going to get rough in a minute.'

In the end, Vitalis had no idea which way the wind had taken them. All he knew was that the weather they had been sailing through was an oasis of calm before the storm proper hit. At the suggestion of the helmsman, he had taken Petronius to the shelter under the awnings where the wind was less and the rain not so constant. Pelagius had barely acknowledged the pair, his mind focussed on the continual rising of his gorge. Weak from vomiting, he had lain on his bed, trying to stay on the framework without rolling across the deck. Vitalis had watched the Saxon ships nearing, then fading as the seas engulfed them. At one moment, they had been close enough to throw their spears and he saw the flaxen-haired bastards briefly, grinning as they were about to take their Roman prize. Then the tide and the wind and the white horses had carried them apart and the moment was lost.

He had heard a roar from the deck above and behind him and had seen, under the madly flapping canvas, the sailors slapping each other's backs. One of the pirate ships had hit the sands, running aground on what looked like open sea. The curved keel had furrowed into the quicksand and the sail bucked and the spar swung. The men on board had been thrown from their decks to flounder and drown in the cloying mud until the sea washed over them.

Night had fallen before they lost sight of the other two ships but they had not come as close again and it was all their crews could do to stay away from the Sands and to stay alive.

In the cold light of the grey dawn on the second day the Roman ship had run aground too, jarring as it hit the shingle of the beach and sliding to a halt at a crazy angle. Pelagius wiped himself down as best he could and tried to stand. He had lost count of the hours he had been flat on his back and day and night had become meaningless. He thanked God quietly for bringing him safe to land but he never wanted to cross a sea – or eat anything – again as long as he lived. They had lost a crewman in the night to a freak wave as it had smashed the ship and swept him overboard, to disappear in the blackness, a sacrifice to Neptune.

Above them on the tilted deck, a sheer cliff of red sandstone rose in the morning, the gulls wheeling above it, watching for any scraps that these exhausted sailors might have with them. The helmsman was first ashore, having secured the ship with his anchors and Petronius was next, enjoying the feeling of the shingle crunching under his feet. It wasn't solid, but it was safer, he knew, than the sea.

'Where are we?' Vitalis joined them on the shore. 'Any idea?'

'Well, not Bononia, that's for sure. The wind drove us north of the Sands.' He screwed his weather beaten face up to the sky, taking in the sea and the lie of the land. The waves had subsided now and it was as if the storm had never been. 'We're standing on Britannia Secunda now, I reckon. Herminius?'

The sailor leaned over the ship's rail.

'This is your old patch, isn't it? Where the bloody hell are we?'

It was Herminius' turn to check the sky and the horizon of

land. He licked his finger and held it up to catch the wind. 'Estuary's to the south,' he said. 'I reckon we're not a million Roman miles from Arbeia.'

'Arbeia?' Vitalis frowned. 'That's the Wall, as near as dammit.'

'That's *your* old patch.' Pelagius was resting on the ship's rail, deciding it was time he joined the human race again.

'It is,' Vitalis nodded.

'They've got their own boatmen there, you know,' Herminius said, tying off ropes and securing hatches. 'They're all the way from the Tigris in Mesopotamia. The Tynus is a bitch of a river and the current's something fierce. Give me the German Sea any day.'

'I doubt *they're* thinking that,' the helmsman grunted. He pointed out to that sea, to where two sails were pale dots on the horizon. 'Our friends the Saxons. Looks like we didn't entirely shake them off after all.'

'Where are they heading?' Vitalis asked him, although he knew the answer already.

'Well,' he said, 'if they keep on that course, they'll reach Valentia. Now what in the name of Neptune would they be doing there?'

Londinium

Severianus had not expected to see Honoria Honorius in his church. True, she had been before but always in the exalted company of the vicarius, an official appearance in which he flaunted her beauty just to annoy, the bishop was sure, the ladies of the Ordo. Yet for the past week now she had come alone, without escort or even maidservant, to pray in the little private chapel. She had nodded to him in the silence of the nave but took no communion. It was all very odd. If anyone had asked Severianus, he would have said that the woman worshipped Bacchus or Isis or worse, no god at all. She had no place in a Christian church, of that he was sure.

'Madam,' he finally said, one cold morning with the fingers of an early frost on the window glass. 'You are troubled.'

She had finished her devotions, lying, as the Christians did, face down on the cold of the flagstoned floor. Now, she pulled her hood up over her head and swept noiselessly to the door. She stopped and looked at him.

'I have lost my son,' she said.

Severianus knew that. All of Londinium knew that. And all of Britannia beyond it. But Severianus was first and foremost a politician and today he was playing the wide-eyed innocent. 'I am sorry,' he said. 'The ways of the Lord are strange sometimes.'

She fixed him with the stare she had used on brothel-keepers, consuls and half Vandal generals. 'It's the ways of men that concern me, priest,' she said.

Severianus bridled. He was not used to being spoken to as a mere priest and certainly not by a woman. But then he remembered that Honoria was not just *a* woman, she was *the* woman of the vicarius. 'Can I help?' he asked, hoping she would say 'no' and leave.

Honoria hadn't moved. 'What does your God say about murder?' she asked.

'It is one of His Commandments,' Severianus explained. 'You shall not kill.'

'And if you do?'

'Then God shall punish you,' Severianus said, 'in His own way and in His own time.'

Honoria shook her head. 'That's not certain or soon enough,' she said.

'It is all I can offer,' the bishop shrugged. 'Perhaps you would prefer the answer of the Lord of Wrong.'

'The devil, is that what you call him?' Her voice rang clear in the echoing chamber.

Severianus crossed himself quickly. 'I do,' he said.

She smiled. 'So be it,' she said. 'I have found no answers here, priest. And I know where the devil lives.'

The logs shifted and crumbled in the hearth that night and Chrysanthos reached out to feel the warmth of the fire. Mother of God, it was cold. The hypocaust wasn't working, despite the ministrations of the vicarius' plumbers. He sensed rather than heard her come into the room, her cloak trailing over the mosaic of the atrium. For weeks now she had shunned his bed, ate her meals alone and avoided his company. At first he had tried to talk to her, to understand. But he was a man. He had never borne a child, never felt the tug of a tiny mouth at the breast or the kick of an unborn infant in the belly. When Scipio Honorius had died, a useful ally of Chrysanthos had gone. But when Scipio Honorius had died, the bottom had fallen out of his mother's world.

Chrysanthos had finished being reasonable. There was a long list of eligible girls, every bit as nubile and accommodating as Honoria and younger. His patience was at an end. 'Lady,' he said as she poured herself a cup of wine. 'It is time this charade ended.'

'Charade?' She arched an eyebrow.

'The sorrowing mother. According to custom …'

'Since when have you and I concerned ourselves about custom, Chrysanthos?' she asked. 'The first time you took me, it was on the floor of the basilica. I seem to remember there were a few startled members of the Ordo waiting to see you on business. And one or two client kings from the north too.'

He smiled despite himself. He stood up. 'I would have those times back,' he said and reached out to stroke her cheek.

'I can't.' She pulled away. 'Not until my Scipio is avenged.'

He let her hand fall and took another swig of wine. 'That old song,' he muttered.

'The devil has the best tunes.'

'What? What are you talking about?'

'Nothing.' Her smile was cold.

'Honoria.' He put his cup down. 'Tell me, who do you blame for Scipio's death?'

'You,' she said. 'Me. Oh, I don't know. The Second Augusta.'

He spread his arms, his point made. 'It's the way of it, Honoria. Scipio, your darling, was a vicious bastard and he was born to die young. You should know – you taught him.'

'Yes,' she said, levelly. 'Yes, I taught him. Perhaps not well enough.'

'He over-reached himself,' Chrysanthos said. 'Here in the shit-hole sewers of this city of ours, here, he was at home. But playing soldier, striving for the purple, that was madness beyond his wildest dreams. It could never have worked.'

'You sent him,' she snapped. 'You gave him a chest of silver and set him on his road.'

'No, I didn't,' Chrysanthos protested. 'Yes, I backed Terentius Marcus and for my own purposes. But Scipio had ideas above his station. He *stole* the silver out from under my nose.'

'You must have put the idea into his head,' she pouted, defiant to the last.

He shook his head. 'Can you hear yourself?' he shouted.

'Whatever ideas were in that boy's head, *you* put there. You and Leocadius Honorius, the hero of the Wall.' He spat out the last words with all the contempt he could muster.

There was a silence. Then Honoria said, 'It's another hero of the Wall I blame the most. Justinus Coelius.'

'Justinus?' Chrysanthos frowned. 'What's he got to do with it?'

'Nothing,' she said. 'That's precisely it. He did *nothing* to those bastards in the Second who hanged my Scip. He sent me a letter such as you would send to your blacksmith. And he sent it by a circitor; two up from the scum of the earth he came from.'

Chrysanthos was still shaking his head. 'Has it come down to this?' he asked her. 'That all this wailing and hair-tearing is about you being a snob?'

Another silence.

'Will you help me?' she asked.

'To do what?'

'To kill Justinus.'

He laughed. 'Since when do you need my help for that?' he asked. 'Even without your malcontent son, you're perfectly capable of doing that yourself.'

'Oh, yes,' she admitted, 'in some dark alleyway or over a friendly cup of wine. But I'd have to reach him first. There's no love lost between us. He'd be on his guard, ready. Unless you,' she closed to him, reaching up and running her finger over his cheek and into his hair, 'you, he trusts. Justinus Coelius is a slave of duty. He's a by-the-book soldier and you represent authority. Order him here, to Londinium, that's all I ask.'

She moved closer, pressing herself against him, grinding her hips against his. Her lips parted and she took his hand, placing it on her breasts.

'No.' He pulled away sharply. 'Not any more, Honoria. I've done all the killing I intend to do. I seem to remember that in your late husband's day, if I may give him his … courtesy title for a moment, you were banished to one wing of this house, the House of the Night, I understand he called it.'

She nodded, scowling.

'Well,' he said, 'I like the sound of that. Consider the arrangements as before and I'll have the builders in by morning. Goodnight, lady.' And he left.

Which was a pity. Because *nobody* turned down Honoria.

CHAPTER XX

Arbeia

Hadrianus of blessed memory had built Arbeia as a supply base for his campaigns in Valentia and Caledonia. The granaries stood there still, although today few of them were full and the garrison was only a fraction of its full complement.

Herminius, the helmsman and the rest of the crew were made welcome while they saw to the repairs to their ship and Vitalis, Pelagius and the boy were put up at the mansio, the old building a prey to draughts and leaks. It was later that night that the men sat talking around the open fire. Petronius was fast asleep in a corner, his dreams full of the rolling sea and the thunder of the wind. There was a knock at the door; Vitalis opened it.

'It *is* you! I don't believe it.'

Calpurnius Succatus stood there, beaming. He and Vitalis shook hands and hugged each other and there were introductions all round.

'You're a long way from Londinium, Vitalis,' Calpurnius said, accepting a cup of warm wine and a hunk of cheese.

'I could say the same of you,' Vitalis said. 'How's Conchessa? Little Tullia?'

'Conchessa's … well,' the decurion said. 'As for Tullia, she's not so little these days. How long has it been since you saw her?'

'Must be nearly three years.' Vitalis told him.

'She'll be turning boys' heads before too long,' Calpurnius sighed. 'Mind you, if I catch any of them …' The fathers sitting around the fire nodded and laughed. They would all of them do the same.

'And Patric?' Vitalis knew he had to ask. 'No news, I suppose?'

'None.' Calpurnius shook his head.

'You know I wanted to come north,' Vitalis said. 'Offer what help I could.'

'I know,' Calpurnius nodded. 'Conchessa keeps all your letters. It was much appreciated, Vitalis, but ... well, we have to be realists. Patric's gone.'

There was a silence.

Vitalis broke it. 'So, what brings you to Arbeia?'

'The line of duty,' Calpurnius explained. 'The vicarius wants a report on the state of the Wall garrisons. I'll pass it by the praeses of the Sixth, of course.'

'And what is the state of the garrisons?' Pelagius asked him.

Calpurnius didn't know Pelagius well. He had met him in Londinium and had heard of the man wherever Rome's imperium stood. He was trouble, a pain in the arse of the church and the establishment. He asked awkward questions to which nobody had an answer. But this was a military question and it didn't sound right coming from his lips.

'Why would you want to know?' Calpurnius asked him.

'We ran into Saxon pirates on our way here,' Vitalis cut in. 'They were making for Valentia.'

'And we were making for Rome,' Pelagius reminded him. 'What can we read into that?'

'You and I once stood shoulder to shoulder in Bishop Severianus' church,' Calpurnius said, 'but, if memory serves, we had differing reasons. You challenged the bishop; I took on the vicarius.'

'And yet, we're still here,' Pelagius smiled. He knew about little Patric, knew about his father's exile. What he had not realised was how much those things would have changed him.

'God's will,' Calpurnius nodded. 'We often have raids along the coast,' he said. 'Saxons come and go. It was just your bad luck that you met them on the high seas.'

Vitalis shook his head. 'I'm not sure luck had much to do with it,' he said. 'Maybe it's the old soldier in me, but I smell trouble in the wind. Calpurnius, I'm not asking you to give any secrets away, but I'm guessing the whole Wall garrison doesn't amount to more than a thousand men, strung out from here to Maia.'

Calpurnius nodded. 'Something like that,' he said.

There was a thud beyond the door and a sharp rattle. It swung wide and a circitor stood here, stained from travel. 'Decurion. Come quickly. There's news from the south.'

Londinium

She'd seen it all before, of course. She'd grown up with it. And before they saw her, she saw them. Julia of the Two Hands was sitting in the Hen's Tooth that night, two men pawing and kissing her, each one about to be lighter of a purse. In the street outside where the open sewer ran to the Thamesis, little Veronica was waiting patiently on her crutches for the first kind heart of the night to cross her palm.

But it wasn't either of them that Honoria wanted. It was that other faithful lapdog of her late son's, the clumsiest drunk in London, Placidus. She saw him wending his way along the path by the bridge, shambling in the dark. Once or twice he swung wide towards a passer-by and when he couldn't quite reach them, he cursed loudly in his drink and broke wind. Honoria lowered the hood as far as she could so that he couldn't see her face. She knew Placidus' targets were usually men, but her cloak was worth a consul's ransom and she knew that Placidus wouldn't be able to resist her.

She let him totter into the gutter and moved out of the shadows so that the fitful moon threw its gleam onto her jewellery and made her rings glitter like stars.

On cue, the big man collided with her, mumbling an apology and she felt the slight tug on her purse. In an instant, she had grabbed the man's wrist and forced it behind his back, swinging him around so that his face hit the brickwork. He cursed and grunted, feeling the blood trickle from his lip.

'No harm, lady,' he mumbled. 'I'm in drink and I stumbled.'

'You're no more in drink than I am, Placidus and the day you *really* stumble, I'll become a Vestal Virgin, whether their fire's still burning or not.' The man hauled himself free and she released her grip.

'Honoria!' he gasped.

'How have you been, you old reprobate?'

'I heard,' he frowned. 'About Scip, I mean. We're all gutted.

Gutted.'

'I'm sure you are,' she said, making sure that her purse was still in place. 'Tell me, who are you working for now? Who's the Rex Inferni these days?'

'Well, he's nothing like your Scip, of course,' Placidus said. 'To be honest with you' – now, that was an odd remark from this man – 'it's all gone to Hell in a handcart, since … well, you know. His name's …'

'No!' She held up her hand. 'Probably better I don't know.' She pulled back the hood and looked at the man. He was stone cold sober, tall and well built. Yes, he'd do. 'Tell me, something, Placidus,' she smiled. 'Ever thought of joining the army?'

Eboracum

The praeses Publius Dio didn't like the sound of it. He hadn't expected to see Justinus Coelius again so soon, yet here he was, bringing rumours of wars. And when a man like Justinus Coelius spoke, it was as well to listen.

'He'd never have got away with that.' Dio was finishing the chicken that he and Justinus had demolished. 'This Scipio whatever he called himself.'

'Oh, I don't think he ever had any intention of marching on Rome,' Justinus said. 'All that was so much hot air. Magnus Maximus had done it and his name, as you know, still moves men who follow the eagles. No, Scipio was too self-centred for that. He was a chancer but he must have known his limitations. With the legions in his purse and the barbarians dancing to his tune, he could have declared himself emperor of Britannia and the rest of the Empire could go hang.'

'Emperor of Britannia!' Dio laughed, waving his cup in the air for the slave to refill. 'This place will never be much more than a pimple on the arse of Rome. Oh, sorry, I keep forgetting you're a local.'

'I was born here, yes,' Justinus said, 'but I'd have to agree with you. The point is, Dio, that the barbarians are still at our gates. That's why I'm here.'

Dio clapped his hands and cleared the room of unwanted ears. 'Should I assemble my officers?' he asked.

'Not yet,' Justinus rinsed his fingers. 'I wanted a private chat first.'

Dio led the way to the couches in the principia's anteroom. 'What do we know?' he asked.

'We know that Scipio was in touch with the Scotti, the Picti and Niall of however many hostages he has now. Possibly the Saxons too. The letters we found seemed to be some sort of diary – a timing phase of the plan. He was to march to Deva to be elected Caesar by the Twentieth, then here where you and the Sixth would pay him the same respect.'

'In his dreams.' Dio shook his head. 'It looks as though young Scipio was confusing us with those fickle bastards in the Second.'

'After that, he was going to meet up with the barbarians.' He got up and crossed to Dio's wall maps. 'The question is, where?'

Dio joined him. 'Depends on the size of the Hiberni contingent,' he said. 'If Niall Mugmedon is serious about this, he could strike anywhere. The Deceangli territory, perhaps. Or the far west of Britannia Prima.'

'Or Valentia.' Justinus was looking at the space north of the Wall.

'Or Valentia,' Dio nodded his agreement. He had been a boy when the rebel Valentinus had welded the barbarians together long enough to flood over the Wall like an unstoppable tide. But he had read the legionary history of the VI and he had talked to men who were there, as he was talking to one now. The VI Victrix had been an island of calm in a raging sea of panic, a sea that threatened to engulf them all and to sweep civilization away with it. And now that tide was rising again.

'Seems likely,' he said. 'The Scotti can cross the Hibernian Sea and the Picti are here in their freezing mountains already. The Saxons, if they're part of this, can land anywhere along the east coast. There's no Pinnata Castra to hold them now. All of the deified Agricola's forts have long gone.'

'How strong is the Wall?' Justinus asked.

'Every milecastle's manned,' Dio told him. 'That's the good news.'

'And the bad?'

Dio went back to his couch. 'I heard from the decurion Calpurnius Succatus the other day. He's a bean counter and he counts less than a thousand heads along those ramparts.'

'And here at Eboracum?'

'Including sick and malingerers, another thousand, give or

take.'

'We'll take,' Justinus said. 'The sick and malingerers too. And we won't give an inch.' He wandered back from the maps. 'I speak with the authority of the Dux Britannorum, Dio,' he said. 'From yesterday, I want your men in training, campaign ready. Can it be done?'

'From yesterday, no,' Dio smiled. 'But from tomorrow, of course.'

'Good,' Justinus said. 'Put your cavalry out from the Wall, north and south for one day's ride. Alert every milecastle and stock them with provisions.'

Dio ran a finger around the rim of his wine cup. 'The Scotti, the Picti, the Hiberni,' he said.

'And the Saxoni,' Justinus added. 'Don't forget the Saxoni.'

'Then I feel it my military duty to point out, Justinus, that we don't have a hope in Hell.'

'Ordinarily, I'd agree with you. But Constantine is coming north. He'll link up with the Twentieth and join us here. The barbarians think they'll be taking on a handful of Wall soldiers. Instead, we'll give them three legions.'

Three legions. Publius Dio was something of an historian. And he knew as a boy what happened to three legions long ago when the Christians' Jesus was a boy in Galilee. The Seventeenth, the Eighteenth and the Nineteenth had disappeared into the blackness of the Teutoberg forest in Germania and had been cut to pieces by the barbarians there. It was the worst military defeat ever imposed on a Roman army. Publius Dio knew it. Justinus Coelius knew it. Yet neither man spoke of it. They were different legions in different days. It couldn't happen again.

Could it?

Britannia Prima

Constantine, the Dux Britannorum, was still east of Abona when the news reached him. Stilicho was dead. The letter spoke of treachery and deceit. The half Vandal had made enemies, that was certain. And those enemies had turned against him now, preferring the weak boy emperor who loved chickens to the only man who could have held the Empire together. They had charged him with treason, with murder, with plotting to take the purple himself. Whatever abominable crime was going, they said, Stilicho was guilty of it. So, in the heat of an August day, they had killed him.

Constantine rode on at the head of his Ala of the II, his staff officers trotting behind him on the road to Deva. He spoke to no one, ignored their cheery small talk and in the end urged his stallion forward so that he was out of hearing range of their prattle. And by the time he reached Deva, his mind was made up.

Din Paladyr

The summer had come early to Valentia south of the Estuary and it had gone already. Tullia was with her bees as she had often been since old Cran was killed. Here, in this field with the buttercups nodding in the tall grass, was the last place she had seen Patric, the big brother she idolised. For a long time she had gone over the details of their last day together and they had haunted her dreams. Now, though, with the passing of the weeks and months, it was all beginning to fade and she hated herself because she couldn't quite remember Patric's face.

'What are you doing?' The voice made her start. She hadn't heard him, any more than she had heard the dark riders of the Danaan who had taken her brother. He was a scruffy boy, not much older than she was. In fact, he was about Patric's age. He was sitting in the saddle of a sturdy mountain pony but she could tell he wasn't much of a rider.

'Minding my own business,' she said. Tullia had all the acquired frostiness of her mother when the mood took her and she had no intention of spending any more time on nattering to a peasant.

'Are they bees?' he asked, mesmerized by the myriad wings fluttering in the sunlight.

Tullia toyed with clapping in mock applause, but she knew that that would disturb the bees so she thought better of it. 'You're quick,' she said, deftly sliding the honey comb from a hive. The boy looked horrified when they settled thickly on her hands and arms. He'd never seen bees before but he knew that they stung and that those stings were the deadliest poison.

'Aren't you afraid?' he asked, sliding out of the saddle. His pony wandered a little way away, as nervous of the bees as he was.

'Of course not,' she laughed. 'Where are you from that you haven't seen bees before?'

'Londinium,' he said. 'That's …'

'I know where it is,' she said. 'I used to live there.'

'Did you?'

She looked him up and down. He was sort of handsome in a peasant sort of way, with dark eyes and curly hair. He carried a knife at his belt but he didn't look like the lads of Din Paladyr who could split willows with their arrows and fought each other with swords and axes.

'Do you like sweet things, Londinium boy?' she asked.

He nodded.

'Try this then,' and she handed him a piece of the honey comb. He sniffed it and put it to his lips.

'That's good,' he slurped, the honey running down his chin.

'Of course it is,' she said. 'The bees make it.'

'What's your name?' The boy was tucking in to the sweet goodness with a vengeance now.

'Tullia,' she told him. 'My papa's the decurion here. What's yours?'

'Petronius,' he said. 'Petronius Borro. I make baskets.'

'What are you doing here?' she asked him. 'You're so far from home.'

'I was wondering that,' a voice called.

The children looked up. Three horsemen sat their mounts at the edge of the meadow. 'Papa!' Tullia trilled. 'Uncle Vit!'

'Uncle Vit?' Petronius frowned, his mouth still full of honeycomb. 'Do you know him, then?'

Tullia paused, despite her mounting excitement. Her papa had been gone for weeks, inspecting the forts along the Wall. And she hadn't seen Uncle Vit since she had left Londinium. And she was only a little girl then. 'Of course I know him,' she pouted. 'He's my uncle.' And she ran to Calpurnius, who swung out of his saddle, Petronius running in her wake.

'When I talked about Tullia and boys,' Calpurnius winked at Vitalis, 'I didn't think Petronius was going to be my first problem.'

Deva

The sun was setting over the estuary of the Deva Fluvius. All day the ceremony had filled the barracks, the arena and the colonia was thronged with people. There was a new Caesar – a proper one this time – and his name was Flavius Constantinus. The XX had stood on the parade ground, wheeled and marched, formed their lines, collapsed into skirmish order, reformed to battle order, saluted their Caesar with the barritus, the thundering battle cry they had learned from all the tribes they had conquered. And if some of the more thoughtful souls in the ranks and among the officers made a mental note that Constantine was the third usurper to assume the laurel wreath in a space of a little over a year, well … there had to be a purpose to it all, didn't there?

Now, as the light faded and the night watch took their turn on the wall-walks, Constantine looked out over the gilded sea. To the west lay the territory of the Deceangli, with their formidable queen, Elen of the Armies, who had been the woman of the last man to attempt what Constantine contemplated now. Only the reasons were different; Magnus Maximus had taken on the emperor to claim the purple himself. Constantine was going to save Rome. There were rumours that were more than rumours. The Suebi, Vandals and the Alans had crossed the Rhenus, something they had been threatening for years and they were thousands. They had their woman, their children, their dogs. This was not a raiding party; it was a people on the march. And now there was no Stilicho to stop them. Just a halfwit boy who talked to chickens and a greedy, vicious knot of political backstabbers who had brought the great Stilicho down for their own greedy, vicious ends.

'To the praeses Publius Dio of the Sixth Victrix,' Constantine was dictating to the scribe who had set up his campaign table on the ramparts. A candle flared in the evening breeze, a pinpoint of light against the gold of the sky. 'I have today been elected Caesar by the Twentieth Valeria Victrix and already hold that exalted post – are you keeping up? – among the Second Augusta and will expect the same honour to be bestowed by your legion. I will be at Eboracum by the Ides.' He waited while the stylus finished scratching on the parchment. 'I'll sign it.' And he did. Flavius Constantinus Maximus left his mark for all men to see. There was another letter he had to write – the one telling Justinus Coelius that there had been a change of plan. The one that said that he, Constantine, had done exactly the same insane thing as Magnus Maximus, Terentius Marcus and Scipio Honorius had done. He had rebelled against his emperor. And the fact that it was for the greater good? How would that count with Justinus Coelius, a man who had never left Britannia's shores, a man who was expecting Constantine's help in whatever local difficulty was brewing? No,

Constantine knew, he could not write a letter like that. He would need to talk to Justinus, man to man and face to face. It was the Roman way.

Din Paladyr

Edern watched them for some time from his position in the rocks. Autumn had come to Valentia and the great fortress of the Gododdin stood grey and solid in the mist. All along the estuary, the fog crept and swirled, so that the shouts of the fishermen and the sailors were muffled and dead.

They were Saxon ships certainly and not the first that had been seen in the estuary. The German Sea brought them, the old grey widowmaker and they had been before. Some of the strangers settled quietly along the river and the coastal bays to the south, selling trinkets and catching eels in the brackish streams. They had women with them and children and Brenna had decided that, as long as they behaved themselves, they could stay. She had even learned a little of their language, that strange, guttural, back-of-the-throat sound that was so different from the soft Celtic of the Gododdin.

But the men that Edern was watching now weren't fishermen and trinket-sellers. They were warriors, bristling with weapons and there were four ships' companies of them. Their helmets obscured their faces, but he could see their flaxen hair woven in braids that hung over their shoulders, the wolfskin cloaks and the round shields painted with monsters only they had seen and symbols only they understood.

The prince of the Gododdin had forty men with him, not enough to win comfortably in a pitched battle. But Justinus Coelius, his father's old friend, had told him once that the best place to stop an enemy was at the coast; hit him while he was floundering in the shallows and battling with the surf. Edern wasn't about to let these raiders come ashore and lose themselves in the wilderness of Valentia.

He signalled his men to their horses and they emerged from their rocky hiding place to trot over the heather. No one spoke. The only sound was the soft thud of hooves and the jingle of bits. Spears were at the upright, swords undrawn. The Saxons were busy, as Edern had hoped, with securing their ships and they saw nothing. He reined in and waited. He could just make out along the dunes his horsemen in position, outflanking the little cluster of ships. There were shouts from the Saxons, barked commands and laughter. Ropes were hauled and sails furled.

'Welcome!' Edern yelled and time stood still.

The Saxons looked at each other, seeing the horsemen in the mist for the first time. They grabbed their shields and crouched behind them, some men kneeling, some standing, expecting a hail of arrows.

'Quite Roman, isn't it?' Edern said to the man at his elbow, who carried the battle standard of Belatucadros. 'A sort of testudo that isn't going anywhere.'

'It's a shield wall, puppy!' a harsh voice rang over the sands. Edern's horse jinked to one side, as surprised as its rider. The man not only had the hearing of a bat, he spoke fluent Gododdin. 'Look on it well; you'll see a lot more of these.'

'Who are you?' Edern asked.

'I am Cynewulf. Who are you?'

'Edern, of the Gododdin. These are my lands and you are trespassing.'

'And you've come to smack my wrists, boy?'

Edern had had enough of this man's insolence. 'No,' he said. 'I've come to kill you. But I'm a generous man. Put your toys away and sail east and we'll just call it a misunderstanding, shall we?'

From nowhere, a spear hissed through the fog, narrowly missing Edern's standard bearer. The prince sighed, drawing his sword. 'Very well,' he called. 'Your choice.'

'I think I should tell you,' Cynewulf said from the centre of the shield wall. 'We're not an advance guard; we're bringing up the rear. Eighty of our ships crept past you in the night. You're surrounded.'

Edern didn't move. What was this? The truth? In which case, whatever he did today would be his last move. Or was it a bluff? If it was, it hadn't worked. And he gave the order.

Iron had rung on iron along the estuary. As the ships had swayed and swung at anchor and the great river had slid past on its tidal journey, the skirmish had swung this way and that. The men behind the wall of overlapping shields had outnumbered the Gododdin but they were penned in by their own tight defences and in the end the sheer weight of the cavalry had told against them. As the Saxons had fallen, they had closed their ranks, until only a tiny handful had stood at the water's edge, knee deep in the rolling tide, parrying Gododdin sword strokes with tiring arms. Cynewulf had been one of the first to die, but his body had been held half upright by the press of his men and it had not been until the middle of that grey day that the fight had finished and the handful had thrown down their shields and surrendered.

Edern had been lucky today. His casualties were slight but he wasn't taking chances. He sent a tired horseman south to the Wall. Justinus Coelius, he had heard, was at Eboracum. It would take the messenger a week to reach him but he must be told about this. The news from Vitalis, now at Din Paladyr, was that a great war was coming; no one knew exactly when or where. And Edern sent another rider west to Din Eidyn. If Cynewulf had not been boasting, but telling the truth, then Taran's stronghold was in danger and he must be warned.

Din Eidyn

The noise in the great hall was deafening. Wine and ale flowed from mouth to mouth and the dancers slipped on the drink-sodden floor. The harps and the pipes were all but drowned out by the war whoops and laughter. In the centre, on the food-strewn table, two huge men, naked above the waist, wrestled each other, gouging and biting, to the wild cheering of the crowd.

Edern's messenger, already aching and exhausted from the fight at the estuary, had left his lathered horse in the courtyard and had struggled through the throng of writhing, drunken bodies. Taran saw him, travel and battle-stained, standing stony-faced in the centre of the hall. His smile faded and he clapped his hands. Slowly, the noise subsided, the wrestlers glad of the pause. The harps and pipes stopped with discordant squeaks and all eyes turned to the messenger.

'I fear you've upset the party,' Taran said before half turning to a near-naked girl on his left and dipping his head to kiss her breast. 'You've come from Din Paladyr.'

'I have, my lord.' The messenger dropped to one knee.

'Well, out with it, man. What's your news that you must interrupt our entertainment?' He winked at the girl and ran his free hand between her legs.

The messenger got to his feet. 'Er … somewhere private, my

lord?'

'This is as private as it gets,' Taran told him. 'Tell me or get out.'

'From Prince Edern, lord ...'

'Yes?' Taran yawned and took a swig of his ale.

'We ran into some Saxons this morning, along the Estuary. They said they were the rearguard of an army. That the rest had gone ahead. Prince Edern believes they may be on their way here.'

Taran's face said it all. He let go of the girl, put his ale cup down and clapped, laughing. 'You see,' he shouted to anyone in the hall who could understand him. 'I told you little Eddi wasn't just a pretty face. Only, his timing is as always, a little off. The Saxons aren't on their way; they're here already. Messenger – say hello to my friend Essegar of the Juti.' He leaned towards a bearded man on his right and translated for him. Essegar roared with laughter and stood up, raising his ale-cup to the messenger.

It was only the man's exhaustion that had made him miss the situation. Now that he looked around him, he realised that half the men in Taran's hall were Saxons, the blond-haired fierce warriors from across the German Sea. His gaze fell on Taran, his lord, his master, the man who would, any day now, be king of the Gododdin.

'I would have said,' Taran was wiping his greasy fingers on what was left of the girl's dress, 'that you can tell my little brother there is no cause for alarm. All is well. But of course,' his bonhomie suddenly vanished, 'I can't do that, can I? Otherwise, *my* timing wouldn't be right.'

No one saw the knife in his hand. No one saw it hiss through the air. And the messenger only saw it when it hit him in the centre of his chest and the impact threw him backwards to sprawl on the sodden straw with the dogs and the drunks. A great roar of approval went up and Taran smiled. 'Where were we?' he asked the assembly. 'Oh, yes, I remember.' And he locked his tongue with the girl's again as the music struck up and the ale flowed.

CHAPTER XXI

Din Paladyr

'No news from Taran?' Calpurnius Succatus sat in Brenna's great hall.

'None,' Edern said, 'I'll go to him. Take a few good men.'

'No,' Brenna shook her head. 'No, Eddi, we're staying together now. Here. Where we're safe.'

Edern looked at his mother. She was a warrior queen like all the female rulers of her people, but she had not drawn a sword for years now. And as for Din Paladyr being safe – Brenna had lost it twice.

She wandered to the window. Beyond the wooden palisade and the huge ditches, Valentia stretched far away into the mists of the south. The Wall lay there, all the power and civilization of Rome. Through the window behind her, had she turned, she would have seen the rolling, white-flecked grey of Boderia and beyond that the mountains of the painted ones where Belatucadros never shone and the world was a cold and godless place. She glanced back at the knot of men clustered around the table. There was Calpurnius, whose wife, men whispered, didn't love him. There was Vitalis, the soldier of the VI who had travelled far and had come home. There was his strange friend Pelagius who worshipped the Christian God – Belatucadros alone knew what drove him. And then there was Eddi, her youngest. She could see his father in him now, Paternus, in the scarlet cloak of a tribune of the VI; Paternus who she had loved; Paternus who was dead.

No news from Taran. That worried Brenna. She had watched both her boys grow and she had grown to like Taran less each day. She had made her apologies for him – even to herself – for so long now that even she half-believed that he was a good man. Her heart was heavy today and she had a sense of foreboding. A little voice inside her head told her that Din Paladyr, the Gododdin, Rome, all of it was about to change. Nothing would be the same. And it would never be the same again.

There was a commotion in the ground beyond the palisade and the gates creaked open. Dogs and geese yelped and hissed, flying out of the way of the horseman who cantered in. She knew him at once, cloaked and fur-capped though he was. Justinus Coelius had got Edern's message and he had come north. Brenna turned back to the men around her table and she smiled.

Deva

With the ceremonies over and the new Caesar in place, the XX Valeria Victrix left the post they had held for more than three hundred years. The tribune left in command of the tiny garrison that remained commanded little more than two hundred men. In the weeks and months to come, he would wander the barracks of the great camp, the only sound his own footfalls echoing down the centuries. And he would watch the estuary and the Hibernian Sea beyond it. If any raiders came now, he could do little more than shake a stick at them. But then, perhaps, it wouldn't come to that.

Eboracum

The VI Victrix had held Eboracum on the river for a little less than three centuries. It was here that the great Constantine had raised his standard long, long ago and the legions had placed him on the greatest throne on earth. Now, another Constantine had come, another soldier and the VI had backed him too. It was a good omen, men said. The name Constantine was worth six legions in the field. None could stand against him.

The praeses Publius Dio stood in his principia, fully armed. His scale shirt was polished, his cloak newly pressed and his hair and beard trimmed. He drew his sword, the gleaming spatha with which he had made his name. The new Caesar had ambitions. He had three legions in his purse and he would take them across the

German Sea, to Gallia, Hispania – who knew where destiny would take them all? For the briefest of moments, Publius Dio toyed with driving the blade into his own bowels, give up his command once and for all. He didn't approve of the new Caesar no matter what his name was. He had come to love this city, its camp, its colonia, even the biting winds that blew along its walls. And he knew, as he stood there in the deserted emptiness of the principia, that he would never see any of it again. He glanced down into the courtyard where the legion's signifers were carrying their standards from the chapel. The raging bull bellowed alongside the silver silence of the eagle and the breeze caught the pelt on the wolf-heads over the signifers' helmets.

Publius Dio changed his mind. Wherever that eagle went, that was his place; not dying in self-imposed disgrace in the darkness of his own soul. He sheathed the sword, trusting that soul to Mithras, to Jupiter, to the god of the Christians, to *any* deity that would look out for him now.

Din Paladyr

The days were shorter now and the nights long in the land. Brenna lay curled in Justinus' arms as the last embers died in the grate. The old wolfhound in the corner stirred and whimpered, chasing hares through the meadows of his dreams and his youth.

'Is it true,' she asked him, 'that the legions have gone?'

He nodded, put his arm around her and hugged her to him gently. 'Constantine intended to talk to me, apparently, at Eboracum. Of course, I'd already left.'

'To protect me,' she said.

Justinus chuckled. 'All one of me,' he said.

She smiled and nuzzled against him. 'Will they be back, do you think?' she asked.

'The legions? Who knows? The man who leads them won't, that's for sure. The first Constantine, Magnus Maximus – neither of those returned. Marcus and Scipio never even got to their ships.'

'And can this Constantine save the Empire?'

He laughed again. 'Stranger things have happened,' he said. 'When they murdered the deified Julius, a lioness whelped in the streets of Rome. The Galilean carpenter rose from the dead. But Constantine holding the Empire together? That might be a miracle too far.'

'So, against whatever is coming, we're on our own?'

He turned her over so he could see her face in the firelight. 'We've been on our own before,' he said.

She smiled and nodded and said nothing. Yes, they had been on their own. But not like this. Never like this.

Caledonia

The Clota froze that winter, in the year the legions left. And across it walked the greatest barbarian army that anyone had seen in the island of Britannia. Their ponies slipped and slithered on the ice sheets, whinnying in their panic. A horse on ice was nearly as bad as a horse in water. The animals lost their nerve and became unmanageable until they found the east bank and felt the good earth again.

Had Justinus been there, he would have been appalled at their shambolic advance. There was no column, no cavalry screen, no ballistae or baggage train. These men lived off the land – the smoking villages and butchered corpses in their wake were testimony to that.

Nectan rode in a war chariot at the head of his painted ones. Their hair and beards were newly cut for the campaign and their bodies shone blue with the swirling paint that kept them from death in the field. Dancing like madmen between the horses, the wild men of the Picti ran naked, serpents coiled over their chests and down their legs, their leather-hard feet crunching on the frost of the heather as they crossed into Valentia.

To their left, the Scotti marched under their green banners, the men of Dal Riata, the warriors from over the Hibernian Sea. Copper brooches shone on their heavy cloaks, bright with the colours of their homeland and the islands of the west. Their tunics were saffron yellow, because saffron, it was well known, discouraged lice. There was more than enough to worry about on campaign without the little irritating bastards that burrowed into the clothes and the flesh.

Niall Mugmedon brought up the rear, his riders of the Danaan protecting the army's back. Of all the leaders of this rabble, Niall knew the Roman way. Most of the men who rode or marched ahead of him had never seen a legion before, had no idea of the way the Romans fought. Or how hard the Romans died.

But they were not marching on the legions; not yet. South of them lay the Wall, the first obstacle of many. What bothered Niall a little was that they had heard nothing from Scipio for months. He was supposed to have sent them all letters, dates when he would lead his legions north to meet them. After that, who knew? The fields of Gallia? The vineyards of Italia? Glittering prizes of the crumbling Empire in places that Niall had never heard of. But there were rumours. Scipio was dead, some said, murdered by his own men. Others said that he had gone mad and had killed himself, lying on the body of his own mother whose love for him was beyond the natural. But the silliest rumour of all was that the legions had elected *another* Caesar and they had sailed away from Britannia like snow melting in the spring sunshine. Niall of the Seven Hostages smiled to himself again when he remembered that one – that would be too ridiculous.

Din Paladyr

They came out of the mist, a straggling line of the Gododdin, old men, women and children bound together by long ropes. It was a raw dawn, the sky low and gloomy with the promise of rain. There were shouts from the ramparts of Din Paladyr as the night watch stirred themselves, then a scurrying along the walls and the bray of war horns.

Justinus, old soldier that he was, had been here before. He was first on the palisades, hauling his winter cloak around him and scanning the hapless line of prisoners. Vitalis had been here too, but he'd never seen this before.

'Who are they?' Pelagius asked him as he reached the wall walk.

'They're the damned,' Justinus spoke for him. 'The forlorn hope.'

'They're our people.' Brenna had reached them now, recognising the Gododdin rags that her women sewed.

'They were,' Justinus said.

'What do you mean?' Edern had arrived, strapping on his sword. 'Where are our scouts?'

'Dead,' Justinus said. 'Before they had chance to get back to us, before they had chance to fart, I shouldn't wonder. But these … well, unless I miss my guess …'

'What is it, Justinus?' Brenna asked him, her voice shakier than she had hoped. 'What's happening?' She strained her eyes into the mist. She heard the snorting of horses and the occasional whinny but saw nothing, just the thin line of people standing beyond the vallum, their hands raised now in silent supplication.

'They're hostages,' Justinus told her. 'Their captors hope we'll surrender to keep them alive.'

'Their captors?' Calpurnius repeated. 'Where are they? Who are they?'

A single horseman rode out of the mist, a gold crown gleaming dully on his helmet and a gold torc at his throat. 'Not they,' Justinus smiled grimly. '*Him*. Niall Mugmedon, the high king of Tara. And it looks like he has a few more hostages now.'

'Justinus Coelius,' Niall shouted. 'Sometime Dux Britannorum.'

'The bastard's speaking Latin,' Calpurnius muttered.

'That's not what bothers me,' Justinus said. 'What bothers me is that he knows I'm here.' He cupped his hands so that his voice carried. 'What do you want, sheep-shagger?' he asked.

'You,' Niall shouted back as his horse caracoled left and right. 'And this dunghill you call a capital.'

'And if I don't choose to consider your offer?'

'Is Brenna there?' the high king asked, 'the queen of the Gododdin?'

'I am here,' she answered, ruler to ruler, in Latin.

'These are your people, lady,' Niall said. 'I will give you until the mist has cleared. Then I will expect your answer. If it's yes, they – and you – will live. If not, you can watch them all die. And you can expect no mercy after that.'

'Until the mist clears?' Calpurnius said, turning to Brenna. 'How long is that?'

'How long,' Justinus answered for her, 'is a Roman road?'

The mist had not cleared by the middle of the day but Din Paladyr was armed and ready. Every fighting man stood on the ramparts to the west, children loading sheaves of arrows into baskets, women manning the steaming cooking pots and tearing cloth for the bandages they knew would be needed.

Justinus had held a council of war with the others and with Brenna's generals. He had no idea how many men waited behind their screen of fog but he doubted they had siege equipment with them. Without that, Din Paladyr could hold for ever, its water supply from the deep wells and its granaries and markets well stocked.

The army outside would starve before they did. But the unspoken question was about Taran. Had Din Eidyn fallen already? Was the prince of the Gododdin dead? Nothing could be done for now. The next move was Niall Mugmedon's and he made it.

'Time's up!' His rough Latin echoed around Din Paladyr's walls. He rode forward again, his helmet gone and his red hair hanging over his shoulders. 'Well, what's your answer?'

'Edern,' Justinus murmured, 'shall we give him a Gododdin welcome?'

Edern smiled. 'Here's your answer, sheep-shagger.'

Niall spoke no Gododdin but he understood what came next. A hundred men stood up on Din Paladyr's ramparts, turned around and hauled up their tunics, flashing their naked arses at the high king of Tara, to much laughter and hilarity.

'So be it,' Niall muttered and raised his hand.

A dozen men darted out of the fog, each of them armed with a sword and they hacked at the trembling line of Gododdin prisoners. Men, women, children, it made no difference. They flopped to the still-frosted grass, dragging down those tied to them along the line. The screams were few and the silence that followed almost painful.

Brenna's face was a mask of horror and her fingers trembled over her mouth. 'Belatucadros, he meant it,' she whispered. 'He really meant it.'

She felt Justinus' arm around her shoulder. 'Of course he did. He's Niall of the Countless hostages. It's what he does.'

She shuddered. 'And I've consigned all those people to death, those women, those children. *My* people.'

Justinus swung her round, gripping both shoulders with his powerful fingers. 'You had no choice,' he said, levelly. 'If you'd given in, opened the gates to that bastard, do you seriously believe he wouldn't have dealt with us all in the same way?'

'He can't kill us all,' Calpurnius said.

'Can't he?' Pelagius asked him, pointing beyond the ramparts. The mist was clearing, as if it had never been. Beyond the line of butchered hostages, the greatest barbarian army that anyone had seen in the island of Britannia stood ready and waiting. With one voice, they broke the eerie silence, banging their swords on their shields, whooping their war cries and blowing their war horns. Banners danced in the noonday and naked madmen ran backwards and forwards, slicing off the heads of the dead captives and waving them in the air.

There was a stunned silence on the ramparts of Din Paladyr, each man alone with his thoughts, trying desperately to stem the sheer panic rising in his throat. Only one man had a sort of smile on his face; Justinus Coelius, sometime Dux Britannorum. He had been right. The barbarians may have their thousands. But they had no siege artillery.

Londinium

The new girl was shaping up nicely. Unlike Honoria she was of good family, from Tarraconensis, with the raven hair and olive skin of her people. Her father had been a decurion in Clunia and Caesaraugusta and his father before him. Her name was Flavia and she was altogether more acceptable than the Londinium harlot that the vicarius used to bring to functions. She was a beauty, there was no doubt of that; and if the wives of the Ordo didn't care too much for how far she turned their husbands' heads, they consoled themselves with the fact that she came of good stock. Now, if only Chrysanthos would do the decent thing and actually *marry* the girl …

'Honoria.' Flavia had been dreading this moment. Ever since she had caught the vicarius' eye, even before he had installed her in the governor's palace, she had known about the House of the Night. It lay beyond the newly bricked-up gate, an annexe to her own quarters. A gorgon lived there, Medusa with her coiling, serpent hair and cruel eyes that could turn a man – or a woman – to stone. And now, here she was. Not even Medusa could get through solid brick, so Honoria had simply walked out of her own gate and into Chrysanthos'. The vicarius was away, on business of state. Now that the legions had gone, there was only a skeleton force manning their bases and no Dux Britannorum to hold them together. It was not an ideal situation.

'You must be Flavia,' Honoria smiled, sizing the girl up. 'I've heard so little about you.'

Flavia couldn't say the same. For all Chrysanthos had ditched this woman for a younger model, he never stopped talking about her. Honoria had said this; Honoria had done that. Would she, Flavia wondered, ever hold such a place in the man's heart?

'Chrysanthos …'

'Isn't here. I know. I may not be welcome in his bed any more, my dear, but my people are everywhere. For instance, your favourite flower is lilac, your favourite colour, green. You have two cats – Scylla and Charybdis. Your brother died when you were ten. You're a dab hand in the kitchen too, working with the slaves to prepare Chrysanthos' favourite concoction. But then, you please the vicarius in other ways, too; mostly on your knees.'

Flavia's eyes flashed fire. For the briefest of moments, she toyed with slapping the woman, lashing out at her still-beautiful face with her nails. But she checked herself. She had it on the authority of the vicarius himself that this woman killed people. Flavia had never met a woman who actually killed people; she didn't know what to expect. True, there were no serpents hissing and writhing in her hair but there were ample hiding place in the woman's cloak and gown to hide a knife.

'What do you want?' she asked instead.

Honoria's eyes softened and a smile played around her lips. 'I'd like us to be friends, child,' she said. 'To get to know one another. After all, we love the same man.'

Flavia gnawed her lip. She hadn't expected this. 'You … you love him still?'

'Of course,' Honoria nodded. 'I have lost two men that I loved and in the space of mere months. It's hard.' The tears welled in her eyes and her lip trembled. Flavia was not a mother yet but she knew all about Scipio. And she *was* a daughter. And Honoria was about her mother's age. Despite all the horror stories from Chrysanthos, despite the warning signs she should have seen all around her, her young heart melted and she held Honoria in her arms.

'Come in,' she said, her cheeks as wet as Honoria's. 'It's cold. Come in and get warm.'

'No,' Honoria shook her head. 'You come to mine. I promise you the House of the Night is nothing like its reputation. We'll talk, you and I, of things that might have been.'

Din Eidyn

Modron clattered into Taran's great hall, shaking the snow off his boots and helping himself to the mulled wine.

'What news?' The prince of the Gododdin was buckling on his sword belt with the help of his latest harlot.

'Well, we're there, lord, surrounding Din Paladyr.' Modron wiped a grimy hand across his all but frozen lips. 'But whose bloody idea was it to start a war in the middle of winter?'

'You know as well as I do, we have to strike quickly. The legions have gone, but there's no telling when they'll be back.'

Modron all but missed his mouth with the next swig. 'The legions have gone? When did you hear this?'

'Two days ago.'

'And when did you intend to tell us, freezing our arses off outside Din Paladyr?'

Taran gently moved the girl to one side. He smiled at the oaf standing before him. Then he whipped free a knife and held it under the man's beard, the point pricking his throat. 'I intended to tell you when I was good and ready,' he said. He jerked the blade free and pushed the man away. 'And don't forget for one moment who's running this show, numbskull.'

Modron muttered what passed for an apology in his world. He waited.

'Are the Saxons in position?' Taran asked him.

'In their ships along the Estuary,' Modron said. 'Nobody'll get out that way.'

'And Justinus Coelius?'

'Oh, he's there, all right. Just as you said.'

Taran chuckled, helping himself to the wine. 'I didn't think it would be long,' he said. 'Mama calls and her lapdog comes panting around her.'

'Do you hate the man that much?' It was an unusually perceptive question for someone like Modron.

Taran scowled. 'Yes, I hate him,' he grunted. 'Ever since he "rescued" us in the rebellion of Valentinus. Ever been on the run, Modron? Not knowing where you are or where you've been or where you're going? Not knowing whether you're going to see your own mother raped in front of you or whether this particular day is your last?'

The oaf shook his head.

Taran tore a loaf of bread apart and took a bite. Modron hadn't eaten yet today, but with his lord and master in this mood, he didn't like to suggest that he might join him. 'You'd think, wouldn't you, that I'd be grateful to Justinus. Technically, I suppose, the Roman who filled our lives then was Justinus' friend, Paternus. He took my dead father's place, slept with my mother and begot that shit who thinks he's my equal. But Paternus was only a pale imitation of Justinus, a mere reflection of all the arrogance of Rome. And now it's Justinus himself who's in my mother's bed, poisoning her and little Eddi with his black arts.' He paused and looked up. 'I want him dead, Modron. Can you do it?'

The oaf shrugged. 'If I can reach him,' he said.

'Yes, and that's the point, isn't it? Reaching him. Get yourself some food.' Modron's eyes lit up. 'And a fresh horse. Tell me, what do you need most, camped outside Din Paladyr?'

'If you're asking me as a man,' Modron chuckled, 'I'd say a hot fire, a hotter woman and plenty of ale. If you're asking me as a soldier, I'd have to say artillery. Then we can smash our way in.'

'They haven't seen you yet, with the others, I mean?'

Modron shook his head. 'We've kept out of sight along the Estuary.'

'Good. I'll deal with that if I have to. In the meantime, I'm taking a ride south.'

'Where to?' Modron asked, reaching for the bread.

'To the Wall.' Taran smiled and winked at the man. 'They've got artillery there, haven't they?'

Aesica

They had artillery along the Wall. Specifically, they had it at Aesica, three wild asses still in their winter wrappings to preserve them from the worst of the weather. The garrison there was small, commanded by a circitor whose gammy leg had meant that he had not marched out with Publius Dio's VI. The raging bull standard flapped on its red field over the tower of the fort and it still stood there after Taran's visit.

All that had changed was that the wild asses had gone, dragged north behind the tough little ponies of the Gododdin. All that had changed was that the small garrison there were dead, their shields picked up in the heather. All that changed was that there was blood on the snow.

Din Paladyr

'Is it going to end here, Calpurnius?' Conchessa stood in the doorway of their private quarters, the sewing still in her hand. 'Tell me the truth.'

Calpurnius had been on the walls for much of the day, supervising the strengthening of the east ramparts. Niall and his people alone could surround Din Paladyr and there was no telling when he would strike or where. Justinus understood siege warfare and Calpurnius understood engineering. That was a combination the barbarians didn't possess. He walked over to her, reading the fear in her grey, glittering eyes. He took the sewing from her and put it down. Then he took her in his arms.

'If it's God's will,' he said.

She pulled away from him sharply, frowning. 'God's will!' she snapped. 'Is that all we are, playthings to amuse God?'

Calpurnius stared at her. The waiting was getting to them all. The snow lay thick on the vallum and powdered the roofs of Din Paladyr. Men and women huddled around their hearth fires and conserved their food. It had been four long weeks since the barbarian army had rolled out of the fog and not a shot had been loosed. The only ones to die were those luckless souls from the outlying villages, the ones that Niall the Hostage-taker had slaughtered like so many cattle, just to make a point. Conchessa had not seen that and Calpurnius was grateful for that. All he could see, as he watched it happen, looking in horror as each throat was slit, was little Patric, the boy who was not his. And each blade that cut through flesh was all but lopping the lad's head.

Calpurnius reached out and took the sobbing woman in his arms again. She hadn't cried like this for so long, not since Patric had been taken; not since they had found each other again after the sewers of Augusta Treverorum. If she sometimes cried over the shade of a man with a twisted smile, she did it when she was alone. 'Conchessa,' he whispered softly, taking in the warm scent of her hair. 'We don't know why we're here, any of us. Why at Din Paladyr; why on this earth. If we had those answers … Don't you think I'd change it all if I could? Go back to Cartago when you and I were first married; when you loved me as I love you? Undo all the hurt and the pain of the years. And be a family again, you, me, Tullia, Patric? Don't you think I would do that?'

She looked up at him, her face red with crying and her lip trembling. He felt her body shaking and held her tighter, never wanting to let go. And he heard her say, softly against his chest, 'Yes, yes, my darling. You would.'

It was a little after dawn the next day when Pelagius was taking his turn at watch. He couldn't feel his feet and the flurries of snow tickled his nose and ears as they fell. He'd be glad to get into the warm, reintroduce his toes to the little thing called life.

Then, something caught his eye. He leaned out over the parapet, peering snow-blind through the grey morning light. He barely heard Vitalis joining him on the wall with warm wine and bread, freshly baked.

'Vitalis,' he said, pointing with a hesitant finger. 'You'll have noticed by now that I'm no soldier, but aren't they ...?'

Vitalis was nodding. 'They're wild asses,' he said, watching the siege engines being limbered up beyond the vallum. 'If you can move your feet, get them pumping. Justinus will need to see this.'

CHAPTER XXII

The great engines were hauled into position by oxen, slipping and sliding on the frosty turf, lowing and rolling their eyes with the effort of the pull.

'They're ours,' Justinus muttered, watching them from the walls. 'From Aesica or Vindolanda would be my guess.'

Calpurnius nodded. 'The bastards will have helped themselves,' he said. 'What's to stop them now?'

Justinus nodded too. What indeed? It could only be a matter of time before the barbarians found out, if they didn't know it already, that the legions had gone, that the barracks were empty and that every town and village in Britannia was there for the taking.

The high king of Tara rode out from his lines on the gentle slope of the hill and called out to the palisades, in Latin. 'This is your one chance, Justinus Coelius. Surrender Din Paladyr or we'll tear it apart.'

His troops were forming up behind him, infantry with spears, shields and swords, their banners bright, their mood ugly. Few people watching from the ramparts understood what Niall had said, but a second horseman put that right. He rode out from the circle of bearded men, his standard-bearer riding beside him. And the standard he carried was the silver face of the sun god, Belatucadros.

There were gasps and mutterings from the walls. The Gododdin looked at each other, uncomprehending.

'That's Modron,' Brenna said, not believing what she saw. 'Taran's general from Din Eidyn.'

'One chance,' Modron bellowed in his native tongue, echoing Niall's words. 'Surrender or we'll tear Din Paladyr to pieces.'

'Too cold to flash our arses this morning,' Edern smiled grimly. 'Think he's within bowshot, Justinus?'

The Roman shook his head. 'It's not likely,' he said, 'but you could give it a try.'

Edern called his archers forward and the best among them took aim. The goose-feathered shaft hissed through the morning to bite into the half-frozen vallum in front of Modron's horse. There was a wild scream and cheer from the men behind him.

'Is that the best you can do?' Modron yelled. 'Din Eidyn has fallen, lady. I rule the Gododdin now.'

There were dark mutterings among Brenna's people. Din Paladyr was her stronghold, but Din Eidyn, on its mountain crags, was more difficult to take. If *that* had fallen …

'I'll take that arrow as a "No", then,' Niall yelled to Justinus. He raised his right arm and brought it down. To his right and left, his artillerymen slammed their rams and the ropes flew wide. Two rocks, black, huge, unstoppable, hurtled through the air. One bounced off the vallum, rolling to a stop. The second hit the palisade, splintering the timbers with its momentum, but the timbers held.

More cheering and whooping from the barbarians. The Picti, naked despite the cold of the morning, leapt and spun ahead of the creaking asses, dancing in their ritual of death and whirling their swords above their heads.

'They'll have to be a hundred and eighty paces away to do any real damage,' Justinus told Brenna and her generals, who had never seen these machines before.

Edern smiled. 'But those madmen are nearer than that, aren't they? Archers!'

Twenty men on the ramparts alongside him aimed for the sky, their arrows hissing like serpents on their way to their targets. One by one, they found their marks, slicing through blue-painted flesh, ripping skin and tearing muscle. Half a dozen of the Picti fell, screaming or grunting in pain and the others fell back. There was no more noise from the barbarians at first, then a growl started. It came from a thousand throats, rising as they battered their shields with their swords and axes, until the whole line was swaying forward in the deadly, hypnotic rhythm of battle.

Nectan, in his chariot, was carried forward by the mob of his own men, but Niall knew better. He hauled his horse out of the way and rode back out of the charging line.

'That won't do,' he muttered to Eochaid. 'I knew it was a mistake to throw in our lot with idiots who paint themselves blue.'

But it wasn't just the Picti who were running headlong towards Din Paladyr. The Scotti were running with them, their tartan tunics flying as the warriors pounded the heather. The noise was deafening, the mad bray of war horns and the roar of their thousands. On the ramparts, Brenna could feel the ground – her ground – shake and tremble.

'Now, Edern,' Justinus yelled, hurrying along the ramparts. 'Now's your time.'

The wall top was suddenly alive with archers, hundreds of them massed to the west of the fort. The thud of gut on leather was the death knell for the men in the front line, skewered as they ran. The iron points bit into eye sockets, rammed into naked chests and there was chaos along the Pictish front. Nectan's charioteer, desperately struggling to keep his horses steady, somersaulted over the back of the cart, an arrow through his head. Nectan hurled his sword away and grabbed the reins but the balance had gone and the chariot swerved and toppled, a wheel cracking and splintering as it hit the ground. The Pictish chieftain was thrown clear but found himself rolling under the running feet of his men. Those who had time leapt over him as they dashed for the palisades, still alive with archers still firing. But the men behind him didn't see him until it was too late and their boots crunched onto his back, his legs, his face. In minutes the man was dead, crushed to death under the weight of falling bodies.

Long before they reached the palisades, the barbarian line had wavered and stopped. There was a human wall stretched across the vallum and dying men lay under the already dead, twitching and writhing in their hopeless attempt to get away. The Picti moved back, melting away out of Gododdin bowshot, behind the safety of the siege engines, to regroup and to count their dead.

Niall of the Seven Hostages, furious, lashed his horse across the lines, riding down two or three stragglers who were stumbling back. He reined in in front of a stunned Scotti chieftain. '*That*,' he barked in his best attempt at a language that the man understood, 'is exactly how *not* to wage war. If you can't keep your bastards in hand better than that, you might as well go home.'

Niall knew he was wasting his time. All the barbarians at the empire's edge had fought this way for ever. They had put their faith in their gods, they had yelled and screamed and run forward to die on Roman swords. It had rarely, if ever, worked and none of them had learned a single lesson from it. At the moment however, Pictish and Scottish pride had been dented. Men were dead and in some numbers. The defenders of Din Paladyr had not lost a man and already, on the first day's fighting, the chieftain of the Picti was a corpse crushed in the heather.

There would be no more attacks that day. Justinus knew better than most what had happened, but he also knew that Niall Mugmedon was a better general than that and he would not let it happen again. He had been watching the wild asses throughout the assault. They had not been reloaded and only two stones had come their way. He had not expected the barbarians to be good shots, but they could only improve with practice. He gave silent thanks to Mithras that the first round had gone to him.

That night, the Picti came for their dead. As the torches flared and guttered in the wind, the burial parties lifted stiffened bodies from where they lay and carried them to the grave pits, fresh-dug in the iron earth. No one shot from the ramparts. No one hurled insults. There was a comradeship in death that all understood. The night watch wrapped their cloaks around them and watched their enemies, the living and the dead, vanish into the night.

Brenna shivered a little as she walked the walls. She wouldn't have her people see that for all the world, but Edern and Justinus, walking with her, knew it had nothing to do with the cold and still less, with fear.

'If Din Eidyn has fallen …' she murmured, giving voice to the thoughts that had filled their heads all day.

'… There was a rebellion,' Edern said, stopping and looking into his mother's face. 'Modron out there proves that. He's in bed with the others. He has to be.'

'And Taran?' Brenna asked him, as though her youngest boy would have the answer.

Edern put both hands on her shoulders and held her firmly as he spoke, choosing his words with loving care. 'He'll have gone down fighting,' he said. 'You know it.'

She closed her eyes. 'Yes,' she said, trying not to let the tears fall. 'Yes, I do.'

It was two nights later that Justinus tested the waters. There was no moon and the clouds that drifted over the estuary hid the stars from view. Ever since the siege had begun, Justinus had wanted to know what the Saxon strength was. He could see them from the north walls but there was no sign of them on the various battle fronts with the others. Was that because Niall of the Hostages, or whoever commanded them, was keeping the Saxoni as a sort of reserve? And if he was, that was a Roman tactic and where had the high king of Tara learned that, a man from a godless land where the eagles had never flown?

Eighty ships, Cynewulf the Saxon had boasted to Edern. Could that be true? Justinus could count thirty two sails from the ramparts of Din Paladyr, but how many more lay along the estuary and in the rocky inlets around Din Eidyn? Justinus had to find out.

Edern had insisted he go, but everybody overruled it. With Taran dead, the boy was the future of the Gododdin. He alone carried the royal blood and the hope of the world on his shoulders. If he had to die, Justinus told him, let it be on the ramparts of his capital, not in some brackish water where the gulls bickered over the corpses of rotting fish.

Justinus had eight men at his back, a contubernium had he been back with the VI again. He had chosen them himself. None of them was a soldier in the Roman army, with dice in his purse and lice in his tunic. They had never sung *The Girl From Clusium* or built a marching camp at the end of a long day on the road. But they were warriors all. This was their land. They knew every inch of it and they would die to defend it. They had all left their armour inside the palisades, travelling light with a sword and a dagger. It cut down noise and increased their pace and these were the watchwords that night – speed and silence.

The wind that sighed on Din Paladyr's ramparts was a roar down at the water's edge where the tide surged in and the white caps that flecked the darkness like flickering corpselights flashed and vanished in an instant.

The Saxon ships rode at anchor off the shore, their sails furled but ready for sea. Others, along the water's edge to the left and right, had been run aground and only their sterns swayed a little with the tide's run, their keels fast in the mud of the estuary. Justinus counted them again, crouching in the trees as he was. He had been right; thirty two. There were no more hidden in the brushwood and the watch fires of the Saxons burned bright further along the coast. If there were any more ships, that was where they would be. Justinus motioned to his warriors to follow him and they scrambled over the water-splashed rocks as they moved west.

They could hear the laughter around the fires now and could see a circle of cloaked men with yellow hair drinking and talking near the flames. Their weapons lay beside them and the ale cups were being passed hand to hand.

Suddenly, there was a shout, guttural and harsh. Justinus' sword flew clear of its scabbard and he whirled to face a Saxon, a huge, two-handed axe in his hand. There was a thud and the man went down, his deadly weapon slicing into the earth at his feet. Behind him, crouching now to retrieve the knife he had thrown, was a smaller man.

'Jupiter Highest and Best!' Justinus hissed. 'Taran!'

'Not a good night to come calling,' the prince of the Gododdin said. There were other shouts in the night now and the men around the fires were throwing away their ale cups and grabbing their weapons. Justinus and Taran led the retreat, hurtling back the way they had come at full speed now that all surprise had gone.

A man slipped on the treacherous rocks and stumbled, his sword flying from his grasp. There was no time to retrieve it and no time for the others to defend him. From nowhere an axe sliced through his head with a sickening crunch as bone and brain gave way to iron.

Two of Justinus' men turned to fight, sparks flying from their clashing blades as they floundered up to their knees in water.

'Back!' Justinus barked his order in Gododdin. 'Everybody, back!'

There was a time for heroics, when there was nothing else left; but this was not it. While both men went down under the Saxon axes, the others left the shore and hacked their way through the underbrush, making for the high ground. None of the Saxoni who followed was carrying a torch – it would make too easy a target for the archers on the walls – but they chased them onto the flat ground of the vallum.

'Volley!' Edern was on the ramparts, watching for the men's return and he saw the situation at once. A hail of arrows thudded onto the vallum, forcing the Saxoni to pull up short. They had seen what those bowmen had done to the Picti days before and had no intention of repeating history. As Edern watched them, the would-be pursuers did a curious thing. They laughed, shook hands and slapped each other's backs. Did the Saxoni win so few victories that this night's work caused such satisfaction?

Taran sat that night with his mother, his brother, Justinus and Calpurnius. The tale he told filled them all with a creeping dread. The barbarians, the Picti and the Scotti, had come out of nowhere, surrounding Din Eidyn as they now surrounded Din Paladyr. The Saxoni had filled the estuary with their ships. Taran had had no time to send word to Brenna and Edern and he had settled down to a siege. He had water and he had food, so he knew he could hold on, at least for a while. But that was before Modron. There had been rumblings among Taran's people from the first day. Why didn't they negotiate? Nobody had to die. The Picti had lived cheek by jowl with the Gododdin for ever. Yes, they had fought each other and raided, but that was the way of it. There was silver in Taran's coffers and even more of it in Brenna's. Every man had his price. The Picti and the Scotti were no different.

Taran, of course, had refused. He was a prince of the Gododdin, he reminded them, an ancient and a proud people. He – and they – would bow to no man. It was then that things had become ugly. The exact details were hazy in Taran's mind now, as he told it by Brenna's fire, chewing heartily on bread and cheese, but Modron had led the mutiny. Modron, of all people; Modron, who Taran had always trusted. He wanted the throne for himself, he said. There was fighting in Din Eidyn's great hall; Taran had lost count of the men he had killed, aware with each thrust that he was butchering his own people. In the end, their numbers had prevailed and he and a few followers had managed to fight their way out.

'And since then?' Justinus asked him.

'For the past weeks, we lived along the estuary. You know the inlets.' His family nodded. 'In the end there were too many of them. The Saxoni were hunting us, day and night. One by one they cut us down. In the end I was alone. That's when you came along, Justinus.'

'Fortuitous,' the Roman nodded.

'Belatucadros was looking out for me,' Taran said. 'How's it going here? Will the well hold out, do you suppose?'

'If Belatucadros wills it,' Edern said. 'There was a strange thing tonight, as you reached the vallum.'

'What was that?' Justinus asked.

'When the Saxoni broke off their chase, they seemed mightily pleased with themselves, as if they'd just won a great victory.'

'Who knows?' Taran threw his arms wide. 'Who knows what madness infects those bastards? None of it makes much sense.'

'The Picti, the Scotti, the Hiberni, the Saxoni and renegade Gododdin,' Justinus murmured, leaning back in his chair. 'Oh, it makes perfect sense, Taran. We're looking into the future.' He looked at every face around that once-impregnable hearth and saw the same fear in each one. 'And I, for one, don't like what I see.'

In the days that followed, Niall of the Seven Hostages took overall command of the army that surrounded Din Paladyr. He tried out the wild asses, creeping them nearer each day to the great wooden walls of Brenna's fortress. He was carrying out target practice, testing the damage his ballistae could cause. Timbers cracked and splintered, earth wedged behind them slipped. There was no headlong charge now, the warriors at the vallum's edge merely watching and cheering every time a hit was scored. Justinus Coelius had presided over dozens of field days like this, putting his artillery through their paces. Calpurnius had used the shelter of night to organize rebuilding parties, the little army of Brenna's people redigging the earthworks and sawing new timbers from the wood piles, lashing them together and healing the wounds that the asses' stones had caused.

'Ever been here before, Calpurnius? In a siege situation, I mean?' Taran stood alongside the man, watching the stakes being hammered into the ground. His breath snaked out on the night air.

'No,' Calpurnius told him. 'No, I haven't. You're living it all over again, of course.'

'Oh, yes.' Taran shuddered. 'They had no siege engines at Din Eidyn, but the slaughter that followed … Your family are here, aren't they? Conchessa? Tullia?'

'They are.' Calpurnius didn't need to be reminded of that.

Taran turned to him. 'Get them out, Calpurnius,' he said sharply.

'What?'

'Before I left Din Eidyn I saw such sights,' Taran's voice tailed away. 'One, I can't get out of my head. She couldn't have been more than ten. She was naked and screaming. There was a man on top of her, jerking up and down …'

'Stop!' Calpurnius shouted and the workmen looked up at him, startled.

'I killed him, of course,' Taran said, 'but the damage, I fear, had been done.'

'Is there a point to this, Taran?' Calpurnius asked, his jaw flexing.

The prince patted the man's shoulder. 'I'm just trying to prepare you,' he said, 'for what might come.'

Calpurnius turned away from him. 'I'm prepared,' he said, quietly.

'You're a Roman, for Belatucadros' sake,' Taran said. 'You don't owe us a damn thing. It should still be possible to get out, under darkness or a flag of truce. Take your family, Calpurnius, save them while you still can.'

Calpurnius turned to him. 'I've abandoned my family before,' he said. 'I ran like a coward. I won't do it again. Besides, I'm a decurion of Rome,' a wistful smile crept over his face, 'and I have reports to send to the vicarius.'

Londinium

Flavia was used to Chrysanthos working late. When he was not at the basilica, he had slaves bring the work home with him and his rooms in the governor's house were littered with parchment, books, ledgers, all the paraphernalia of a government outpost at the edge of the empire. She longed to help him. For all she had misunderstood Honoria and had misjudged her, she could never see Chrysanthos through her eyes. More of a father than a lover, he seemed distant these days, withdrawn. And never more so than tonight.

In the light of the candles he looked old and drained. He had run this province for more than half of Flavia's life and every day, every month, every year was beginning to show. He had survived Magnus Maximus. He had survived Stilicho and the warlord usurpers who had raised their standards in recent months. And he was still here. Chrysanthos never talked politics with Flavia. She was too young, too naïve. But tonight … tonight was different. He watched her cross the room and smiled as she stooped to kiss his forehead. She poured some wine for them both and he held up a piece of parchment, dangling with the seal and purple ribbon of the emperor.

'Well,' he said softly, looking into her beautiful, trusting face. 'It's official. We're on our own.'

It was not what he said; it was the way that he said it that frightened her. 'What do you mean?' She sat down, holding his free hand.

'It's a rescript,' Chrysanthos said, 'an edict from Honorius, or whoever writes the boy's letters for him. There are problems, apparently, in Italia. Alaric the Goth is marching on Rome. The emperor cannot restore the legions appropriated – and I quote – "by the usurper Constantine from Britannia".' Chrysanthos let the parchment fall to the table. 'He's sent this message to every town in Britannia, as if I don't exist outside Londinium. Already, we have no Dux Britannorum. Now, we have no vicarius either.'

She reached out and stroked his cheek, all the pain he felt etched on her face.

'But that's not the point,' he went on. 'The point is that we have no army. When I blow these candles out, Flavia, my child, we shall be in darkness. Rome has gone.'

Din Paladyr

The candle had all but died and Justinus Coelius, sometime Dux Britannorum, was finishing his letter. For days now, the stranglehold on the Gododdin fortress had been growing tighter. Spring was coming to Valentia but it was slow, dripping wet and unkind. Every now and then there was a day of high winds, and the rain drove in torrents along the estuary, battering the ramshackle encampments of the barbarians, scattering, if only temporarily, the ships of the Saxoni. But there was no hope in that wind from the east. Calpurnius and Conchessa and, in his most optimistic moments, Justinus, prayed to their different gods that that wind would blow the legions back, but none of them believed for a moment that that would really happen.

Vitalis cleared his throat, realising that Justinus was lost in thought.

'Come in,' Justinus said, sealing his letter, 'both of you.'

Vitalis and Pelagius had received the summons at the same time and they had hurried through the night camp. Justinus looked up at them, both haggard and tired with the endless routine of the watch that they shared, ragged and unshaved. He didn't offer them ale or wine or even a seat.

'You, preacher.' He looked at Pelagius. 'If I put a sword in your hand, would you fight?'

Vitalis turned to look at his friend. In all their time together, it was a question he had never asked.

'No,' Pelagius answered. 'I would not.'

'Not even against the barbarians?'

Pelagius shook his head. 'Especially against them,' he said. 'They are just men, Justinus, like you and me. They freeze on their ramparts, as we are freezing on ours. They miss their families, their homes. And they have no God, as Vitalis and I have, to comfort them through the night.'

Justinus snorted. 'That's what I thought you'd say. So ...' he held out a package, 'will you deliver this for me?'

Pelagius blinked. Had the man gone mad? Was the strain of command getting to him? 'What is it?' he asked.

'It's a ring,' Justinus told him. 'Just like this one,' he held up his left hand. 'Like the one Vit still wears, despite himself.'

Pelagius glanced down. An identical ring, jet and gold, shone on his friend's hand. 'The Wall ring,' he said. 'The ring given to all four of you Heroes of the Wall.'

Justinus nodded. 'That one,' he pointed to the package now in Pelagius' hand, 'belonged to Leocadius Honorius. He gave it to his son, the late Caesar Scipio Gratianus. I took it off his dead body and I should have sent it to his mother, the lady Honoria. I'd like you to do that for me. You know her by sight at least.'

'I do,' Pelagius said. 'But my place is here.'

'No, it's not, Christian,' Justinus said. 'Whatever happens at Din Paladyr in the days ahead and whatever you believe, your god has no place here. I'm not sure Mithras has.'

Pelagius smiled. 'You're wrong, Justinus,' he said. 'God is everywhere. Always. You have a different name for him, but, believe me, it's all the same. I'll take the ring, if I can get out of this place, that is.'

'There are ways,' Justinus said. 'Leave that to me.'

Pelagius nodded. For a long moment, he and Vitalis looked at each other. Then they shook hands and clapped each other on the back. 'Deus vobiscum, Vitali,' the preacher said.

'Et tu, Pelagi,' Vitalis whispered. 'See you on the other side.'

'That you will,' Pelagius laughed and he was gone.

When his footfalls had died away, Vitalis spoke to Justinus for the first time. 'That was kind,' he said. 'A kind thing to do.'

'Hmm,' Justinus nodded, handing him a letter. 'Now, it's your turn.'

'Oh, no,' Vitalis held up his hand. 'You're not fobbing me off. We go back too far, Justinus, you and I. Pelagius may have no place here, but I do. I was a pedes, remember, not far south of here, slogging my guts out under a miserable bastard of a circitor. Now, what *was* his name?'

Justinus laughed. 'So, if I put a sword in *your* hand?' he asked.

Vitalis was suddenly serious. 'Then I'd use it,' he said. 'God or no God. It's funny. If you'd asked me this at another time, in another place, I'd have answered you as Pelagius did. But now …'

Justinus stood up. The pulled the man towards him by the back of his neck and gave him the soldier's kiss on his forehead. 'I'm not saving your life,' he said. 'I'm giving you a chance to save mine. To save all of us.'

Vitalis frowned. Justinus was still holding him by the neck so that their foreheads were together. 'That letter,' he whispered, '*must* be delivered.'

Vitalis turned the parchment towards the flame and nodded. 'When must I leave?'

'Tonight,' Justinus said. 'By the sally gate. Pelagius has gone that way already. If he finds Honoria, all to the good – I'll have cleared my conscience.'

'I'll say my farewells.' Vitalis half turned as he spoke.

'No.' Justinus' harsh word stopped him. 'No farewells. Not even to Conchessa. *No one* must know where you've gone or why.'

'Why not?' Vitalis asked, confused.

'Because we have a serpent in our midst,' Justinus said. 'My problem is, I'm not quite sure who it is.'

It was the next day that the news began to spread. Pelagius, the mad preacher, had got out in the middle of the night, running who knew where. He had stolen a horse and galloped out of the sally port, riding hard for the south. And what was worse, Vitalis had followed him. Pelagius was no loss. He talked rubbish on street corners to anyone who would listen and spent hours locked in deep, philosophical argument with Gwydyr and his priests. Nobody understood him. But Vitalis, he was a friend of Justinus Coelius, who lay with the queen. He had been a soldier of the VI Victrix, the legion that had kept the Roman peace along the Wall and north of it for three centuries.

'And if someone like him runs,' Taran was saying to his

generals, 'what does that tell us about the true state of things? I've seen it, gentlemen. I watched Din Eidyn burn. Do you think it can't happen here? I don't want to sound defeatist about this, but there may have come a time to parley, talk to these barbarians man to man. You've been on the ramparts as I have. You've seen them freezing their arses off, burying their dead. They're losing more men than we are and by now the game must be running out. They'll have to forage ever further afield to find fresh meat and it's a long time until the harvest. I think we should consider it, don't you, in all reason?'

The generals looked at each other in the great hall and muttered.

'It's the queen's call,' one of them said, finally. 'Brenna must make it.'

Taran closed to the man. 'Justinus,' he whispered in his ear.

'What?'

'I'm not speaking for myself when I suggest a parley. No, the queen and I have talked this over, long and hard. All that's keeping her stubborn at the moment is Justinus Coelius.' He paused and looked around the dubious, shifting room of men. 'And I don't have to remind you all that he's a Roman.'

CHAPTER XXIII

Petronius Borro woke with a start. It wasn't dawn yet and the night was cold. His master's door was open and he could see, in the dim light, a bed that was empty; a bed that had not been slept in. Then, he remembered; his master had gone and had left no word for him.

Petronius had made friends here in Din Paladyr and had picked up a little of their language. They, in turn, had learned a little Londinium Latin, mostly words their mothers wouldn't approve of, but it made for friendship. There had been no time for Petronius to settle to his old trade of basket-making. The Gododdin made their own. And in any case, Vitalis was only supposed to be here for a while, paying his respects to his family before he and Pelagius took ship again for Rome. Now, suddenly it was all different. Vitalis and Pelagius had gone. And Petronius Borro had no idea what to do.

Tullia was sewing in their quarters on the slope of the hill. She watched dawn creeping over the smoky huts of Din Paladyr and saw the soldiers patrolling the walls. She wondered, as she did every morning, how the bees were coping without her. There was a Pictish camp on the meadows now and the noise and the nearness of so many men and horses would have frightened them, she was sure, and they would have gone away.

The voices of her parents downstairs reached her. It was a variant of the same conversation she had heard for the last two days; they talked of little else.

'But why didn't he tell us?' Conchessa asked. 'Why just go

like … well, like a thief in the night?'

'He'll have had his reasons.' Calpurnius was trying to defend his wife's brother. Running was not Vitalis' way. There had to be another answer.

'What are they saying?' she asked him, as she prepared their jentaculum, with her ever more meagre rations, 'out on the streets? In Brenna's hall?'

Calpurnius looked at her and frowned. 'It's not good,' he said. 'Some of them think Vitalis is a coward.'

'That's rubbish!' she snapped, at them more than him.

'I know it,' Calpurnius said. 'You know it. Anybody who knows Vit knows it. But what's happening out there is panic. I've seen it before. At Cartago, Augusta Treverorum, even Rome. Somebody starts a rumour, however wild, however stupid and before you know it, the rumour is reality.'

'And our reality?' Increasingly these days, Conchessa was coming to rely on Calpurnius and his experience. Septimus Pontus she loved; Calpurnius Succatus she needed.

'Our reality,' he said softly so that Tullia could not hear, 'is that we have food for a month, perhaps two. Niall and his murderers have all of Valentia to steal from, an endless supply. It's all a matter of arithmetic really; the abacus doesn't lie.'

Conchessa was silent for a moment, pouring some of the milk back into the jug. 'He'll have gone south,' she said suddenly. 'Vit will have gone for help.'

Calpurnius looked at her. Had she understood nothing of the last months? 'Where will he have gone, Con?' he asked. 'The Wall? A thousand men strung out along seventy two miles – Niall would have them for a snack and not even belch. Eboracum? Deva? Between them, they could only field a vexillation. It wouldn't be enough. Vitalis knows that.'

'Londinium,' she said, clutching at straws because her one remaining baby's life depended on it. 'Lucius Porca's men. Vit will have gone to Londinium.'

Londinium

'Thank you for seeing me, Lady Honoria.' Pelagius half-bowed in the atrium of the House of Night. A pale sun's rays kissed the marble columns and the mosaics sparkled with a life of their own.

She looked up at him from her couch and narrowed her

eyes. 'Pelagius the preacher,' she said. 'Does the vicarius know you're here?'

Pelagius smiled. 'Are you going to tell him?'

'That depends,' she said.

'On what?'

'On what you want.'

'I have something for you,' he said, 'from Justinus Coelius.'

For the briefest of seconds, Honoria's eyes flickered to her left, to the folds of a curtain in the corner. She smiled and patted the couch beside her. 'Sit,' she said. 'I will be delighted to accept anything from the great Justinus Coelius.'

Pelagius hesitated. He was a brave man; he had proved that countless times. But he was not an idiot. He had heard that the Lady Honoria Honorius, whore of the vicarius Chrysanthos, killed people. And sitting beside her on a couch was well within dagger thrust. Even so, he took a chance and handed her Justinus' package.

It had taken Pelagius six days to reach Londinium and he had exhausted three horses to do it. He had slept where he could, in copses, under rocky outcrops, but he had seen no soldiers on the way, not until he had reached Londinium and he noticed that Lucius Porca's men watched the north as anxiously as they watched all other points an astrolabe could divine.

When she opened the package, Honoria couldn't help herself. She let out a cry; 'Scipio's ring,' she said through sudden tears.

'Justinus thought you should have it,' he said.

For a moment, Honoria's broken heart softened. For a moment, she was back in the old days, when Leocadius had been the consul of Londinium and Justinus was a distant Dux Britannorum, and all was well with the world. But Justinus was still distant, Dux Britannorum or not. Her heart hardened again.

'Couldn't he have bought the ring himself?' she asked.

'No doubt he would have liked to, lady,' Pelagius said. 'But he's in the middle of what I believe the army calls a little local difficulty.'

'Oh?'

'He's at the Votadini stronghold of Din Paladyr under siege.'

'By whom?'

'Barbarians, lady,' Pelagius told her. 'Thousands of them.'

A smile played around Honoria's lips. She reached out and

patted the preacher's hand. 'You've ridden far,' she said. 'My house is yours. Rest yourself and take refreshment.' She looked at the man, rather less plump that he used to be. 'You look half-starved, man.'

He stood up. 'Thank you,' he said, 'but I must get back.'

'To Din Paladyr?'

He nodded.

'I didn't take you for a soldier,' she said, standing up with him.

Pelagius laughed. 'I didn't either. You probably take me for a madman, lady,' he said, 'but I hear a voice in my head from time to time. Call it God, call it my conscience, I don't know. Right now, the voice is telling me to go back.'

She nodded. A madman indeed. 'Take a horse, at least. The stables are that way. And Pelagius …'

'Lady?' He paused in the doorway.

'Thank Justinus Coelius for me. I shall repay him one day.'

Pelagius bowed again and left.

When he had gone, dashing down the steps that led to the courtyard and the stables, the curtain in Honoria's rooms billowed open and Placidus stood there. For months now, the clumsiest drunk in Londinium had been riding all over Britannia in search of Justinus Coelius. He had stolen the uniform of a circitor of the II Augusta so that his sudden appearance at army camps looking for the man had the semblance of routine. But he had ridden in vain; the man who was once Dux Britannorum had vanished as surely as the legions.

'Lucky you were here today, Placidus,' Honoria said. 'We've found him. Din Paladyr. That's north of the Wall somewhere – you'll find it; I've every faith in you. Well?'

Placidus stood there. He had only arrived this morning and was glad to get out of that bloody uncomfortable armour at last. He was looking forward to a few days' leave, back at the Hen's Tooth with his mates and the girls. 'Er … didn't I just hear that lunatic say Din Paladyr was surrounded? Under siege?'

Honoria smiled and closed to the man. 'It's a long ride to the north, Placidus,' she said. 'By the time you get there, Justinus Coelius may well be dead. I would have liked to feel my blade across his throat, but I'll settle for yours. I'll even be happy if some barbarian does it for us.'

'But … lady,' Placidus felt that Honoria had missed the

point. 'From what we've both just heard, it's a bloody war up there. I didn't bargain for …'

Honoria sighed and took the man's heavy cheeks in her hands. 'Tell me, Placidus,' she purred, 'what you dream about in the still watches of the night.' She stepped away from him. 'Is it this?' she said, and let her robe fall so that she stood naked in front of him, the sun gilding her honey skin. Placidus gulped, his eyes bulging. She took his hand and placed it on her breasts. 'When you come back from Din Paladyr,' she said, 'all this will be yours.'

He licked his lips and didn't know how to answer her. He knew men who would kill to spend the night with Honoria Honorius, the whore of the vicarius. Men who would die for it. Was he, he asked himself, one of them?

She smiled, reading his fevered mind and she knelt down on the shining mosaics, unbuckling his tunic belt and lifting the linen out of the way. 'Here's a little something,' she whispered, 'on account.'

Din Paladyr

Calpurnius' first month of food supply had nearly come to an end. In the old Roman tradition in which he had been brought up, the day and night hung in equilibrium with twelve hours each. The sun was in Pisces, the fish, a symbol the Christians used now and the month lay under the protection of Minerva, goddess of wisdom. There had once been sacrifices to Mamurius, Liberalia and Quinquatria.

But today, as he walked the ramparts of the Votadini fortress high over the estuary, another sacrifice filled his mind. The words of Taran burned through his head like wildfire. Vitalis and Pelagius had got out, men said, by the sally port, the tiny gate to the south-east that was hidden from the barbarians' view. Surely, he could get Conchessa and Tullia out the same way? But then, the dilemma. If he went with them, he would be deserting his post, as he had done before at Cartago when his world had unravelled. If he let them go, what chance would a woman and a girl stand getting through the ring of iron that the enemy had forged? And this morning, the ring was tightening.

Justinus had sensed it too. For weeks now, he had heard the sound of hammering and sawing in the low woods that fringed the estuary, out beyond the camp of the Scotti to the west. This was

Din Paladyr's weakest side, where the rocks were low and scaleable beyond the vallum. The soldier in Justinus knew perfectly well what that noise was all about and this morning, for the first time, he saw it.

'Calpurnius,' he murmured to the decurion, 'get Brenna and Edern. It's starting.'

The three wild asses had stood in their position for days now, the slings empty and swaying slightly in the breeze. But now, others were being hauled into place alongside them, dragged by the grumbling oxen. The timber was new, gleaming bright in the crisp, bright air and the leather slings were oiled and greased with animal fat. The Scotti were busy dragging heavy carts into place by hand, each cart filled with stones, sharp and murderous at every facet.

'They've built their own,' Calpurnius muttered when he got back to Justinus. 'And I thought they were barbarians.'

'We don't have a monopoly on killing people,' Justinus said. 'And I also think we may all have underestimated Niall Mugmedon.'

The high king of Tara was sitting on his horse in the centre of the enemy lines, supervising the loading of the asses. To his right and left, Modron's Gododdin formed a screen of shields and behind them the Scotti and the painted ones carried ladders. They too had been newly sawn and planed.

Edern reached the ramparts along with Brenna. 'What's happening?' he asked.

'He's concentrating his strength,' Justinus said. 'How many asses do you count?'

'Eight.' Edern didn't like those numbers. Din Paladyr had no siege equipment – the wall walks were too flimsy to take the weight and they had no stone platforms from which to fire.

'Two stones hitting the same spot will crack a few timbers,' Justinus said. 'They've done that already. But eight? Then eight more and eight more? That'll blow a hole to sail a Saxon ship through.'

Niall's arm sliced downwards through the air and the first ass bucked and brayed, the thud of twisted gut on timber followed by the high whine and hiss as the first stone sailed across the walks.

'Let him who is without sin ...' Calpurnius muttered, but the words of his Lord carried little weight in Valentia. His musings were punctuated by the crash of timber and the whole wall shook. A second followed it and a third. As each stone found its mark, the barbarian lines roared their approval. Justinus and Calpurnius scrabbled sideways, pushing past the men crowded on the palisades to check the damage. A section of the wall had gone, the timbers shattered and the earth behind it sliding to the vallum.

'They've got better, haven't they?' Calpurnius said, trying to steady a slipping rock.

'There's no doubt of that,' Justinus agreed. 'Can you fix that?'

'If I've got an hour or two and enough timber,' Calpurnius said.

Justinus looked up to where the second volley was coming at them, all eight asses firing together now. 'In the meantime,' he said, dashing back, 'I don't think this is a very good place to stand.'

The stones crashed into the timbers over their heads, showering them with splinters and the earth gave way. Calpurnius slipped, losing his footing as a flying sliver of wood sliced into his thigh. Justinus grabbed him before he could fall any further and hauled him to relative safety. The man was hobbling and bleeding heavily. 'Over here!' Justinus yelled to the nearest man. 'Get him to a medicus, quickly.'

'I'm all right,' Calpurnius insisted through clenched teeth. 'My place is on the wall.'

'You were nearly *under* the wall,' Justinus steadied the man as the others took his weight. 'Anyway, don't think I'm doing you any favours. The medici up here are the Votadini priests. If one of them offers you broth to drink, take my advice and don't touch it! On the other hand,' he grinned, 'it might just keep you alive.'

Again and again, Niall's wild asses bucked and the stones crunched with unerring accuracy on the same spot. When the dust and debris had cleared, where a strong wall had stood was now a gaping hole beyond the vallum. Niall's commands were lost in the terrifying noise, the guttural roar that rose from the massed ranks. As one, they moved forward, the Picti, the Scotti, the Hiberni. Still there were no Saxoni in their lines. Still, they kept to their ships, to the estuary and to the north.

Edern's focus was on the Gododdin, his own people who marched forward under Modron's banner and the captured standards from Din Eidyn; Taran's banners. Come to think of it, where *was* Taran?

The elder prince of the Gododdin skulked at the far ramparts, above the others in the inner ring of defences. Niall's ballistae couldn't reach this far and this would be where a last stand would be made, if it came to that. Here was the fabled silver of the Gododdin, hidden underground. Here was the largest well and Brenna's hall and the temple of Belatucadros himself. If all that fell and the people with it, Din Paladyr would be no more.

Justinus and Edern both shook their heads. The enemy were coming on slowly, deliberately. There was still a handful of Picti, battle-mad, who danced and cavorted in their savage blue ahead of the line, but the line itself was steady, rolling forward over the vallum at a walking pace. Their shields were held high and overlapping, like those of the Saxoni that Edern had met at the water's edge, like a Roman testudo on the march. They gave as much protection as they could to the ladder-carriers marching stolidly behind them. Niall's cavalry of the Danaan waited on the wings, making no move at all.

Shit! Justinus had to admire the Hostage taker more than ever. Not only was he keeping his Saxoni in reserve, he was keeping himself out of the action so that he could direct matters as the best Roman generals did. He signalled to Edern but the prince had long ago earned his laurels and knew exactly when to unleash his archers. Justinus smiled to himself. He had taught the lad well.

Below Taran on the inner ramparts, a number of Gododdin women waited, their hair lifting in the breeze, their eyes watching their men on the walls in front of them. Conchessa was with them, her golden hair braided in the Roman way and Tullia stood with her. Not far from them, Petronius Borro had found himself a Gododdin helmet and sword and stood, waiting patiently to die for the women beside him, as he knew his master would do, as he knew his father had done all that time ago in the temple of Isis, far to the south.

The arrows hissed deadly, clattering on the upraised shields like hail in winter. Here and there men went down, screaming and groaning but the ranks closed, the shields slid together and the tide of death came on.

'Reload,' Edern yelled along the line, dashing backwards and forwards, urging the archers on. A second volley hit home and a third. More men fell, more shields crumpled to the grass, but this time there was no stopping them.

'We taught them,' Justinus muttered to himself on the ramparts to Edern's left. 'And we taught them too bloody well.'

By the time Edern's archers released their fifth volley, the barbarian line had reached the breach in the outer wall and the ladders were being lifted, clattering onto the timbers that were still upright. Now the front line was running, the shield formation broken up and swords flashing in the morning. Iron rang on iron as the two sides met in the narrow gap. The first man there was hacked down by the defenders, spears jabbing and probing, swords slicing and slashing. In the confined space, men slipped in the blood of others and their own, stumbling over fallen bodies in their desperation to get inside or to hold them out. Oaths and screams filled the air and briefly the banners of Belatucadros, carried by both sides, clashed as their bearers buffeted against each other.

Edern ordered half his men to stay on the ramparts to slow a second wave now forming up under Niall's command. The rest abandoned their now useless bows and joined the others at the breach, forcing the attackers back with their numbers. In the centre, where the press was greatest, men were crushed to death, their faces blue, their tunics dark with their piss. Justinus knew there was no chance of holding this gate. If he'd had a legion with him, a vexillation, even a contubernium, he could have formed battle order and stopped the enemy advance. As it was, each man on either side was fighting for his life and when Niall led forward his second wave, there was a danger of a rout.

The high king of Tara had dismounted now and was striding over the vallum, Edern's men's arrows bouncing around him as though he were immortal. The Gododdin who saw that, reloaded and aimed at him specifically, the gold on his helmet a bright target. The iron tips ripped his mail and glanced off his headgear, but none found its mark. Justinus saw none of this, busy as he was at the breach. He recognized the signs. It was not the men at the front who broke and ran – they had nowhere to run to. It was those at the back. That was why, in Justinus' army, the optiones were there, hard men who terrified the pedes under their command far more than the enemy did. He still remembered the crack of a vine stick across his back in the days of long ago.

But the Gododdin had no optiones and Justinus' screamed commands to hold could barely be heard. In the end, after Mithras and Belatucadros and God Himself knew how long this slaughter had been going on, Justinus began hauling men out of the back line, wavering as they already were. He ordered them back to the inner wall, not as a running, stumbling rabble, but in good order, Roman style, their shields to the front and their wounded dragged behind their protection.

Brenna, on the inner ramparts, ordered the gates opened and her soldiery streamed in, grateful for the respite. Edern's archers dashed from their walls and loosed their arrows into the advancing mob, cutting across the space between the ramparts. By the time Niall Mugmedon reached the breach, standing on the pile of corpses, the fighting had stopped, both sides exhausted. The only sound now was the whimpering of dazed and frightened men, men in pain, men staring death in the face.

The light was fading as both sides counted their dead and licked their wounds. Gwydyr's priests were busy with their rattles, their chants and their potions. Brenna's women stitched the worst cuts and smeared honey on angry wounds. Calpurnius was still hobbling as night fell but the wooden spike had been pulled from his leg as four men of the Gododdin held him down and he used language that would bring a blush to the cheeks of many a lady at the emperor's court, or even that of the vicarius.

The torches that guttered along the inner ramparts of Din Paladyr lit a ghastly scene. The dead had been hauled away from the breach where so many had fallen and they lay in heaps beyond the vallum. Niall could not man the outer palisades because his men would be in bowshot from the inner stockade. But he could and did consolidate his position all round the fortress. The outer concentric ring was his and as night fell, he brought his Saxoni up from their ships to mount guard on the northern ramparts.

From here the raiders from the German Sea could look down on the defenders huddled around the great hall. Every space on the inner walls was filled with an archer or a spearman and if the fighting had gone hard today, it was impossible to imagine how it would go tomorrow. Tomorrow there would be no more tomorrows and every man and every woman would put their life on the line.

That night, Brenna sat in her great hall. It was cold, but no one lit a fire, perhaps because they all instinctively knew that fire was the one weapon that Niall of the Seven Hostages hadn't yet tried. Yet the situation cried out for it. If he could reach the inner palisades and pour pitch over those timbers, they would go up like a torch and Brenna and all her people would vanish in the flames. The queen had been here before, long ago when Taran was a little boy and Valentinus of the silver mask had stolen her stronghold.

She had no Justinus then, nor Paternus. She had met them when she was on the run in the wilderness south of the Wall, her world destroyed. And here she was again, staring into the cold blackness of the empty grate. The great wheel of Belatucadros had come full circle.

'Where the hell were you?' Edern's voice made her jump. He was striding across the hall, past her servants to where Taran sat in a corner. There was dried blood on his tunic and his cheek was livid with a puffy bruise.

Taran was on his feet. 'What's the matter, little brother?' he asked.

Edern stood toe to toe with the man, scowling at him. 'Timing again?' he spat.

'What are you talking about?'

'You know what I'm talking about,' Edern said. 'The game. Your lead. My lead. I attack, you follow. You attack, I follow. Where was that today, Taran? Or was I too busy to notice?'

'I would have come to your aid, brother,' Taran wheedled, 'as always. It's just that there wasn't the time. Better to hold the inner ramparts than for both of us to die on the outer ones. Tell him, Justinus.'

The Roman had just come from the makeshift hospitals. The head count was worse than he thought. He took in the situation at once. 'He's got a point, Eddi,' he said, softly.

'You're a prince of the Gododdin,' Edern felt obliged to remind his brother. 'You're supposed to set an example, to lead from the front.'

Taran rounded on the younger man. 'Correction, little brother,' he said. 'I am *the* prince of the Gododdin. You don't think any of this is chance, do you?'

'What?' Edern asked. 'What do you mean?'

Taran's jaw flexed. He looked at his mother, torn as she always was between her boys. He looked at his brother, the snivelling little shit who was a Roman's bastard. And he looked at Justinus Coelius, the biggest Roman bastard of them all. For a moment, his hand hovered over his knife hilt, then he swirled away, barging past Edern into the throne room.

The candles burned here around Brenna's great carved chair where she held court. Monsters coiled in the oak of the arms and the legs and the high back. Taran stood and looked at it. Then he half-turned to Brenna, who had followed him.

'That's mine,' he said, like a spoiled child. 'When am I going to get it?'

She looked at him in astonishment. She hadn't heard her son talking like this since he was a child and could barely climb onto the throne he pointed at now. 'When I'm gone,' she said coldly. 'When Gwydyr has said his words and shaken his rattles over me. But with the enemy at our gates, does any of this matter now?'

'Oh, I think it does.' Justinus and Edern had joined the pair. 'It's remiss of me,' the Roman said, 'but in all this excitement over the past few weeks, I'd completely forgotten to give you this.' He held up a piece of parchment that gleamed briefly in the candlelight until it fluttered to the floor at Taran's feet.

'What is it?' the elder prince asked.

'Oh, you know what it is, Taran,' Justinus said levelly. 'But for the benefit of your family here, I'll explain. That is a letter from the late Caesar, Scipio Gratianus. True, it is unfinished, unaddressed. But it was meant for you, wasn't it, Taran? The others were to be sent to the Picti, the Scotti, the Hiberni, all to arrange for this little party we're all enjoying so much at the moment.'

'You're mad,' Taran said, picking the parchment up. He read it, briefly. 'As you say, no salutation. This could be to anybody.'

'Brenna.' Justinus turned to the woman he loved. 'When Eddi discovered the Saxoni along the estuary, what did you do?'

'I sent a messenger to Din Eidyn, to warn Taran.'

Justinus nodded. 'Yet, according to Taran, he received no such warning. He was caught napping by the barbarians. Odd, that, isn't it?'

'I received no warning,' Taran insisted. 'There was no messenger.'

'Did he come back?' Justinus asked the others. 'Did he bring reports of Din Eidyn?'

'No,' Edern remembered. 'No, he didn't.'

'He must have run,' Taran bluffed. 'Panicked. Got the hell out.'

'Now, why would he do that, brother? He was a good man. Cut his teeth on raiding parties, Saxoni, Picti or any other godless breed. It would take more than that to rattle him.'

'Eddi, when I found Taran at the water's edge, as the Saxoni reached the vallum, what happened?'

'They clapped,' Edern said slowly. Everything was falling into place. 'They were pleased with themselves.'

'Because they'd just done a good job,' Justinus said. 'They'd made sure that Taran had got to the safety of Din Paladyr and that we'd taken him in.'

'I don't understand,' Brenna said, her world turning upside down. 'What are you talking about, Justinus? Eddi, what's happening?'

'Shall I tell her, Taran?' Justinus asked. 'Or will you?'

Taran smiled and sauntered across to the throne; the throne that was his. He spun on his heel and sat on it, running his fingers over the worn patina of the arms, resting his head against the back. 'You seem to have all the answers tonight, Roman,' he said.

Justinus looked at him with contempt. 'Modron wasn't the traitor in the Gododdin camp, Taran, *you* were. You made some unholy deal with the Picti, the Scotti, Niall of the Seven Hostages, the Saxoni and poor, deluded Scipio who thought he could command the legions. I applaud your ambition at least,' he said. 'As a confederation goes, it was probably unbeatable. But we're none of us masters of our fate, are we? You got yourself into Din Paladyr to sow discord, worry everybody, spread doom and gloom. At some point in the fighting, what would it be, an arrow in Edern's back? Well, these things happen in war, don't they? Calpurnius is out of action. So that just leaves me. What plans did you have for me, Taran?'

The elder prince of the Gododdin pounced without warning, a knife glittering in his hand. But Justinus had been caught like this once, when his attacker had been a mad girl. He wouldn't fall for it a second time. He jerked aside and drew his sword.

'No,' Edern drew his knife. 'No, Justinus. This fight is mine. It always was.'

The princes circled each other in that cold, dead room where the candles danced. One by one, Brenna's people crept closer, whispering to each other, watching with horror as the royal family tried to rip itself apart.

'Justinus!' Brenna shouted. 'Stop them!' and she darted forward herself. Justinus caught her arm and swung her back into his grip. Short of using her own knife on him, she wasn't going to break free of that.

Iron clashed in front of the throne the pair were fighting for. But only Taran was fighting for the throne. Edern was fighting for all the years of pain, for those times long ago when the bigger, older, tougher Taran always won the mock fights, with fists and feet and wooden swords. For those times when he had not watched his little brother's back as he should. And now, especially for now, when he had sold his birthright for a wooden chair and was prepared even now to hang him and his mother out to the tender mercies of the barbarians.

The blades slid together as they circled, flashing silver in the candlelight.

'Give it up, Eddi,' Taran chuckled. 'You know you can't beat me. You never could.' He feinted to the right, then smashed Edern in the face with his fist. The boy fell back, his eyes blurring and blood gushing from his nose. He felt his head jerked backwards as Taran gripped his hair and he was driven to his knees.

Through the tears and the pain, Edern saw a tall soldier looking down at him. He was wearing a fur cap and he was smiling in the sun. 'Use your left, Eddi,' he whispered. 'Use your left.' For the briefest of moments, Edern was back in the bee meadows beyond Din Paladyr's walls and Justinus Coelius, the Dux Britannorum, was bending over him, helping him up and drying his tears and giving him good advice. The best advice in the world.

Edern threw his knife from his right hand to his left and rammed upwards. Taran jerked against the impact, his own knife clattering to the floor. As the blood pumped out over Edern's hilt and Edern's hand, Taran sank to his knees. He clutched his little brother convulsively, then reached up to grab his sleeve. 'Timing, brother,' he gurgled as his lungs filled with blood. 'Timing.'

CHAPTER XXIV

There were no dirges for Taran. He was a traitor. He was a prince of the Gododdin. He was a snivelling dog who got his just deserts. He was a casualty of war. Men would argue over his passing as long as the memory of him lasted but it was all too raw this morning to get the measure of things.

All night, Brenna and Edern had talked and finally she had collapsed into Justinus' bed, her body wracked with convulsive sobs, not for what was, but for what might have been.

In their quarters, Calpurnius and Conchessa made love for the first time in months, their bodies locked together, their eyes focused on each other. And for the first time in years, Conchessa no longer saw the handsome, twisted smile of Septimus Pontus who had taken her all those years ago in the meadowlands of Augusta Treverorum. All she saw was Calpurnius, the man she loved after all, the man who, along with them all, would die this morning.

Tullia was still sleeping as her father left. His leg was numb with pain and the stiffness of the Gododdin bandages, but his place was on the wall and he went there now. He bent down and kissed her forehead and the girl murmured in her sleep, running through the waist-high grass with Patric as the bees danced in the air and sang to them both. Calpurnius nearly fell over Petronius Borro, curled up asleep outside the girl's door. The lad started up, a Gododdin sword in his hand, a Gododdin war cry half forming on his lips.

'You'll look after them, Petronius?' Calpurnius said and the boy nodded.

'Face front.' Justinus was wandering the ramparts of the inner palisade. He had not slept. He wore his old uniform of the Dux Britannorum, the spare he kept at Din Paladyr. Because today he was going to die and it was important that he look his best. He hadn't buckled the helmet in place yet, so that the men on the ramparts could see his face.

'Look to your dressing, lads. Keep that formation tight.' He knew that his old friend the tribune Paternus had taught the Gododdin warriors and they had passed it on to their sons. They would never equate with a legion of Rome, with the VI Victrix, the XX Valeria or the II Augusta, but they would do. And this morning they would go to Belatucadros like soldiers.

There was an unholy scream from beyond the outer palisade. Justinus looked up to the sky. An hour after dawn, he judged. He clapped on the helmet and murmured, 'Mithras, also a soldier, teach me to die aright'. A shower of arrows sailed over the timbers to thud into the hut roofs and the churned mud of the open space beyond. Even in the spangelhelm, Justinus could hear the roar of the torches being lit and could smell the woodsmoke. He'd been right. Niall was going to use the fires of Vulcan to burn them out. That made sense. He couldn't use his asses at this range and marching across open ground in battle formation would leave him at the mercy of Edern's archers.

Those men crowded the ramparts now, the one remaining prince of the Gododdin with them, watching the black smoke drift upward. Edern turned back. Behind him, the troops of his people filled the streets and the yards. Their women and children sheltered in their houses and he shook his head, knowing how easily that thatch and that wattle and daub burned.

'Water!' he and Justinus were yelling at their different points along the ramparts. 'Now!'

Calpurnius was yelling too, pushing men into line, handling the slopping buckets himself as they formed a human chain from the deepest well. Outside the palisade, all was silent for a moment. Then the flying arrows and the flying brands came hissing and tumbling through the air to bite into the timbers of the palisade and thud into the huts in the inner vallum. The tongues of fire took hold here and dozens of them caught light, a raging inferno of terror and choking black smoke.

Edern cursed his dead brother to Hell. His archers couldn't see their targets now and when the barbarians scaled the outer walls with their ladders, there was no way on earth he could stop them. Neither was there any way that Justinus or the bucket-men could put those fires out. Any arrow that reached the ramparts was quickly extinguished but it was the smoke screen that was the problem. Any minute now there would be enough chaos for the barbarians to pour through the outer breach and drive their way up the hill, smashing down the burning buildings and using their ladders on the inner defences. After that, it would be hand to hand along the walls, north, south, east and west. And, Justinus knew – they all knew – the Gododdin did not have enough men for that.

It was difficult to know who heard it first above the roar of fire and men. It was a war horn, a single one at first, then a second and a third, echoing the first over the estuary. Calpurnius, on the north wall, watched in disbelief as the Saxoni formation on their hill with the sea at their back crumpled and broke. There was an army, huge, wild and fast, streaming against them from the west, driving them to their ships. A few of the Saxoni threw their axes or spears then they panicked and ran, a litter of weapons in their wake. Calpurnius joined the Gododdin, cheering and clapping. He had never seen these banners before and had no idea who they were.

There was more black smoke now, rising beyond the outer palisade to the west. That wasn't coming from Niall's firebrands or from Niall's arrows. That was coming from Niall's camp. Justinus had to see for himself. He ordered the barricades torn down from the inner gates and, taking a cohort of men, ran down the slope, past the burning buildings to the outer walls. Edern got there as he did and the limping Calpurnius wasn't far behind.

Justinus was laughing, pounding the timbers his men had abandoned only yesterday. Smoke and flame was rising from the barbarian camps, all of them to the west and the barbarians, hit in the rear by a force they had never expected, fell into their tribal groups. They fought and died around their clan chiefs, the plaids dark red in the morning and the green banners of Niall Mugmedon going down in the press of men. There was no cohesion now, no false Roman tactics, just desperate men caught wrong-footed and dying for their complacency.

'Look, there, Eddi,' Justinus laughed, unable to believe what he saw. 'There's a sight to tell your children about. Gentlemen, I'd like to introduce you to an old friend of mine. There,' he pointed, 'on the black horse in the centre. That's Elen of the Armies. And those are the Deceangli.'

All eyes were on the tall woman on the black, her long golden hair streaming under her spangelhelm. Stretching out to either side of her, her banners straining against the wind from the estuary, her people of the Deceangli from Britannia Prima marched in an unstoppable line, roaring their battle cries and driving the barbarians of the confederation before them.

'Well, let's give them a hand, Eddi,' Justinus beamed. 'How about a few arrows in those bastards' arses to help them on their way?'

Edern obliged, his bowmen who had joined them on the wall letting fly with their deadly shafts, cheering as the Picti and the Scotti littered the vallum again, their ladders forgotten, the wild asses abandoned.

Justinus was laughing again and he nudged Edern. 'Who's that, riding with Elen, that ugly bastard in the stolen Deceangli armour?' Edern was laughing too. 'He rides like a basket maker I used to know.'

Before Elen of the Armies had reached Din Paladyr and while her warriors were mopping up around the great stronghold's perimeter, rounding up their prisoners and helping themselves to weapons and armour, Justinus led a troop of horsemen over the slope to the west. Stragglers from the besieging army were stumbling away here, dazed and confused by the sheer speed of the Deceangli attack. Justinus ignored them. There was only one man he was after and he knew, in his heart of hearts, that he would not be lying broken on the battlefield behind.

It was the middle of the afternoon before he found him, resting with a knot of his riders of the Danaan on a rocky outcrop far from the estuary. His crown had gone. So had his helmet. And he was bleeding heavily, his right arm stiff and useless. His men circled him at the Gododdin approach, their shields high, their spears bristling.

'Niall Mugmedon,' Justinus called. 'Sometime high king of Tara.' He was speaking Latin.

The shields dipped a little and the high king looked out from their defensive ring. The Gododdin outnumbered him four to one and there, at their head, was Justinus Coelius, his Nemesis.

'Come to finish our fight, Roman?' Niall called.

Justinus urged his horse forward and the others followed. They threw a circle around the dismounted Hiberni and drew their swords. Justinus had not drawn his. 'I don't fight cripples,' he said, nodding towards Niall's ripped arm.

The Hibernus looked up at him, silhouetted as he was against the sun of Valentia. 'How *are* you still alive?' he asked.

'Thank Belatucadros,' Justinus shrugged. 'Or Mithras or Jupiter Highest and Best. You can even thank the Christian God if you like. But I expect you have gods of your own.'

'We have,' Niall said. He was exhausted and beaten and he was staring those gods in the face.

'Go home, Niall Mugmedon,' Justinus said, hauling on his rein. 'Go back to Tara where the eagles have never flown.'

The Gododdin looked as startled as the Hiberni. 'You're letting me live?' Niall asked. 'Why, after all I've done to you?'

'I can do that,' Justinus said, 'because I am still alive to do it. And that's because of a Christian friend of mine. You won't have heard of him – his name's Vitalis and he believes in turning the other cheek; it's the Christian way, apparently.'

'Is it?' Niall asked, wincing as the pain hit him again. 'And how many cheeks have you got left to turn?'

Justinus laughed. 'I'll let you know,' he said and wheeled his horse's head.

'I owe you,' Niall called.

Justinus halted and turned the horse back. 'Yes,' he said. 'Yes, you do. And I'll call in that debt now.'

'How?' Niall struggled to his feet.

'You have seven hostages,' he said. 'I want one of them, sent back where he came from. You know which one.'

The fires roared into the black of the sky at Din Paladyr that night. Gododdin, Deceangli, Roman, they all drank and ate and danced away the darkness. Whatever gods they prayed to had answered them today and the impossible had been achieved. Justinus had formally thanked Elen of the Armies and she had smiled.

'You brought me Macsen Wledig,' she said, as her warriors made ready for the road days later. 'It was the least I could do.'

The circitor of the II looked a little out of place this far north. His legion had never tramped the heather north of the Wall and they would never do that now. Even so, he seemed genial enough, smiling and beaming at people he met by the roadside. Anybody with a smattering of Latin told him snatches of what had happened. There had been a great battle and the queen of the Gododdin, Brenna, had triumphed. Oh, there was some small help from a tribe somewhere in Britannia Prima, but that was a sideshow, really.

The circitor was fascinated. But he had a job to do, his praeses had insisted. He had an urgent message for Justinus Coelius, who, not too long ago, had been the Dux Britannorum. Justinus? Oh, yes, everybody knew Justinus. He was the hero of the hour, just as he'd been one of the heroes of the Wall all those years ago. Yes, he'd be in Din Paladyr, with the queen.

'It's time I gave it all up, Justinus,' Brenna said. She had buried her boy as a prince of the Gododdin and Belatucadros help the man who so much as hinted that the man had been a malevolent traitor.

'Gave what up?' Justinus asked, easing himself onto one of Brenna's couches.

'This,' she smiled, waving her arm around her hall. 'Din Paladyr, the Gododdin.'

'Never!' he laughed.

'I'm serious,' she said. 'Eddi's ready now. In fact, he's been ready for years but I couldn't see it. What do you say that you and I retire and grow old disgracefully together?'

He leaned across to her and kissed her, smiling. 'You know,' he said, 'I think I'd like that.'

'Lady.' A servant hovered in the doorway.

'What is it?' Brenna asked.

'There is a messenger, madam. For the Dux. He's a circitor of the Second Augusta.'

Justinus frowned. A circitor of a ghost legion. That was odd. 'Show him in,' he said.

The circitor marched in, helmet in hand and threw Justinus a rough soldier's salute. Justinus *had* seen it done better, but if this was the best the man could do, it wasn't surprising that Constantine had left him behind.

'What's your name, circitor?' Justinus asked, wandering back to the couch, 'and what's your news?'

'My name's Placidus,' the circitor said. 'And my news is this.' His right hand jerked forward, a knife hissing across the hall. There was a cry and a thud.

'Justinus!' somebody shouted and a cloaked figure hurled himself in the way of the knife. The tip hit him in the chest and bounced off and the man sprawled across the floor.

In a second, Brenna was alongside Placidus, her own knife buried deep in his ribs. A startled Justinus leapt to her and caught the man as he went down, blood oozing over his mail. 'Remind me,' Justinus said when he had caught his breath, and pointing to her reddened knife, 'to be gentle with you in our retirement.'

Their eyes turned to the man who had taken Placidus' knife in the chest. He was hauling up his cloak and pulling aside his tunic, looking for the wound. There wasn't one. Then he saw the silver crucifix that dangled around his neck and he roared with laughter.

'Pelagius!' Justinus bellowed and hauled the man upright.

'My God just saved my life,' the preacher said.

'I think he's saved both of us today,' Justinus said. He crouched over the body of Placidus. 'Who *is* this?'

Pelagius shrugged. 'He and I came north together,' he said. 'He sort of bumped into me on the road north of Verulamium. I'd have been here sooner, only I lost my purse. Have you any idea how hard it is to get a horse and a bed for the night with no money? But I'm afraid I become a little suspicious of friend Placidus. He was a nosy fellow but not in general. All he wanted to know about was you. So I ended up following him. And when I got here … well.'

'You're a good man, Pelagius,' Justinus said. 'If you every get tired of … whatever it is you do, I can find a place in my command …'

'Justinus!' Brenna growled.

'Oh, sorry,' Justinus beamed. 'I'd forgotten. I don't actually have a command any more.' And that didn't bother him one bit.

'That's just as well,' Pelagius said, 'because you and I both know I wouldn't make any kind of soldier. Besides, Vitalis and I are off to Rome. I trust he's well.'

'He is,' Justinus said, 'and he'll be delighted to see you. There's just one thing, though. We hear that Alaric the Goth is marching on Rome. Is it a sensible place to be at the moment?'

Pelagius shrugged. 'Alaric is a Christian, at least. No offence to either of you, but it'll be nice to be back in God's keeping again.'

They held each other close, as they had each time they had left each other.

'You saved us,' she said, looking up at him through a film of tears. 'You saved us and now you're going away.'

'It's the way of it, Con,' he said. 'Call it the Lord's way, if you like.'

'We need you here, Vit,' she sniffed.

'No, you don't,' he laughed. 'You have Calpurnius, well, anyone can see you're a family again. Little Tullia is nearly big Tullia now and something tells me you'll have your hands full with her.'

'You won't be here to see it,' she reminded him.

'Now, don't try that old blackmail on me, Conchessa Succatus. It won't work.' He held her again, tighter than before. His cheeks were as wet as hers. 'I'll write to you,' he whispered, 'from Rome.'

'I can't lose you again, Vit,' she sobbed. 'I have lost so many people I have loved.'

'You won't lose me,' he smiled through his tears. 'I'll be with Pelagius, remember? And you can't get closer to God than that.'

And he was gone.

Londinium

Chrysanthos was burning the midnight oil as usual, the lamps low and the weather warm. Summer had come to Londinium and Chrysanthos was still here even though he no longer sent his reports to the emperor, even though he had no army to preside over and no Dux Britannorum to lead them.

He was surprised as he watched Honoria glide noiselessly into his chambers. Flavia had gone to bed hours ago and the servants too. 'Why have you left the House of Night,' he asked her, 'without my express permission?'

'Chrysanthos,' she looked at him, her eyes bright in the lamps' glow. 'Can't we leave all this bickering behind, at least for one night?'

He looked at her. He had loved her once. Perhaps he loved her still. But there was so much blood between them and so much murky water under Londinium's bridge. 'All right,' he smiled. 'For one night.' He poured them both the newest batch of red wine he had imported from Italia. He thought he'd better strike quickly before fact caught up with rumour and Alaric sacked Rome. They raised their cups to each other and sipped. She sat on the couch, smiling.

'Know what this is?' he asked her, holding up a piece of

parchment.

'No.'

'It's the latest report from Calpurnius. Can you believe it, he's still there, in Din Paladyr or whatever they call it. They fought a battle apparently, *without* the legions. And they won. What does that tell us, eh?'

'What indeed?'

'He says – and I quote – "the Saxon is conquered, the ocean calmed, the Picti broken and Britannia secure." Quite a poetic turn of phrase, don't you think?'

She chuckled, crossing the room to replenish their wine. He didn't notice the ring she slipped off her finger. It was Leocadius' ring, the ring of the Wall heroes, the one that had passed to Scipio and had been returned to her by Justinus Coelius by way of Pelagius. Honoria had had it altered recently, by the finest Londinium craftsman, who had given it a hollow ground below a hinged lid. The cavity contained a little white powder and she sprinkled it into the wine now.

'You're going to miss all this, aren't you?' she asked him, smiling as he drained the cup. She did the same.

'What?' he frowned.

'The reports, the paperwork. The gossip. All the fuss and bother that is Britannia.'

'Miss it?' he echoed. 'Oh, I know times have changed, what with Constantine and the legions. But Alaric hasn't actually *got* to Rome yet. And things here will go on much as they always have.'

'Do you remember,' she looked into his grey eyes, dancing in the lamplight, 'do you remember asking me who I blamed for Scipio's death?'

'Yes,' he said and coughed, an odd burning sensation rising in his throat. 'Yes, I do.'

'I told you the Second Augusta, didn't I? But I couldn't kill them all.'

'No.' He could hardly speak for coughing now.

'Then I said Justinus Coelius – and, despite my best efforts, I don't think I've been successful there either.'

'Honoria …' Chrysanthos was on his feet, clawing at his tunic's neck. His throat was on fire, so was his stomach and the room was spinning.

'Then I said, "You",' she reminded him. 'Actually, I don't think I said it in that order. I think I blamed you first. So that's all right, then, isn't it?'

'Honoria.' Blood was bubbling from the tight lips of the vicarius. 'What have you done?'

She tried to smile, but the blood was trickling down her chin and dripping onto her gown. 'What I should have done a long time ago, Chrysanthos,' she wheezed. 'A long time ago.'

Din Paladyr

The bees came back to the meadowlands of Valentia that summer and Tullia was there, as usual, tending them. She was glad, on balance, that Petronius Borro had stayed in Din Paladyr after all. He was torn between making baskets on the great fortress over the estuary and going to Rome with his master. It was Vitalis who had persuaded him he should stay; Vitalis and a girl who had eyes a boy could drown in.

That girl was with her bees now, a necklace of buttercups tied around her neck and her hair flowing long and free in the Gododdin way. She hadn't heard him walk through the long grass. She hadn't heard him as he pulled a grass blade and chewed it in his crooked smile.

'A thousand, thousand wings,' he said softly, 'fluttering in the air, darkening the sky. They dance in the sun, telling of new pastures with the sweetest flowers. They sing about their loves and the sights they have seen up there, where the winds play and we humans will never go.'

She dropped the honeycomb and the tears fell like rain. 'Patric,' she whispered.

Niall of the Six Hostages had paid his debt to Justinus Coelius.

Justinus Coelius wandered above the estuary as the sun set that night, Brenna beside him. They heard the sighing of the wind in the heather and saw the lights of Din Paladyr in the distance.

'Do you think they'll come again, Justinus?' she asked him, linking her arm through his and looking out over the sea.

'The legions? Or the Saxons?' he asked.

'Either,' she said. 'Both.'

'I don't know,' he said and turned to face her, holding both her hands. 'All I know is that that part of our life has finished for ever. But we mustn't forget. And we mustn't let our children forget, or our children's children.'

'Forget what?' she frowned.

'That there was once a place called Valentia,' and he held her close, breathing the scent of her hair, 'that there was a Wall and there were heroes of the Wall. And there was once a Britannia ...'

GLOSSARY OF PLACE-NAMES

Abona: Bristol
Aegyptus: Egypt
Aesica: Great Chesters, Northumberland
Anderitum: Pevensey Castle, East Sussex
Aquae Sulis: Bath, Gloucestershire
Aquileia: Italian city near Venice
Arbeia: Fort in South Shields, Tyne and Wear
Augusta Treverorum: Trier, Germany
Belgica: Tribal region that roughly covers modern Belgium
Boderia: Firth of Forth, Scotland
Bononia: Bologna, Italy
Branodunum: Saxon Shore Fort, Norfolk
Britannia Prima: One of five provinces of Britannia, covering Wales and south-west England
Britannia Secunda: One of five provinces of Britannia, covering north England
Caeseraugusta: Zaragoza, Spin
Carthago: Carthage, Tunisia
Cataractonium: Catterick
Clausentum: Bitterne, Hampshire
Clota: River Clyde
Constantinople: Istanbul, Turkey

Dal Riata: Irish Kingdom which ruled lands in Ireland and Scotland
Deva: Chester
Din Eidyn: Edinburgh
Din Paladyr: Traprain Law, Scotland
Dubris: Dover
Durnovaria: Dorchester
Eboracum: York
Flavia Caesariensis: One of five provinces of Britannia, covering central England
Gallia: Part of the Roman Empire that roughly covers modern France, Luxembourg and Belgium
German Sea: North Sea
Hadrianopolis: Edirne, Turkey
Hasta: Asti, Italy
Hebros: River Maritsa, Turkey
Hibernia: Ireland
Hibernian Sea: Irish Sea
Hierosolyma: Jerusalem
Icena: River Itchen
Isca Augusta: Caerleon
Isca Dumnoniorum: Exeter
Lindum: Lincoln
Llyn Tegid: Bala Lake, Wales
Maxima Caesariensis: One of five provinces of Britannia, covering south-east England
Mediolanum: Milan, Italy
Mona: Anglesey
Narbonensis: Province in Gaul
Natiso: River Natisone, Italy
Oceanus: Atlantic Ocean
Onnum: Halton Chesters, Northumberland
Pinnata Castra: Inchtuthil Fort, Perth and Kinross
Pollentia: Pollenso, Italy
Portus Adurni: Portchester Castle, Hampshire
Portus Leminis: Lympne Fort, Kent
Regulbium: Saxon Shore Fort, Kent
Rutupiae: Richborough Castle, Kent
Saxon Shore: Coastal defences from Norfolk to Hampshire
Sorviodunum: Old Sarum, Wiltshire

Tarraconesis: Roman province of Spain
Thamesis: River Thames
Tynus: River Tyne
Valentia: Short-lived fifth province of Britannia, perhaps north of Hadrian's Wall
Vectis: Isle of Wight
Venta: River Wensum
Verulamium: St Albans
Vienna: Vienne, France
Viroconium: Wroxeter
Vindolanda: Bardon Mill, Northumberland
Vindovala: Rudchester

www.blkdogpublishing.com

CPSIA information can be obtained
at www.ICGtesting.com
Printed in the USA
LVHW051559240920
667015LV00002B/234